A BROWN PAPER BAG *and* A FINE TOOTH COMB

A Novel

CLAUDETTE CARRIDA JEFFREY

D1603750

INFINITY PUBLISHING

ISBN 978-0-7414-7903-7 Paperback
ISBN 978-0-7414-7904-4 eBook
Library of Congress Control Number: 2012947111

Printed in the United States of America

Published December 2012

INFINITY PUBLISHING
1094 New DeHaven Street, Suite 100
West Conshohocken, PA 19428-2713
Toll-free (877) BUY BOOK
Local Phone (610) 941-9999
Fax (610) 941-9959
Info@buybooksontheweb.com
www.buybooksontheweb.com

To my sons
Todd
and
Timothy (1960-1994)
who have given my life meaning and purpose

ACKNOWLEDGEMENTS

My sincere gratitude to: Mary Gehman, Gay Jones, Mitzie Neisz, Connie Paddock, Robbie Williams, Mark Homer, and Todd and Denise Cooper for reading as well as critiquing my work, but most of all for their encouragement and continued belief in me whenever I wanted to throw in the towel.

Thank you to a cousin I wish I'd had a chance to meet, Darrlyn A. Smith.

I could not have finished this project without the technological knowledge of my son Todd and my daughter-in-law Denise. It is certainly an illustration of the many times our children become our teachers.

My special thanks to the authors of the following books that were invaluable to me:

De Caro, Frank. *Louisiana Sojourns*. Louisiana State University Press, Baton Rouge 1998.

Gehman, Mary. *The Free People of Color of New Orleans: An Introduction.* Margaret Media, Inc., New Orleans, LA 1994.

Gehman, Mary and Reis, Nancy. *Women and New Orleans: A History.* Margaret Media, Inc., New Orleans, LA 2004.

James, Rosemary. *My New Orleans*. Touchtone, New York 2006.

Kein, Sybil. *Creole: The History and Legacy of Louisiana's Free People of Color.* Louisiana State University Press, Baton Rouge, LA 2000.

Kein, Sybil. *Gumbo People*. Margaret Media, Inc., New Orleans, LA 1999.

Smith, Darrlyn A. *The New Orleans 7th Ward Nostalgia Dictionary 1938-1965*. JADA, Inc., Seattle, WA 1996.

Also:

Center for New Orleans Studies/ Road Scholar/ Elderhostel, New Orleans, LA
The New Orleans Public Library
The Historical New Orleans Collection
Faulkner House Books, New Orleans, LA

Your life is like a tapestry
being woven by God and history
on an enchanted loom. Every
bobble of the shuttle has meaning,
every thread is important.

Richard Nelson Bolles
American Writer and Educator

LIFE JUST IS.
You have to flow with it.
Give yourself to the moment.
LET IT HAPPEN.

Jerry Brown (1938-   )
American Politician

INTRODUCTION

I was eight when my mother went off to live with her boyfriend. My grandmother promised me she'd come back as soon as the "old man" threw her out. I turned ten and she still wasn't back. I didn't care because my mother's parents, Gustave and Philomene Soublet, took better care of me than she ever could. I never wanted to be at her mercy ever again.

I called my grandparents Big Mama and Big Papa. I don't remember knowing why they, like other grandparents, were called those names nor did I ever ask. Eventually I used my own interpretation as to how the names might have originated. The words seemed to literally translate from the French, *grandmère* and *grandpère*, to big or maybe older mother and father.

Mr. Joe, my mother's boyfriend, was an old man - as old as Big Papa - and he didn't like kids. I wasn't allowed to visit my mother at his house; she always came to my grandparents' home to see me. I called her by her first name, Iris, because she never acted like a mother to me. She was more like an older sister.

Mr. Joe and Iris drank a lot, mostly beer. When somebody else was buying, they drank whiskey. They hung out in a notorious bar on St. Bernard Avenue where my mother had met Mr. Joe. The bar was in the heart of my neighborhood, the Seventh Ward in downtown New Orleans, where most of the Creoles of color lived. Everybody knew everybody, and everybody knew everybody else's business. And due to segregation in the 1940s, you did most of whatever it was you did in the Seventh Ward. So there was no place to hide; someone always saw you.

I often wondered why Iris had chosen such an old man. One night when Big Mama thought I'd fallen asleep on the sofa, I heard her whispering to Big Papa, "Gustave, Iris will never meet anybody decent right now. There aren't any young men her age left in town. They've all gone to war."

"Well, Philly," Big Papa told her, "New Orleans is a port city; it's always gonna be a wide-open town. There's a war in the Pacific and one in the Atlantic, so *boocoo* soldiers and sailors from all the bases nearby are flockin to the city night and day lookin for some real *bazah*. And you know what bazah I'm talkin about. You oughta be glad she's latched on to Mr. Joe, cuz if not, she might be draggin the street all night foolin around with some of those troops passin through. Some of them are real no-count and down-right mean. You know what, *bay*, I heard they beat up a lot of the women they fool around with and then hightail it out of town."

My grandmother reluctantly agreed Mr. Joe was the better choice, but she said she thought he, as well as all the others, might be dangerous.

"I pray every night for Iris, Gustave. I ask God to straighten her out and keep her safe while He's doing it," Big Mama cried. She stumbled out of the front room with her shoulders heaving. Big Papa shook me. "Claire," he said, "it's time to go to bed."

What seemed strange to me was in spite of all the gossip that floated around, we never found out what Mr. Joe did for a living. My grandfather thought he might be a gambler or a dope dealer because he always seemed to have money and was usually at home during the day. Whatever he did, he hid it well...and so did Iris. He rarely came to our house, and when he did, he stayed only a few minutes.

Sometimes when Mr. Joe got drunk, he'd put a handful of paper money in my mother's hand and tell her to buy something special for her little girl. She never did. She'd tell me about the money, but I never saw a cent of it, nor did she ever buy me anything, let alone something special. I guess she drank up all the money because she didn't spend any of it on clothes for herself. Iris seemed to have only two outfits, and as Big Mama put it, they were always *crotay*. We went to Sunday Mass together a few times and I always walked into church with my head down. I was ashamed to be seen with her.

My grandparents and I lived across the street from an old three-story, brick building. It took up one square block and was surrounded by a lacy, cast-iron fence. It looked as if it had been plucked right out of France and dropped down into the center of New Orleans. A nursing home for elderly Whites, it was owned and operated by The Little Sisters of the Poor, an order of Catholic nuns.

On our side of the street there were three houses; we lived in one side of the last house, a *double-shotgun* that sat in the middle of the block. From our house to the corner, there was a beautiful garden shaped like an obtuse triangle. It was bordered by giant, sycamore trees. All year long the garden was filled with vegetables and flowers. It, too, belonged to The Little Sisters of the Poor. My grandparents were the garden's caretakers. Big Papa built a gate so that we could enter it from our yard.

My grandfather was a first-class carpenter and a boat builder until he suffered a heart attack and could no longer do strenuous work. He did light, odd jobs to make ends meet and somehow we managed to squeak by. He even found a way to make sure I went to a Catholic elementary school within walking distance from our house. Big Mama always waited for me on the front porch swing when I'd come home from school, and when I'd come home for lunch, she'd have my favorite meal waiting: a bowl of vegetable soup and a ham sandwich.

The library was like the home of a friend who lived close by; I dropped in often, especially in the summer. There was no air conditioning, but it was always cooler than my house. I read everything I was permitted to read, but sneaked a peek at the books that were off limits to me, especially the anatomy books kept on a shelf behind the librarian's desk. Because I could only get a quick glance into these books, my curiosity was whetted even more.

My best friend Emily lived around the corner from me. When our appetites for knowledge fused, we found ways to learn whatever we wanted to know. We didn't dare ask my grandparents or Emily's mother about sex. They thought the subject unsuitable for discussion. In those days, children were seen and not heard and you stayed a child a long time. So most of what we wanted to know, we had to search out on our own.

Emily's neighbor Erica, a young nurse, usually helped us in our searches. We, in turn, helped her hang her family's laundry in her backyard whenever she did the wash. She'd let us borrow her nursing textbooks which we'd take to Emily's house, lock ourselves in the bathroom, and read until we were bleary eyed.

Erica was our "go to person" for about two years. She made us promise never to tell anyone where we were getting our information.

"Don't y'all tell nobody Ah loaned y'all these books, okay?" she said. "Emily, if your mama finds you with ma books, she'll give ma mama a piece of her mind and probly never talk to us again. Then she'll tell your gramma, Claire, and Ah sho don't want Miss Philly beatin down my door because she thinks Ah'm corruptin y'all."

"My grandmother won't come, Erica. She'll send my grandfather to see your daddy. And that's a lot worse." I could picture Big Papa, with his 6'2" frame, staring down at Erica's father who was only as tall as Napoleon Bonaparte.

We were brokenhearted when Erica got married and moved away.

My grandparents always spoke in Creole French whenever they didn't want me to understand what they were talking about. They didn't teach me to speak it for that very reason. I'd catch an occasional word, but could never string enough of them together to make a coherent sentence. For months, every Monday night while witnessing a man and a woman meet on the corner of our house, I'd hear Big Mama and Big Papa use the same words. Between my mother and Emily's mother, I managed to find out what the words meant. When they asked where I'd heard the words, I told them in the girl's bathroom at school.

After months of never being allowed off the porch after the couple arrived, I finally figured out a way to find out what they did that was so shameful.

Claire Soublet

PART ONE

– 1 –

BLUE RENDEZVOUS

"She's here!" I muttered deep in my throat, then quickly put my hand over my mouth to trap the words as they were leaving my voice box so that they wouldn't escape and explode into the quiet New Orleans night. It felt like my ten year old heart went from ninety to one hundred-sixty beats in three seconds. I started to tremble with excitement.

My grandmother pointed to the corner as she shook her head from side to side. She mumbled to my grandfather, "*La putain!*" He craned his neck in the darkness looking in the direction my grandmother was pointing. "*Honte, honte, honte!*" she hissed. "*Petite cochon!*"

I called the woman "Lady Blue" because she always wore the same cobalt-blue dress with blue, high-heeled, sling-back shoes. Her hair was long and dark and she wore it loose around her shoulders. Even when she walked near the streetlamp, I couldn't see her face and couldn't tell if she was Black or White. Her exposed body-parts were fair, but in a city like New Orleans that didn't mean a whole lot. Creoles of color are of many different hues and range from milk-white to chocolate-brown. My family, the Soublets, certainly proved that.

Lady Blue's lover was a Black man – there was no question about it. He was tall, muscular and ebony black. He must have had light-colored eyes because they shone like a cat's in the partial darkness under the tree. One leg was shorter than the other which caused him to rock from side to side when he walked. I called him "Wobble." His disability must have kept him out of military service because it was 1944 and everyone his age and older was off fighting in the war.

3

When Wobble arrived, that was my cue to bid my grandparents goodnight. While the couple sauntered up the block, crossed the street, and darted behind one of the gigantic trees, I tip-toed through the house and sneaked out the back door. I went through the garden gate, then crept along the rows of vegetables to find a spot in which to crouch next to the cast-iron bars on the fence. There was just enough reflected light from the windows of the house on the other side of the garden to allow me to see everything.

Lady Blue and Wobble didn't touch until they were securely behind the tree. Then Lady Blue hiked up her dress around her waist and against that solid slab of sycamore, bark and all, the love dance began. There were no garters, garter belts, panties, or stockings to remove. She had come unencumbered and fully prepared for instant action. She did all the kissing, moaning and groaning until Wobble seemed compelled to join in. I could hear him grunt while he slapped her behind. She scratched and clawed at his arms and back until he slapped her hands away complaining she was taking his skin off.

It was the end of May and the nights were already warm and sticky. I was close enough to smell their body odors mixed with Lady Blue's sweet perfume. The salty, sweet scent penetrated my nostrils and made me sick to my stomach, but I knew if I gagged I'd be discovered. So every few seconds, I held my nose and breathed through my mouth.

When their lovemaking was over, the pair sat on the exposed roots of the tree and talked.

"I can't give you much this week, I hope that's okay," Lady Blue said as she handed Wobble some paper money. He gave her a small packet and she slipped it into her pocket.

"Fifteen dollas!" Wobble snarled after he counted the money. "Baby, you shawt, way too shawt. Ah'm wert mo than fifteen bucks."

"I couldn't get anymore without making my husband suspicious. I got this from my mother. But if she accidentally mentions it in front of him, I'll be in big trouble. I'll bring more next time, I promise." Lady Blue's small voice sounded pathetic.

"Looka here, woman, Ah got ma own problems. Ah cain't run faeva. Dey gonna git me one a dese days. Ah need cash, not scuses." Wobble smacked her lightly across her mouth. "You don

4

wan me mad at you, huh? Ah can git good and mean, yeah. You cain't have me and a bag a weed fa fifteen dollas."

"No...I know. Please don't be angry with me. I'll have more for you next week. I won't let you down, I swear."

"Dat's mo like it, baby." He stood up and pulled her to her feet, then grabbed her by the shoulders and roughly drew her into his body. "Ah'm sho you wan some mo a dis," he said as he pulled up her dress again and rubbed up against her. "You sho don wan ma fis in yo face, do you?" He laid his huge fist against her cheek and then smacked her hard on her behind.

"Nooo, baby." Her response was quick and trembly as she put her arms around his neck.

"Gotta go." Wobble slipped out of Lady Blue's embrace. "Don fawgit what Ah said, *na.*" He groaned loudly as he yanked the condom from between his legs. He handed it to Lady Blue who quickly removed a small, paper bag from the pocket of her dress and dumped the bulging rubber inside. Wobble zipped up his pants, tucked in his shirt, and left her under the tree.

As he sprinted toward the corner, Lady Blue pulled down her dress, smoothed her hair, then rolled the paper bag into a small ball and put it under some leaves in the gutter. She walked up the street and disappeared into the night.

Even though I didn't understand most of what they said, the strange mutterings that came through the fence bars that night was my first encounter with words spoken in the heat of passion. I couldn't comprehend why the couple's behavior was supposed to be pleasurable. They seemed to be inflicting pain on one another. How could they have enjoyed that? Besides that, he'd threatened to beat her up and she didn't seem to mind. I vowed that if that was what I had to do to have a boyfriend or a husband, then I would rather be a nun! I realized reading Erica's nursing textbooks had not prepared me for seeing the real thing. And there was no one with whom I could discuss my concerns and fears.

June arrived bringing horrible weather. Rain fell every day and all day without letup. I was sure the lovers wouldn't meet in the pouring rain. At first I wasn't sure if I'd go back into the garden to watch them. I hadn't quite gotten over my first experience. But the decision wasn't mine to make. Lady Blue and Wobble kept their regular meeting time but I couldn't go into the garden because it was too wet and muddy. I suddenly felt left out.

In spite of my fears and some feelings of self-reproach, I knew their meetings were going to be as addictive to me as they must have been to them. I couldn't wait for the rain to stop and the garden to dry out.

The following Monday arrived fair and dry, but Lady Blue and Wobble didn't show up. The next morning I went to examine their special rendezvous tree. Out of pure childishness, and in an effort to leave a permanent marker in that spot, I carved the names I had given them on the tree trunk with a piece of metal I found in the gutter. There was a chunk of newspaper lying near the tree, and when I kicked it, two blue shoes poked out at me. I knew right away they were Lady Blue's. I picked them up and wrapped them in the newspaper, then I ran into the house with them under my blouse so that my grandmother wouldn't see them. I cleaned off the mud in the bathtub and hid them in a brown paper bag in the hall *armoire* until I could find a more secure location. My grandparents seldom used the old relic; they stored old books and papers in it. I knew my treasure would be safe for a while.

The rain returned and with it intense humid heat. Two Mondays came and went. There was no sign of Lady Blue and Wobble. I was on summer vacation; I had time to come up with hundreds of scenarios. I concocted different theories about what might have happened to them. Had they found out I was watching them and changed their meeting place? Could they have found out my name was Claire Cecile Soublet and they planned to kill me so I couldn't tell anyone about them? Perhaps her husband caught her in a lie and killed her. Had Wobble killed Lady Blue because she hadn't brought him enough money? Maybe her husband found out about them and had just killed Wobble. Even though some fear had set in, I didn't feel the need to tell anyone.

My secret was too exciting to share. I kept it to myself as long as I could. It bolstered my self-esteem. It was the first time I hadn't shared something that important with Emily. I think I was a little jealous of her because she had a mother and two brothers. Several days later, I told her about Lady Blue and Wobble and I thought she'd be jealous of my big secret. Instead, she was furious. She couldn't believe I'd withheld it from her for so long. After she gave me a tongue-lashing, I didn't tell her I'd found the shoes. She went away angry. I didn't see her for a few days. We promised never to keep secrets from one another again. I was lying. Was she?

When the rains filled the gutters, Emily and I always took off our shoes and romped in the cool water. The fact that it was muddy didn't faze us. We never checked for broken glass or sharp objects – only for the dreaded leeches that we knew hung out in the murky water. A cut foot could be tolerated, but the thought of those creepy parasites sucking blood from our legs or feet gave us shivering fits.

The day the rain stopped, we walked in the gutters on both sides of the street. But the water near the bridge had such a bad smell, we stopped walking on that side. The water receded two days later and the stench was worse than before. Everyone believed there was a dead animal under the bridge, but no one could see under it beyond a foot or so on either side. My grandfather called the Board of Health.

Mud and debris had clogged both sides of the bridge which was made of two massive iron planks laid side by side. The men had to use long, hooked probes and eventually pulled out a blob of rotting flesh - a Black man. His shirt and pants had adhered to his decaying flesh. His upper body had become blue, muddy plaid; it was ripped open in places where the hooks had gored it.

With further probing, they pulled out a second, swollen lump.

As soon as I saw the cobalt-blue, shredded cloth, I gasped, "That's Lady Blue! That's the dress she always wore. And that must be Wobble." I pointed to the first body they had recovered. "No wonder they didn't come back." I remember how proud I felt because I wasn't hysterical.

My grandparents and I were standing in the street near the bridge watching what was happening. Someone had already called the police and they had just arrived.

Big Papa nudged me. "Be quiet," he snapped. But it was too late. One of the policemen standing near us heard what I said.

"You know those people, little girl?" He motioned for me and my grandparents to follow him to stand on the sidewalk in front of our house.

"Not really." I looked at Big Papa. I'm sure he could see the terror in my eyes.

"Didn't you call them by name?"

I didn't answer.

"Answer the policeman's question, Claire." Big Papa's tone wasn't angry but it was sharp.

"I don't know their real names. I gave them those names. I called the woman Lady Blue and the man Wobble." I explained why I called them those names. I was so glad Emily wasn't there because she would have blurted out everything I had told her without being asked.

"Where do you live?" The policeman asked.

"Right here." I pointed to the house behind me.

"Do you know anything about those people?" The policeman seemed to be a very nice man. He didn't have a southern accent. I was shocked he was so courteous to me and my grandparents. Shocked, but grateful.

Big Papa answered. "They've been comin here every Monday night at 9:00 for a few months, na. They used to run and hide behind that tree," Big Papa pointed to it.

The cop stared at me. "Did you see what they did under the tree, Claire?"

My grandmother answered this time. "We sent her to bed before they ran under the tree."

The policeman didn't take his eyes off me.

"Did you go to bed, Claire? Or did you find a way to see what was going on under that tree?" He could tell I was petrified and afraid to answer in front of my grandparents.

"Speak up, little girl. If you know somethin, tell the policeman!" The tremor in Big Papa's voice betrayed his forceful demeanor.

"Once I hid in the garden and watched them do their business." I told the cop about the bag of weed Wobble had brought to Lady Blue and the money she had given him. He asked me about their conversations and if I was sure I had never heard their real names.

"They didn't talk a lot," I lied. "They only called each other baby."

The cop asked me if I could remember anything else. I told him I couldn't. He had no way of knowing I had Lady Blue's shoes and I wasn't about to tell him.

My grandparents refrained from bringing up the subject to me after the policeman told us he no longer needed us. But I could tell how disappointed in me they were because for the rest of the day they tried not to look at me or speak to me. They spoke to each other in Creole French.

The shock of my ordeal didn't set in until that evening when I started to shake uncontrollably and cry. I bit my lips until they bled. And when I began to taste the blood, I cried even harder. The tears had more to do with my grandparents learning my secret than about seeing the dead bodies.

I hadn't ever been afraid of the dark, but after that experience I was too frightened to stay in the house alone. For a long time I even refused to go into our yard or into the garden alone. Much to my surprise, my grandparents were sensitive to my fears.

We never found out if the case was ever solved. There was nothing about the murders in the newspaper or on the radio. It was as if it had never happened.

Those blue, high-heeled shoes are still in that brown paper bag. Eventually, I moved them to the bottom of the cedar chest in the front room where the rest of my grandmother's collectibles were stored. I knew my mother wasn't interested in what was in the chest and the rest of my grandmother's children seemed disconnected from us. So I was sure the collectibles would one day be mine.

– 2 –

OLD ENOUGH TO KNOW

The nightmares didn't begin until months after Lady Blue's and Wobble's murder. Each time I'd see their bodies being pulled out from under the bridge and I could hear them calling my name. My grandparents would often find me curled up on the floor at the foot of their bed.

My mother was coming less often to visit us now and my grandparents rarely mentioned her name. I started to dream about her, too. In those dreams, the neighbors would taunt me whenever I walked on the *banquette* in front of their houses. "Your mama doesn't want her own child. She'd rather run the street with a lot of different men. Where's your daddy, little girl?"

I never told Big Mama or Big Papa how much those dreams frightened me. Instead, I asked God for help.

"Lord, it's me again...Claire." I'd cup my hands over my mouth and plead, "Please don't let me turn out like my mother; protect me from her bad blood that runs through my veins; she's no-good...everybody calls her a *boozan* woman, and...and if I'm not asking too much, let my grandparents live a long time because I feel safe with them...and...ah, God, if I have to be like my mother...then before I grow up...I want You to strike me dead!"

This was a part of my nightly prayer before the awful day I heard that frantic voice fill my head..........

"Miss Philly! Mr. Gustave!" Someone was yelling and pounding on our front door.

I ran ahead of my grandmother and opened the door. Edward Labouche burst into the front room. Big Papa must have been in the side yard because he suddenly appeared and ran up onto the porch.

10

"Sit down, Miss Philly, please." Ed pointed to the sofa and waited for Big Mama to sit. Then he looked out at my grandfather who stood behind the screen door looking into the house. "You too, Mr. Gustave, come in and sit down." Ed finally looked at me. "Go back to the kitchen, Claire," he ordered me. "This news is for grownups."

I looked at Big Mama for confirmation. "Go on," she said.

I left the room but quickly doubled back on all fours to my grandparents' bedroom. I lay on the floor on my belly on the side of their high, four-poster bed. I could see all of their bodies, but not their heads. I could hear everything.

While Ed stood quietly as if waiting for me to be out of earshot, Big Papa came in and sat on the sofa next to Big Mama. He put his arm around her shoulder.

"Ed, tell us what's wrong. Has something happened to Gus...or to Iris?" My grandmother pleaded as she wrung her hands in her lap. Big Papa grabbed her hands and held them.

"I dunno. I'm not really sure, Miss Philly." Ed started to cough and clear his throat. The room got very quiet.

"Jesus, Mary and Joseph, Ed!" Big Papa roared.

"Listen, Mr. Gustave, this is real hard for me. I've known you my whole life; you're like a part of my family." Ed stopped again. "Well...early this morning I was walking my dog and I found a woman's body in the gutter near the corner." He pointed toward Laharpe Street. "She was lying under a piece of canvas...naked. I ran across the street to Mr. Joseph at the home and asked him to call the police. I had to go to the morgue with the police and the body. They weren't too eager to believe I had only found the body and that I wasn't the one who killed her. I was questioned all the way to the morgue and even after we got there. They finally believed me and let me go, but I was there all morning."

"Ed! Was it Iris?" my grandfather asked impatiently.

"There was a lot of dried blood on the woman's face, so I couldn't tell. It wasn't until they cleaned off a lot of it at the morgue that I thought it looked like Iris. But I'm still not positive."

Big Mama cried out, *"Mon Dieu! Mon Dieu!"* as my grandfather tried to comfort her.

11

Ed didn't say anything more. He walked toward the front door as if he were giving my grandmother time to compose herself.

He was around thirty years old and still lived with his parents about four blocks away. Although he had a college education, he was a carpenter like his father, an old friend of Big Papa's. He and Iris had gone to school together and also dated for a short time.

Ed walked back to where my grandparents were sitting and knelt down in front of the sofa. "The morgue has her listed as a White female Jane Doe because I couldn't positively identify her. I didn't tell them who I thought she might be because if I was wrong, I'd cause you a lot of trouble and hurt for nothing. So you need to go to the morgue. You'll know if it's Iris."

I stopped listening. First Lady Blue and Wobble...now my mother. All of them murdered. Who knows who else had been killed under those giant sycamores? After all, trees can't talk..........

I was reliving my mother's death again. When I closed my eyes, I could still see the newspaper article: *Transient woman found murdered in the 1500 block of North Johnson St. Her throat had been slashed. She was found nude lying in the gutter covered with an awning. A man walking his dog discovered the body just after dawn on Tuesday. It is believed she was murdered elsewhere and her body dumped at the Johnson St. location.*

That small article, without my mother's name, was all that appeared in the paper. Colored people were rarely written about in the 1945 New Orleans newspapers, and when they were, it was usually when they were murdered or had committed some kind of crime. Any additional news that ever circulated was pure conjecture or gossip, and there were plenty of both going around about my mother. The police hadn't told my grandparents much and my grandparents told me nothing. At almost twelve, I thought I was old enough to know everything. The truth couldn't be worse than the gossip.

The rustling of the tree branches and the singing locusts filled the warm, spring night. I stood in one of the little wing doors peeking at my grandmother who seemed lost in sadness as she sat on the front porch swing gently rocking herself. She was probably thinking about the same thing I had just been thinking about.

I quietly came out of the house and sat next to her on the swing. We were alone for the weekend and had lots of time to talk, and this was one night I was going to insist on answers. My grandfather had gone to his fishing camp in North Shore. All three of us used to go, but when my grandmother's hips and legs started to give her trouble, my grandfather went alone or with some of his friends. While he was gone Friday through Sunday, my grandmother and I took care of the nuns' garden. They gave my grandparents a small stipend and some of the vegetables that were grown.

Even in late April that year, the city was a warm, humid, stagnant swamp and that made the mosquitoes happy. It was the kind of weather they thrived in and rapidly multiplied. At seven o'clock in the evening, the females were sharpening their high-performance needles to lay siege to the exposed skin and blood of the Crescent City folk. I shivered when I thought about how many bites I'd have by the end of the night.

Big Mama started a fire of leaves and rags in the yard close to the porch. Mosquitoes hated the smoke created by the burning of that strange combination, so we could sit without constantly slapping ourselves as long as the fire smoldered and smoked.

"Big Mama, if I ask you about my mama, would you tell me?" I closed my eyes waiting for her answer. I was praying she'd talk to me because I had a lot of questions. I felt grown-up enough to handle whatever she'd tell me.

No answer came. There was only the crackling and popping of the rags as they burned.

"I'm sorry. I know you hate to talk about my mama. You're not crying, are you?" I opened my eyes and looked at her.

"I'm not crying, Claire. It's almost a year since your mama died and I can't bring her back. I'm all cried out." Big Mama's eyes glistened with tears but none spilled out. "What do you want to know?"

"Do you think that soldier my mama was running with behind Mr. Joe's back killed her, or did Mr. Joe kill her because he found out she was running around on him?" I could feel my grandmother flinch each time I said the word kill.

"Ooooo…" she groaned, "I think I'm gonna change my mind. We don't need to talk about that right now. Wait until Big

13

Papa comes home, then he can talk to you insteada me." She looked at me like a wounded dog. "Can't you wait?"

"Big Papa won't be home until Sunday night and I need some answers before Sunday morning," I said in my small, angry voice.

"Settle down, little girl. Don't you cut your eyes at me! And cut out that sass, right now. You don't need to know anything. You want to know and I want to know why you want to know?" My grandmother had her hand positioned and ready for her infamous backhand slap.

"I need to know before I go to Mass Sunday morning. I never told you, but one Sunday when I went to church with my mama, she showed me a man she said was my daddy. She told me his name is Lester. Is it true? Because if it is, I'm going to ask him if he knows he's my father." I moved forward quickly out of range for a slap.

"You will do no such thing! That man is married with a set of children. Do you want to be responsible for messing up his life and his family's?"

"Why not? He messed up mine. I'm Claire Soublet; I have my mama's last name...your last name. Everyone already knows I'm a bastard." This time I didn't move fast enough. My grandmother's hand flew through the air and managed to catch part of my cheek and my ear.

"Don't you ever say that again, you hear me! You'd better thank the good Lord you're not an imbecile or deformed or something. You're healthy and you've got ten fingers and ten toes. What you need to do Sunday is thank God for being a Soublet and not a Menard." Big Mama was trembling.

"Wait a minute...Lester's last name is Menard? But that's your maiden name." I was beginning to understand and my mouth hung so wide open I could have caught flies.

"That's right...Lester is your mother's first cousin and he already knows you're his child. His father, Augustin Menard, is my brother and he hasn't spoken to me since he found out your mama was pregnant for his son. You wanted to know. Well, there it is."

The shock that Augustin Menard was not only my great uncle but also my grandfather suddenly became too real and I realized why my grandmother said I needed to thank God I wasn't born an imbecile. I remembered hearing the grownups talk about how members of the royal houses intermarried and had all kinds of physically and mentally impaired children. Now I understood perfectly what she meant.

"Big Papa and I tried to talk to your mama when we found out Lester was engaged to marry Dr. LaCroix's daughter. She wouldn't listen when we reminded her he was her first cousin and that we knew he wouldn't give up a doctor's daughter for her. No...not my brother's son. Lester only wanted one thing from your mama...and he got it. But Iris was determined to make him marry her. I think she got pregnant on purpose thinking that would force her father to go to Augustin and demand Lester marry her."

"Did Big Papa go?" I asked.

"No, he wouldn't go. Your mama told Lester herself that she was pregnant and he hurried up and married the doctor's daughter and left your mama flat. She was never the same after that. She started drinking and dragging the street. After you were born, she'd leave and be gone for days at a time. Then she started living with first one man then another. That's why we kept you with us no matter how many times she moved in and out."

Even though I had insisted my grandmother tell me the whole truth, I now regretted knowing it. I felt sick inside. No wonder right after my mother's death there was all that behind-the-hands whispering whenever I passed people in my neighborhood. I tried to imagine what they were saying about me and my mother. At least, they could see I hadn't turned out to be an imbecile. Now that I knew who Lester was, how could I go to church again and see him without wanting to kill him? He had planted his seed in my mother, then he'd left her to sink or swim — and she'd sunk. Now I had no mother and no father. I hadn't wanted to make my grandmother cry, but she'd ended up making me cry. She tried to take me in her arms and hold me, but I pushed her away. I couldn't stand to be touched. I felt like I wanted to die.

"Claire, I knew you'd ask me one day and I was hoping you'd be older when I'd have to tell you. As for who killed your mama, the police couldn't find the soldier she was supposed to be going with because there was more than one. Most of them were passing through on their way home from the war or on their way to it. Your mama hung around Freddie's then, the bar on the corner of Johnson and Lapeyrouse. The people who always drink at Freddie's told Big Papa they saw her leave with a lot of different soldiers."

"What about Mr. Joe? Did the police question him?"

"Yes, but they couldn't find anything that made him look guilty. And right after that, he had that stroke, and they never went to question him again. It wouldn't have made any difference if they had; he was paralyzed and couldn't talk. He died about two months ago, you know."

"I know, it was announced in church. So...my mama is just another dead slut, huh? The police never found out who killed Lady Blue and Wobble, or if they did, we don't know about it. Now, my mama. And I know why they'll never find their killers. They were all Colored and nobody gives a good goddamn."

"Claire! When did you start cursing? You'd better watch your mouth in front of your grandfather. He won't tolerate that kind of talk from you."

"I've always cursed; you just never heard me. I'll watch my mouth around Big Papa, don't worry."

Just then a car pulled up in front of the house. Miss Odelia, my grandmother's club's secretary, had come to collect the dues. She didn't turn off the ignition but sat in her shiny, black Model A Ford with the windows rolled up looking toward the porch. I knew she was hoping to avoid letting in a couple of blood suckers every time she stopped.

Big Mama waved and yelled to her, "Okay, I've got it ready for you."

Wow, I thought, she's driving her own car! I'm going to do that when I grow up. I'm not going to need a man to drive me where I want to go the way a lot of women do. I'll drive all over the country and probably go out to California with my grandparents to see my aunts. I'm going to do a lot for them when I get my fabulous job. First, I need to graduate from college. Suddenly, I felt Big Mama tugging on my arm.

"Claire? Claire, didn't you hear me? I said go in and get the dues money off my dresser and take it out to Miss Odelia."

Miss Odelia rolled down her window about an inch and I slipped the envelope with the money to her. She quickly rolled up her window and spoke to me through the glass.

"Tell your grandma I'm sorry I can't stop to talk. Honey, these damn biting bugs are too much for me. I'll see her next time.

Claire, get down off the running board, *cher*, so I can take off."
Then she motioned for me to step back.

Damn! How far back do I have to be, I wondered? She's
going straight, not sideways.

When I got back to the porch Big Mama got off the swing
and I could tell her mood had changed.

"I don't want to talk anymore, Claire," she told me.

"Nooo! Big Mama, you promised," I pleaded.

"My head is suddenly *gros comme ça.*" She put her hands
out beyond her ears. "I need to take some aspirin and go to bed."

"But it's still early."

"I know, but my head doesn't care." My grandmother tried
to laugh, but I could tell she was in pain.

"Okay, but will you finish telling me tomorrow?" I asked her
in a calm voice even though I was really pissed.

"Yes, I'll tell you more tomorrow. Now go in and go to bed.
I have to put out the fire before I come in. Goodnight." Big Mama
walked off the porch to get the hose in the alley. I watched her
spray the fire several times before I went in.

- 3 -

EMILY DIGS FOR DIRT

I jumped out of bed, swung my door open and stepped into the kitchen. Big Mama was already dressed and rummaging around for something to eat. I watched her break off the end of one of the hot French breads we had delivered every morning and generously spread it with butter. It was the perfect size to enjoy with her cup of coffee. She called the knobby end of a loaf of bread a té té. And you never cut bread in Big Mama's house; it was always broken.

"Good morning," I chirped.

"Good morning, Claire. Emily was here a few minutes ago. She's going to the market and the bakery for her mama. So she wants you to meet her at the library at 9:00 to work on your report for school." I watched a pleased look envelope my grandmother's face.

"Oh shit! I forgot." Hmmm, I thought, Big Mama thinks she's home free.

"I'll never get used to your cursing, Claire, it continues to shock me. You know, it's really low-class to use that kind of language. Well...never mind. This morning I have some weeding and vegetable picking to do. And later on this afternoon, I'm going back- a- town to visit Miss Arnette. She had a stroke last week."

"Oh, I'm sorry. Can she still talk and everything?"

"I don't know. Can you make your own breakfast this morning? Why don't you have some warm bread, liver paté and café au lait? The bread is really crispy today."

"What time will you be home after you go to Miss Arnette's?"

"Probably about 3:00."

"Hmm…I'll stay at Emily's and come home when I think you're back."

"I'll pick you up on my way home, Claire. But you know, one day you'll have to get over being afraid of the dark and an empty house – and sooner rather than later." Big Mama seemed unable to speak to me with even a little warmth in her voice. I wondered if she was angry because I was forcing her to think and talk about things she was trying to forget.

Emily was waiting for me outside the library. She'd brought me a glazed donut from McKenzie's Bakery. We couldn't go inside until I finished eating it.

"Cee Cee, did you ax your gramma about your mama? Did you find out anything?" Emily wanted the dirt right away. She loved to gossip and enjoyed hearing about everybody's dirty laundry.

"Nothing I didn't already know. We'll probably never know who killed my mother."

"Not that…I mean about your daddy. Was it the man your mama showed you that time in church?"

"Nope. Big Mama told me my mama was lying about that man because my mama really didn't know who my father is." I lied to Emily with a straight face. She had stung me pretty badly when she chewed me out for not telling her about Lady Blue and Wobble in a timely manner. I didn't want to give her that much information about me knowing she couldn't wait to tell everyone what she knew, especially her mother who also liked to gossip. I was learning to keep my business to myself – best friend or not.

"Girl, you sure have a messy family. I'm damn glad my mama's alive and I know who my daddy is." Emily patted me on the head as if I were a poor little mutt.

"You're really lucky, Em." I had to turn away from her because my lips were puckered in anger. "I'm finished with my donut. Let's go in."

It took two and a half hours for us to write a report on Spain. Emily and I had teamed up for the report and had picked Spain out of twenty other countries. I did all the research and Emily did the writing. She claimed I was the better reader and her handwriting was better than mine. We had learned longhand together and the nuns seemed to have a special way of teaching it, so it was hard to distinguish her handwriting from mine.

We left the library and went to Nick the Greek's grocery store. Nick made lots of different types of ice cream and sherbet and all kinds of candy. We each bought a bag of caramel twists and walked home slowly making sure we ate all our twists before we reached the house. Emily's mother would have been upset had Emily arrived eating a bag of candy before lunch.

Mrs. Valcour was cleaning what looked to be about five pounds of shrimp and about a dozen crabs. That much seafood meant she was getting ready to make gumbo that night to serve to her club members the next day. When she saw us, she stood up and ripped off her apron.

We knew we had come home too soon.

"Girls, take over for me, please. I forgot to have you get the hot sausage, Emily. I've got to go back to Vaucresson's before they close for lunch. You don't mind helping Emily, do you, Claire?" Mrs. Valcour looked at me with her usual wry smile waiting for my answer.

"I'd love to help," I said. I'd never just sit and watch Emily do it all by herself. Emily's mother and I had a strange relationship and I didn't know why. Even though I was always at her house, we never had much to say to each other. It seemed I was respectful and she was tolerant.

"Good, thank you, Claire. Go wash your hands, girls. No wait! Let me get in the bathroom first. I need to clean up before I go to the market."

"Hey, Ma, where's Johnnie and Matt? Why can't they help us?" Emily was staring at the pile of seafood to be cleaned. She constantly complained about her brothers who liked to eat but never helped in the kitchen.

"Johnnie's at Aunt June's helping her unclog her kitchen sink and Matt's on the back porch sleeping."

After Mrs. Valcour closed the bathroom door, Emily took me by the hand, and with a finger pressed on her lips, she led me out on the back porch. Matt's six-foot frame was stretched out on a pallet and he was fast asleep. Emily picked up the glass of water near his head and poured half of it on top his nose and mouth. He woke up frantic - snorting and clawing at the air. Emily quickly ran back into the kitchen, but I wasn't fast enough to get away.

Matt caught me by the top of my braid and held on as he ran toward the sound of Emily's giggling dragging me behind him.

"You lousy brats!" he screamed. Matt was notorious for his temper. He was always in trouble at school for fighting. But he was tall and good-looking and a big, high school, football star, so the nuns at Xavier Prep were never too severe when they punished him.

"I didn't do that to you, Matt." I was laughing but I was scared.

Still holding on to my hair, he yelled to his mother, "Ma, where's Emily?"

"She was here a minute ago...I don't know where she is. Look for her yourself. I have to get to the market." Mrs. Valcour came out of the bathroom and stood near the side door.

"Let go of that child's hair, Matt. That mean streak is back and I don't like it. You're too old to get upset like that with your sister and her friends. Listen...I don't want any shit to go on while I'm gone, okay?"

"Yeah, Ma," He reluctantly let go of my braid and went out to the back porch.

As soon as her mother closed the side door behind her, Emily opened it and came into the house. She was still giggling. She had been hiding in the alley.

Like a lightning bolt, Matt appeared in the kitchen doorway, and before Emily could turn to run, he threw his shoe at her and it slammed into her forehead. She screamed. The side door burst open and Mrs. Valcour rushed into the house. It was clear she hadn't left the alley. She must have suspected Matt was going to retaliate against Emily and her daughter might need her to intervene.

Matt stopped in the middle of the kitchen on his way to doing more damage to his sister. "Saved again, huh. You do all kinds of shit to me, then you hide behind Mama. That's not right and you know it, Ma. But one of these days you won't be so lucky, Mama's pet, no one's going to save you." He glared at Emily and his mother and then returned to the back porch.

"Claire, get the arnica in the bathroom and some salt for me to rub on Emily's head." Mrs. Valcour was pressing a large *hickey* that had formed on Emily's forehead just above her right eyebrow.

21

"Matt, get your ass back in here. You have inherited the job of cleaning the seafood, all of it. I'm putting you on notice today, if this violent streak you have continues, you're going to find yourself living with your father and his other family in Baton Rouge. I won't put up with it much longer." When he appeared in the doorway, his mother picked up his shoe and threw it on the floor near his feet. "One of these days you're going to kill somebody or they're going to kill you."

Without a word, Matt put on his shoe, sat at the table and began to clean the shrimp and the crabs.

His mother dabbed arnica on Emily's forehead and then rubbed salt on the area. Emily winced and groaned the whole time. I watched Matt, full of anger and contempt, look over at her as she gave her victim's performance. I thought, boy, if looks could kill.

"Girls, go out and sit on the front porch while I'm gone. Do not come back into the house. I'll only be gone about twenty minutes." Mrs. Valcour pushed us out of the side door in front of her.

We were hungry but dared not go back into the house. And true to her word, Emily's mother was back in a short time. She made us sandwiches and lemonade and brought it out to us on the front porch. She asked us to stay there until my grandmother picked me up.

It was the first time I had seen Emily so subdued. From the things she talked about, I realized she was afraid of her brother and what he might do to her when her mother wasn't around.

"You don't think Matt will really hurt you, do you?" I asked.

"You mean worse than today? Yeah! Girl, you don't know my brother." I heard the fear in her voice. "It started when I was about five and he was twelve. He used to sneak and show me his thing, then he'd tell me I had to show him mine. He made it like a game and I was too young to know better. He was my brother and I didn't think he'd make me do anything wrong. And I liked getting away with stuff my mother didn't know about."

"You actually did it, Emily?" I was shocked until I saw the faint smile on her face.

"Yeah, it was fun at first. We'd go out on the back porch when my mama was busy and play around. After a while he said we should touch each other. I didn't feel anything, but he started wiggling and then he tried to put his finger in my coochie. But when his weenie got hard, I got scared. I thought I'd hurt him, so I stayed away from the back porch for a while. He got mad and did mean things to me. I thought if I did what he told me, he'd stop being mean to me."

"Emily, tell me you didn't let him touch you again." I really hated Matt now. I was afraid to hear what else he had done to her. I thought about Lady Blue and Wobble having sex.

"Girl, I sure did. I let him put two of his fingers in me and he showed me how to pull on his weenie so that it made him feel good. One afternoon, my mother caught us."

"Oh, thank you, God!" I was never so happy to hear anything in my life.

"My mama blamed Matt for everything. She was screaming at him and telling him he was committing incest. She wanted to know if he'd put his thing in me and she beat him until she believed he hadn't done it. She told him I was only a baby and that he'd ruined me for life. My mother never said anything to me. She didn't even try to tell me about the birds and the bees. She just petted me while Matt looked at me with hate in his eyes."

"Has your mother ever forgiven him? The way she looks at him and talks to him, I don't think she has." I was beginning to understand the Valcour household. Emily didn't seem to care that her mother now saw her son differently. It seemed as long as her mother petted her and sniped at her brother, Emily was happy. No wonder Johnnie was rarely at home. It was not the happy place I had always thought it to be.

Emily seemed calm and unaffected. I, on the other hand, was totally unprepared to deal with incest. I knew this would affect the way I felt about Matt. I knew in the future, I would never be anywhere near Mathieu Valcour when no one else was around.

I was happy to see my grandmother when she arrived. I wanted desperately to go home and concentrate on something other than Emily and her vicious brother.

– 4 –

ENOUGH PREJUDICE
TO GO AROUND

After my grandmother built her leaf and rag fire, we sat on the front porch swing as we had the night before.

"Are you ready for part two, Claire?" Big Mama looked a bit apprehensive, but I didn't think she'd dare disappointment me.

"I've been waiting all day for it." But when my grandmother yawned, I realized I'd better get her to start talking in a hurry. "Tell me about my mama. You stopped talking about her even before she died. I don't really know anything about her. Did she always look like a dried-up old hag? She wasn't even thirty when she died, but she looked like an old woman in her coffin."

"Your mama was a beautiful girl, Claire. I wish I had some pictures to show you, but we were never big on taking pictures. Oh, that auburn hair! It was natural, you know, she never had to dye it. She had those light brown eyes like her daddy, and that pretty, creamy skin. She coulda had her pick of husbands if she had stayed a good girl. But..." Big Mama stopped to give a long sigh. "Iris loved to dance and never missed a party or a ball."

"Did my mama ever go to a party wearing a pair of red velvet overalls? I think I remember seeing her in them, but I was so little I don't know if it was a dream or not."

"No, you weren't dreaming. She went to a Mardi Gras party wearing that outfit."

"I thought she was a beautiful fairy. She looked so different; I didn't think she was my mother." In my mind's eye I could see how my mother looked that night. Her silver cape was draped around her shoulders as she went out the front door with long, reddish curls bouncing off her back.

24

"Big Papa and I had a time with your mama. She had no interest in school. We finally gave in and let her quit. Iris could wriggle anything out of her papa, so when she wanted to go to all those parties and dances, he made sure she had a new dress or a new costume for each one of them. Big Papa is one of the founders of the Autocrat Club, you know, and that was the only place he forbid her to go." Big Mama stopped talking and I could tell she was hesitant about continuing.

"Don't stop, Big Mama. I want to know everything. I don't do what you call *conte* and I don't tell my family business to my friends, if that's what you're worried about."

"Okay, but if I ever hear what I'm telling you from anybody, I'll know you're the *mashuquette* who told because only your mama and I ever knew about it. And when I tell you, it'll be just you and me who know." My grandmother shook her finger at me.

"I promise I'll never tell a soul." I didn't take a breath waiting to find out what it was. I was almost giddy because I knew it was going to be big and juicy.

"When your grandfather was active in the Autocrat, they used to have a lot of different kinds of things going on. Every holiday, and of course Mardi Gras, there was some kind of special dance or ball. And every Friday they'd have fish fries. I guess they still do those things."

"Did you ever go to any of the dances or balls with him?"

"No, the club is for men; well...that's what Big Papa told me. They made money for the club by holding dances, but they didn't attend any of them. The only reasons the members were supposed to be at the dances were to collect the money at the door, chaperone the young people who came, and to keep out the riff-raff who liked to cause trouble. Me, I never worried about not being able to go to anything the club gave."

"Boy, you sure did trust your husband."

"Well...not completely. But back then, oh, I guess even now, if your husband tells you something's not for women, you just as well accept it because you can't do anything about it. Anyway, when your mother was fifteen, she asked her father to buy her some material to make herself a costume for a Mardi Gras party one of her friends was having. He had no idea she was planning to go to the masked ball at the Autocrat. Your mama was sure her father wouldn't recognize her if she was masked. Iris made herself a Cleopatra outfit and it was some pretty. She bought a plain mask and when she got finished adding to it, it was really something."

"Big Mama, did you know she was going to Big Papa's club?"

"No indeed, child. If I had known, I probably woulda told her father."

"Big Mama! You woulda ratted on my mama?"

"I don't really know. Let's just say I'm glad I didn't know. The night of the dance, guess who picked up your mama?"

"I don't know. Wait...Lester...my daddy, the bastard maker?" I quipped.

"Not nice, but you're right. It was Lester. He was the one taking your mama to the ball. That's the first time I saw him grown up. My brother is a *passablanc,* so he never did see my sister and me much. Your mama is the one who used to see my brother and his family at the uptown movie show all the time, you know, at the Saenger Theater."

"Damn, if my mother saw them, then that means she was passing for White, too."

"Honey, your mama passed whenever she wanted to. She went everywhere she wanted to go and nobody told her a thing. White people can't tell who's Colored or who's White. Too many of them look like us," Big Mama chuckled.

"I know your sister Seraphine became White, didn't she? *Nennaine* told me she did." My great-aunt used to tell me family stories before she changed and didn't make sense anymore.

"Seraphine had White fever bad. My father told us she went to work for his sister uptown, and one day she ran off with a White man. No one ever heard from her again. My father and my stepmother said she was a lost cause, so they never even tried to look for her. Me, I never really believed them."

"You and Nennaine look White. Did you ever pass?" I knew my grandfather hadn't. He was café au lait just like me. We could pass the brown-paper-bag-test, but not pass for White."

"No, we never wanted to."

"Is it true about the test a man has to pass to get into the Autocrat Club? They hold a brown paper bag next to his skin, and if he's darker than the bag, he can't become a member?" I had heard Emily's mother talking to one of her friends about it.

"Or...they pass a fine tooth comb through his hair and if it breaks, he doesn't get in? Is all that true?"

"Ask your grandfather about it one of these days," Big Mama's face was flushed as if I'd embarrassed her. "I want to see if he'll admit it to you. He doesn't tell me too much about what goes on at the club. But I've heard that's what they do."

"So, some people are too black for the Whites and too brown for the Creoles. That makes us as prejudiced as the White people." I had never given that much thought, but suddenly realized that after all the Creoles of color had been through because of discrimination, they were doing the same as the Whites – discriminating.

It was clear my grandmother didn't want to discuss it. "I'm off the track again," she said. "What was I talking about? Oh...Lester. Lester was dressed up like the King of Siam. Your mama made his costume, too. Him and your mama made a great-looking pair, yeah. When Iris and Lester got to the club, Big Papa was taking the tickets at the door. At first, Iris was afraid and she kept her head down. But when he took their tickets and told them to have a good time, she knew he didn't have any idea who she was. That's when she decided to really test her father."

"Big Mama, c'mon! How could my mama's own father not know who she was? How could he miss her eyes?" I was indignant.

"Well, I don't know. It might have been because she had put colored netting over the eye parts of her mask. All I know is, she said he didn't know who she was. But wait, you haven't heard the best part. When Gustave came into the dance hall, he was watching your mama dance and she said he didn't take his eyes off her. So she went and asked him to dance with her."

"What! How could he dance with her...touch her...hear her voice and not know her?" I jumped off the swing unable to restrain myself. My grandmother pulled me down again.

"I'm telling you, he didn't recognize your mother. He even tried to squeeze her closer to him, but she wouldn't let him. He asked her to save another slow dance for him because he thought she was the most beautiful girl at the ball. Iris told him she couldn't because her boyfriend wouldn't like it. So he invited her to come to a dance after Lent was over and he gave her a free ticket so she would come alone." My grandmother laughed like crazy. "If Gustave ever found out it was Iris and that I knew about it, he'd drop dead of a heart attack."

"You didn't hate Big Papa after that? I woulda killed that old, son-of-a-bitch." Big Mama glared at me over her eyeglasses. "Oh, I'm sorry, I shouldn't have said that. Big Mama, did my mama say the other men in the club danced with the women at the ball?"

"Honey, they all drank their liquor and danced with any woman who'd dance with them.

Iris watched her papa dance with a bunch of women. Me, I wasn't surprised at all because I knew he had a roving eye long before that dance." Big Mama laughed again. Nervously this time.

"You know what I think? I think he knew it was my mama and the joke was on her. I know he had to know his own daughter, especially when she talked. Maybe he was drunk."

"Maybe he was drunk and didn't recognize his own daughter." Big Mama shrugged her shoulders. I think she knew he did know but had kept it to himself. "But it doesn't matter now."

"Big Mama, how could you let him mess over you like that? Shit, you're too good. His ass would still be paying if he'd done that to me. Damn! What else did he do?" God, how stupid she was. Not me! No one will ever do that to me. How would I ever look at Big Papa the same way again? I'd always see him as a cheating husband. A sudden pain shot through my head.

"Hush your dirty language and just listen. I found out about a woman Big Papa was going with right before your mama was born. He hurt himself helping to move an icebox off a boat and into his friend's camp in North Shore and was in Charity Hospital for a week. Do you know that hussy had the nerve to come to the hospital to see him? She musta thought I wouldn't be there because she walked straight into his room. I was standing outside talking to the doctor when I saw her go in. I listened for a little while outside the door and I heard him tell her, 'Priscilla, you must be crazy coming here. You'd better get out of here before Philomene comes back and finds you.' But it was too late. I rushed in that room with my big belly, grabbed an umbrella out of Priscilla's hand, and beat her with it all the way down the hall. A nurse grabbed me and held me until Priscilla got on the elevator. Why are you holding your head, Claire?"

28

"Just a little ache. I think my head hurts because of all the new stuff I learned tonight. As for your husband, he needed his ass beaten, too. But it's funny, because when I look at you and Big Papa, I can't believe you ever had problems. Do you still love him, or are you together because you're getting old and you need each other?"

"How did you get so smart, little girl? I didn't know anything about life when I was your age. In fact, I didn't know anything until after I got married. Gustave and I, I guess like a lot of people our age, are married the way people ought to get married...for life. When we took our vows in front of the priest, we knew it would be forever." My grandmother's face softened and I could tell she was thinking about the good things her husband had brought to their marriage.

"Yeah, all that's true, but he had another woman on you, maybe more than one. I know I'd never forgive any husband of mine for doing that."

"Yes you would, Claire. You'd forgive him if you knew he was a good man, and your grandfather is a good man. But...he's a man. And for some reason, they have to stray once in a while. It must be their nature to be like that. Aren't you glad we stayed together so we could raise you?"

"I am glad, but what I'm really happy about is that we're not White." I had suddenly thought about something else that I needed to get off my chest.

"What are you talking about, child? I thought we were talking about your mother."

"I know, but look, Big Mama," I pointed to the old folks' home, "Look at that place with all those old White people in it. All they do is stand at the fence or sit on the balconies outside their rooms waiting for their children who never come after they put the old people in there. Most of them just get dumped like garbage. There are a lot of old people in there. But all I ever see are five or six families who come to visit on Sunday. Those old people were put there to die. Then after they die, that's when their families come back. They go to Mass and then follow the hearse to the cemetery. Then they spend the old people's money."

"Claire, who..."

I didn't let my grandmother finish. "Who told me that? I heard you and Nennaine talking one day. That's exactly what you said and I remember thinking how glad I was Colored people didn't leave their old people to die by themselves. I'm never going to put you and Big Papa in a place like that." I touched my grandmother's arm but then quickly pulled my hand away.

"You're a good child, Claire. I hope we leave this earth before we become a problem for you or your aunts. I know your Uncle Gus won't lift a finger to help, especially where I'm concerned. But I don't want to talk about my son because I'll surely cry." Big Mama dabbed at her eyes.

"I watched you take care of your sister until she died. Did you ever get tired and want to put her in a place like that?" I pointed to the old folks' home.

"*Mais non!* She was my sister and she needed me."

"But she was so mean to you. She used to call you stupid and jackass. She did that even before her head got messed up." I remember staying out of my great-aunt's room after her behavior started to change. I had no idea what was wrong with her.

"She was senile, Claire. Lots of people get that way when they get old. My sister was good to me, my husband, and my children. That's why we called her Nennaine. She was everybody's godmother. Think about something. When Gustave married me, I told him he had to take Aurelia to live with us. She didn't have anyone else and I wasn't going to let her live alone. She couldn't count on our brother, and Seraphine was gone, so there was no one else for her to live with except me. Aurelia never wanted to get married and she didn't. She finished raising my brother and me after we left my father's house. Our life was horrible after my mother died and my father remarried. One day I'll tell you that story."

"Big Mama, I know why you think Nennaine was good to you and your family. She was a teacher and always had a paycheck to pay for the house and to buy food for the family when Big Papa couldn't work because of the rain, huh?"

"That's right, but how do you know that?"

"You don't always speak in that funny kinda French. So when you think I'm sleeping, I'm usually not. I'm always listening to the conversations and arguments between you and Big Papa and the ones you used to have with Nennaine, too."

"You...uh..." my grandmother swallowed the other part of what she was going to say. Instead she said, "If it hadn't been for

Aurelia during the Depression in the '30s, we would have starved. She didn't believe in banks, and when the bank failed with the little money Gustave and I had, her money was in the armoire, right there in the hallway." Big Mama gave a loud, deep sigh. "Do you think I would ever put my sister in a home because I was tired or she was too much trouble? No indeed not."

"Did Big Papa get along with her?" I asked. I had always thought he didn't like her. He rarely spoke to her.

"They got along, but they never had much to say to each other. Maybe Gustave didn't like her because she came along with me like a part of the marriage and she never left. Aurelia told me she thought Gustave hated her, and the only reason he put up with her being here, was because she had a steady job. I never told her about the other woman or about Iris going to the Autocrat Club. I'm sure..." My grandmother suddenly stopped talking, twisted her head toward the sidewalk, and squinted her eyes in the dark.

Miss Anne Marie was passing the house and heard us talking. She came up the walk as far as the stoop to have a few words with us. "Good evenin, Philomene. Claire." She dipped her chin down toward her chest giving us the classical southern nod. "I bet you enjoyed that trout your son caught. I went *bummin* round to Gloria's yesterday and ate me some. He brought her more than a dozen of some big ol fish. Ain't nothin *chinchy* bout that son of yours."

"No...ah...I didn't get any. I wasn't home yesterday. He musta come by when no one was here." I could tell my grandmother was embarrassed because she was lying. She was home yesterday, like all the other days.

"Girl, you sho missed some good eatin." Miss Anne Marie fanned herself with her hand. "It's some sticky this evenin. Lemme get on home so I can get outta these sweaty clothes. I sho hate walkin in this dark, spooky block. But I got me my hat pin ready for any sumbitch who tries to fool with me," she flashed something silver in the darkness. "Goodnight, y'all."

My grandmother walked down to the fence with her to say goodbye. "I'll watch you until you get to the corner to make sure you're okay. Goodnight, Anne Marie."

I wondered why Big Mama bothered. Miss Anne Marie couldn't run back to my grandmother if she needed help, nor could my grandmother run to her to help.

31

Miss Anne Marie was a huge woman with the widest behind I'd ever seen. Her full name was Anne Marie Bogass and I wondered if she knew she was known as Anne Marie Bigass in our neighborhood. In New Orleans we attached a Miss or a Mister to peoples' first names instead of their last. If I hadn't done that, I'm sure I would have called her Miss Bigass more than once.

When my grandmother returned to the porch, she had slipped into her depression once again. This time I knew my Uncle Gus was the reason. I couldn't stand him! He always made her cry by telling her mean things when no one else was around to hear. She would never tell us what he'd said to her.

Big Mama didn't want to talk anymore. We went in and cleaned up the kitchen. Even though it was a Saturday night, we'd had a meal without meat – leftover codfish balls from the night before. Since all our Fridays were meatless, we usually had one of three dishes: egg stew, codfish balls or some kind of seafood. It was always my job to wash everything; Big Mama dried them and put them away. I didn't mind washing the dishes, but I hated to scrub the pots and pans used to cook any kind of seafood, especially codfish. I vowed when I'd have my own kitchen, I'd never cook codfish or any kind of seafood in my pots. Whenever I'd tell my grandmother how I felt, she'd laugh and tell me, "You're Creole and Catholic; you'll always have seafood cooking in your kitchen."

After the kitchen was done, we listened to the news on the radio. The war seemed to be winding down, but most of the news was still about the fighting.

My grandmother managed to tell me a little more while we were cleaning up. She told me when my mama met Lester she was only fifteen; he was already twenty. She met him at a party and didn't recognize him at first. She kept him away from Big Papa because she knew he'd disapprove. Lester came to the house only once, the night he picked her up for the masked ball at the Autocrat Club. They saw each other only about a dozen times when she found out she was pregnant. Big Mama said she begged my mother to go to California where my aunts lived. Her sisters would have helped her to get a fresh start. She had such a gift for sewing, especially for making costumes. They would have helped her get a job in Hollywood where they worked, but she refused to go.

My grandfather blamed my grandmother for my mother getting pregnant. He told her she should have put an end to Iris keeping company with Lester the minute she found out about it. Big Papa wanted to know why she didn't tell him it was happening. He said he would have forced Iris to go to California. Big Mama said he never gave her a chance to tell him she didn't find out they were seeing each other until well into the relationship.

When my grandmother started to cry, I knew it was time to stop talking and let her go to bed. I could hear her sobbing for a long time before I finally went to sleep. I didn't know if she was crying about my mother or my uncle. And if it was my uncle, I wanted God to let me be a man for just one day so I could kick Uncle Gus's ass until he puked.

– 5 –

LIVING A DREAM

That night, I slept in fits and starts. I had the same nightmare over and over again. Each time I'd wake up to find it was only a dream, I'd go right back to sleep and the same dreadful vision would start again.

In each dream I arrived home from the library to find a giant snake coiled in the corner of the kitchen near the stove. It was yellow and black with huge, yellow-green eyes, and the strangest thing of all was that it had a wide fish mouth with a long, scaly, red tongue. The snake's eyes bore into me as it told me it was waiting for my grandmother to come home from the market. I knew that wasn't true because she always went to the market before noon. I had never come home to an empty house ever since Lady Blue's and Wobble's murders. The snake seemed to sense I didn't believe it and quickly told me that Big Mama probably needed some meat from Vaucresson's butcher shop and had gone to St. Bernard Market to buy it. It suddenly moved its head closer to me and widened its fish mouth into a grin.

"I really don't know where she is. I was just guessing," the snake said. His crusty tongue darted in and out of its mouth close to my face.

"Why are you waiting for my grandmother?" I asked as I jumped away from the snake and hit my back against the table. "Awww...why...?"

The snake grinned enjoying my pain. "Why do you think I'm waiting for her?" It followed me as I moved toward the back door.

"I...I...don't know," I stammered.

Fully uncoiled, the snake was as long as the kitchen. Terror was now churning in my belly.

"When she comes back, I'm going to wrap myself around her and squeeze her until every last drop of life oozes out of her body. I'll crush you too if you try to help her." It thrust out its tongue and stung me on my chin.

My mouth flew open but no screams came out. I ran out the back door, through the alley and out to the sidewalk. I had to get to the market to stop Big Mama from coming home to her death. I ran up Johnson Street then turned right on Laharpe. And as I passed Emily's house, I saw her standing on her porch laughing and talking with a boy whose back was turned toward me. I didn't have time to stop, so I didn't call out to her.

Up Laharpe until I reached Claiborne...darted across the street...crossed over the *neutral ground*...DAMN...the market's closed. Back across the street to Levashe's drugstore...Big Mama could be picking up her medicine...noooo...it's CLOSED!

I fled up Claiborne Street a few blocks toward Esplanade. Was she walking home that way? NO! Street empty. Back the other way to St. Bernard Avenue...looked in Sacred Heart Church...looked through the big window of Belfield's Drugstore...in some alleys...over a bunch of fences all along the way to Corpus Christi Church. Maybe she's lighting candles. Church empty. No Big Mama! She wasn't anywhere I looked.

I was winded when I started running back to the house, but I didn't stop to suck in air, I ran clutching my chest. And then I spotted my grandmother walking about two blocks ahead of me. "Big Mama, Big Mama!" I called out to her. She seemed not to hear me. She continued walking despite my frantic, breathless screams. "Big Mama...don't go in the house...the snake is waiting for you...it's going to kill you. Stop! Please, Big Mama, stop." I ran faster and faster trying to catch up to her. But it was no use. By the time I got to the house, she'd already gone in. As I galloped through the alley, I could hear her screaming, screaming, screaming..........

I never made it to the kitchen in any of the dreams.

The next morning while I was getting ready for Mass, I heard a knock at the back door.

After my grandmother opened it, I could hear my uncle's angry voice. The door was closed between my room and the kitchen, so I cracked it open just enough to hear what they were saying.

"Who told you I gave Gloria a buncha trout?" Uncle Gus yelled.

"Never mind. That somebody didn't just see trout, that somebody ate trout. But you didn't think enough of your family to bring us some. I don't understand what we did to you for you to hate us so much. What did we do to you, Gus?"

"You gave birth to me, Ma, that was enough. Look at me...*I look like mortal sin dipped in hell.* How many times do I have to tell you that? I don't look anythin like my three sisters, well two, anyway, now that Iris's gone. How'd you get me, huh, Ma? Some joker must have hopped the back fence while Papa wasn't home. Look at me! Don't look at the floor." There were three loud smacks on something hard.

"Is that table a substitute for what you'd like to do to me, Gus?" My grandmother's voice was a little shaky but strong. "You don't scare me, son."

"Yeah, Ma, I sure would like to put a hurt on you. But first, tell me where this nappy, hay-colored hair comes from and these yellow-green eyes? You and Papa bein my parents, I'm not supposed to look like this. Nobody in this family has nappy hair, why me? And what about these color eyes? People tell me I look like a jungle cat...like a damn leopard. Your eyes are blue and Papa's are hazel. What did you do, Ma, to make me look like this? I know it ain't Papa's fault. I blame you. I'm the only monster in the whole goddamn family. Even the army didn't want my ass cuz I'm born with a heart defect. I couldn't even go to war to fight and die. I hate you for that and for all the other damn thins you done to me. And there you go, na...you and them goddamn crocodile tears. Shut up...just shut the hell up!" Uncle Gus yelled at Big Mama.

I rushed into the kitchen pulling my dress over my head and I stood between my grandmother and my uncle.

"Get out of this house and leave Big Mama alone. I'm sick of you mistreating her. I hate the things you tell her and I hate you, too. Get your ass out of here! And when Big Papa comes home, I'm gonna tell him what you've been saying to your ma..." Before I could finish what I was saying, Uncle Gus snatched me by my hair and dragged me out to the back porch where my grandmother wouldn't be able to hear what he said to me.

He smacked me hard across my face. "If you tell Papa," he whispered, "I'm goin to come back and kill you and your gramma, you hear me." He dragged me back into the kitchen and threw me into Big Mama's arms. "You better remember what I told you, too. I ain't playin. As for you, Mother Dear," he put his finger close to his mother's face, "You ain't never gonna get none of the trout or anythin else I catch. I wish Papa had never married you." He started to move closer to her as if he was going to hit her.

I moved backward near the corner of the stove where we kept a small baseball bat for "emergency" situations. But before I could pick up the bat, the screen door slammed open and Big Papa walked in.

Uncle Gus started to open his mouth to speak when my grandfather's fist knocked him square on his ass before he could get a word out.

"Apologize to your mama and your niece, boy." Big Papa roared. "Apologize to them or get the hell outta here and don't ever come back. Well...whatcha gonna do, boy?"

My uncle got up off the floor and walked to the back door, then he stopped. "Sorry, but I ain't apologizin for nothin and I never will."

"Then get out and stay out or I'll whip you until you go blind." Big Papa started to go after his son again but Big Mama grabbed his arm and held him back.

Uncle Gus tore out the back door, across the back porch, and his long legs hit the alley running.

"Come here, little girl," Big Papa pulled me close to him. He hugged Big Mama and me at the same time. "You're a good girl to protect your gramma the way you did. I was standin in the alley under that kitchen window." He pointed his chin toward one of the open windows above the alley. "I heard it all."

"What are you doing home so early, Gustave?" Big Mama asked him.

"Nothin was bitin, Philly. So I thought I'd come back early and take y'all to Lavata's to get some oyster loaves. Go on to church, little girl. We'll be ready to go when you get back."

"I'm scared, Big Papa. Uncle Gus might be waiting for me in the next block or somewhere around the church. He said he was going to kill Big Mama and me. Last night I even dreamed this was going to happen." I could see the big snake in my mind's eye; it had my uncle's head and its wide fish mouth was grinning as it wrapped itself around Big Mama and me.

I wasn't feeling so brave anymore.

"Don't let bad dreams scare you. They're just dreams. And as for your uncle, he's long gone. He'll crawl back here one day when he needs money. Here," Big Papa dug in his pocket and put a bunch of nickels in my hand, "light some candles for all of us, especially for your Uncle Gus and your mama. Go on na and hurry back. Your gramma and me are hungry."

– 6 –

THE BISHOP'S RING

The neighborhood was abuzz about a visit the bishop, head of the Catholic Archdiocese of New Orleans, was going to make to the old folks' home. Mr. Joseph, the gatekeeper, told everyone who passed his guardhouse that the bishop was coming to the home's church to say Mass.

Our neighborhood was racially mixed and almost everyone in it was Catholic. So, for Blacks and Whites, the event was going to be big. It was May 1946 - the Germans had surrendered ending the war in Europe and the atomic bombs had been dropped on Japan bringing the war in the Pacific to an end. Everyone knew there were many things to be thankful for and used any occasion to celebrate. I was especially thankful we lived across the street from the home and would get a special view of everything that would go on.

The nuns asked my grandparents to decorate the home's church with flowers for the bishop's visit. My grandparents and I were overjoyed because we'd get to play an important role in the event.

After Big Mama cut and arranged the flowers for the altar and the ones that would adorn the ends of the pews down the center aisle, I helped Big Papa set them up in the church. They took my breath away. Upon seeing how beautiful the church looked, it occurred to me that was the only opportunity I'd have to see the flower arrangements. My maturing mind suddenly grasped the impact of being forbidden to attend the special Mass for one reason only – the color of my skin.

The Catholic churches in the city were segregated – they were either White or Colored. We had one church in the Seventh Ward that was considered a mixed congregation, but even at

Sacred Heart the division was enforced - Whites sat up front while the Coloreds sat in the last three rows in the back. The city's priests were White, as well as the nuns. There was one order of Colored nuns, the Sisters of the Holy Family, who operated a school for Colored girls. You knew the rules without them being spelled out to you – what churches you could go to and the ones you couldn't. If you caused a commotion over discrimination, you were often arrested.

The Coloreds would be allowed to greet the bishop and give him their many gifts, but outside the gate before the bishop entered the home. The Whites would also greet him outside, but they could enter the gate and the church to attend Mass. They would be served refreshments in the dining hall.

In a few weeks, I would be confirming at Corpus Christi where I went to church and attended elementary school. That same bishop would be presiding over the Confirmation. I had been excited because Emily and I would get to see him and be blessed by him twice. I slowly began to lose my enthusiasm. Every time I thought about the grand procession that would take place when he marched up the driveway and into the church with his White flock trailing behind him – the church my grandparents and I had decorated – I could feel the anger welling up inside me. I wished I had magical powers, so that with my mind I could cause all the beautiful flowers in the church to wilt and dry up just before everyone entered the church.

I asked Big Mama if there'd be any flowers left for Corpus Christi's altar when I confirmed. She pacified my concerns when she showed me all the tiny buds that would be open in a few weeks. My grandparents always provided the flowers that filled our church on holidays and special occasions and everyone knew they came from our yard. I beamed like a fluorescent bulb every time I sat in church, especially on Easter Sunday when I saw all the beauty that I had helped Big Papa and Big Mama create. You couldn't tell me all eyes in the church were not on me, and for a change, it was for something positive.

My grandparents' flowers, fruits and vegetables were known all over the Seventh Ward, especially during the war when most of the men were off fighting and almost everything was either rationed or in short supply. Our victory garden was the most productive in the neighborhood. There was something grown, picked, sold, and delivered every season. Delivery was my job – from pans of figs to bags of persimmons, pomegranates, peppers, mirlitons, eggplants, and tomatoes. There were Easter lilies, red and white roses, hydrangeas, violets, and a score of other flowers that I remember putting in the basket on my bike and delivering to our neighbors' for their tables on special occasions. We even sold brown eggs from the dozen chickens we raised.

Big Papa's heart condition changed the way he provided for us. We relied on the stipend he received from the nuns, some non-strenuous jobs he did for the neighbors, the rent from the other side of the house, and the money from the sale of the things we grew in our yard. Occasionally, my aunts in California would send us a few dollars. That dribbled away and finally stopped altogether.

I would have given anything to have my grandfather robust again and able to do the things he loved to do. Emily and I talked about what we'd wish for when we'd kiss the bishop's ring during Confirmation. The superstition was, if you made a wish when you kissed the ring, whatever you wished for God would grant. I believed this body and soul. I wanted Big Papa's heart repaired. I wanted him to be able to work again so that he could buy another fishing camp in North Shore and I'd be able to see the smile come back to his face. He hadn't been happy since he'd sold his camp because we needed the money. He not only missed fishing on the weekends, but his catch was part of our meals for the following week. There was no more Nennaine to fall back on. I knew my grandmother missed her, and although my grandfather would never admit it, he must have missed her, too. Even if it was purely monetary.

We hadn't seen Uncle Gus since Big Papa hit him when he'd refused to apologize to my grandmother. Every week Big Mama sent me to Gloria's, Uncle Gus's friend, to ask her if she'd seen him. The answer was always no. But one day she didn't answer right away. She asked me to go home and ask my grandparents to return the money Uncle Gus had borrowed for them. When I told her he hadn't borrowed any money for them, she went home with me to confront them.

"Hey, Miss Philly and Mistah Gustave," Gloria greeted them as she walked ahead of me through the back door. I noticed how she took long strides and planted her feet solidly each time they hit the floor. Big Mama said she walked like a longshoreman and that there was nothing lady-like about her; it must have been running a barroom that made her that way. But it didn't matter; we liked her anyway.

"Y'all musta sold boocoo flowers for the bishop's visit. Ah'll be over here in the mornin wit y'all." Gloria hugged Big Mama and nodded to Big Papa.

My grandmother looked anxious about Gloria's visit and suddenly jumped to her feet. My grandfather grabbed her hand and tried to make her sit down and calm herself.

"What's happened to Gus, Gloria?" There was a rift in Big Mama's voice when she said her son's name. She held on to Big Papa's hand to steady herself knowing bad news was coming.

"Nothin, Miss Philly, calm down. Nothin's happened to Gus. Well, nothin Ah know about anyhow," Gloria said. "Ah'm here cuz Claire tells me Gus didn't borrow no money from me for y'all. Gus musta lied, then. Cuz about three months ago, he told me y'all was hurtin bad for money since you got heart trouble, Mistah Gustave. Gus said y'all was too embarrassed to ask anybody for help. Ah loaned him $200 to give to y'all. He told me y'all would pay me back in a coupla months." Gloria stood nervously licking her bottom lip. She didn't seem to know what to do with her hands, so over and over again she smoothed her straight, light-brown hair from her crown down to her shoulders. Looking at her closely, I realized how pretty she was. She would have been beautiful had she done something to look more feminine. According to Big Mama, she could try wearing something frilly and some lipstick and rouge once in a while.

"We haven't seen Gus for four months now. We had a falling out. Didn't he tell you about it, Gloria?" Big Mama looked at her husband for support, but he seemed too shocked to speak. He was a man of few words, and when he was angry, he said even less.

"Yeah Miss Philly, he told me. But he said he didn't hold no grudge toward his father or any a y'all. He was gettin the money to help y'all and to show y'all there wasn't no hard feelins. There was some six-month job over in Mississippi he talked about. Maybe that's where he's at all this time."

"Sit down, Gloria; I'll make us some coffee." My grandmother pulled out a chair for her. "Claire, walk over to Gus's girlfriend's house on Derbigny and ask her if she's seen him. What's that girl's name again?"

"Angelique." Gloria and I said it at the same time. Gloria's teeth were clamped together as the name, laced with venom, forced its way out of her mouth. She looked at me and grinned showing me her firmly-pressed-together teeth.

"Ask Angelique if she knows your uncle's whereabouts. Gloria's gonna wait here until you get back." Big Mama turned to Gloria realizing she hadn't asked. "Can you wait?"

"Sure, Miss Philly, Ah can wait," Gloria said. "You can bet Ah ain't goin nowhere until Ah find out where that bum's done gone."

"Go on now, Claire, and come right back. I have a bad feeling about this." My grandmother looked so disheartened. She stared at the floor shaking her head from side to side as she spoke. Big Papa stared at her with frozen, lifeless eyes.

As I left the house, I carried with me the anguished look on Gloria's face. She loved my uncle, but at forty-three years old she couldn't compete with Angelique who was Gus' age, ten years younger. Gloria was the owner and operator of a bar-restaurant and was every bit the independent woman. Whenever Gus needed a temporary place to live, a few bucks to tide him over until payday, or when he needed sex because Angelique wasn't available, Gloria was there to provide whatever he needed. She never asked for a commitment and believed he'd realize how important she was to him and eventually marry her. Even if they were married, she said, she'd allow him to have Angelique or any younger woman on the side, as long as he came home to her.

Gloria didn't know I'd heard her tearful confession to my grandmother as they sat on the swing one afternoon. I was quietly sitting behind one of the little wing doors I'd cracked open in order to eavesdrop. Big Mama told her how much she wanted Gus to settle down with her and how much she liked her, but there was nothing she could do to help. She urged Gloria to move on with her life before she got too old. She asked her how long she planned to "accommodate" Gus. Didn't she think ten years was long enough?

I ran all the way to Angelique's house about eight blocks from where I lived. I was tempted to stop at the small grocery store on the corner of Prieur and Columbus for a box of Smith

Brothers licorice cough drops. I loved those more than any candy bar. I decided to buy a box and had my hand on the shop's screen door, but my conscience prevented me from going in. My grandmother had asked me to hurry back, so no cough drops. I resumed my run.

Angelique's mother answered the door before I had a chance to knock. She must have been peeping through the shutters the way she always did. She seldom came out of the house. She preferred to peep at everyone and see everything through her cracked shutters. Her neighbors called her "*queen of do poppin.*"

"Come on in, cher. Nobody's home cept me," she told me.

I went into the cluttered, dusty front room. "Miss Ines, is Angelique home? I need to ask her something." I stayed close to the door. Everywhere I looked there was a reclining cat staring at me. The house smelled like catpee and the floor was covered with catshit. Goosebumps popped out on my arms and legs and I started to shiver. I swallowed hard trying not to vomit.

"You know Angelique ain't here. Why you axin me fa her?" Miss Ines shook her bent finger in my face. Her long fingernails were packed solid with black gunk. "Your uncle stole ma daughter and took her with him to California. They got married last month. Don't y'all know that?"

"No! We haven't seen or heard from my uncle in four months. We didn't know where he was. I came here to ask Angelique if she knew."

"*Lord today!* That uncle of yours is some dirty bastard. Ah'm sorry for talkin that way, cher, but that's just what he is. He knew if ma daughter axed me if she could go with him, Ah'da said no. So he talked her into sneakin off in the night like some common floozy. He knows Ah don't have nobody else to help me, but he made her leave me anyhow. He ain't right, cher, and God's gonna punish him for what he done. So Ah *put him in the hands of the Lord.*"

"I'm sorry, Miss Ines. He used to hurt my grandmother, too. So I know what a dirty bastard he is." I had a feeling she wouldn't object to my language because I was agreeing with her. I moved closer to the door and opened it.

"Wait, cher. Don't you want a cool glass a lemonade? I just made some."

"No, ah…no thanks. I have to go now. My grandparents are waiting for me."

"Okay, but tell Philomene to come and see me, so we can talk about this *comass.* Tell her Gus is workin as a chauffeur for a big time producer in Hollywood. He's makin good *la shon.* Angelique's workin, too. They oughta be sendin both of us some of that la shon insteada writin to me to brag about it." Miss Ines started to cough and wheeze. Then she spit into a rag she took out of the pocket of her grimy dress. I quickly squeezed out of the door.

"Good day, cher," she managed to mumble between the coughs that rocked her body.

I ran home as fast as my legs would go. My grandparents and Gloria weren't as shocked as I thought they'd be. Gloria was willing to let the money go as a loss, but Big Papa wouldn't hear of it. It would take him a while to pay it all back, he said, but she'd get every penny of it. He wanted to start with fifty dollars which he took out of a pocket in his overalls, then three more payments of fifty dollars, he told her, one every other month.

Gloria tried to talk him out of feeling obligated to repay her, but Big Papa said Gus was his son, so it was his responsibility to make things right. I wondered how he'd do it. We were always in financial dire straits. My grandmother's face was pale and expressionless. I knew she too was wondering how her husband planned to pull it off. She must also have felt a degree of guilt because she knew it was because her son hated her that he'd done such a horrible thing to us. She confirmed what I was thinking when she told Gloria she pitied Gus's new wife because she may become his new object of hate. Big Mama said she'd go and see Angelique's mother to warn her that nothing ever pleased Gus and her daughter may be in trouble.

When Gloria left, the three of us were too mired in grief and worry to say anything else about Uncle Gus. Someone else had not only been lost to us, but to make matters worse, he had left us his bold rejection: the financial hardship to repay his debt which could very well kill his father. And…my uncle had escaped from me, from my revenge. Faithfully in my prayers every night, I asked God to punish him now that he was out of my reach.

"Gustave," Big Mama broke the awful silence, "the money you gave Gloria...was that the money we made selling flowers for the bishop's visit?"

"Yes, but I don't want to talk about it right now, Philly. I need to go and see Albert. We'll talk when I get back." Big Papa picked up his keys and walked out the back door. A few minutes later, we heard him recklessly drive out of the yard and take off down the street with his tires squealing. His Model A Ford was always in excellent condition. Albert, his friend, was a first-class mechanic, and he and Big Papa benefited from each other's skills.

"Listen to him and that car. He's angry, that's why he's driving like a crazy man. I'll bet he's gone to ask Albert to get him a couple of jobs, even though the doctor's told him not to do anything strenuous, to stay calm, and not to lose his temper so much." My grandmother grabbed the back of her neck and squeezed it. "I'm trying so hard to keep Big Papa alive, I think it's gonna kill me in the process." She gave a nervous little laugh.

"Well, Big Mama, I'm about to make you feel better." I took thirty-two dollars out of my pocket and handed it to her. "Here," I said, "This is the money I hadn't given Big Papa from my deliveries the last two days."

"Claire, I think you have some kinda special gift. You seem to do things just when they ought to be done. I think you know about things before they happen," Big Mama told me as she shook the money in the air.

"No, wait, Big Mama. I didn't hold onto that money on purpose. I just never had a chance to give it to Big Papa. Are...are you saying I have *hoodoo* power?" My mouth suddenly got dry and my top lip began to twitch. I was remembering my dream about the snake before Uncle Gus's last visit.

My grandmother saw the fear in my eyes. "No, child, no." She took both my hands in hers and rubbed them briskly. "I didn't mean to scare you. I meant you have a good gift, a gift that God gave you, not the kind you get from the devil. Remember a few days ago when you asked me if we had the money to get the things you needed for your Confirmation, well, think about that. If you had given this money to Big Papa, he probably would have given it to Gloria, and then I don't know where we'd get the money for your Confirmation. But look, here it is. That's the kinda thing I'm talking about."

46

"Whew, thanks, Big Mama. You had me really scared for a minute. I thought you were comparing me to *Marie Laveau*," I said and patted her shoulder even though I wasn't a hundred percent convinced. "Tomorrow, Emily and I have to be across the street early so we can get a good place to stand. Are you and Big Papa staying on the porch?"

"Yes. Anne Marie and her husband, Gloria, Albert and his wife, and maybe a couple of other people will be here. I'm making coffee and somebody's bringing hot donuts from Liuzza's Bakery. You and Emily come back for some donuts and café au lait before you go to Mass."

"Okay, thanks, but after Mass. We're going to Communion. I think I'd better get my clothes ready for tomorrow." I left my grandmother sitting in the kitchen with her head in her hands waiting for my grandfather to return.

The next morning just before seven o'clock, Emily and I were in a choice spot right in front of the big gate of the home. We had on our church clothes because we were going to Corpus Christi to attend Mass right after the bishop went into the home and the gate was closed.

We watched the nuns scurry from floor to floor rounding up the old people who were able to walk and bring them to the church for Mass. I didn't see the woman in the yellow, chenille robe who always hung over the third-floor, balcony railing screaming, "Help! Help me!" Missing too was the man who stood for hours at attention in front of the closed, church doors, or the other man who often came out to pee on the flowers because he thought they weren't getting enough water.

Twenty minutes later, we were surrounded by people standing five deep waiting for the bishop to arrive. They had brought all sorts of gifts for him: flowers, cookies, cakes, pies, hand-crocheted lace to trim his vestments, embroidered doilies, fudge, pralines, homemade wine and brandy, freshly-caught crabs, shrimp and fish, even freshly laid eggs. They were giving the things they could afford or could make themselves. Emily brought a cash donation for the poor in an envelope. I had decided to give nothing. I had already given my family's gift of the flower arrangements in the church – that was enough. And because I was angry about the discrimination issue that was about to take place, I thought it was certainly more than the bishop and the home deserved.

The bishop arrived shortly before 8:00 – minutes before he was scheduled to say Mass. His long, black, highly-polished car pulled up in the front of the iron bridge. He did not get out until after his driver had loaded the gifts into the trunk of the car.

Short, round, and red-faced with bright, orange hair that glistened in the sun, the bishop's smile was so wide and artificial that his mouth looked like the mouth of a jack-o-lantern with a full set of teeth. As the bishop walked across the bridge, he kissed the small children and the babies, but only the White ones. The Colored babies and older children got a pat or a rub on their heads, then he'd stick his hand in their faces making his ring available for them to kiss.

When he got to me and raised his hand to give me the ceremonial pat, I put my head down and quickly moved back into the crowd. As I turned to leave, I saw Emily bend over and kiss the bishop's ring. I stayed in the back as he made his way up the driveway and into the church with the Whites following him in for Mass. Mr. Joseph quickly closed the gate. The bishop's Colored driver waited in the car.

On our way to Corpus Christi Church, I blasted Emily for kissing the Bishop's ring. I was angry because she chickened out and I ended up being the only militant one.

"Why did you kiss the damn ring after we said we might not do it? You saw me walk away; why didn't you?"

"Because I wanted my wish to come true," Emily screamed. "Maybe you didn't give a shit about the thing you wanted to wish for, but I did." She threw it right back at me.

"I did care about my wish and I still do," I screamed back at her. "But after I watched that man take everybody's stuff, saw him kiss all the White kids, and then rub 'dem po little niggas' haids,' I was so goddamn mad, I thought my head was going to pop open. There was no way I was going to put my lips on that prejudiced bastard's hand."

"Okay...that's you. But goddamnit don't tell me what to do. And, Claire, stop talking all that blasphemy stuff." Emily rolled her eyes at me and started to fastwalk.

I let her walk ahead and I lagged behind so that I could think.

Now what would I do? I needed to make the wish I'd planned when I'd kiss the bishop's ring during my Confirmation. I needed God to grant it. How else was my grandfather going to get his heart fixed? The more I thought about it, the more I realized that I'd have to let it go just as I had Santa Claus, the Easter Bunny and the Tooth Fairy. I'd have to find another way because I was certain I'd never kiss that man's ring. I knew when the bishop would shove his fat, pasty hand in my face at the Confirmation; I'd turn away in disgust again. There would have to be a direct line to God to get Big Papa cured – the middle man idea wasn't going to work.

- 7 -

JUST THE TWO OF US

My grandmother knew what was wrong the moment Mr. Albert appeared at the back door. We had no telephone then, so he had to come to the house. He stood on the back porch and looked at her through the screen door.

"Gustave's dead, Albert?" Big Mama was asking but she already knew the answer.

With his aging, lean body more bent than usual, Mr. Albert opened the screen door and stepped into the kitchen. "He didn't make it to Charity Hospital, Philomene. Ah'm sorry."

I screamed. My grandmother told me to be quiet. As I whimpered, she stood motionless while Mr. Albert told her what happened.

"Gustave complained all day yestiddy, even on our way to ma fishin camp." Mr. Albert suddenly remembered he still had on his cap and snatched it off his head. "We wasn't five minutes out of Nu Awlins when he started sayin he had intagestion. He said he ate some cabbage and stewed chickin you had fixed fa him. This mawnin he told me he walked the flo all night, but Ah neva heard him. Ah gave him some bicarbnut a soda and Ah thought it done him some good. But about 11:00 when we was out crabbin, he keeled over in his skiff. Maurice was with us and Ah was some glad. He helped me get Gustave back to Nu Awlins as fas as we could. Ah thought cuz North Shore wasn't too far we'd make it, but he died on the way." Mr. Albert's voice shook as tears gathered in the corners of his eyes. He rubbed his dry hands together and then as gently as he could, he leaned over and patted my grandmother's shoulder. I couldn't take my eyes off the empty spaces where three of his fingers had been. When he and Big Papa were out hunting one day, his shotgun misfired and blew off part of his left hand.

"Did Gustave suffer much, Albert?" Big Mama was crying now.

"No, Ah don't think he did. He neva come to after he fell over in his boat." Mr. Albert sniffed and blinked back his tears.

"What do I do now?" Big Mama asked.

"You don't worry bout nothin right na. Maurice and me, we called Blandin's Funeral Home to pick up Gustave's body from Charity. But firs, you gotta go and idenify him. Come on, Philomene, Ah'll take you up to the hospital."

Mr. Albert waited in the kitchen while my grandmother took off her apron and went to brush her hair and get her purse. I sat with him at the table with my head down on my arms. He reached over and patted my cheek. "Ah'm sorry, sugah, Ah know how much you gonna miss your grampa. He sho wanted to see you grow up to be a fine, young lady."

"Stay here, Claire," my grandmother told me as she rushed into the kitchen, "I don't think you should come with us."

"No," I cried, "I don't want to stay here; you have to let me come. I'm afraid to stay here by myself."

"Okay then. Hurry up and put on a dress and comb your hair. We'll wait for you in the car," Big Mama said. She hated the boy's overalls Big Papa let me buy. So even though death had just arrived at our door, I still needed to be dressed like a lady.

After Big Mama identified my grandfather's body, Mr. Albert took us to Western Union to send a telegram to my aunts in California. The next day we received their reply telling us they were unable to come for the funeral because they were planning to get married soon. They sent a hundred dollars to help with the burial expenses.

That telegram completely destroyed my grandmother. She started muttering to herself day and night. How could her daughters not come home for their father's funeral? Where was her only son, Gus? She questioned herself about whether or not she should try and find him to let him know his father had died, but she knew he probably wouldn't come. He was angry with his father and he hated her, his own mother, so why would he care? She knew the people who loved and respected her husband would be there – the two of us and all his friends - so who cared if anyone else came. Big Mama didn't seem to care that I heard her talking to herself; she was behaving like a woman possessed. I thought I needed to talk to someone about her, but I didn't know who. And if she found out, I knew she would think I betrayed her.

The purple and black mourning crepe that hung on our door didn't help. In order to avoid looking at it, my grandmother and I didn't use the front door. We walked up and down the alley using the back door. I didn't wait for the undertaker to take it down; I did the morning after the funeral.

We kept my grandfather's body at the funeral home for viewing and the rosary and we held his wake at our house. Gloria and Mr. Albert and his wife came to the house early in order to set up the food and drink. There were soft drinks and punch, and some hard liquor, mostly for the men. Large platters of boiled ham, bologna and salami, different kinds of cheeses, all sorts of salads, and an assortment of bread and crackers fed our guests. Our friends brought various cooked dishes and baked goods.

It was at the wake that we first heard the rumor. Francine and Clementine, my twin aunts in California, were passing for White and were going to marry White men – two brothers who worked as cameramen in Hollywood.

My aunts were seamstresses in the wardrobe department of MGM Studios. They had gone to California in 1941 just after World War II started. When my grandparents learned of their plans to leave, they were hurt and couldn't understand why their children wanted to leave home. The twins told them there was no future for them in New Orleans. They wanted good jobs which they couldn't get; they wanted to marry men who weren't poor and Creole; and most of all, they wanted to live where the rain didn't constantly interfere with everything they did. With heavy hearts my grandparents let their daughters go and wished them good fortune. At first the twins wrote every week, then once a month, and eventually we rarely heard from them.

One of Big Papa's friends told Gloria he'd seen the twins in California and that he'd gotten the information straight from their mouths. My aunts planned to cross over and disappear into the White world. That news instantly spread through the house.

A lot of whispering started as everyone sat around the front room, the kitchen, and the front and back porches eating and drinking. Most of the talk, especially the nasty aspersions cast by the women, was about my aunts when it should have been what they remembered about my grandfather.

The men were the ones who reminisced about their friend. They recalled how Big Papa had helped all of them build their homes. Together they had donated their time and their talents to build their church, Corpus Christi, and their private men's organization, the Autocrat Club. Whatever they shot when they hunted; they shared. When the seafood catch at the fishing camps they owned in North Shore was abundant, those who had camps shared with the ones who did not. Big Papa was an essential part of that tightly-knit community. Anything wood that needed to be built or repaired, his hands helped do it. He made himself available whenever he was needed.

Gloria was upset because the women had picked Big Papa's wake to gossip about my aunts. To her that showed a lack of respect for his widow.

She told my grandmother and me, "Don't y'all listen to all that conte. You don't know if it's even true. Let me handle their bahinds. They ain't never gonna talk like that at nobody else's wake!" I don't know what she said to the gossipers, but as quickly as the jabbering had started, it stopped.

Big Mama went through the wake, the funeral Mass, and the burial in a daze. Now and then, she cried. But most of the time, she was quiet as she listened and looked around with her soulful eyes. Her face had grown flushed and it stayed that way. Mr. Albert's wife told me to make sure my grandmother paid a visit to the doctor because her blood pressure might be high. Big Mama refused to go. We had so little money, she said, she couldn't afford to spend any of it on a doctor and medicine. I begged and pleaded with her, but she wouldn't go. She made me promise I wouldn't tell Dr. La Croix, the family doctor, about her condition, and swore she'd go to see him as soon as things were financially better for us.

Father O'Mara, at Corpus Christi Church, knew about our situation and offered my grandmother a chance to make a few dollars a week washing and ironing his vestments. She jumped at the opportunity to earn some money. He also gave us a discount on my school tuition.

I felt humiliated. Growing flowers for the nuns was one thing, being the priest's washerwoman was quite another. How could she wash a White man's clothes? Please God, don't let it be true. You couldn't tell me Big Papa wasn't having a conniption in his tomb.

After all the praying I had done asking God to fix my grandfather's heart, He hadn't heard my prayers. In my thirteen year old mind, I knew I was being punished, and it was because I refused to kiss the bishop's ring...twice. Now, God not only hadn't granted my wish to repair Big Papa's heart, He had let him die. And to make matters worse, we were poorer than we were before. Big Mama was probably sicker than she was telling me and was going to die leaving me alone in the world. How could this happen? Except for not kissing the bishop's ring and cursing, I knew I was a good girl. I couldn't correct the kissing-of-the-ring incidents, but I swore I'd stop saying bad words. Maybe then, God would stop punishing me? My daydreams and my nightdreams were of nothing else.

I grew silently angry. Why had Big Papa died before I could enjoy going to North Shore with him again? He'd promised me he'd teach me how to fish and crab. And I'd never gotten the chance to ask him about the brown paper bag and the fine tooth comb. What would I do when I outgrew the overalls he'd bought me? He'd spoiled me. Big Mama never would.

Before my grandfather was even put in his grave, the nuns hired someone else to tend their garden. The rent from the other side of the house, the money Big Mama made at the rectory, and the sales we made from the fruit and flowers we grew allowed us to get by. But we had a paper-thin existence; there was nothing extra. All of Big Papa's friends slowly disappeared. Big Mama claimed she understood. She knew they were busy trying to keep their own families afloat. We pinched pennies to make sure her dues in the Ladies Sodality were always paid because she was depending on the Sodality's death benefit payment and her small insurance policy to pay for her burial. She didn't want a wake, she said, just quietly put her in the vault on top of her husband.

My grandmother had no idea how much pain and fear I felt every time she talked about her death. My grandfather was dead, my mother had been murdered, my uncle had gone away angry, and there'd been no further word from my aunts in California. We were essentially alone and too full of pride to outwardly show our struggle to survive. When I heard my grandmother cry in her bed every night when she thought I was asleep, I knew I had to do something to make things better for us.

Bobby, a friend from school, told me Colari's Drugstore needed another person to make deliveries a few hours a day after school and all I needed was a bicycle. He worked there, but lately there were more deliveries than he could handle. I applied for the job before I told my grandmother about it. Mr. Colari had known my family for many years. He knew I'd be a good worker because I'd delivered fruits and vegetables to his wife many times. He usually hired boys fourteen or older, but even though I was a girl and had just turned thirteen, he hired me anyway.

I worked every afternoon, Monday through Friday from 3:30 to 5:30, and all day Saturday. I had my own bicycle, so Mr. Colari didn't have to buy one for me to use. Big Mama wasn't too pleased I'd gotten the job without her permission, but because she knew the Colaris and the drugstore was only a few blocks from our house, she didn't fuss too much. I earned three dollars a week and my tips were good. Almost every week, I'd collect at least four dollars from my customers.

Mr. Colari also sold some groceries: canned food, sugar, coffee, tea and other non-perishables. He also sold bread, apples and oranges and occasionally other perishables. Whatever perishables he didn't sell in two or three days, Bobby and I were allowed to split and take home.

A few days before Christmas, we received a letter from my aunts. Enclosed was a picture of their double wedding. Big Mama put the letter away without letting me read it. I was hurt. But the look on her face when she'd read it told me it was another heartache she'd have to get over. I wondered how much more she could take. A week later she handed it to me and apologized for not letting me read it when it first came. "Remember," she said, "everybody does what they need to do to survive, so don't blame your aunts. I think I always knew this would happen. I think Big Papa did, too."

I took the one page letter out of the envelope.

December 14, 1947

Dear Mama,

We guess you can tell from the picture that we were married a month ago in a joint ceremony. We married brothers and live in apartments next door to each other.

About six months ago, we saw one of Papa's friends here in California. We're sure you've heard about it by now. That's why we decided to write this last letter to you.

Our lives have completely changed and we don't intend to go back to the way things used to be. We've made a decision that we know will hurt you, but we have no other choice.

Our husbands are White and they think we are, too. We have let them believe we're orphans without any living relatives. Living as White has forced us to cut all ties and contact with everyone we knew before and ask that you don't try to find us. This is our way of erasing our past. We hope you understand and will forgive us. We'll always love you in our hearts.

Goodbye,
Francine & Clementine

The envelope had no return address and the postmark was smeared and illegible. As for the picture, Big Mama had torn it to shreds and threw it out the day the letter came.

I knew my aunts would have no trouble passing for White. They had fair skin with hazel eyes and light reddish-brown hair - a young version of my grandmother, except for the eye color. Why shouldn't they change their lives? Even though I didn't blame them for switching sides, I couldn't forgive them for deserting their parents. But I did wonder, given the chance, if I'd do it.

I didn't know then how everything that happened before I was fourteen would profoundly influence who I'd turn out to be. I sat for a long time with the letter in my hand watching Big Mama try to conceal her pain. Her children, every single one of them, were gone. Four ungrateful pigs who didn't deserve the parents they'd been given. But I, who loved my grandparents, had already watched one of them die and knew the other would soon follow.

What was going to happen to me? I knew that's what kept Big Mama sad all the time. I wondered what I could do to keep her alive so that I could have her with me while I finished growing up.

My aunts' letter had put a hex on Christmas that year. But then our Christmases had never been what you'd call joyous...that is celebrated with lots of presents, a decorated tree and a big special meal. They were low-key: a few presents, sometimes a small tree and the meal was more like a Sunday meal, not particularly sumptuous, but more than what we had on a weekday. I always knew we didn't have a lot of money and realized things didn't come to you out of thin air. So I learned to expect little and that way I would be less disappointed when there was little or nothing at all. The Christmas I remember most was the year I was nine. I got a shiny, new, blue and white bicycle.

– 8 –

MEETING SERA MENARD

One afternoon while I was sorting my deliveries, I came across a bag with the name, Sera Menard, almost identical to my grandmother's sister's name, the one who'd left home and never returned. Although the name wasn't exactly the same, I still held out hope it would be her. A "what if" popped into my head. What if it was my great-aunt and she had shortened her first name hoping she'd never be found? But she still had her last name, so that didn't make sense.

According to the address, this Sera Menard lived on Esplanade near Galvez in one of the enormous, two-story houses with the wide, wrap-around porches. All the properties in that block had magnificent gardens that fronted and encircled the houses. Several had beautiful courtyards with working fountains, birdbaths and palm trees. No Creoles of color lived on Esplanade near Galvez. The people who lived in those homes had to have enough money to maintain them, and Whites were the only ones with that kind of money. Creoles of color could not live in those houses even if they could afford them. Segregation dictated where everyone lived, even in a mixed neighborhood. Pushing my curiosity to the back of my mind, I started out on my bicycle to make my deliveries.

When I arrived at the Menard house, I stood outside the gate for a long time afraid to go in. My whole body shook; every nerve cell seemed to be firing at the same time. Mentally, I wanted to get it over with; emotionally, I didn't know if I could handle it. If she was my great-aunt, how would I tell my grandmother? And if she wasn't, then I'd be disappointed.

Finally, I sunk my top teeth into my bottom lip in an effort to steel myself against my own timidity, pushed in the heavy, cast-iron gate and walked with my bike up the path that wound through a lovely flower garden. I thought if Sera Menard was anything like her beautiful garden or smelled as sweet as its bright flowers, then I couldn't wait to meet her. I rested the bike against the steps, walked up onto the porch and banged the big, brass knocker on the door. I could hear a fragile, female voice telling me she was on her way. When the door opened, a small, frail woman with piercing eyes stood looking me up and down. She gave me a big smile as she held out her gnarled hand to receive the bag I was delivering. Slowly and deliberately, she leaned her curved back against the door frame for support. She closed her eyes and sighed before she spoke again.

"You're new. What happened to Bobby?"

"He...ah, he...ah," suddenly I couldn't talk. I was paralyzed as I stared at the woman. She smiled at me as she took the bag out of my hand. She was old but still beautiful. Her silky, white hair was loosely piled on top her head and held up with two, large, mother of pearl combs. The loose tendrils fell helter-skelter around her ears and neck. Her face was exquisite without a drop of makeup. The eyes...I'd seen them before. Someone I knew had those spectacular eyes: sky-blue, ringed with a black circle. The woman's skin was fairer than my grandmother's, but despite that, I thought they resembled each other. Perhaps I forced myself to think they did. Big Mama spent so much time in the sun tending her fruit and flowers, I didn't know what color she was under her dress. I promised myself I'd find a way to peek at her when she was naked.

"Young lady, I just asked you a question. Didn't you hear me?" the woman asked.

"Yes...," I had to quickly look at the invoice because her name had evaporated out of my brain. "Miss Sera, I heard you. You remind me of someone and I was trying to think who it is."

"I don't look like anyone you know; I look like myself. And, young lady, I'm still waiting for you to tell me what happened to Bobby." She had grown annoyed with me.

"Sorry! Bobby had more deliveries than he could do by himself, so I was hired to help him. I'll be coming here now. But if you want Bobby, I'll tell Mr. Colari."

"No, no, no, cher; you'll do fine. What's your name?" she asked me.

"Claire Soublet. I live with my grandmother, Philomene Soublet. Her maiden name was Menard, just like yours. We live on Johnson Street across from the old folks' home."

"I'm sure your grandmother having the same name as mine is pure coincidence." Miss Sera's cheeks and her nose suddenly blazed red. She looked away and I could have sworn I saw a few tears well up in her eyes.

My heart shook hard in my chest. What if she's lying to me? She might be too embarrassed to admit who she is because she's been passing for White all these years. Maybe if I push her a little more she'll have to tell me the truth. "Do you know my grandmother, Miss Sera?"

"How would I know your grandmother?" She sounded perturbed as she glared at me.

I ignored her scowl. "Maybe you met her at the market or somewhere else in the neighborhood." I looked straight into her eyes hoping I could tell if she wasn't being truthful.

"No, I've never met her. I don't do my own marketing. I'm confined to the house. Why do you think you're making this delivery?" The sarcasm in her voice seemed out of character.

"You never go out at all!"

"I haven't been out in many years...too many to remember now."

"I'm sorry you never get to go out, Miss Sera." I had a lump in my throat. I was disappointed she wasn't who I wanted her to be. But I decided then and there that it didn't matter who she was, we'd get to be friends anyway. "Miss Sera, why don't you get a renter or a relative to live in this big house with you? You shouldn't be here all alone."

"Listen, you don't have to keep calling me Miss Sera. You can just say: yes ma'am or no ma'am. Wouldn't that be better?"

"Not really. I don't like to say ma'am or sir. In fact, I won't say them. Slavery's over."

"Oooo! All right, Claire. You certainly know your own mind. I like that about you. And as for someone living with me, I tried that. You can't trust most people and I don't have any relatives left."

"Oh, I know all about that. My grandmother and I are alone." I glanced at Mr. Colari's old watch he'd given me to make sure I got back before the store closed and realized I'd taken too long on her delivery. "Miss Sera, I have to go; I have to finish my work."

"Here, Claire, this is for you." She put a dollar bill in my hand, then handed me an envelope addressed to Mr. Colari.

For every delivery I made to Sera Menard's house, she gave me a dollar tip. There was often a pitcher of lemonade and a plate of cookies set up on a table on her porch for us to enjoy together. I made sure she was my last stop. I would ride like a monster was chasing me to get all my other deliveries done, then I'd be able to spend a half-hour or more at her house. I liked to sit and talk to her. She was so kind and interested in me that I eventually told her all about my life.

Bobby and I had become good friends. I found I was spending more time with him than with Emily. I hardly saw her at all outside of school. She was jealous and teased me about having a crush on him. I vehemently denied it, but in my heart I knew she was right. My grandmother liked Bobby, too. He came to our house in the evenings and the three of us would sit on the front porch swing and talk. Bobby did all sorts of odd jobs around our house. He could fix anything. Big Mama said he reminded her of Big Papa because he was a jack-of-all-trades and that endeared him to her.

Bobby was also from a poor family, one even poorer than mine. His mother had thirteen children and a disabled husband. She worked as White in one of the canning factories trying to support the family, despite having one baby after another. Her three eldest sons had quit school to go to work full time when they each reached fourteen. Two of them had joined the army during the war and had their allotments sent to their mother. Whatever money Bobby earned working after school, he gave his mother every cent of it.

We were together the entire school day because we were both in Sister Agatha's seventh grade class. Bobby had been held back twice in the early grades and was two years behind his friends. This always embarrassed him. So I wasn't surprised when in eighth grade he dropped out to become an apprentice carpenter. Even though I knew he was almost sixteen and older than his brothers had been, I didn't understand how he could deny himself an education, especially after all the conversations we'd had about the importance of getting one. I begged him to reconsider, but he refused to change his mind.

On my next delivery after Bobby quit his job and left school, I told Miss Sera what he'd done.

"He's a good boy, Claire, and he's going to be a good man whether he gets an education or not," she told me.

"That's the same thing my grandmother told me. But I thought I might want to marry him when we're older, and I sure as he...heck don't want to marry a carpenter. I refuse to end up like Big Mama. I want a better life for myself."

"I know you do, Claire, but I don't think he'll ever be the kind of person you'll want to marry. You're going to outgrow him. Don't throw him away, though, keep him as a friend."

"I guess I will because I'll never marry him now." After I said it, I wasn't sure I meant it. The future seemed too far away to make such an important decision.

I told her how we were beginning to see less and less of Bobby. He worked hard and was usually tired evenings. Sometimes we waited all evening for him and he wouldn't show up, but we still didn't have a telephone so he couldn't call when he was too tired to come. He always came on weekends, though. He was excited about the trade he was learning and that's all he wanted to talk about. I usually got so bored I'd get up in the middle of his prattling and go in and go to bed. Big Mama was always attentive to him. So I'd leave her to hang on his every word.

"Maybe one day he'll take the hint," Miss Menard said. We both laughed.

"How is your grandmother, Claire?"

"I think she's okay. She never tells me if anything's wrong. It seems she talks to Bobby about everything, and of course, he won't tell me anything. She probably tells him not to tell me because she thinks I can't handle it. She sold him my grandfather's car and I didn't even know until he showed up driving it. He gave her fifty dollars and plans to give her the rest when he starts to earn a real salary."

"Do you have enough money now that it's summer and you're working more hours?" Miss Sera always asked about my financial situation. She had increased her tips to two dollars each delivery and I seemed to have one every week and sometimes two.

"I guess we're okay."

"Did Mr. Colari hire someone to take Bobby's place?"

"No, I make all the deliveries. When I start high school in September, they'll have to get another person."

"What high school are you going to, Xavier Prep?"

"No, we can't afford it. I'm going to Clark High School. My friend Emily is going, though. I took the entrance exam with her just for the hell of it. Oh, sorry, I forgot myself." I tried never to use bad language when talking to Miss Sera.

"It's all right. I already think of you as an adult. You're very grownup and you've got a lot of responsibility. How did you do on the test?"

"Pretty good, I think. The school sent me an acceptance letter and a whole bunch of papers I'd need to fill out if I intended to register."

"Claire, if I offered to pay your tuition to Xavier Prep, would you accept it and go?"

"I couldn't take your money, Miss Sera. My grandmother would have a fit. She raised me to work for whatever I get."

"Tell her the nuns at Xavier Prep know about your situation, and when they saw how well you did on your test, they offered you a scholarship. Would she believe that?"

"No, she wouldn't. Anyway, she'd check with the school, so I know better than to lie to her. Why would you do that for me?"

"You're a smart girl, Claire. I want to see you do something special with your life. If I can help you in anyway, I want to. I don't want your life to be like your grandmother's and certainly not like your mother's. And I don't want to see you go to that...that school...over there." Miss Sera pointed in the direction of Clark High School. I wondered what she had really wanted to call the school. "Nigger school" came quickly to my mind. But just as quickly, I dismissed the thought.

"Did you have a bad life, Miss Sera?"

"I wasn't always poor, but my life was...well...maybe one day I'll tell you about it."

"What about today? I've got time. You know you're always my last delivery. Tell me a little bit today, please. I'll bet you had an exciting life. Look at the house you live in. You must have had a rich husband or else you made a lot of money by yourself."

"Not today, Claire." She seemed suddenly nervous.

I knew no amount of begging would work. So I tried a different strategy. "Miss Sera, can I ask you one question about your life today?"

"Go ahead…but only one."

"Is your name really Sera Menard?"

"No. I was a businesswoman. I didn't use my own name and I still don't. I put two names together that I liked, but I used only the first name on the window of my store. I had a shop in the Vieux Carré. I designed and made ladies clothing."

A businesswoman! Damn! I knew she had no idea how much she'd ratcheted up my curiosity by telling me that. How would I contain it now? It didn't matter because whenever I asked her to tell me about her life as she'd promised, she'd put me off every time.

Sera Menard's hands were getting worse. She wore white, cotton gloves all the time now and she treated them with a liniment that seemed to relieve some of the pain. Turning the knob to open the door had become difficult for her, as well as picking up objects, especially cups and glasses. Bringing lemonade and cookies out to the porch had become impossible for her. So that summer with some of the money from my tips, I started to bring snowballs for us to enjoy. No matter how hard they were for her to eat, she never complained. I grew to care deeply for her. That she was White no longer mattered.

One day I suggested it might be time for her to find someone to live with her. I knew she had a woman who came for a couple of hours every morning, but I couldn't understand how she managed the rest of the day. Miss Sera was outraged I had the audacity to suggest such a thing to her.

"Don't get into my business, little girl. Stay in your place. Can't you see I'm able to manage and I'll continue to do so? Don't ever say anything like that again, you hear me?" She shook a gloved hand in the air as she spoke and the pungent smell of the liniment made my eyes tear.

"Okay, but I only said that because I can see you have a lot of trouble opening the door. I didn't mean to get in your business. I'm sorry! Okay? I have to go now." I got up and started to walk across the porch. Anger and hurt were burning my throat, and the liniment tears, already in my eyes, spilled out. Damn! Why should I bother about what happens to this old witch?

"Claire, wait! Please forgive me; I've been in a lot of pain today. I'm not really angry with you; I'm angry with myself for being old and broken down. Before you came, I was thinking about how I used to be...used to look...when I was young, and I started feeling sorry for myself. Forgive an old woman, please, cher."

"Sure, Miss Sera, I'm sorry you're not feeling well today. Can I do anything to help you right now?" I instantly forgave her.

"No, you go on. I'll be alright." She quietly made her way to the door and went inside.

I stood for a long time on the edge of the porch feeling sad, not only for Miss Sera, but for my grandmother and me. The three of us had such difficult, lonely lives. But Big Mama had me and I knew I'd change my life. Miss Sera, though, would probably die alone.

- 9 -

COULDN'T CARRY
THE CROSS

Eighth grade graduation gave Emily and me the giggles. We looked as if we were getting married. All the girls were in long white gowns, white opera gloves, with white flower wreaths in our hair. The boys wore black suits, white shirts with dark ties. We were in church all morning, had a lunch break, and then languished in the auditorium for the ceremony well into the afternoon. Finally about 3:00 that May in 1948, with our diplomas in hand and giggling, we burst out of Corpus Christi Elementary School ready for high school and a journey to adulthood. I knew there were some graduates who'd test the strength of New Orleans's laws. The nuns and priests already considered them parochial outlaws.

During the presentation of the diplomas, I thought about what Bobby was missing and wished he hadn't dropped out. Although he'd been a slow student, he had excelled in one area – math. The nuns were upset when he quit school, and they tried repeatedly to convince his parents to force him to return, but they refused. His father told them his son was using his math skills in the contracting business because you had to know how to measure in order to build a house, so he didn't think there was much more his son needed to learn. But then Bobby's father had never gone to school. Most of his life he'd worked as a janitor in the office buildings on Canal Street and in the hotels until he became disabled.

My grandmother asked Bobby to accompany her to my graduation, and when they arrived shortly before the ceremony, the nuns and the priests crowded around him as if he were a celebrity. You would have sworn he was her grandson the way Big Mama was puffed up full of pride. She stood off to the side watching the hullabaloo with the widest grin I had ever seen on her face. I wasn't surprised, though, because she constantly extolled his virtues and talked about how impressed she was with the plans Bobby was making for his future.

Almost daily, she told me I couldn't go wrong if I married him as soon as I was old enough. It always left me wondering: how old was old enough? Even though I'd said I wouldn't marry him, I still thought about it sometimes. But the more Big Mama told me I should, the more I grew to hate the idea. Eventually, I convinced myself it was totally out of the question. I knew she wanted me to have someone to take care of me when she died, but I also knew there was something much more important to her - Bobby's silky, black hair and blue eyes. "Think about your children," she would say.

Oh, how I hated that tired, old, Creole crap that always managed to rear its ugly head again and again. I needed to marry someone with my skin tone or fairer to insure light-skinned babies. And of course, he had to have *good hair* so that the children would have it, too. Bobby's hair and eyes fulfilled the expectations my grandmother had for me. I loved her, but my love didn't run deep enough for me to sacrifice myself to please her, or to make my children fit the Creole profile.

Bobby's seventh grade education, in my mind, automatically labeled him. I didn't care that he'd breezed through his carpenter's apprenticeship and was in the process of setting himself up as a contractor. How else could he end up but like my grandfather? I was positive he'd work when the weather was good and be at home when it rained. And sure as hell exists, I'd pop out a baby every year. "Not me!" I screamed in my head.

I didn't want to leave Big Mama, but I desperately wanted to get out of New Orleans. I was emotionally mature far beyond my thirteen years and understood how trapped many people are in the lifestyles they lead or are born into. I needed to escape the one I was handed or I'd surely die. I had to find a way out, but not with Bobby. I refused to be married to a semi-literate carpenter and spend the rest of my life in New Orleans.

My aunts – how had they gotten away so easily? I wished I could talk to them. They went to California and made a life for themselves, and seven years later, they were married and happy. No happiness for my grandmother and me, though, knowing we'd never hear from them or see them again. They sacrificed us with little or no regret. Passing for White as they did was something I couldn't nor wouldn't do; I needed a different kind of change. And since there was no one to consult, I had to find out where I was headed on my own.

Of course, I did have Miss Menard. I began calling her that because I liked the way it sounded. Miss Sera sounded too southern – too slavish. I grew to feel emotionally and spiritually connected to her...a mysterious woman who guarded her secrets with great care. I liked that about her. It intrigued me. But...a woman alone? Is that the way I wanted to end up at her age, all by myself with no husband, no children, no relatives to help me out if I needed someone? I knew how it felt to have so few relatives in my life and I didn't like it. I wondered if Miss Menard was sorry and regretted the way she had lived her life. I knew she had to be lonely, even though she wouldn't admit it. I was all the more grateful I had my grandmother. Curiosity was gnawing at me again; it was hard keeping it at bay. I didn't want Miss Menard to die without ever telling me about her life? Oh, there seemed to be so much thinking and planning for me to do! I was at it again, taking on a new worry.

It was the beginning of summer and I would be entering high school in a few months. I was excited to finally leave parochial school – no more white blouses and blue-serge, pleated skirts. Clark High was a public school and I'd be able to wear regular clothes, but Xavier Prep, where Miss Menard had offered to pay my tuition, was another Catholic school where uniforms were mandatory. I often thought about her generous offer, and knew even if Big Mama had agreed, I was too proud to have accepted that kind of handout. If I had worked for her, and not the drugstore, perhaps I might have considered it.

My grandmother seemed to be feeling better since she'd finally begun seeing the doctor regularly. The flush had left her face and her eyes had more life in them. I think the grief from my grandfather's death and the pain from my aunts' desertion were beginning to subside. But she had become extremely quiet and seldom engaged me in conversation the way she used to. The only time she had a lot to say was when we talked about Bobby.

Although everything seemed okay with Big Mama's health, I noticed another change in her. She was starting to be forgetful. Each time she made a batch of biscuits, she forgot to put in the baking powder and then forgot to take them out of the oven on time. The biscuits came out hard enough to be used as baseballs. She'd shrug off the mistake and quickly bake another pan. She also never had her club dues ready for Miss Odelia to pick up. So many little things were now forgotten.

I gave her most of the money I made working at the drugstore and I relaxed when, at last, she stopped complaining about how little money we had. I knew because she sold Big Papa's car to Bobby and he began paying her a little at a time, the extra money was allowing her to go to the doctor. It helped with the household expenses. She stopped talking about money altogether which made me happy. It was the first time in my life I felt I didn't have to worry about not having enough.

About two months after graduation, Bobby came over for his usual Saturday evening visit. Big Mama and I, in our usual fashion, were sitting on the front porch swing waiting for him. Upon his arrival, my grandmother casually excused herself and went into the house.

Bobby was full of talk. He babbled on and on about the plans he was making for when his contracting business started raking in the money. He already had more jobs than he could handle with the crew he had, so he was in the process of hiring more men to work for him.

"I got a big future ahead of me, Claire. I mean…ahead of us." Bobby grinned sheepishly and tapped his toes on the porch. I always thought his shyness made him more attractive, especially when his wide grin exposed his two, deep dimples. When he started to giggle and dropped his head, a patch of wavy, black hair fell onto his forehead. He quickly pushed it back off his face and gently started to rock the swing. "You get what I'm saying, right? Our future, yours and mine."

"You're kidding me, right?"

"No, our future, that's what I want. And your gramma wants it, too. What's this 'you're kidding me' stuff? I thought you wanted that, too."

"Bobby, I'm not even fourteen, yet. The only thing I think about is going to school. I start Clark in September, remember?

Plan your future, not mine. There's lots of things I want to do and I have a long way to go before I can do them."

"Ohhhh...no you don't! I got plans for you...for us. Do you think I'm working like a mule just for myself? It's all for us, Claire."

"Look, Bobby, you're not even seventeen, yet. You quit school so that you could help your family and that's what I think you ought to do. You and my grandmother always talk about your plans and you automatically make them my plans. Did you ever ask me what I want for my life? Not once. You talk as if my dreams don't count."

"Never mind how old I am, I'm a man! I have my own business, and I need a good woman by my side so I can do all the things I want to do. Don't you have the brains to understand that?"

I ignored his insult. "You need a woman, huh. Well, Bobby, I'm not a woman; I'm a girl and I'll be one for another four years. Now, would you like to hear my plans?"

"No! Listen, Claire, my plans are bigger and better than yours. I'm gonna make a lot of money. No way you can do that. One day I'm gonna own a lot of businesses. I'm just starting as a contractor but I ain't stopping there. I'll probably run for mayor one of these days. I'm gonna make a name for myself in Nu Awlins and I want you with me. Doesn't Mrs. Robert Villagoso sound good? Wait...don't answer, yet." Bobby jumped off the swing. "Be back in a second." He leaped off the porch and ran to his car.

When he returned, he handed me a small, gift-wrapped box he'd taken off the front seat of the car. "Go ahead, open it," he said as he pulled at the ribbon and untied the bow.

"Oh, wow, it's really pretty, Bobby," I said as I looked at the gold cross and chain. "But my birthday isn't until the eighth of September."

"I know, but it's not a birthday present. We're engaged now. That's gotta take the place of a ring; I couldn't afford one right now. I'll buy you one later on. I had Father O'Mara bless it. Let me put it on you."

"Bobby, I'm thirteen...well, fourteen. I don't want...to be engaged. I've never even kissed you or anybody else. If I don't even know what it's like to be in love, why would I think about getting married?" I wouldn't let him put the cross and chain on me.

"Ha, I can fix that right now." He slid over on the swing, threw his arms around me, and planted a big, wet kiss squarely on my lips.

I wiped off his kiss with the back of my hand. "Don't you ever…ever do that to me again."

He laughed. "After we get married, I'm going to do more than that to you. In fact, I might not want to wait." He put his hand on my thigh and I quickly slapped it away.

"I don't want to marry you, Bobby. I was going to wait to tell you, but now I know I'd better tell you right now. I'll…NEVER … want to marry you!" I let it roll out of my mouth like a Gulf Coast hurricane.

"Are you crazy, girl? I already told everybody, my family and all my friends. You ain't making me look like no fool." His whole body jerked with the realization I had rejected him. He had reverted to street language.

"You should have asked me first."

"I didn't think I had to."

"If you had asked me, I would have told you I couldn't marry you because I won't be happy being a carpenter's wife. You need to marry someone who will be happy married to you. I wouldn't be! I want an education and I want to marry somebody who's not a carpenter or a Creole. And the one thing he's got to have is an education. Those are my plans, Bobby, the ones you didn't want me to tell you about."

Slowly Bobby got up from the swing, looked down at me, then slapped me as hard as he could across my face. I was too stunned to move or cry out.

"Give me back my goddamn cross and chain, you stupid bitch." He snatched the box out of my hand. "I don't need to marry your po nigger ass. I'm gonna make me a lot of money and I'm willing to bet on my mama's life, your ass is gonna regret the day you let me go." He walked off the porch and then turned toward me again. "You lucky I even looked at you. Look at me, girl," he ran his hand over his hair and with his forefinger touched his cheek, "with this white skin, I can have any kind of woman I want. I don't need nobody with as much coffee in her as you got. Yeah, that's right, don't look surprised. You only light-brown; I'm damn near white." He raised up one pant leg. "Look here, this is where the sun don't shine. I look like any White man anywhere. So I sure as hell can do better than you. Some of your friends are running after me behind your back. Did you know that? Nooo, you too busy getting an education." He put his hand over his mouth and snickered into his hand. "You better remember what your gramma told you and think about what your children gonna look like. You need a man like me to give um to you. If you don't marry me like your gramma thinks you are, you gonna cause a whole lot of trouble. Listen, girl, I don't think you know this, but I just about own y'all already."

In one sprint, I shot inside the house, latched the screen door, and then stood behind it. "You've got about twenty seconds to get your ass in that car, Bobby."

"You think you bad, na? What you think you gonna do, bitch?" He was sounding more and more like a thug as he stepped back onto the porch.

"I'm going to get my grandfather's shotgun and blow your goddamn head off. Is that bad enough for you?"

He could tell I meant what I said. Laughing and muttering to himself, he scurried off the porch, walked to his car and jumped in. His tires screeched as he burned rubber pulling away from the house.

Suddenly I felt a light touch on my arm and I jumped. In the shadowy darkness I could faintly make out my grandmother sitting behind one of the little wing doors she'd cracked open.

"You scared me, Big Mama. Have you been sitting there the whole time?"

"I heard every word you said to that boy. Shame on you, Claire. Bobby's a good boy and you really hurt him," she told me. "When he calms down, he'll come back, you'll see. Even though he told you all those terrible things, he didn't mean them. He's planning to marry you, I'd bet my life on it."

"Don't, because that bastard will never marry me. And if he ever comes back here, I will get Big Papa's shotgun and blow a goddamn hole in that son-of-a-bitch."

"Claire!"

"Claire, nothing. That dumb piece of shit slapped me. No goddamn man is ever going to do that to me again. Maybe Big Papa treated you like crap and my mama got treated like a damn dog by every man she ever had – one even murdered her – but that's not going to happen to me."

"Never say never," Big Mama said with a wait-and-see tone to her voice.

"I'm saying it. I'm not going to end up like you or my mama; you can bet your life on that. I won't be another dead Iris or Lady Blue. My aunts got out of this rat hole, and when I can, so will I!" The cover of darkness allowed me to avoid seeing the hurt that had probably enveloped my grandmother's face. But then I realized I hadn't said everything.

"I'm sorry I hurt you, Big Mama, but I'm not going to marry anyone who hits me or makes me miserable from the beginning. I'm still a young girl, and I don't want to be engaged, much less think about getting married. I want an education and a career of my own. We've had a hard life for as long as I've been alive. I want a better one and I don't need Bobby to give it to me. I can make a good life for myself...and for you. But you have to stop trying to set me up with him. I don't...want him! I don't care how much money he plans to make; he'll always be a dumbass Creole to me."

My grandmother quietly closed the wing door and left me standing in the dark. I stood there for a while trying to feel some remorse for the things I'd said to her, but I had none. My face began to sting, and touching it, I found I had four, wide, fingerprint welts on my cheek. In the dark, I made my way through our shotgun house to my room. When I passed through Big Mama's room, she was lying on her bed facing the wall. I said goodnight to her. She didn't answer.

While I was holding a piece of ice on my cheek, Bobby's last statement started rolling around in my head. What in the hell could he have meant about practically owning us? I was too weary to try to get my grandmother to tell me what he meant. It would have to wait. I knew just as Bobby would get over me not wanting to marry him, so would my grandmother. We were holding our own now. I was entering high school soon and nothing was going to stop me from going to college.

"Good morning, Big Mama." I didn't get an answer. My grandmother continued frying the *lost bread*. It was her Sunday morning special. The kitchen smelled like cinnamon and sugar.

"Why are you angry with me? I'm the one who should be mad. Bobby smacked my face." I moved close to her so that she could get a good look at my bruises. "See...pretty, huh?"

"Oh!" She seemed surprised to see the four, raised marks on my cheek. They were still red and tender. She quickly made an herb poultice for me to hold on my face.

"Big Mama, can I ask you something?"

"I know what it is; it bothered me all night. Listen, Claire, I'm going to die one of these days, and who knows, it might be soon. I have been trying to protect you and make sure you have someone who will take care of you. I thought that person was going to be Bobby."

"If you had asked me if I wanted to marry Bobby, I would have told you I didn't. But you didn't ask me. You and Bobby made plans for my future without asking me what I wanted. Did you two do something that you haven't told me about? Did you promise Bobby something? Tell me!"

"I didn't promise anything, Claire, I've already done it." Big Mama sat down and grabbed her regular stress spot - the back of her neck. She squeezed and massaged it with the tips of her fingers, and then shook her head as if she could fling away the panic she was feeling. I also knew she was buying time hoping I'd get hot under the collar and storm out of the kitchen giving her a temporary reprieve.

"You can't put me off, Big Mama, what did you do?"

"I let Bobby pay off the house and I signed it over to him."

I ran out of the room and slammed the door between the kitchen and my room. My heart was pounding and my legs were shaking so violently I could no longer stand. I fell on the floor and curled up in a ball. What had she done? My grandmother had sold the car, given away the house, and next she'd give me away – all to Bobby.

"Claire, get up." Big Mama rushed into the room and tried to pull me up off the floor. I slapped her hands away. "Let me tell you why I did what I did. Please, cher." She had never referred to me with an endearing term. It shocked me. I sat up and looked at her.

"Why, Big Mama? Why would you do that?"

"Because I don't have to work for the priest anymore, I quit last week. I can live in this house for the rest of my life and still collect the rent from the other side. We finally have enough money to make it month to month. When you marry Bobby and move, you won't have to worry about me. He's already bought a lot and he's going to build you a house on it. Claire, give him a chance to grow up. He'll make a good husband. Don't cut off your nose to sp..."

I cut her off screaming, "I'll never marry Bobby! I hate his guts now. So get him out of your head because he's definitely out of mine." I stood up without her help and couldn't control the hateful look I gave her. "What's he going to do, throw us out? We'll just find another place to live, that's all. I'll be damned if he'll own me. How much was it to pay off the house?"

"Twelve hundred dollars."

"Damn! Where is Bobby getting all that money? First the car, now the house."

"Claire, he's not a worker anymore; Bobby's a contractor. His company is already making good money."

"Maybe I can work two jobs and give him back his money - a little at a time - the same way he paid you for the car."

"How can you make twelve hundred dollars? You can't work all the time and go to school, too. The job at the drugstore is enough. And another thing, who else besides Mr. Colari is going to hire a fourteen year-old?"

"Well, I guess we'll just have to wait and see what Mr. Villagoso does, won't we? Maybe, he won't do anything."

"Let me deal with him, Claire. I doubt if he'll give me any trouble. I went into those agreements with him, so I need to handle it. Lord today! I know one thing; Big Papa is turning over in his grave." Big Mama grabbed the back of her neck again and groaned.

"Turning over? He's probably doing flips. I'll bet *he'll pull your toes tonight* to let you know you've been a bad girl." I laughed and Big Mama did, too. "I don't have time to eat right now. I'm going to 9:00 Mass, are you coming?" She had started going to Mass with me every Sunday after Big Papa died.

"No, you go ahead. I've got a big head this morning," she said. "I'll keep the lost bread warm for you."

"Have you been taking your pills?"

"Every day. This is a Bobby and Claire big head, not a high blood pressure one."

"Sorry. I'll light an extra candle for your big head, okay?"

"Okay," she smiled while rubbing her temples, "but hurry home after Mass, Claire. You know what fried bread is like when it's kept warm for a long time."

– 10 –

MISS PRISS BETRAYED

The summer had gone by so quickly that before we knew it, it was the day of our party. Emily and I had decided not to celebrate our graduation in May. So many other kids were having parties that we wanted to wait and have a "going to high school to-do." We planned it for the Friday before Labor Day. Because Fridays were meatless days, that's when many of the Catholic kids had their parties. We could serve tuna, salmon, or egg salad sandwiches and not have to buy expensive cold cuts. Potato chips weren't popular as party snacks back then. We had a big dish of pickles and olives.

I had worked my last morning at the drugstore. After school started, I'd have to go back to making my deliveries after school on weekdays. My weekends would be completely free now that Bobby wouldn't be hanging out at my house. I'd have more time to read, study, and finally, I could spend a little time with Emily.

It had been about a month since the engagement fiasco and Bobby hadn't been back. In my mind it was hallelujah time. I would be fourteen in a few days – light years away from being married to anyone. Every time I thought about being asked to become engaged, I closed my eyes and shook my head in disbelief. Actually, I wasn't asked, I was told. Bobby was a horse's ass and I was thankful he wouldn't be a part of my future.

After checking to see if my grandmother needed me for anything, I headed around the corner to Emily's to help her clean house and get the food ready for our party. Mrs. Valcour always allowed us to have our parties in their front room. The room was enormous and had only a few pieces of furniture giving us lots of room for dancing. And because no one smoked or drank liquor, she thought her furniture was fairly safe from ruin. However, for extra protection, she covered everything except her lamps with plastic drop cloths. Big Mama would never have agreed to a party under any circumstances and I never asked to have one. She always said parties belonged in *dance halls.*

While we were making the sandwiches, Emily asked me why I started talking funny.

"Every time I turn around," she said, "you change something about the way you talk. I wanted to ax you that question for a long time, but I didn't want to hurt your feelings."

"Then it must be okay to hurt them now, right? Why are you asking me such a silly question? Is it because we're going to different high schools? You're at the Prep and I'm at a public school?" I was already feeling hurt and now I felt she was insulting me. "Don't you care about my feelings? Or maybe you think we aren't going to be friends anymore. Is that it?"

"Girl, Claire, don't say things like that. You know we'll always be friends. I only axed you that because I thought you should know people always talk about you and the way you talk. They say you ain't got a pot to piss in and you got the nerve to be stuck up. They say you talk that way to get attention. I just wanted to find out if it's *for true.*"

"You've known me almost all my life. You shouldn't have to ask me anything; you should know by now. I know everything about you."

"Oh no you don't! You only think you do."

"Well, excuse me. What don't I know?"

"Never mind, chil. That's for me to know and you to wonder about." Emily sucked her teeth and rolled her eyes at me.

"Okay. I'm not going to play a guessing game to find out. I don't care to know if you don't want to tell me. But I do want you to tell me what you mean by...the way I talk. What way do you mean?"

"You don't sound like everybody else. You sound like you from Nu York or somewhere like that. I remember when you used to call my mother Miss Beatrice, now it's Mrs. Valcour. That sounds like you putting on airs to me. Nobody else around here talks like that."

"You mean I don't have a real southern accent...a New Orleans way of speaking. You're right; I don't. Most people here have a lazy way of speaking, like you, for instance. All the grammar the nuns taught us, you still say, 'you sound like you from,' instead of, 'you sound like you're from.' Why do you say axed instead of asked? You do all sorts of crazy things with the king's English and I try not to. It isn't because you don't know the correct thing to say, you're too damn lazy to say it. You're even worse than you used to be because you want to make sure you sound like everybody else. Well I say, shit on the way everyone else speaks."

There was a loud knock on the side door. We were the only ones home, so Emily went to answer it. She returned with a large, brown package and stuck it in the refrigerator. It was Friday, so it had to be a meat delivery from Vaucresson's Market. It must have been Mrs. Valcour's meat for her weekend meals now that the market delivered. I had the urge to be nosy, but I refused to ask Emily and sound like the pisspoor little girl people thought I was.

My grandmother always went to the store to get whatever she needed to cook. Our meals had been more vegetables, which we grew; chicken, from our yard or from the fresh-kill place on Claiborne Avenue; meat when Big Papa went hunting and all sorts of seafood he or one of his friends had caught in North Shore. Now that he was dead, it was vegetables, chicken, and seafood on Fridays. Meat, rarely.

"Where were we? Oh yeah, you was telling my ass off about the way I talk. And I say, girl, you got some ca-ca with you. I'm gonna forgive you for putting me down for the way I talk. I guess you don't know no better." Emily flipped her hair and gave me a shit-grin.

"Forgive me? Didn't we just put each other down? We traded insults, that's all. If you really want to know who's to blame for the way I speak, then blame my great-aunt. She even changed the way everybody in my family speaks, but she didn't do much with my grandfather because he resented being corrected. Every time I'd open my mouth, she'd correct what I'd say. She would tell me she wanted to hear the consonants on the end of words, especially the sound of g. I had to tell her if a word had a long or a short vowel sound. She listened for the correct tense of a verb and made sure all my subjects and verbs agreed. I was never allowed to use slang around her. And now, when I learn something I've been saying is wrong, I correct it. That's why I call your mother Mrs. Valcour. It may be southern to call her Miss Beatrice, but it isn't correct. Anyway, Mrs. Valcour sounds better than Miss Beatrice to me; I don't care what anyone else says. And the biggest reason I speak the way I do is because I don't want a southern accent."

"I know you don't. See, you a stuck-up heifa, girl." Emily's tone was sarcastic.

I ignored her. "Every Saturday, Nennaine used to take me to the river where we'd catch the ferry at the foot of Canal Street. We'd ride back and forth from New Orleans to Algiers."

"All day?" Emily tried to look stunned and interested. "For true, girl?"

"Emily...stop making fun of me. You know I used to do that with my aunt...all day."

"Noooo, I thought you went for one ride and then did something else. What did you do all day on the ferry?"

"Lessons, that's what she called them. You remember she was a teacher, right?"

"No."

"You used to know, you just forgot. Anyway, that's all she ever did in her life. I was her class and the ferry was her classroom. I went to school all those Saturdays. We used to stop at Solari's in the Vieux Carré and buy our lunch. We'd get all sorts of delicious stuff...Italian salami and mortadélla, huge dill pickles from big wooden barrels, Greek olives, dates, French bread...and, oh God, I almost forgot, cream puffs for dessert." By the time I finished talking, my eyes were full of tears. Nennaine had been a blessing. Why did she have to die?

"You crying? You never cry. You must really miss your aunt. I don't know, girl, that whole thing sounds boring as hell to me. I gotta go to the bathroom."

I knew Emily left the room so that I could get myself together and I was grateful. I hadn't realized how much I missed my aunt and the things we did together until I was telling Emily about her. My aunt was responsible for a lot of good things in my life. My grandparents took care of me and loved me, but my aunt gave me the things that really mattered to me. She taught me to read when I was three and that's why I love books so much now. Getting an education was important to her and I'm sure that's one of the reasons it became important to me.

Who had Emily become overnight? She wasn't the person I thought I knew. Even she had made that clear. Maybe I had spent too much time with Bobby and she had grown up and left me behind.

"Hey, girl, whatya thinking about?' Emily swept into the room with a flourish.

"You."

"What about me?"

"How different we are now. We used to think alike, but not anymore."

"You damn right. You want an education and I want to get married and have four or five kids as soon as possible. I want a husband, chil, to sit me on my butt and work to support me and my children."

"Damn, you sound like you just graduated from high school instead of grammar school."

"Honey, you ain't kidding. Do you think we grew up too fast? I feel like I'm damn near a woman already. What about you?"

"No, not me. I'm thirteen, well, fourteen, and I want to be a teenager and enjoy high school. Would you get married if you could before you're out of high school?"

"In a second, baby. Think about it, girl. I would have my own big ol house to take care of and I could screw every night. Yeah, baby...*can't beat that with a stick.*"

"Four or five kids, huh. I guess you will have to screw often. But, Emily, what do you know about screwing?" Wow, I thought, she really is a lot closer to being a woman than me. I looked at her suddenly with fresh eyes. She was developed top and bottom and fully filled out. I was tall like a reed with a flat chest and a flat rear end. Her cheeks had a hint of rouge and her lips were also tinted with lipstick. I, on the other hand, had a freshly washed face with glossy cheeks and a shiny nose full of freckles. Her hair was jet black and lay in curls spread out on her shoulders. I pulled my frizzy, thick, brown hair back and tied it with a ribbon. She was beautiful and looked every bit like a woman and I had been too busy to notice. While she had been changing, I had stayed a little girl with a shiny, freckled face.

"Hey!" Emily yelled at me. "Where are you, in a trance?"

"No. I was still thinking about you and what you think you know about screwing."

"I know more than you think I do. Don't look at me like that, Claire. Close your mouth. I ain't done it yet, but I sure want to. Don't you?"

"Hell no! I want to do a lot of things, but screwing isn't one of them. I daydream about traveling to exotic countries...all the places I've studied and read about. That's what I can't wait to do. As for screwing, after watching Lady Blue and Wobble, I don't know if I ever want to do it."

"Girl, you weird! Hey, maybe we'll both fall in love when we're in high school and then you'll change your tune. I plan on beating you to the punch, anyway."

"Go right ahead, fall in love first. Don't wait for me; I'm not interested. Damn, Em, believe it or not, we're finished with the sandwiches. Come on, let's mop and wax the linoleum in the front room, then we'll make the punch. I hope there's room in the refrigerator for all the stuff we have. Your brothers aren't going to eat our food, are they?"

"No, my mama's gonna police the kitchen. I'll also put a note on everything. But, honey, it ain't gonna matter. You know they gonna sneak and steal a coupla sandwiches, no matter what we do."

Emily always talked a lot more than she worked. I knew I'd end up doing most of the party preparations, but I was used to it. She was my best friend; I didn't mind. I'd do almost anything for her. She quickly draped the plastic cloths on everything and plopped down on the couch as she watched me mop the floor.

"Hey, Cee Cee, I already got my eye on somebody. But I got to wait and see what's gonna happen with the girl he's going with now." In an effort to be coy, Emily covered and uncovered her eyes as if she were playing peek-a-boo.

"Bullshit! As spoiled as you are – you're going to be someone's second choice. I don't believe that." I laughed, but I was shocked. She had changed so much in so short a time; maybe she would be willing to play second fiddle. "And, please, don't tell me he's a goddamn carpenter or a bricklayer."

"Yes, ma'am...he's a carpenter. Ain't nothing wrong with that. See...that's why people say you stuck up. You think you too goddamn good for one, don't you?" Emily's mouth had drawn up in a sneer.

"How can you ask me that as many times as we've talked about Bobby? I don't intend to stay in this dump to make gumbo, boil crawfish, have a bunch of snotty-nose brats, and wait on a beer- drinking husband hand and foot. No, no, no...hell no!" I realized I was yelling, so I put my hand over my mouth to try and stop myself from saying anything else.

"Okay, Miss Priss. One of these days somebody's gonna snatch Bobby right out from under your nose and you gonna be sorry when he gives her a real good life insteada you." Emily had fully stretched out on the sofa. She had begun *sweating bricks* on the plastic, so she pulled it back and lay directly on the cushions. "You missed a spot, Cee Cee," she pointed to a place around one of the piano legs, "over there."

"Back to Bobby – I hope he finds someone else because I don't want him. I recently made that clear to him."

"What!" Why didn't you tell me that happened?"

"Because I've been angry about it. And my grandmother's been fuming mad...at me. She thinks that bastard is coming back. But he'd better not. I don't want to see his ass at my house or anywhere else, Emily."

"Oh, shit!" she groaned.

"Oh, shit, what?"

"I invited him to come tonight," she giggled. "I did it for you, Claire. I didn't know you two had split up. He didn't say anything about it when I invited him to the party."

"Split up...we were never together. We were just friends, and you know that. Cut the crap, did you really invite him?"

"Yeah."

"Damnit, Emily!" I screamed at the ceiling. "Well, I'll finish helping you get the stuff ready, but I'm not coming back tonight. I've had enough of Bobby."

"Honey, you nuts to let somebody keep you away from your own party. Claire, this might be the last one we give together. Maybe you'll find new friends at Clark, and I'll find some at Xavier. You know, anything could happen between us. Uh...I mean...uh...we could go in different directions. Please, Cee Cee, please come."

"Let me think about it for a little while," I said.

When I finished mopping the floor, I pushed the bucket with the mop in it into the next room and then opened the front door so that the floor would dry quickly. I grabbed the can of liquid wax and two cloths. I threw one of them on the couch next to Emily.

"Okay, kiddo, get off your ass and get to work. Are you sure you want a big house and five kids as lazy as you are? Oh…wait…on second thought, if I know you the way I think I do, you're planning on having a maid, right?"

"Girl, you sure know me." Reluctantly she got off the sofa and got down on her knees to help. But I knew if past behavior was any indication of what she'd do at that moment, it would be to start in the corner of the room and stay there talking while I did the rest of the floor.

"Listen," I told her, "if I come to the party, you have to do something for me."

"Yeah, sure. What?"

"If Bobby starts something with me, I want your mother to throw him out, okay?"

"Okay, she will. But I don't think he'll bother you. You worry too much."

"I don't think you know him well enough to say that. But I'm sure your mother won't stand for any of his mess. All right, I'll come."

We waxed without talking. I felt we were both thinking about the enormous differences that had grown in our thinking and how that would eventually work against our friendship. But nothing had changed about the way we got things done. Emily waxed in one little circle and I managed to cover the rest of the room.

"We're done. While I clean the bucket and the mop, why don't you make the punch, Emily. Go easy on the sugar, okay. You always make it too sweet."

"There you go again, worrying…and being bossy. Oh, I forgot to tell you, my mother plans to test the punch before, during, and after the party to make sure there's no liquor in it. That's stupid because the boys will probably pass around a bottle and everyone will pour it right into their cups."

"When did this start happening? I know you can't be telling me that there was liquor at our parties when we were twelve and thirteen. I was there, Emily. I don't believe that could have happened and I didn't know about it."

"Damn, Claire, shut up and grow up. You need to get your nose out of a book sometime and find out what everybody else is doing. Girl, I'm surprised you're not still wearing plaits and pinafores."

"I'm okay just the way I am. I'm not interested in finding out about everybody else. But tell me, Miss Valcour," I teased her, "who's the carpenter? Does your mother know?"

"Yeah, she knows. She says we're both young and I need to be patient. She thinks he's just in puppy love with that girl. Shit…what I say is, *tompee,* cuz when I put my *gris-gris* on him, he's damn sure gonna marry me."

"Oh really," I laughed. "Come on, tell me who he is?"

"He's a *gahbe* just like us. But that's all I can tell you until I get him."

"Damn, some best friend you are!"

"Don't say that. You don't understand."

"Then make me understand."

"I can't!" Emily burst into tears.

"Hey…oh my God, Emily, I'm sorry. It's okay. I don't have to know." I tried to grab her hand but she quickly put it behind her back.

I suddenly felt pangs of guilt not having spent the amount of time I used to spend with her. Bobby and my grandmother had caught me up in their evenings and weekends and I had neglected my best friend. That summer I'd worked lots of overtime hours, and when Bobby stopped coming to my house, I kept my nose stuck in a book. I seldom saw Emily. While she was occupied with growing up, I was either working or reading.

We'd always lived around the corner from each other and we'd had eight years of school together in the same classroom. I looked at her small, gold, hoop earrings, and then touched their counterparts in my ears. When we were eleven, we pierced each other's ears and had to be taken to the doctor when we ended up with infections. We had always been the "two musketeers." But now she was almost a woman and I was in no way her equal.

How was I going to get through the party? I sat in the middle of my bed holding my face hoping I'd suddenly have some creative ideas. I had no desire to see Bobby, much less exchange words with him again. There had to be a way I could gracefully get out of staying for the whole party but I needed to come up with a plan before I got there.

My grandmother had finally relented. The week before the party we got a telephone. I had convinced her by telling her we had to have one for emergencies. She knew that wasn't the only reason I wanted one, but she gave in.

The telephone, it occurred to me, would be my way out.

Half of the forty-four kids we graduated with and ten of their friends came to our party. Emily's mother demanded we play only a few records for slow dancing; she didn't want to see all the couples pressed together dancing on a dime all night. Mrs. Valcour always sat in her bedroom, the room behind the two big French doors of the front room. She'd crack the doors slightly to see everything that was going on. She allowed 40 watt bulbs, but no red or blue ones.

After a bite to eat, a few dances, and talking with some of my friends, I excused myself saying I needed to call my grandmother because she wasn't feeling well when I left her. I had avoided Emily after our initial meeting at the very beginning of the party. The telephone was in Mrs. Valcour's room and she gave me permission to use it. I didn't allow the call to go through, but made believe I was talking to Big Mama and she was asking me to return home. I asked Mrs. Valcour to tell Emily why I had to leave and I left quietly through the side door. As I walked up the alley, I heard Bobby's voice. He was just arriving and had stopped on the porch to talk to some of his old friends from school. I stood in the alley and waited until they all went inside before I ventured out and ran up the street.

The next morning I called Emily to apologize for leaving the party early and not helping with the clean up.

"That's okay, Cee Cee," she said, "my mama helped me. How's your gramma?"

"Much better today, thanks. How'd the party turn out?"

"Girrrrrrl, you missed everything. We had some fun. A few pints of something went around, and after a few cups of spiked punch, all the girls started giggling. We drove my mama crazy, especially when Sydney kept turning off one of the lights and I kept playing the same slow record over and over again. Girrrrrl, my mama threatened to make everybody go home, and then we quit doing it. But it sure was fun while it lasted."

"Your mother must have been foaming at the mouth," I said. "Did she fuss at you after the party was over?"

"You know it, but it didn't matter by then because I got a big surprise from somebody." She began to screech into the telephone, "Surprise, surprise, surprise, sur..."

"Emily, stop it!" I moved the phone away from my ear for a second. "Tell me the damn surprise."

"I can't tell you; I have to show you. Meet me on the corner in a coupla minutes."

I shot out of the house and ran to the corner of Laharpe and Johnson. And as usual, we arrived at the same time.

"I have to hurry; my mama's waiting for me. We're going to Canal Street to buy my uniforms for school and get me some shoes." Emily was bouncing up and down with one hand holding the top of her blouse closed.

"Okay, well hurry up and show me."

"Look." She opened the top of her blouse and pulled the cross and chain away from her chest. "Isn't it beautiful? I got it last night as a present."

"That's...that's your present?" I stammered.

"Yeah, from my secret admirer. But I can't tell you who, remember?"

"You don't have to; I already know. Bobby gave it to you."

My childhood friend's eyes froze in terror as she looked at me. But the shock had been enormous for both of us. We stood there staring at one another, each waiting for the other to speak; Emily, with the inevitable end to our friendship looming in her mind, and me, with her betrayal exploding in the middle of my heart.

"Don't look at me like that, Claire. You didn't want him, you selfish bitch! He wasn't good enough for you, but you don't want me to have him. And...whether you like it or not, he's mine now."

I tried not to react to her hateful dressing-down. "Emily, did he tell you that cross and chain is the one he gave me last month as a so-called engagement gift? He was going to buy me a ring later." I watched her mouth drop. "Yesterday when I started to tell you what happened, you told me you invited Bobby to the party and I never got the chance to finish telling you. Now, I don't want to. Ask him what happened."

"I don't give a shit what happened. All I know is last night he told me he's been wanting to get close to me for a long time, but your gramma kept on pestering him to promise himself to you. He said he finally told her he wanted somebody else...and...I guess that's me."

"That's not what happened and you're a fool if you believe that. But go ahead, be my guest. You deserve that mangy animal. And in case you haven't noticed, he's grown over a foot a year in the last couple of years. With his pigeon toes and his black, hairy knuckles, he looks like a goddamn, seven-foot, blue-eyed gorilla. Haven't you asked yourself why he wears long sleeve shirts all the time, even in the summer? It's because his arms look like his knuckles. I hope the two of you will be very happy and have lots of little blue-eyed apes. You have my blessing, Emily." I walked away and left her standing on the corner.

– 11 –

THE GLOW FROM TRUTH AND LIGHTNING BUGS

Needing to calm down and get my mind off Emily and Bobby, I went to the early show at the Circle Theater and then to Belfield's Drugstore for an ice cream soda and a few school supplies I thought I'd need when school opened.

My grandmother must have heard me come up the back porch steps. As I opened the screen door, she opened the back door, grabbed me by the arm, and pulled me into the kitchen.

"Sit down," she ordered me. "Bobby called while you were gone. Did you call that boy a blue-eyed gorilla, Claire?" Big Mama was beside herself. "He told me you said that to Emily. How could you talk about that boy like that?"

"He went after my best friend, Big Mama."

"How do you know he went after Emily? Maybe she went after him. I've been watching her lately. She's flirty. I noticed how she acted at your graduation in May. She wanted to make sure all eyes were on her. She gets that from her mother."

"What do you mean she gets her flirty ways from her mother? Mrs. Valcour is always in church, and when she isn't, she's with her club members. She's not a loose woman."

"Claire, you're young. You don't understand. You have to be careful of those women who are always in church trying to show everyone how pious they are. They're just as treacherous as the women who sell themselves. They go after your boyfriends or your husbands and money is usually at the root of it." After what she'd told me about my grandfather, I knew she was speaking from experience. "And...don't you believe your mother was the only one gossiped about. Mrs. Valcour has always gotten her well-deserved share."

"Who's the mashuquette, now, Big Mama?"

"Never mind. As for Bobby, a lot of girls are going to want him; he's a good catch. You're the only one too stupid to see the promise in that boy; *you can't see for looking.*"

"Okay, I get what you're telling me, but have you forgotten the nasty things he said to me when I refused to marry him? I sure as hell haven't. He's a rotten, dirty bastard and I'll never forgive or forget what he said to me. And shit, don't call me stupid! Your precious, drop-out Bobby is the one who's stupid."

"Stop that kind of talk, right now! You sound like a street woman. I've let you get away with that filthy language for far too long. So...I'm putting you on notice, no more cursing in this house, you hear me?" I wondered if she regretted abandoning her back-hand slap. She looked as though a real, hard slap would have helped to drive her point home to me.

"I hear you. But I know what's really got your goat. I won't be marrying your precious, blue-eyed Creole. Tell me the truth, Big Mama, isn't that why you're upset?"

"Shut your sassy mouth! What I want you to do is call that boy and tell him you're sorry. He'll forgive you. He doesn't want Emily; he still wants you."

"I don't care if he does. I don't want him," I screamed at her. "Why can't you understand that? I'm not calling him because I'm not sorry for what I said. He is a long, lanky, blue-eyed gorilla. If you want him in this family...you marry him!" I ran out the back door, up the alley, and out to the sidewalk. I stood there not knowing where to go. No relatives, and now no best friend. There was no place to go, and no one to go to.

My grandmother opened the front door and shouted at me, "Claire, you come back in this house, right this minute!"

Wordlessly, I walked up the street in the direction of the drugstore as Big Mama continued to yell after me. Dusk was departing letting the night move in. I was usually going to my house, not leaving it. I knew I shouldn't go too far because I was still afraid of the dark. I was always grateful we slept during the night and not the day. To me nothing good happened at night and I preferred not to be awake when it did.

I turned on Esplanade Avenue and soon found myself in front of Miss Menard's house. She had befriended me from her very first delivery and I had grown to trust her. She knew everything about my life. I needed someone to talk to and I didn't think she'd turn me away. I pushed in the gate and slowly went up the walk. Suddenly, I got cold feet and turned around to go back out. Why would this old White woman care about what was happening to me?

"Claire? Is that you?" Miss Menard's fragile voice called out to me.

"Yes, Miss Menard, it's me." I turned again and walked toward her voice. She was sitting in a dark corner of the porch wrapped in a blanket. A shawl covered her head and shoulders. Her shaky voice and the smell of liniment told me she was in pain.

"What are you doing out here so late?" I asked her. When I got past the pungent, medicinal odor, I inhaled something sweet in the air. I tilted my head back and breathed in the fragrance and wondered why life wasn't as gratifying. "Mmmm...what smells so good?"

"Night jasmine. It's right here on the side of the porch." Miss Menard turned her head toward the jasmine and sniffed loudly. "That's why I'm sitting out here. I want to enjoy my garden while I still can. Oh look, there's dozens of lightning bugs under the tree over there! I'll bet you used to smash them on the front of your clothes, didn't you?" She looked at me for a moment. "Why are you here, cher? Tell me the truth, now."

I plopped down dejectedly in a chair next to her, covered my face with my hands and started to cry. There had been no tears since my grandfather's death, but this was the second time in two days I'd let my emotions take over. Every part of my body quivered with despair and I felt as if I was going to break apart.

"My...my..." I couldn't continue. The sobs prevented me from speaking.

"Oh, my goodness, is it that bad?"

I nodded.

"I had a feeling something was wrong; I've felt it for weeks. You haven't been here in a long time. I called the drugstore several times for a few things, but Mr. Colari delivered them himself. How come?"

I managed to get out, "You...you...you always called after I left on my deliveries."

"Oh, I'm glad to hear that," she said, "I thought you were tired of looking at my old, twisted face and body. I wondered if you'd deserted me, Claire."

"I wouldn't desert you, Miss Menard. You're the only one in my life now who encourages me to do the things I want to do. My grandmother's sister used to. I really know how much I miss her now."

"Doesn't your grandmother want you to get an education?"

"No."

"I don't believe that, Claire."

"You don't know the half of it, Miss Menard."

"Then tell me."

I told her everything that had happened with Bobby, Emily and my grandmother.

After listening to my story, she said, "Listen, cher. Don't let your anger make you miserable. Never use up your energy to hate people who do terrible things to you. They're not worth it. As for Bobby, I'm disappointed in him. He was a nice boy when he delivered to my home and I thought he was going to turn out to be a good man. I think you injured his pride, Claire, that's why he insulted you. But you have to forget what he said. Don't let his words hurt you and take you off the course you've set for yourself."

"I'm trying. But you don't know how ashamed I was a few minutes ago to tell you he'd called me a poor nigger and told me I needed him to give me light-skinned children. He owns the house now. God! I know him and he's going to use that to get back at me. He might even be nasty enough to make us move. But you know what hurts the most; he took my best friend away from me."

"No, cher, he did not. You said he told you some of your friends were after him. Didn't you realize he was giving you a message about who not to trust? You let it pass because you thought Emily couldn't be one of those friends. But she was, Claire, and you certainly don't need a friend like her. Good riddance. And don't worry; she'll regret what she's done."

"Miss Menard, you remember the dream I had about the snake, well...in it I ran pass Emily standing in front of her house talking to a boy. His back was turned to me. I wonder if that was a warning of what was going to happen. Because the morning after the dream, my Uncle showed up and caused a lot of trouble. Maybe the boy in the dream was an omen about Bobby."

"Oh cher, don't believe in all that hocus pocus. Emily was not a good friend to you, that's all."

"What about Big Mama? How am I going to live with her when she seems to be more interested in what Bobby wants? What I want doesn't matter to her."

"You have to forgive her. Everything she's done, she's done for you. You can make her understand why you can't marry Bobby. But you have to give her a chance to do that. She's been counting on him to take care of you when she dies. Trust me, cher. You can make her understand. Go home now and talk to her, you'll see."

"I'm afraid."

"Don't be. She'll be glad to see you. I'll bet she's chewing her fingers waiting for you on the front porch swing. Go home, Claire."

"How do you know all these things, Miss Menard? Did you go to college?"

"No, I'm self-taught. I've been reading too ever since I'm a little girl. I had an older sister who taught me to read just like your Nennaine taught you. Everything I've learned since then, I've learned the hard way. In other words, life taught me the rest of what I know. I'm really not smart, just experienced. It's getting late; you'd better be getting home."

"Okay. Do you want some help getting into the house before I leave?"

"Yes, if you can help me into the foyer, that'll be fine. I haven't used the upstairs for years. I use one of the rooms off the kitchen that used to be the servant's quarters. I had that part of the house converted for my use. That way when I'll need someone to give me round the clock care, I'll have a room for that person."

Getting her out of the chair was a struggle. I don't know how she would have managed without me. Her legs were so weak they could barely hold up her withered body. I had to practically carry her inside.

When I finally got her into the house I told her, "Please don't be angry with me, Miss Menard, but you shouldn't be in this house all alone. If you have an accident and can't get to the telephone, you might lie where you fall and die."

"I'm fine, you worry too much. Go on now, get yourself home and remember what I told you." She dragged herself along holding on to the wall as she made her way toward the back of the house. 'Goodnight, cher," she called to me, "make sure my door is locked."

Big Mama was waiting on the swing just as Miss Menard said she would be. I sat down next to her without a word. I had cold feet. I couldn't think of a way to begin telling her what I needed her to understand.

"I thought you were afraid of the dark." She looked at me as if she'd caught me in a lie.

"I am. That's why I'm out of breath. I ran all the way home."

"Where did you go?"

"I went for a long walk...all the way to the Rivoli," Now I was really lying.

"What! Are you crazy? It's dangerous around the Rivoli Theater at night. Did you go to a movie?"

"No. I just walked and tried to think about this mess with Bobby. I didn't know I'd end up there. When it got really dark, I ran all the way back." As soon as the last word left my mouth, I remembered telling Miss Menard I never lied to my grandmother. My life was changing. I was changing and I hated it.

"I'm glad you're home. Come on, let's go to bed. I'm worn out worrying about you."

"I'm sorry I worried you, Big Mama. Can we talk for a few minutes before we go in?"

"Okay, but only a few minutes."

Calmly I explained to her why I couldn't marry Bobby. I told her all the things I hoped to do in my life: get a college degree and get a job where I'd get to travel to all the places in the world I'd read about. I wanted to make her life better and show her how much I appreciated all she'd done for me. As for marriage, it might come later in my life, or maybe not at all. Nennaine never married and she never regretted it. I told her I couldn't do any of those things if I married Bobby and I asked her to believe in me and encourage me; the rest I could do on my own. My grandmother started to cry and I stopped talking and held her hand.

"I thought about what I needed to do while you were gone, Claire. You have a good head on your shoulders. You're not only book smart; you're strong-willed and you understand what it's going to take to get where you want to go. I have to trust the decisions you make because I think you know what you're doing. I've been quietly planning for your future for a while now, so I'm going to step aside and let you take charge. I'll ask God to watch over you."

"You mean it?"

"I said it, didn't I?"

"What about the house? Do you think Bobby will...?"

My grandmother cut me off. "You go to school. Let me figure out what to do about him and this house."

She was startled when I threw my arms around her and gave her a big, loud kiss on her cheek. Displays of spontaneous affection had never been our family's strong suit.

"What was that for?"

"Oh, just for the hell of it. Oh, oh, sorry. I forgot the new rule." We chuckled as we went in to bed.

PART TWO

- 12 -

HIGH SCHOOL DRAMA

Clark High School reopened for Blacks in 1948. It had been a White school, but was closed several years before due to declining enrollment. The school's new population came from all over New Orleans: above Canal Street, down in the Ninth Ward, and Creoles of color from the Seventh Ward. I had never had to deal with the rough, tough, in-your-face kind of classmates, so I spent ninth grade as a loner. I didn't attend any of the football games or the sock hops after the games; I focused on school. My homework, reading, and my job kept me busy with not a lot of time to think.

Getting to school was a short walk. I felt fortunate it was only eight blocks from my house and only five from my job at the drugstore. The trip to Xavier Prep took at least an hour and required a transfer of buses. I never would have been able to keep my job after school had I gone to the Prep.

Feeling fortunate did nothing to alleviate my loneliness. Only a few of the kids I graduated with from Corpus Christi had come to Clark High. And the ones who came, I considered acquaintances not friends. I refused to admit I missed Emily, even to myself. After eight years as best friends, it was painful to think a boy had come between us. She knew it wasn't that I didn't want her to have Bobby that had hurt me; it had been her lies and her theatrical betrayal. I knew to trust anyone from that point on was going to be difficult, especially a female friend - one who smiled in your face and laughed behind your back.

Emily and I hadn't seen each other since that Saturday morning in September. My fourteenth birthday, a few days later, was a sad one. It was the first one I'd spent without Emily since we were six years old.

She dated Bobby openly now that I knew about them. One of my gossipy classmates saw them together and couldn't wait to tell me. With Emily attending Xavier Prep and me at Clark, there was little chance I'd ever see her unless we sought each other out. I often asked myself if I were jealous of her because she could afford to go to the Prep and I couldn't. The answer was always a solid no, but deep inside I also knew I would like to have gone where all the good students went. I consoled myself by knowing without a doubt that one day, no matter how difficult it got, I'd be able to realize most of my goals. Emily wanted a man – a man who would give her a home and five babies. I wanted an education, and after getting it, I'd get whatever else I wanted from my own abilities and the money I'd earn.

Bobby stayed away from my house and me. He called my grandmother occasionally, but she never told me what they talked about. Behind my back she had been his ally; she had accepted his guarantee that I would be well taken care of so that she could die in peace. My refusal to be conscripted into marriage had foiled both their plans.

Big Mama seemed to accept that the marriage would never happen. She stopped mentioning Bobby's name to me altogether. I'm sure she was apprehensive about the deals they'd made; I was nervous about the ones she might be making to keep the wolf away from the door. It had been months, and he still hadn't made a move to throw us out. Big Mama certainly seemed calm enough. Her composure allowed me to settle into ninth grade and focus on my studies.

In my sophomore year, I joined the drama club. Our English teacher, Mr. Fields, was our drama coach. We were allowed to use several minutes of our class period to meet. For rehearsals we used study periods and lunch breaks. Several of us worked after school and couldn't meet at any other time.

In my junior year, we won the city championship performing the play, *I'm a Fool*, by Sherwood Anderson. I played a rich young woman wooed by an imposter.

Neal Fontenot, the grandson of one of our neighbors, was also in the group. We often rehearsed whatever play we were working on when he came to visit his grandmother on Sunday afternoons. The front porch swing was an ideal place to run our lines. Mr. Fields often wrote one act plays expressly for Neal and me to perform for our class and occasionally for the entire school.

Neal was extremely shy and only shed his shyness when we rehearsed or he was on stage performing. Acting together for almost two years, we became close friends. I watched him change from a loner to an outgoing person. Many of our classmates automatically assumed we were dating and started to tease us. No matter how many times we denied it, no one believed us. One Sunday I decided to talk about the gossip.

"Does all that talk about us bother you, Neal?"

"Not as much as when it first started. But, Claire, I need to tell you something about that. I like you, but not like that." He looked embarrassed, as if he'd hurt my feelings.

"Same here."

"Really?"

"Really. I'm not interested in boys or dating right now. I can wait." I watched him relax and then I continued, "I don't listen to all that garbage and you shouldn't either. We know we're just friends and we're the only two who count."

"Can I tell you something in confidence, Claire?" He suddenly folded his arms across the top of his body and pressed them hard against his chest. His whole body shook and his lips quivered.

"No! I don't want to hear anyone's problems, okay? Sorry." I jumped off the swing and pulled Neal up, too. "Let's go for a walk. Maybe you'll be able to shake what's bothering you. But give me a minute."

I opened the front door and yelled, "Big Mama, Neal and I are going for a walk. Be back in a little while." I must have assaulted my grandmother's eardrums because she was sitting a few inches away from the door. I knew there was no way she'd missed a Sunday afternoon of sitting behind a cracked, wing door listening to Neal and me. She'd rather swallow fire.

I turned toward Neal and put a finger on my lips. When his eyes widened, I knew he understood. We didn't say a word until we were halfway up the block.

"Was your grandmother eavesdropping?" Neal was still shivering.

I nodded. It was my turn to be embarrassed.

"Did you know what I was about to tell you?"

"No, but I could tell it was damned important because you looked really serious."

"You saved my life just now. I was about to tell you that if I liked girls, I would definitely pick you. But I don't, I like boys." Neal stopped walking and scrutinized my face while I digested what he'd told me. "You're the only person I've told because I trust you."

I was speechless. If he had given me ten guesses, even a hundred, I would never have guessed what he planned to tell me.

"Say something, Claire, don't just stand there. Call me a sissy, a ginny woman, anything, but say something." Tears were streaming down Neal's face. He yanked a handkerchief out of his pocket and quickly dried his face and blew his nose. His red nose and red-rimmed eyes didn't detract from his handsome face.

It was the first time I had looked at him closely. He had dark, mahogany skin with sharp features and curly brown hair. His eyes were chestnut brown. A magnificent set of teeth enhanced his best feature – his smile. I had never seen him without it, until now.

"Neal, I'm shocked, but not too shocked to realize what my grandmother would have done with that information. She would have gone straight to your grandmother. Then I imagine all hell would break loose at your house. But wait...does your mother know?"

"We don't talk about it, but I think she does. My father definitely knows. He's really mean to me and calls me all kinds of names behind my mother's back. But she knows he does it even though I've never told her. They fuss all the time and I think because of me, they're close to getting a divorce." Neal started to cry again.

"Listen to me, Neal; I don't care about what you told me. We're friends and we'll always be friends. Nothing will change that. So don't worry about your secret. I'll never tell anyone."

I wasn't sure if I had helped him or not. We walked another block and then returned to my house. Neal left me at my gate and went back to his grandmother's.

I sat on the swing to think about Neal and how complicated his life must have been. There was nothing particularly effeminate about him that I had ever noticed. He was always a sharp dresser, had a fresh haircut and carried himself with pride – but so did a lot of other boys. He didn't walk or talk funny that I could see. And there had never been any of that kind of gossip about him in school or in the neighborhood. The door opened and my grandmother looked at me for a while before she spoke. She stayed inside and spoke to me through the screen door.

"Well, you and Neal seem pretty close. If you couldn't talk on the swing, he must have had some big secret to tell you." Big Mama didn't mince words. "Exactly how close have you gotten?"

"We're friends...today, tomorrow and forever. We're not interested in each other romantically. Didn't you hear us say that when you were listening behind the door?"

"I don't believe everything I hear, Claire."

"Well, believe it. I'm sure that should make you very happy. He's a little too dark for you, right? I'll bet his hair is too curly." The Creole crap had once again resurfaced. I could never use the term Negro or Black to refer to "our" people in my grandmother's presence. Creoles of color had a separate ethnicity, she'd say. And all of the people who accepted being part African and talked about going back to Africa could go; she hadn't come from Africa so why would she go back.

My grandmother's eyes flashed anger, but she chose not to act on it. "What was Neal's big secret?" This time she didn't hint; she asked directly.

I knew I had to tell her a believable lie. Then it occurred to me a half-truth might do. "Neal's mother and father aren't getting along. They argue all the time, mostly about him. He's afraid he'll be the cause if they get a divorce."

"That's old news. Maria hates her daughter-in-law, always has. She agrees with her son when he tells her how Neal's mother spoils him. So she's encouraging him to divorce her and then he and Neal can move in with her. She'll love that because she's lonely."

Even though I liked to mind my own business, I felt compelled to tell Neal what my grandmother had told me. I couldn't wait to go to school the next day.

Neal wasn't surprised. He told me his grandmother didn't disguise her hatred for his mother. She'd even tell him nasty things about his mother and when he'd try to defend her, his grandmother would tell him he had a sassy mouth and would send him home. Neal's mother told him she was reaching a breaking point and it might mean big changes for him. He was scared.

After we won the city championship, we were to compete at the state level at the end of May. But it was not to be. Neal withdrew from school and he and his mother left the city without his father's knowledge. The only person who knew about it was Mr. Fields. The day after Neal left, Mr. Fields told me Neal had asked him to give me a message. He told me Neal would contact me as soon as he and his mother were settled and that he would write to me and send the letters to Mr. Fields to give to me. That way, my grandmother would not be privy to Neal's and his mother's whereabouts.

For months I waited to hear from Neal, but he never wrote. I wondered if his mother had forbidden him to write because she feared Mr. Fields or I would accidentally tell someone where they were and then her husband would be able to track them down.

- 13 -

WHEELS ON LUNDI GRAS

Miss Menard's arthritis was progressing rapidly and she was rarely able to go outdoors. Every day I rushed to complete my deliveries in order to spend some time helping her before I went home. She was spending most of her day in bed. And on the days Lena, her housekeeper, wasn't there to make sure she ate, if I hadn't gone to heat food Lena had prepared and stored in the refrigerator for her, she would not have eaten anything.

I had grown as close to her as if she were a family member. And even though she never said it out loud, I knew she felt the same way about me. It didn't matter to her that I wasn't White, or to me that she wasn't my grandmother's long lost sister. I had found her by accident and I don't know what I would have done without her to advise me when things got really bad.

Miss Menard gave me a key so that I could let myself in. I started bringing my bicycle up on the porch and stashing it behind the metal glider. I didn't want to leave it in plain view while I was in the house because it would surely be stolen. I think I was even afraid Big Mama might pass the house, look in the yard, and recognize it.

I'd signal Miss Menard before I entered by banging the door knocker four times. Some days I found her sitting on my favorite piece of furniture, the mahogany Parson's bench in the foyer. She'd be waiting for me with a big smile on her still-beautiful face.

I loved the setting around that big old house. The two enormous oak trees on the street-side of the banquette grew until they met and fused, then they grew toward the house several feet above the roof. When the tips of the branches brushed together in the wind, they made a wonderful rustling sound above the patio, and when they hit the roof they made a big, flopping sound. I would often stand on the front porch and stare at the branches of the trees as they fanned out above my head. I loved the shade and the shadows they imposed over and around the whole house. Just as I did with clouds, I'd look for special shapes and faces in the shadows and imagine all sorts of scenarios with me as the lady of the house. Daydreaming had always been the place I'd go to hide when I needed to shut out the world. It was convenient; I never had to physically move or even close my eyes. I could daydream wonderful fantasies with them wide open. I possessed virtual reality even before I was seven.

Before I realized it or was ready for another big change in my life, my senior year was upon me. I spent from October to December filling out applications for college. Unless I received a full scholarship, I hadn't the slightest idea how I was going to pay for the next four years. My grades were good and I expected to graduate near or at the top of my class, so I was praying one of the schools would offer me one.

During Mardi Gras week, we got Monday through Wednesday off from school. I told my grandmother I was going to pick up some history notes from one of my classmates, but I really was going to see Miss Menard. I knew her housekeeper wouldn't be there for two days and she'd need my help. I was still hiding my special relationship with her, too afraid to tell Big Mama. What would I do if she'd forbid me to see her?

After I put the bike behind the glider and stood it on its kickstand, I decided to look around before I knocked. I had been so distracted with things related to school; I hadn't noticed how rundown the garden was beginning to look. Miss Menard had always done a lot of her own gardening, except for the hedges, the grass, the fruit trees, and the large, magnolia trees that needed a gardener's care. Why hadn't her gardener taken care of what needed to be done? He had to know she no longer worked in the yard.

The beautiful rosebushes in front of the porch and the ones that lined the walkway were starting to dry up from lack of watering and they needed pruning. The hedges had not been shaped and now grew higher than the cast-iron fence. Most of the fern were still succulent, but many of the flowers that grew around them seemed to be dying. Only the night jasmine in the side yard was flourishing. Every tree, bush and plant around the patio had died. The banana trees in the back yard were drying up and their big leaves were drooping, almost touching the ground. Even the two giant magnolias seemed to be crying out for water.

I felt sick as I looked around at what had once been a magnificent garden. It appeared to be dying right along with Miss Menard. I didn't want to lose either of them; I had to do something. I ran past the patio and into the back yard to a small, brick garden house and grabbed a hose and a big pair of pruning shears. I had watched my grandparents and often helped them in the nun's garden and also in ours. I knew what needed to be done and I did it. When I was finished and was standing on the porch admiring my handiwork, I heard tapping on the window behind me. Miss Menard was in a wheelchair sitting in the middle of the open drapes in the front room.

Were my eyes deceiving me? Did she look better than she had in months? I knew I had watered only the dying plants, but it looked as if some other miracle liquid had found its way to my frail friend, and like the plants, she had rebounded with new life. In seconds I unlocked the door and was inside the house. She met me in the foyer.

"When did you get it?" I asked staring at the wheelchair. "You didn't have it when I was here Friday, did you? You didn't tell me, you sneaky dog!"

"No, I wanted to surprise you," Miss Menard's face was flushed with excitement. "Lena brought it to me Saturday. I ordered it last month. Rolling myself around is still troublesome because of my curled fingers, but I'm managing. I just need to take my time."

"I couldn't believe my eyes when I saw you through the window. I'm so happy to see you getting around again. You look beautiful. I like the way you look when you're smiling. How's your pain today?"

"Not so bad, Claire. I think getting up and around the last two days has helped me. For a long time I've said I wouldn't have one of these things. I was wrong, wasn't I?"

"Yes, but I knew you weren't thinking straight. You didn't even want to talk about it." I watched her face as I spoke waiting for her to react, but she didn't. She just sat there smiling at me.

"Lately, Claire, I've been thinking about what a short time I have left on this earth, and I don't want to lie in my bed and waste away. I want to be sitting up when I die."

"Oh," the word die made my heart flutter. My eyes were immediately overrun with tears. "Don't say things like that, please, Miss Menard." I couldn't hold back the tears and they scurried down my cheeks.

"Don't cry, cher. I'm an old woman and I'm going to die soon, whether you want me to or not. But...not right now. I need a little more time. I've got unfinished business to take care of."

"What business?"

"My business, you nosy little girl. When I get it done, I promise to tell you what it is." Miss Menard was firm but not annoyed. In fact, she was still smiling at me.

"Okay," I said.

"Claire, what are you doing here on Lundi Gras? On Fat Monday, you're supposed to be getting ready for Fat Tuesday," she laughed. "I didn't think I'd see you until Wednesday. Don't you celebrate the Mardi Gras holidays with your grandmother or your friends?"

"No, I think it's a stupid holiday just like Halloween."

"Oh, cher, your life is too bare for such a young person. You should be having fun with your friends."

"I don't have any friends. Anyway, I don't care about all that stuff."

"I care. You're just seventeen, but you've never had a chance to be a child." Miss Menard quickly changed the subject. "What possessed you to work in the yard today? Is that why you came?"

"No. I thought Lena wasn't coming until Wednesday and maybe you might need me."

"You're such a sweet girl, Claire."

"Thanks. I just happened to stop and look at the garden and saw how neglected it was. Thought a little water and some pruning might help. What happened to your gardener?"

"I let him go a few weeks ago. If you don't stay on those people, they do as little as they can. I had to constantly tell him what he needed to do."

"What people?" I snapped. Was she bashing Colored people?

108

"Gardeners. I've had a bunch in the last ten years. They all did everything as fast as they could and hightailed it out of here. When I could, I used to finish a great deal of their work."

"Do you realize how much yard you have, plus the patio? You need a trustworthy gardener. I think I know someone who would do a good job for you."

"Who is this person, Claire? Can I trust him? Remember, I don't like strangers hanging around my house. How well do you know him?"

"He was my grandfather's friend. His name is André Dejean and he's been a gardener all his life. He took over Big Papa's job caring for the nun's garden. He's good, that's why he takes care of some of those big homes on St. Charles Avenue. I think you'll like his work, and him, too."

"Where does this Mr. Dejean live?"

"Close by...near Kerlerec and Claiborne."

"Well, bring him to see me on Thursday. I want you here when I talk to him."

"Okay, I'll take care of it. Can I do anything in the house to help you today?"

"Lena came early this morning and gave me two hours. I think she needs the money. Or maybe she thinks I'm going to kick the bucket soon and she'll be out of a job," Miss Menard snickered.

I laughed with her, but then I turned serious. "You're going to fool her, aren't you?"

"I'm going to try. You know what you can do for me today; you can take me out on the porch and visit with me for a while. How's that?"

"Okay, let's go." I grabbed the back of the wheelchair and pushed her out on the porch. It was a little chilly, so I went back in and got her another blanket. I knew I'd enjoy her so much more than a catty bunch of teenagers who pointed and laughed at everyone they saw.

- 14 -

SIX WEEKS NOTICE

Mardi Gras morning Big Mama and I decided to have breakfast before we left the house to catch some of the parades and then walk the length of Claiborne Avenue up to Canal Street. Everybody walked the neutral ground on Claiborne at least once on Carnival Day, masked or not. Most Creoles of color didn't venture above Canal Street, particularly during the Mardi Gras season. That was the time for all kinds of violence: Black vs. White or Black vs. Black. Vendettas and criminal acts were carried out from behind a mask, especially after the masker got tanked on liquor. There was no time better than Mardi Gras for revenge.

In the middle of our breakfast, Bobby walked through the back door as if he lived there. He plopped down on one of the kitchen chairs.

"Good morning, Miss Philly." He looked directly at my grandmother ignoring me. "Coffee sure smells good."

"Good morning," she replied suspiciously without an invitation to have a cup.

"No need to beat around the bush, y'all need to find a place to move to. I'm moving my family in this house when y'all move out. Six weeks ought to do it. After all, I did give y'all almost four years. So, I want y'all out by the end of March."

"Bobby! Why are you doing this? We just talked two weeks ago. I thought we'd settled it. You know damn well you don't deserve this house because you paid off the $1,200 balance on the mortgage." Big Mama had cursed. She'd never done that in my presence. "All the rest of the money in this house came from my husband's and my blood and sweat. I thought I could trust you to take care of my granddaughter. I was on your side, remember? But

110

do you think I'm going to let you walk away with her home just because you say she jilted you? Claire doesn't want to marry you and I thought you had accepted that. She's going to graduate from high school in May, and we're not going anywhere before that. And maybe I'll see to it that we won't have to move at all."

"That ain't your call, Miss Philly. You better check with your lawyer, that's what I did. I own this house. I got the deed and it's in my name. You and your granddaughter need to be outta here in six weeks."

"Why do you need this house, Bobby? I thought you were going to move into the house on Pauger Street."

"I am, but not with my family. I'm getting married one of these days and that house on Pauger is for me and my wife. This house," Bobby made a sweeping circle in the air with his hand, "is for my family. I'm gonna tear out some of that wall," he pointed to the wall separating the two sides of the house, "open it up, and then add a coupla rooms in the back. My mama and daddy still got eight of my brothers and sisters at home. The addition ought to be enough room for everybody."

Big Mama closed her eyes and put both hands on top her head as she tried to digest what she'd just heard, while Bobby, looking smug, waited for her to respond.

I had held my tongue long enough.

"You're a lousy bastard. You're doing this to get back at me. You cheated my grandmother out of this house, and probably that goddamn car, too. You're a crooked son-of-a-bitch, and so help me God, you're going to pay for what you've done to us."

"I guess that's supposed to be some kinda threat, right? You need to shut up, bitch. You don't figure in this one bit. I got y'all by your titties, so pack up your shit, and get the hell outta my house."

I ran to get the bat on the side of the stove. I intended to bash in his brains, but Big Mama grabbed me and held me.

"Get out of here, Bobby, or I'll let Claire loose on you."

"Six weeks, that's what y'all got," he hurled his parting shot over his shoulder as he wasted no time walking out of the back door.

My grandmother spent the rest of Mardi Gras in bed with cold towels on her forehead. She rubbed garlic on the back of her neck trying to prevent her blood pressure from rising any higher.

For the first time in my life, I didn't know what to do. After all my big talk about finding a new place to live if Bobby ever threw us out, I didn't know how to go about finding that place. But I did know I couldn't sit and wring my hands or curl up in a ball on the floor. I needed to talk to someone; someone who could point my nose in the right direction. Big Mama was trying, but I knew she couldn't handle it anymore. I was afraid she'd have a heart attack or a stroke and die. I had no choice; I had to take charge of things.

As soon as Big Mama dozed off, my feet flew over the uneven, brick banquette and they carried me to Miss Menard's as though I were borne upon the wind. She'd know what to do.

It was already dark and all the Carnival revelers were beginning to stagger home. Most of them were rushing home to dinner, often the last big meal before Lent started. I heard the final, *"Hey la bas,"* for that year's Mardi Gras. The next day, Ash Wednesday, fasting would begin and their sacrifices would be pledged. Liquor, food, cigarettes and candy were the most popular things "given up for Lent." Abstinence for almost forty days once a year made even the biggest sinners feel self-righteous. I wondered what Bobby had given up?

After running the whole way, I entered the gate without breath and my legs shaking from overuse. When I stopped halfway up the walk to lean over and try to breathe, I raised my head and my eyes came to rest on Miss Menard quietly sitting on her moonlit porch. She had already seen me.

"Claire, what's wrong? Has something happened to your grandmother? Why do you look so frantic?"

I didn't answer. I bounded up the steps and fell on my knees in front of her, buried my face in her lap, and began to cry.

"What is it, cher? Tell me!"

"O...o...o...kay...but...I need ...to...st...op crying first." I was sobbing so hard I started to choke on my saliva. Miss Menard waited patiently as I fought to calm myself. "He did it," I finally blurted out, "and it's going to kill my grandmother."

"Who did it? Bobby?"

"He's making us move. We have to be out in six weeks."

"Oh, that dirty, no-good, little bastard!" Now Miss Menard was shocking me with her curse words. "What's he going to do, move in?"

I told her what he'd told Big Mama and me.

"Who is he going to marry? Emily?"

"I don't know."

"It doesn't matter. Listen to me, Claire. I have an old friend I can ask for help. Leonard Stern owns a lot of property all over New Orleans. I'm sure he has some rentals in the Seventh Ward. Let me find out if he has a vacancy."

"I don't know if we'll be able to afford it. We'll just have the salary from my part-time job. We won't be getting the rent from the other side of the house or the few dollars Big Mama makes selling the fruit and flowers she still grows in our yard. She's talking about asking Father O'Mara for her old job back. I don't think she can do it anymore. I'll have to quit school and go to work full-time and that will kill me."

"Stop thinking bad thoughts. I'm going to help you, cher. I'll probably know something by the time you come here after work tomorrow. Try not to worry." Miss Menard started to touch my face then remembered the liniment-soaked glove on her hand. She patted my back instead.

"I can't stop worrying. Big Mama looks sick. What if something happens to her? Then what? I don't have anyone else. I'll be left alone." I burst into tears again. Miss Menard patted me gently on the back with both hands as my head lay vibrating in her lap. She sat very still and let me cry it out.

All sorts of thoughts started running through my mind as I spent myself weeping. Through my tears, I could see my grandmother in bed unable to walk or talk. We lived in one room in the back of a large house. I was apparently someone's maid because I had on a white uniform. There was no more house; no more school; no more Miss Menard. How would I get along without her? And then I saw someone else. He was sitting in the rain under one of the trees near the house on Johnson Street. I sat up abruptly drying my face with my hands.

"I just thought about something else that's probably upsetting Big Mama," I sniffled.

"There's Marcel, a homeless man we help. Everyone calls him Crazy M and they shoo him away every time they see him in the area. When he comes to our house we give him something to eat, and when it rains we let him sleep on the back porch. If he didn't have lice and sores, we'd let him sleep in the kitchen. I don't think he's as crazy as people think he is because he talks to Big Mama and me all the time. When we leave, he won't have anyone who cares about him."

"Child, child...Claire! Stop trying to carry all the ills of the world on your shoulders. That homeless man has had you and your grandmother to care about him for a long time, now he'll have to find someone else. Your main concern should be about you and your grandmother. Get up!" she ordered me. "Pull that chair over here and sit down.

I jumped up and obeyed like a three-year-old.

"You won't be alone, I promise you. Besides, your grandmother is tough. Where do you think you got your toughness? Do you think she's lived as long as she has without facing tough times before now? I remember how tough it was when we were kids." Miss Menard's eyes flickered. "You know...when we grew up. I think your grandmother and I are close in age. Well...back then...we had a lot less than people have today. Things were tough for everybody; it didn't matter whether you were White or Colored." She had to stop several times to clear her throat or swallow in order to finish what she was saying.

"I know. Big Mama told me her mother died when she was a small child and that she had a really, mean stepmother. One of her sisters ran away when she was fifteen. That's who I thought you were when I first saw your name. Nennaine is dead, Big Mama's brother and my aunts are all in California passing for White, so I don't think my grandmother has any toughness left. I'm all she has now." Each time I looked at Miss Menard's eyes I knew I'd seen them in someone else's head. Big Mama's brother? I saw him only once; his face was now out of focus.

Miss Menard's face became deeply cloaked in sadness, but when she saw me looking at her she quickly commented. "Hmm...that sounds a bit like my life."

"Miss Menard, are you sure you're not my great-aunt? You and my grandmother have a lot in common. That seems really strange to me."

"No, but I wish I were. There are many strange things in life, Claire. But listen, it's late and you need to go home. Help me in, cher."

After I got her settled in the house, I locked up and walked behind a group of people headed in my direction. I recognized the

Maillot family, Bobby's cousins. I hoped no one would turn around and see me, so I deliberately slowed down and fell far behind them. When I saw there were people on the other side of the street, I crossed over and walked close to them. With each step I took, I wondered whether Miss Menard knew what she was telling me to do when she told me not to worry. It was a lot easier for her to say it, then for me to do it. I quickened my pace and caught up with the group when we got to my block. I wished them a good evening and dashed across the street to my house.

And there was Big Mama, sitting on the swing waiting for me with a worried look on her face.

– 15 –

FIRST THE RAIN
THEN THE FLOWERS

Leonard Stern had no rentals for Coloreds. I found it strange Miss Menard wasn't more upset when she told me.

"I've been doing some thinking, Claire. Before I tell you, though, I need to ask you something important. Does your grandmother know about me...about you coming here?"

"No. I've never told her about you."

"Why?"

"When you turned out not to be her sister, what was the point? Why are you asking me?"

"When I tell you what I have in mind, you'll know why."

"Before I forget, Miss Menard, Mr. Dejean is going to be here at 5:30 tomorrow. I'll try to get here by then, if not, I'll only be about ten minutes late. I asked him to wait for me on the porch."

"That's fine, Claire." She took a deep breath and then rolled herself out of her room toward the kitchen. "Do you drink coffee, yet?"

"Only café au lait."

"Good, that's what I drink, too. I'll make some."

"You can do a lot of things now from your wheelchair, can't you?"

She nodded in agreement as she wheeled herself about making the coffee. Even with her gnarled fingers and twisted hands, she maneuvered her chair around the kitchen effortlessly. Everything she did was done with a surgeon's precision – in a meticulous and particular manner. My grandmother worked the same way in the kitchen. When I tried to assist Miss Menard in getting the milk out of the refrigerator, she dismissed me with a flick of her wrist. One by one, she managed to get each cup of coffee with boiled milk to the table.

"Sit down, cher. I'm ready to tell you what I have in mind." She waited for me to sit and taste my café au lait.

"Do you think your grandmother would agree to live here, Claire?"

"Oh, God, I don't know! Probably not. What are you telling me? You want us to live here with you?"

"Why not? You need a place to live and I need someone to live here and help me. We need each other. I'll provide room and board for you and your grandmother, and in exchange, you both will take care of the house and me. Doesn't that sound like a fair exchange?"

"I need to think for a minute, Miss Menard. You just shocked the hell out of me."

"Drink your coffee. I know it's a big decision. Take all the time you need."

I couldn't look at her while I tried to make sense of what I had just been offered. I looked down at the embroidered tablecloth and traced the bright-colored thread of the flowers with my fingers. Could I trust this woman to get us out of our dilemma, or did she want to possess me and my grandmother for her own selfish purposes? Was she reverting back to slavery with us as her human chattel? She had no one in her life. Could it be she was so mean everyone had run away from her? Would I be putting us in a worse situation? The one person who had been helping me solve my problems had now become one of them.

I lifted my head and looked at Miss Menard as if I would find the answers boldly written across her forehead. Before I could say anything, she shook her finger at me and smiled.

"I recognize that look. It's about trust. I know; I've had lots of experience in that area. I don't expect you to give me an answer today. Take some more time and think about it. It might turn out that you don't trust me enough to put your lives in my hands."

My whole face burned from embarrassment. She had figured out exactly what I was thinking. I had to say something. "I will think about it some more, but I can't wait too long. Big Mama has a lady in the next block from our house and Father O'Mara looking for a place for us."

"Okay, you decide how to handle things: my offer and your grandmother."

"Maybe I'll talk to her tonight. I'm scared, though. She's going to be hopping mad I didn't tell her about you from the beginning. Oh, Miss Menard, I'm so tired worrying about everything. I feel as though my head weighs a thousand pounds."

"Did something else happen yesterday?"

"Yes, something did. Bobby came back after I left the house to come here. Marcel was there. My grandmother had given him something to eat and they were sitting on the back porch talking about what was going to happen with the house when Bobby showed up. He started screaming and cursing at Marcel telling him to get away and stay away from the house and not to ever come back. He told that poor man if he ever caught him hanging around again, he'd kick his ass. Poor Marcel ran away crying and Bobby ran down the alley behind him shouting curses at him. Big Mama is still upset. This morning she said she doesn't know how she could have been so wrong about Bobby. Personally, I'd like to see a bunch of bad luck fall on the bastard's head for what he did to Marcel, my grandmother and me."

"I thought he was getting married? What happened?"

"Damn if I know. I've been too involved in school to pay attention to half of what's going on around me. There's been no gossip about him lately...that I know about, anyway."

"Bobby sounds like an angry young man to me. Stay away from him, Claire. I don't trust him. You have to let Marcel take care of himself now. Has your family always been there for him?"

"For as long as I can remember."

"Even your grandfather?"

"Sure. Big Papa knew Marcel ever since he was a young boy. I think he's been roaming around the street since he was a teenager."

"How old is he?"

"Late thirties, maybe early forties. But he looks like an old man."

"You and your grandmother have such good hearts. Not everybody does, and certainly not Bobby. He's out for revenge. Please, stay away from him."

"I will, but it doesn't stop me from wishing I could get back at him. I guess we both want revenge. I wish I knew someone who practices hoodoo. I'd put some gris-gris on that son of a...," I giggled suddenly remembering Bobby's fear of *voodoo*. "He's afraid of that stuff. He swears some woman *put bad mouth on* his father and that curse gave Mr. Villagoso some kind of muscle disease. He says that's why his father's legs don't work. I think it's because he's mean to his wife and kids. Big Mama says he still likes the ladies, paralyzed or not. Sooo, what I really think is that Bobby's ol pappy probably put his peepee in one too many holes and the Good Lord paralyzed his ass." Miss Menard and I howled laughing. "The old geezer still managed to give his wife thirteen children," I continued, "maybe his legs didn't work anymore, but his weenie sure did." We laughed so hard we cried.

"Oh, Claire, I should tell you not to say things like that because God will punish you, but," Miss Menard said still laughing, "that's funny and you make me feel young again."

"Damn, look at the time. I'm late." I dried my eyes with my fingers. "I have to get to the drugstore before it closes so that I can turn in my cash." I jumped up from the table. "I'm sorry I have to run off without helping you clear the table."

"No, no...go on. I'll leave these things for Lena to clean up in the morning. Are you coming tomorrow?"

"Of course. Remember I'm supposed to meet Mr. Dejean here at 5:30. I won't be able to stay long, though. I have to study for my tests on Friday."

"Go on, cher. I'll lock up behind you."

My house was dark when I got there. Something was wrong. My grandmother was always home when I arrived. I ran through the alley and flung open the screen door. I felt around the wall in the dark until I found the switch for the kitchen light.

Big Mama was lying on the floor in front of the stove. She was sprawled out on her back, arms and legs spread apart. Her eyes and mouth were open. I froze momentarily afraid to touch her. When I did, she was so cold her skin felt like unused clay. I knew she must have been lying there all day. I curled up in a ball on the floor next to her and tried to scream, but I had no voice. The tears came with no sound. Finally, I realized there was no use lying there, Big Mama was dead, and all the screams and tears in the world wouldn't bring her back.

I got up and called Dr. La Croix. He was on his way out to make a house call, and in a "matter of fact" manner, he told me he'd send an ambulance. Then I dialed Miss Menard. She told me to stay strong and that she was sending Lena to help me. She started to cry as she apologized for being an invalid and not able to come herself. I heard her mutter, "Why, Lord, are you making this child's life so hard?" Before I could comment, she hung up.

Lena was there in ten minutes and was with me when the ambulance arrived and pronounced my grandmother dead. I found Big Mama's papers for her Sodality and called the club's president. She told me what funeral home to call to have the body picked up and assured me all the expenses would be taken care of. She promised to come in the morning and help me with whatever arrangements I wanted to make. Lena called home to tell her husband what had happened and he encouraged her to stay with me as long as I needed her.

Mrs. Montoya came to help me the next day as she'd promised. We honored my grandmother's wishes that there be no wake or rosary, so there was only the Mass and the burial to arrange. The funeral was small and quiet with Father O'Mara officiating. A small group of Big Mama's friends and neighbors, the Ladies of Sodality, Anne Marie Bogass and Gloria attended the Mass and followed the hearse to the cemetery. I buried her in St. Roch's with the family: my grandfather, my mother and Nennaine.

When we arrived at the bank of vaults, there was a beautiful arrangement of flowers propped up under the row where my grandmother would be placed. The card was hidden among the flowers. It simply read, "Bobbie." I asked the cemetery attendant to remove it and do with it whatever he wished.

I didn't cry until we left her coffin in front of the vaults and drove away from the graveyard. Everything I had feared might happen had indeed happened. There was no way anyone could have comforted me.

When Lena dropped me off at home, she told me she needed to get home to her family. She said Miss Menard wanted me to come and live with her permanently, if I wanted. I'd be a fool not to accept, she said. I refused Lena's offer to drive me. I told her I needed time to pack some of my clothes, tidy up the house, and lock it up securely until I knew what I was going to do. Getting the house in order didn't take a lot of time because of my grandmother's spotless housekeeping. As I was locking the backdoor, I heard Mr. Trevigne, my neighbor, calling me over the partition on the back porch.

"Claire? Claire, is that you, dawlin?"

I unlocked the door and stepped out on the porch.

"There you are, sweethawt. I was some sorry to hear about your gramma, honey. I just got back from Texas this morning. Mr. Joseph told me what happened. I wish I coulda been here for you, sugah. Is there anything you need me to do for you?"

"No, but thanks, Mr. Trevigne. Do you know what's happening with the house?"

"Oh, yes indeed I know. Your gramma told me. That's why I was gone them days, to find out if I wanted to live with my daughter in Beaumont. And yeah, that's where I'm going. Say, just before you come home, Crazy M was hanging around back here calling your gramma and you. I told him about Miss Philly and ran his butt outta here. He was screaming and crying when he ran down the alley. I don't know how you people stood him all those many years."

"He's not a bad man, Mr. Trevigne, and he's not crazy. He was crying because he knows my grandmother was one of the few people who really cared about him...and...I'm another one." I looked at the old man with disgust on my face.

"Well, have it your way. I won't miss his butt in Texas." He wished me good luck and told me he was packed and would be leaving early in the morning.

I sat at the kitchen table and held my head in my hands the way my grandmother used to do. I suddenly remembered where Big Mama kept her secret money stash, even when Big Papa was alive. She said he didn't always think about the next day when it came to money. She had to put a little away in case they got into a real big hole. Whatever was in her secret box had to be more than I had.

I ran to her room and opened the door to the hat compartment in her chifferobe to search for the small candy tin she'd shown me a few years back. It wasn't there, but there was a cigar box sealed all the way around with wide, adhesive tape. I slowly peeled the tape off the box. As soon as I lifted the lid, the smell of tobacco went straight up my nostrils and made me dizzy. There were still half a dozen cigars left in the box. My grandfather had enjoyed a good smoke every now and then. Several envelopes were buried under the cigars.

The first one held Mr. Trevigne's February rent. The next one had Big Mama's wedding ring, gold necklace and bracelet, Big Papa's silver pocketwatch, and a ruby brooch I remembered Nennaine wearing. The last envelope had a bank book and $400 in twenty dollar bills. The bank account was in my name and it had a balance of $2,100. There was a note inside the bank book.

Claire,

I started saving for your college the minute I realized how smart you were. I know the money won't see you all the way through, but I hope it will at least get you started. I'm sorry I'm not there and you'll have to do it alone, but I'll be watching you and helping God to protect you.

Stay a good girl, and you'll get everything you want. Try to help Marcel if you can. Maybe you can get him to go to a home for Colored people where they'll take care of him. I'm afraid for him. Be good! Big Papa and I will see you in heaven.

Big Mama

There were no tears left to cry; my ducts were dry. I placed the box in the bag of clothes I was taking to Miss Menard's. Deep inside, I knew since there were no relatives I could go to, I'd probably end up living with her permanently. I decided to take the one picture album we'd somehow managed to fill, the tapestries, the lace doilies my grandmother had crocheted, the pair of vases from Czechoslovakia that had been a wedding gift to my grandparents from Nennaine, and, of course, Lady Blue's sling-back shoes in the brown paper bag. For years they'd all been stored in the cedar chest in the living room. Afraid someone might steal them when I wasn't there, I packed them in two large shopping bags and then made two trips to Miss Menard's getting everything to her house.

- 16 -

GOD BLESS THE FIRE BUG!

At 7:00 the next morning, I heard Lena calling us as we sat having coffee in the kitchen. "Miss Sera and Claire, y'all wanted in the front room. There's some young guy and a policeman here. They need to talk to bota y'all. Ah'm goin out to *make groceries.*" We heard the front door slam.

"Good morning, Miss Sera," Bobby greeted Miss Menard as we entered the living room. He darted a quick glance at me but didn't say anything. "Mawnin," the cop flashed his badge. "Mike McArdle, ma'am," his voice indicating his unwillingness to be there.

"What's this all about?" Miss Menard looked past Bobby to the cop. "Why are you in my home this early in the morning?"

"Ah, ma'am, this hea man's double shotgun on Johnson Street got burned down las night. He tol me this hea girl threaten him recintly. He said she tol him somethin was gonna happen to him. Whea was you las night, girl?" The policeman glared at me and put his hands on the handcuffs hanging from his belt. "Tell the trut, na."

"Look at this child! She can't even answer you. Just yesterday she buried her grandmother who died in that house. Now she finds out her home and everything in it is gone."

Miss Menard grabbed my hand and held it.

Numbness had set in. I stood there like a dead tree stump.

"Look at her, Bobby. Do you really think she burned down that house? You ought to be ashamed of yourself for all that you've done to this child and her grandmother. You too," she screamed at the cop. "And another thing, how did you know Claire was here?"

Bobby fired back, "I got my ways."

123

"Look hea, ma'am, Ah'm jes doin ma job. Ah had a check out this hea man's accusations." The cop cleared his throat. "Er um, that fire wasn't no axident. You can still smell the gasaline that somebody sprinkled even outside the house."

"Oh God, Mr. Trevigne!" I moaned.

"You talkin bout dat neighbor a yawrs. He got out awright. As a matta a fac, he's the one called the fire in," the policeman said. "He's on his way to Texas right na."

"Is the whole house gone and everything in it?" I was thinking about how glad I was that I had thought to take those things out of the cedar chest and had brought them with me.

Bobby sucked his teeth and rolled his eyes, but it was the cop who answered. "Yeah, look hea," he was eyeing me up and down as he tugged at his pants trying to get them up over his huge belly, "Ah don't think you done it, but you got any idea who mighta? Maybe it was some fella you gave the ol heave-ho and he wanted to do you some hawm. You got a boyfrien? Whea you livin na?" There was a lascivious sneer on his face as he flung the questions at me. He was a White man, and it was obvious he had no respect for me. I knew he wouldn't have minded taking me behind the bushes for a fast fuck, but to speak civilly to me was out of the question.

Miss Menard spoke out again before I could answer. "Claire is her name. She's going to live here with me as my live-in nurse. She has no kin. And no, she doesn't have a boyfriend."

"Claire been hea all night?" the cop asked her. "Don't you lie fa her, ma'am. She might git you in a worl a trouble, too."

"Yes, she arrived here about 4:00 yesterday afternoon," she told him.

The policeman turned to Bobby. "Look hea, fella, Ah don think dis girl burn down yawr house. We gotta look fa somebody else. Ah'm tru hea." His words had a commanding tone. "Ah'll be back if Ah need any mo infamation."

Bobby had spoken only two sentences since he'd arrived; he mostly rolled his eyes, groaned and grunted. As he turned to leave, I saw his hate filled eyes riveted on me. He and the cop walked out and the door slammed behind them.

A few days later, the policeman returned; this time with information for me. The body of a man had been found in the kitchen area of the ruins and was identified as a vagrant who hung around the neighborhood. The cop theorized that the man must have broken in, and when he couldn't find anything he wanted to steal, burned down the house. Something must have happened to him that prevented him from getting out and he was trapped and died in the fire. My neighbor had said he heard something around midnight, but assumed I was still in the house and that it was me bumping around in there. Mr. Trevigne went back to sleep until the fire woke him up three hours later. Because it was a frame house, it was fully engulfed by the time the fire department arrived. Everything burned except the cement front steps, the brick chimney, and the cinder blocks the house sat upon.

Marcel, poor Marcel! The policemen didn't seem to know much about the man, and I didn't volunteer anything about him. I was sure Bobby wasn't going to tell the cops anything either because of the way he had treated Marcel. He also had to know the fire was probably Marcel's revenge.

I was left with only one thought: God bless Marcel!

I learned the source of Bobby's anger several days later. Emily was pregnant and he was being forced to marry her. He was almost twenty, but she was just seventeen and underage. Her mother promised to shoot him if he didn't marry her. Emily had already dropped out of school and the wedding was planned for early summer when Bobby's work was slow. Emily still wanted the church wedding she'd always planned – pregnant or not.

Weeks later, I remembered I hadn't met Mr. Dejean at Miss Menard's to discuss the gardening job. But he'd come at the appointed time and she'd hired him. He was already coming two mornings a week and the garden was beginning to look verdant again.

I came to realize that I really had no decision to make. I would live with Miss Menard indefinitely. Where else could I go? Except for the bags I moved the day of the funeral, everything I owned burned in the fire. The only items I managed to salvage when I finally looked through the charred rubble were the metal crucifix that had hung on my grandmother's bedpost and the set of silver combs she wore in her hair. Standing in the ashes, I remembered what Big Mama had told me about Big Papa's life, and I knew even though our young lives were similar, I was much better off than he had been.

When he was two years old, my grandfather was abandoned in the French Market. An elderly White woman found him wondering through the stalls. She took him by the hand and as Big Mama put it, "just walked off with him." She was a widow who lived alone on the fringes of the French Quarter. She named Big Papa, Gustave Soublet, but he never knew if Soublet was her last name. She told him to call her, Madame. She fed him and once in a while bought him a few pieces of clothing, but that was the extent of her nurturing.

Madame was severely hard of hearing and rarely spoke to my grandfather or anyone else. She communicated with a few French words and hand gestures. He did not speak in complete sentences, in French or English, until he was seven when he began to roam the streets of the Quarter, the Marigny and the Tremé areas.

In those areas he found shops where he'd work for free in order to learn the crafts and eventually he was hired for a few hours in some of them. When he was seventeen, he returned home after being gone a few days and found Madame had died and her house had been boarded up. He was left with the clothes on his back and no place to live. Big Papa went to the Tremé district where Creoles of color lived, people who looked like him. He went to work for a Colored cabinetmaker, met my grandmother and married her three years later. He had never gone to school, so Big Mama and Nennaine taught him to read and write.

Miss Menard wasn't Madame; she was happy to have me with her and I was glad to be there. She cried when she told me she wished Big Mama had lived. They would have had a lot to share and would have been able to watch me get the education I so desperately wanted. When I showed her the contents of the cigarbox, she was overjoyed and told me to put all the money in the bank and add to it as a nest egg for the future. In exchange for my nursing and household duties, she was going to give me room and board, pay for any extra college expenses, and give me a small salary for all my day to day needs.

There were times when I thought I'd never smile again. Then I'd remember something my great-aunt used to tell me. She'd say, "Compare life to what happens in spring - the April rains are our tears; the May flowers are our joys and we cannot know one without knowing the other." It was strange how Miss Menard always gave me similar advice.

There was less than a month and a half before graduation. I'd heard from only three of the six schools I'd applied to, but it didn't matter. As lofty as my goals were, and as much ambition as I knew I had, I still chose Xavier University. Not only had they offered me a four-year scholarship, but it was in New Orleans which allowed me to continue to live with Miss Menard. Even though for years I'd told myself I couldn't wait to leave, there was no way I was leaving the city. My need to get away would have to wait. I had lost too much and too many and I needed to stay where I knew someone cared about me.

– 17 –

PEOPLE YOU MEET
AT CHURCH

Still mourning my grandmother's death during my high school graduation, I had no desire to participate in the senior activities. I wasn't asked to the prom and probably wouldn't have gone had I been asked. But I did wonder if Emily had convinced all the friends we'd shared that I was snooty and they'd decided to steer clear of me? Perhaps I had become a recluse and had kept to myself after our friendship ended. I didn't have those answers. What I did know was that it was hard to be seventeen without friends. Even though it hurt, I knew deep inside I had developed a profound distrust for people in general and I didn't want anyone to get too close again. I had Miss Menard and I would let her become my whole world. After all, hadn't she been the only one I could turn to when everything began to happen?

My father had taken his family and moved to California to live as White and his father Augustin had followed. My twin aunts had never written again and my grandparents' friends seemed afraid to talk to me for fear I might ask them for something. I saw most of them at church on Sundays and holidays. Mr. Albert's health was failing, so he and his wife moved to Baton Rouge to live with their daughter. Gloria sold her bar and moved to Texas to live with her brother. Angelique and Uncle Gus sneaked into town to put Angelique's mother in the Colored old folks' home even before Big Mama died, and then returned to California without my grandmother and I ever knowing. I found out when Gloria came to my grandmother's funeral.

Weeks after Big Mama's death, Anne Marie Bogass was the only one of her friends I thought cared about what I was going through. One Sunday after Mass, she invited me to her home for cinnamon rolls and café au lait. She gave me some money at the church and I ran ahead to Liuzza's Bakery to wait in line for the fresh, hot rolls they made for 10:00 every Sunday morning. By the time I got out of the bakery, Anne Marie was just reaching the corner of Johnson and Lapeyrouse, so we walked to her house together. I made the coffee and served it with the rolls on her side porch. For a few Sundays after that, we ate together after Mass. It took me a few weeks to realize that after a round of questions that first Sunday, she never again asked me how I was doing.

Anne Marie lived in the corner house where Emily and I used to meet to walk to school together. The house sat far back on the property and faced Johnson Street, while her yard also faced Johnson Street, it wrapped around the corner and took up part of the block that Emily lived on, Laharpe Street. Her garden was beautiful with the flowers planted along the perimeter of her elaborate, cast-iron fence. The middle of the yard was all green, velvety lawn. In the back of the house, there had once been several fruit-bearing trees: cooking pears, Japanese plums and pomegranates. Emily and I used to help her husband glean the trees until he became ill and they had the trees cut down. The foot-high stumps were painted white and each held a large flower pot planted with perennials.

I loved sitting on Anne Marie's wrap-around porch and being able to enjoy her blooming flowers and lush grass. I looked forward to our Sunday's together. After that first Sunday, though, our conversations were only about her garden and about how much she missed her husband who died just months before my grandmother. She'd cry and ask me to get her a wet face cloth from her bathroom. After she dried her tears and was emotionally spent, she needed to relax quietly on her bed for a while. Then she'd ask me to wash, dry and put away the dishes we'd used and to see myself out when I was done.

After four Sundays of the same routine, I realized what I was needed for was to stand in line at the bakery, to be a coffee maker, a dishwasher and a good listener. What I was going through as a young girl or the fact that I was her dead friend's granddaughter meant not a damn thing to Anne Marie Bogass. I began attending 10:00 Mass instead of the one at 9:00. The rolls were still warm at 11:00, so I'd stop and get some for Miss Menard and me. She'd have the café au lait waiting when I arrived. I never told her about my Sundays at Anne Marie's.

At my cap and gown ceremony, there was no one in the audience to represent me. Although Miss Menard had promised me she'd try to make it, she was in an unusual amount of pain that day and could not attend. Having graduated second in my class, I gave my Salutatorian speech to polite applause. I envied the clapping and stomping the other students received from their families and friends. My tears of grief had finally stopped, and like my grandmother, I walked through it all in a quiet daze. I knew if I wanted to bring happiness into my life, I needed to learn how to do it – without family or friends. I'd have to forget about what I'd promised myself earlier. I'd have to let my old age take care of itself.

The Sunday after graduation, I saw Mrs. Valcour at Mass. I had seen her several times at the St. Bernard Market and at Saturday Confession at the church, but she'd always looked the other way to avoid speaking to me. But this Sunday, she chose to speak.

"Claire? I didn't recognize you. You're all grown up. Look at how tall you are! Don't worry, one of these days you're going to fill out in all the right places." Mrs. Valcour looked me up and down a few times, then she took my hand and led me away from the front of the church where all our fellow parishioners were standing and talking. She didn't stop walking until we moved up the block and away from the groups of people who were standing around.

Mrs. Valcour looked old, tired and sad, not at all the fashionably dressed, attractive woman I remembered. I knew with the Korean War still raging and both her sons having been drafted, she had every reason to look distraught. Before I could ask about her family, she abruptly let go of my hand.

"Claire, sweetheart, I'm sorry I need to get back home. I forgot I have a couple of things simmering on the stove for Sunday dinner. I just ran out to Mass. I've got to run. I'll talk to you next time." She ran across the street and walked quickly toward Prieur Street taking the long way home.

I didn't see her again for several months. I had already learned her eldest son was dead. At Mass in early June, it was announced that Mathieu Valcour had been killed in action. One of his Xavier Prep classmates told me he had only been in Korea a short time when American war planes mistakenly took his infantry division for North Koreans and bombed it. When no banns of marriage were announced in June, I knew Emily and Bobby's marriage must be postponed or something else was wrong. Then John, Emily's youngest brother, returned with his right foot missing. He'd lost it to frostbite while on a march with his unit in the bitter Korean winter. He had been recuperating all spring in an army hospital back east.

When Mrs. Valcour greeted me after Mass, she wasted no time pulling me away from the church crowds as she'd done before. I could feel her tension as she pressed her fingers into my arm. I knew how much she loved her sons and how hard she'd worked to send them to Xavier Prep and then Xavier University.

"Did you hear about my boys, Claire?" She was whispering to me with her eyes full of tears. "Johnnie's really bad off. He's home, you know, but he's suicidal. I've had my hands full with trying to take care of him. I've...had...had to take a leave from my job to watch him." She was a bookkeeper at an insurance company on Claiborne Avenue.

"I'm really, really sorry, Mrs. Valcour." I didn't know what else to say to her. As I looked at her with sympathy, I was trying to picture tall, handsome Johnnie with only one foot. He, like his brother Matt, had been a football star and a big man on the campuses of Xavier Prep and Xavier University.

"He says he's half a man now and he can't and won't accept that. He thinks no woman is going to want a gimp. That's what he calls himself. What am I going to do with my boy, Claire? I have to go back to work." Mrs. Valcour covered her face with her hands and sobbed. Not knowing what else to do for her, I gave her my handkerchief, took her hand, and walked her to the corner.

"With everything that's happened with my boys, Emily and Bobby were married quietly in the rectory a few weeks ago." Mrs. Valcour was suddenly calm now. "Have you heard about Bobby, Claire?"

"No, and I'm not interested in hearing anything about him. I tune people out when they bring him up to me." I knew she was about to piss me off and I was trying to head her off.

She ignored me and told me anyway.

"When Bobby received his draft notice, he went running to get his physical. He wanted to go to war thinking that he'd get off the hook with Emily once he was in the service. But the army rejected him. He's a 4F. The examination showed he's already in the beginning stages of the same kind of muscle disease his father has. He hadn't told anybody he was having a lot of muscle pain and tremors in his legs. We knew he was doing less and less physical labor with his work crews and that he'd delegated all of that work to two of his brothers. We thought he did that because he was the boss and that's what bosses do."

"Mrs. Valcour, please, it's too bad that Bobby's sick, but you certainly can't expect me to feel sorry for him." I was hoping she'd stop telling me about him. She didn't.

"Your old house on Johnson St. is being rebuilt and his family is waiting to move in. Bobby and Emily live in the house he built on Pauger St. A couple of months ago he bought and completely renovated a small store on Orleans Street, just off Claiborne. He turned it into his main office. In the fall, he's planning to add a real estate section to his business. He's going to buy a lot of buildings around the city, fix them up, and then cut them up into offices and rent them out." Mrs. Valcour was all puffed up. "I have no doubt he'll be rich one day, crippled or not. He's not no-count like a lot of boys his age, you know." She was breathless when she finished. She seemed to want to make sure she told me all of it whether I wanted to hear it or not. She also knew I was too well-mannered to walk away and leave her standing there.

"Well, good for Bobby," I said through my teeth. "Excuse me, but I have to…"

"I'm telling you, Bobby's going to make a lot of money, Claire. He's not a louse like his father. I'm so glad he married Emily. He's not going to let that disease stand in his way. Bobby's going to be a good husband to Emily, there's no doubt about it."

"Okay, bully for both of them! But I think I already told you, I don't give a shit." So much for my being too well-mannered. "I thought you were upset about Johnnie a minute ago. Now I know where Emily gets her personality and it ain't from her daddy! Gotta go, bye." I turned from her and walked away as fast as I could just as her mouth was opening to unload a reprimand or more unwanted information.

When I was two blocks away, I heard someone running behind me and calling my name. I was reluctant to find out who it was for fear it was Mrs. Valcour. Finally I stopped and turned around.

"Hey, Claire. Whew! Boy you walk some fast." Donovan Auberge was out of breath and grinning as wide as his mouth would open. I hadn't seen him since our graduation.

"Hi, Don. What do you want?" My tone was abrasive; I was still fuming from my conversation with Emily's mother.

"Say, Claire, where do you live now? I know your grandmother passed away before graduation but I never found out where you moved to? I wanted to ask you to go to the prom with me, but my mother thought it was too soon after your grandmother's passing for you to go to a dance. So I didn't ask you. I'm sorry about your grandma, Claire."

"Thanks, Don. I'm glad you didn't ask me because I wouldn't have gone. It was too soon after losing my grandmother. But thanks, anyway…I mean for wanting to take me." I started to walk again and Don, with his long legs, fell in lock step with me.

"Claire, why can't you tell me where you live?"

"I can tell you. But first, tell me why you want to know."

"So we can go out on a date…to a movie or something. I have to know where to pick you up, don't I?" Don's face was bright red as well as his ears. His freckles glowed on his cheeks. I wondered how he had come through high school with the bunch we'd gone to school with and still come out shy. He was 6'2" and had a face like Van Johnson and a lot of girls always followed him around at school. Despite all the girls, he'd been a shy loner. We often had study period together and we talked, mostly about our studies. I invited him to join the drama club, but he refused. I never understood his so-called shyness because he always seemed so outgoing. I was reluctant to ask him about it. I didn't think it was any of my business.

"Look, Don, I'm not dating right now."

"Huh, what do you mean 'right now?' I'll bet you haven't ever dated." He jumped in front of me and started walking backwards. "C'mon, go out with me, Claire. Don't make me beg like a dog." He put his hands together under his chin, stuck out his tongue and started to pant.

I tried not to laugh but I couldn't help it. I quickly got my composure back and again in my gruff voice said, "I said I'm not dating. That's the only answer you'll get."

"Okay, okay. But for your information, I haven't dated anybody either and I didn't go to our prom. Did you know we're both going to Xavier U?"

"No, I didn't. What does that have to do with me dating you? And how the hell do you know I'm going to Xavier U?" As private as I knew I was, how did he know what university I planned to attend?

"I saw you on Xavier's campus during senior visitation day in May. I figured you were there because you'd chosen to go there in the fall. You have, haven't you, Claire?" Don's voice sounded a little anxious.

"Yes, I'm going to Xavier U this fall...so?" When the last word of the sentence left my lips, I heard the nastiness in my voice. I knew being defensive was a sorry excuse for my behavior, especially to a nice boy who apparently liked me and had finally gotten up the nerve to ask me for a date. "Don, I'm sorry for the things I just said to you...well...not for what I said, but for the way I said them. It isn't about you. I really don't date." After I finished my apology, I had the beginnings of a headache. I was not in the habit of apologizing for anything I said. I usually thought about it before I said it and then that was the end of it – no matter the consequences.

"You're already forgiven, Claire. Say, since we're going to the same school in the fall, I can give you a ride to school every day. My parents gave me their old car as a graduation gift. I'm getting my license soon."

"What the hell! Is your car supposed to excite me?"

"Does it?"

"Damnit, Don! Okay, I'll tell you. I live in the two-story..."

"Never mind," Don interrupted. He turned again and began to walk next to me. "I'm going to find out where you live today without you telling me. I'm walking you home."

"Suit yourself. It's a free country." When we both giggled, I was pleasantly surprised.

I was so wrapped up in talking and laughing with Don that I forgot to stop at the bakery and we had to backtrack several blocks. Don, in spite of his bashful ways, tried to invite himself in for coffee and rolls. I wasn't ready to make him privy to my living situation, so he had to settle for a warm roll without the coffee and eat it outside the gate. Before he left, I tore off a corner of the pastry bag and gave him my phone number. He gave me his.

Donovan Auberge didn't wait until September to see me. The next Sunday at church he quietly slipped into the pew and sat next to me at Mass. I was so nervous and giddy I dropped everything I put my hands on. I think he thought I did it on purpose because each time he picked up something I dropped, he mimicked the way I said I was sorry. The last time he did it, we both burst out laughing. Not only did everyone turn and look at us, but the usher came. "Shame on you! Be quiet or leave the church," he whispered. We really did try but we couldn't stop. We were infected with the giggles and thought it best we leave while the priest was giving Communion. We had both planned to take the sacrament, but thought we'd better not go up to the altar in our euphoric state of being.

After we left the church, I agreed to go to Belfield's for an ice cream soda, only if I could buy my own. That way it wouldn't be considered a date. I was glad the soda fountain in the drugstore wasn't crowded and I didn't see anyone that I thought knew me well enough to gossip. Having to leave Mass early had paid off after all!

While Don walked me home after our sodas, I gave him an abbreviated version of what had happened before and after my grandmother died. I asked him not to ask me out again because I was still unsure if I was really okay at that point, or if there was still more "bad stuff" to come. I felt like a stranger in a strange place, I said, and I wasn't ready to cope with anything or anyone new in my life. I had only one focus: to work and get ready for college. I liked him, had fun with him, but being friends was all I wanted to be. He said he understood. I told him I'd call him soon but just to talk.

My job at Colari's Drugstore changed significantly. I trained two fourteen-year-olds to replace me making deliveries. One boy was the son of one of our old neighbors on Johnson St. He was a lazy cuss and didn't want to work. Mr. Colari bought my bicycle and Bobby's old bike so that he'd be able to hire kids who didn't have one. Alfred, the lazy one, broke one of the bike's the second day he was on the job. He was fired. I started training someone else.

Two days after he was fired, Alfred's parents came to the drugstore and begged Mr. Colari to rehire him. He told them that not only had their son broken the bicycle, but he wasn't a good worker. He was slow; he complained about how hot it was riding in the sun; he complained about how long he had to knock before "those old people" answered the door. After only two days on the job and with that attitude, Mr. Colari said he felt compelled to let him go. The father began to cry. He was a bricklayer, he said, and had recently been told he had a hernia and needed to be operated on as soon as possible. With six children, he needed Alfred to help out until he got back on his feet. His wife had started a small, childcare business in their home to help them make ends meet. They needed every cent they could make and he begged Mr. Colari to take Alfred back. Mr. Colari said he was sorry but he couldn't do it. His customers came first and he wouldn't be able to trust the boy to do a good job for them. He paid Alfred's parents the two days wages and a "little extra" to help them. I found out later the little extra was $50. No wonder they had gone away smiling.

My new job for the summer was helping Mr. Colari in the pharmacy. I typed and labeled all the prescriptions. When I wasn't busy with that, I stocked the shelves in the drugstore. Mr. Colari was happy that I had gotten a scholarship and I'd be going to college in the fall, but he hated to see me leave the drugstore. He asked me to look around and find him someone, someone like me, to take my place before September. He couldn't count on his two daughters to help out in the store any longer: one was already in college, the other one would be starting like me in the fall. I didn't know anyone or where to start looking. I decided I'd ask Father O'Mara to help me find someone.

I called Don the next evening after Miss Menard had gone to bed for the night. He asked me to call him again in two days because he was getting something special and wanted to share it with me.

Although I knew Miss Menard couldn't hear me, I spoke very softly and talked only about five minutes. I felt guilty, like a sneak, all because I didn't want anyone to know about Don, not even Miss Menard. And especially not Lena! I kept my door locked when I wasn't home and never let her clean my room or my bathroom. I did them myself. I didn't trust her and at the time I didn't know why.

- 18 -

FENDING OFF A
HUNGRY WOLF

Donovan's summers were spent working full time in his family's grocery store. He'd get off most evenings around 7:00. The store was closed on Sundays. My job at the drugstore was Monday through Saturday until 6:00. I was also off on Sundays. Calling him after 8:00 in the evening was good for both of us.

On Thursday, when Don's phone rang, it hadn't even completed the first ring when he answered.

"Hey, Claire. I was waiting for your call."

"Damn, were you sitting on top the telephone?"

"Yep. Say, promise me you won't say no when I ask you something, okay?"

"Sorry. Until I know what it is, I can't say yes or no."

"Okay, here goes. Yesterday was my eighteenth birthday and..."

"Happy Birthday, Don!" I interrupted. "I hope your surprise isn't that you're going to invite me to a party. I won't come."

"Claire, you didn't let me finish. There's no party. I was going to tell you I got my license today and I'd like to take you for a spin around the lake when you get off tomorrow. I'll get off an hour early so I can get to the drugstore by the time it closes. How's about it? Do you want to go? I promise I'll have you back in less than an hour."

"Well, I guess I could." At the same time I was saying yes, I was wondering what I'd tell Miss Menard about being an hour late. "Okay, I'll go, but I can't meet you in front of the drugstore. Mr. Colari talks to Miss Menard all the time and I don't want him to mention he saw you pick me up. Can we meet a block away?"

138

"Wow! You really are embarrassed to be seen with me, aren't you?"

"That's not true and you know it," I snapped. "Tell you what...forget it, okay?"

"Claire...I was kidding! You know me."

"Don't kid me about that. I've explained my situation to you more than once. Do you want to be friends? Last offer. Take it or leave it."

"I'll take it; I'll take it!" Don yelled into the phone. "Say, where should I meet you? Is Galvez and Esplanade okay? On the same side as the drugstore."

"No, I'd have to pass the house. Miss Menard might be on the porch waiting for me."

"Oookay, a block in the other direction, then. How's Prieur and Esplanade?"

"That's good. Try to be there about 6:05 sharp, okay? That corner's going to be deserted that time of evening. I don't want to have to stand there to wait for you."

"I'll be there. You won't have to wait. I promise."

The next night when Mr. Colari closed the door behind me, I ran up the block toward Prieur St. Never having seen Don's car, I didn't know what kind to look for. So when a car pulled up to the curb behind me and tapped the horn, I turned around and went up to the car.

It wasn't Don. It was the cop Bobby had brought to investigate the fire on Johnson St. He was driving an unmarked car and he was drunk. When he slid across the front seat to the passenger's side, I jumped back away from the car door.

"Hey, girlie, Ah sho recanize you with dose long legs a yawrs. Member me? You ain't got that White lady to hide bahine na. You gotta talk fa yawself. What you doin on this heah islated corner? You sellin somethin?"

I didn't answer. There were no cars passing in either direction; no one walking on my side of the street. I was trying to think about what to do next when the cop jumped out of the car and rested his back against the back door in order to hold himself upright. He pulled his badge out of his pocket, held it up for me to see, then dropped it but couldn't bend to pick it up.

"Git in the caw, girlie, or Ah'm gonna arres you for prostitutin. You ain't gonna sell nothin to me, you gonna give it to me. Me…Officer Michael McArdle," he slurred his name and when his knees started to buckle, he grabbed onto the open car door and held on.

"Git in this caw, you skinny nigger bitch! You gonna give it to me this night. Thea ain't no White mother hen protectin you na. Ah'm gonna make you suck ma prick. Oh, wait a minute, what y'all niggers call it? Oh, yeah, y'all call it a dick. Well, you gonna be a dick sucker tonight when you suck Mike McArdle's dick. Then, Ah'm gonna put ma dick in yawr ass. You know why? Cuz Ah ain't gonna have no mo fuckin half-breeds running round Nu Awlins. Ah already got me some, all kins, too. Got me niggers, injuns, dagos – you name um." He patted his chest.

I started to turn to run but as drunk as the cop was, he pulled his gun from his waist band and pointed it at me. "Run, go head, yawr back as good as yawr front," he said. "But Ah retha fuck you then shoot you. You like them dago bitches Ah had. Ah had to tell um Ah was gonna kill dey mafia husbans to get um to do what Ah wanted. And if dey tol on me, Ah'd have to kill dey churen."

My brain was frozen. I didn't think I could even scream. I stood paralyzed trying to thaw it out so that I could think of what to do next.

"So, girlie, you ain't goin noweah. Git in the caw! Ah'm gonna injoy piping yawr ass like you was one a dem faggots in the Quawters." He stumbled toward me and my fist shot out and caught him in his throat. The hit wasn't hard enough to hurt him, but it threw him off balance and down he went. The gun flew out of his hand and landed under his car. I started running down the street toward the house. I don't think the cop could have caught me even if he were sober.

Officer Michael McArdle couldn't get up much less run after me. All he could do was prop himself up on one elbow and yell at me as I ran. "You cain't hide from me. Ah'll git you. You ain't going noweah. You ain't got noweah to hide!"

I only turned around once and that was to make sure the cop was still on the ground. I didn't stop running until I was inside the gate – two blocks away. I fell as I stumbled up the steps and landed hard on my right elbow. I cried out in pain.

Miss Menard screamed, "Oh my God, Claire. What's the matter?" She was sitting in her favorite spot on the porch. As I got up she rolled toward me in her wheelchair. "Cher, what's wrong?"

140

"Go in the house, please Miss Menard, hurry!" She didn't hesitate. She wheeled herself in and I quickly locked the door behind us. She rolled to the sofa and thrust her hand down into the side of the cushion and pulled out a small revolver.

"Is someone chasing you?"

"I don't know...I don't think so. I don't think he could get up." I knew she didn't understand what I was talking about. But here I was caught in the act – again – just like the time I watched Lady Blue and Wobble without my grandparents knowing. This time it wouldn't be about what I saw, it would be about who I was meeting. I was unable to justify, even to myself, why an innocent ride to Lake Ponchartrain had to be hidden from Miss Menard. What would I say when she'd ask me why I needed to hide it from her?

"Give me a minute to catch my breath, please." I took a couple of deep breaths as we headed to the kitchen. Miss Menard gave me a glass of water and put the tea kettle on. "No tea, please, I'm burning up inside and out."

Miss Menard still had the gun in her hand. It looked strange for this gentle woman to be packing a pistol. If I'd had the time to make up my usual, dramatic scenarios, I would have ended up placing her on the "ten most wanted list." She realized I was watching her and shoved the gun in the pocket of her robe.

"I didn't know you had one of those in the house," I told her.

"It's the best equalizer I know," she chuckled. "I don't just have it to scare some bastard; I'll drop the son-of-a-bitch where he stands. Let him come. He'll be sorry, just like the other one." The sharp edge to her voice made her statement bold and believable.

This was not the woman I thought I knew, certainly not the soft-spoken lady who called me "cher" and always urged me to forgive. Oh, there was no doubt she'd had an exciting life. I was sure of it now.

"Claire, stop whatever you're thinking about me and a gun. I can see in your eyes you're trying to write a story about me in your head. I'm not a Calamity Jane. I've lived here alone for a long time and I needed something to protect myself. If you have a gun, you have to know how to use it...and be willing to use it if you're threatened. I have two of these," she patted her pocket. "I keep one in the living room and the other one in my bedroom in the top dresser drawer. So, if ever you're in trouble...," her voice trailed off and she left the unfinished statement hang in the air, then watched me to see if I got her message.

"Oh, no thanks. I'm afraid of guns. I could never shoot anyone."

"Really, with your temper! We'll see. At any rate, I want you to know where I keep them. You never know what might happen. Enough of that. Tell me what happened, cher."

"Okay, but don't fuss with me until I tell you everything." I didn't give her a chance to comment. I ploughed right in with the whole story, including the language the cop used. I was no longer afraid to let Miss Menard see the imperfect, cussy side of me. I had just seen hers and it made me feel a little more relaxed.

Miss Menard's expression seemed frozen the entire time I was relating what had happened. She didn't react to anything I said – not even the dirty language. When I finished, she calmly asked me to jot down his name on a piece of paper.

Until that moment, I hadn't realized that my right arm was stiff and I could hardly move it. I wouldn't let Miss Menard touch it. She called her doctor, but when she told him the house call would be to see me, he refused to come. He told her to send me to Charity Hospital. She made an ice pack and helped me to wrap it around my elbow. After half an hour, the swelling was down and I could almost straighten it out without groaning.

"I think you just have a bad tissue bruise, that's all, "Miss Menard told me. "You wouldn't be able to straighten out your arm that much if something were sprained or broken, Claire. Take two aspirin before you go to bed."

I didn't know how I'd be able to work with a stiff, achy arm. Maybe I shouldn't go in tomorrow, I thought. I was glad Lena had already gone and was off for the weekend. She'd have made this into a much bigger deal than Miss Menard. It wouldn't be that she gave a damn, but she'd fuss and hover over me to make sure she got every last detail about what happened. And that information would give her something to gossip about. She sneaked in short telephone calls all day long passing along gossip to and about all her friends.

"Should I wait to ask you about why you didn't trust me enough to tell me about your friend, cher?"

"No, I can tell you now. He's only a friend. His name is Donovan Auberge and he's a boy I graduated with from Clark…a friend, that's all. I know it and he knows it. I didn't want you to think there's anything more between us."

"Is that the real reason, Claire, or is there something you're not telling me."

"There's no other reason," I lied. How could I tell her that after all she was doing for me that I didn't trust her or anyone else a hundred percent?

"This is the first time since I've known you that you've lied to me. But I'll let it go tonight because you've been through enough with that animal. What about work tomorrow? Afraid to go?"

"Yes."

"I need you to trust me, cher. Can you do that?"

"Yes." Another lie left my lips.

"Good. Now listen to me. I don't want you to worry about Officer Michael McArdle," she was using that ten-most-wanted-list voice again. "Leonard and I are still owed one big favor. We have some good friends in this town who can make sure Mike McArdle doesn't make that mistake again. I promise you he'll never bother you again. What I do want you to do, though, is to stay in this weekend. He might be lurking around somewhere in this area."

"Don't worry; I have no plans to go anywhere. I just want to call Donovan to find out if he ever came. Because if he did, I'll have to tell him why I wasn't on the corner waiting for him."

"No. You'll tell him nothing. That's an experience you have to keep to yourself. You need to forget it ever happened. And telling someone who might keep asking you if you've seen the cop again is not a good idea. If your arm is black and blue, tell people you fell. That's true, isn't it?"

"I guess so." I tried not to let on she was scaring me, plus I was too shaky to argue. It was beginning to sound like a real-life, suspense story. "Can I call Don now?"

"Go ahead, but only talk a few minutes. I need to make that call."

There was no answer at Don's house.

I called Mr. Colari the next morning to tell him I wouldn't be coming in to work. He asked me if I'd seen the commotion the night before when I left the drugstore. A drunken man had been arrested in the next block from the drugstore near Prieur St.

Someone reported him when they saw him lying on the sidewalk screaming incoherently.

We hadn't heard anything. But when we were in the back of the house, it was impossible to hear what was taking place on our street, much less two blocks away. There was nothing in the Saturday or Sunday paper about the incident.

I tried to call Don all weekend without success. It was difficult for me to believe he'd not only stood me up but he didn't think enough of me to call and tell me why. Something had to be wrong.

– 19 –

WHO DISPENSED JUSTICE?

Early Monday morning before I went to work, I called Don again. His mother answered. She told me she knew who I was because Don talked about me all the time. She hated that we were getting to talk for the first time under such circumstances and was sorry Don was too distraught to talk to me. He and his daddy had been very close.

"Thank you for calling, Claire. I'll have…"

"Excuse me, but what happened to his father?"

"Oh, I'm sorry, I thought you knew. Our store was robbed Friday minutes before Don was to leave to pick you up. Two men pistol whipped my husband when he wouldn't give them the cash in the register. After Don gave it to them, they fled. He stayed behind to talk to the police while I rode to the hospital in the ambulance with his daddy." Mrs. Auberge related what had happened without emotion. She'd probably done it a hundred times before I called.

I suddenly remembered she'd said Don and his father had been close…that could only mean his father had died. I couldn't think of how to word what I needed to say to her. While I was mentally searching for what to say, she spoke up filling the awful void in the conversation.

"Claire, my husband died Saturday morning. I'm sorry to just dump all that on you. Your silence told me you were shocked and didn't know what to say to me. It's okay, I understand. Don is too upset to talk to anyone. I'll have him call you when he feels better, okay?"

"Sure, Mrs. Auberge. I'm really sorry you lost your husband."

I was skittish when I went back to work, but I got through the first day. Each day without incident made me less afraid. By the end of the week, I was back to my old self again.

While I waited for Don to call, I sent his family a condolence card and put a note in it for him. He called a few weeks later.

"Hey, Claire. Sorry it took me so long to call. We got your card."

"I'm sorry about your father, Don."

"Thanks. You know they caught those men who robbed the store and beat my daddy. You might know...a bunch of ziggaboos!" He said the word as if he was used to saying it.

"That was fast. I'll bet you and your family are pretty happy about that, aren't you?"

"Yeah, I guess so. But that's not stopping my mama from selling the store and our house."

"Where is your house?" We had never talked about where he lived.

"My house is behind the store on London Avenue. It has the same address as the store. My mama refuses to continue running the store or living in the house. She says we're getting out of New Orleans because she can't finish raising us in this place...too many bad niggers here. We're going to California to live with one of my aunts."

"Oh, what about Xavier U.?" I tried to keep the disappointment out of my voice.

"I have to put college on hold for a year, but that's another long story."

"Tell me, Don."

"Not right now, Claire. I have to go. I'll call you before I leave. Maybe we can get together before then to say goodbye." Don hung up before I could say anything.

He never called and I was too proud to call him. Miss Menard tried her best to get me to understand what grief does to a person. I told her I'd gone through it and I hadn't behaved that way, and to me if you make a promise, you shouldn't break it under any circumstances.

The last day of August was my last day at the drugstore. I thanked Mr. Colari for everything he'd done for me. He forgot himself and gave me a big hug and a kiss. If I hadn't turned my head, he would have planted it on my mouth. Then he looked around to make sure no one was in the store. Sheepishly he said, "You understand, don't you, Claire?"

"I certainly do, Mr. Colari. I understand perfectly well. Don't worry, I won't tell a soul you kissed me," I whispered. He gave a nervous little snigger.

As I watched him check the store again to make sure he was safe, I laughed to myself. Poor Mr. Colari, that sneaky, lascivious bastard. He knew it was his last chance to feel what a café au lait seventeen-year-old felt like, but he still had to make sure no one caught him. Not as slimy as the cop, but who knows what that White, self-righteous, pillar-of-the-community, up-standing pharmacist was thinking while squeezing me. One day he might ask me to do more than stock his shelves and wait on customers. All I knew was that I was leaving just in time.

The day after Labor Day, I went to Canal St. to shop for school clothes. I usually banked half my salary, but I decided to splurge and spend all of my last paycheck along with $200 Miss Menard had given me to use for whatever I needed. I had a helluva lot of shopping to do. And shop I did. Although my list was long, shopping didn't take as much time in those days because Coloreds weren't allowed to try on anything in many of the stores. You had to hope whatever you bought fit when you got it home. So, I was in and out of the stores that allowed try-ons. And the ones that didn't: Maison Blanche, D.H. Holmes and others, I bought there too, but carefully.

On the way home, I thought I'd surprise Miss Menard with an oyster loaf from Lavata's. I hadn't had one since eating there with my grandparents just before my grandfather died.

Johnnie Valcour was there waiting for an order. I hadn't seen him since before he went to Korea. He greeted me quite warmly and bought me a soft drink.

"How's your mother, Johnnie?" I wasn't sure I really cared, but I did need to try and make conversation.

"She's doing better. She's trying to get used to my brother being gone and Emily and all her mess. I'm guilty, too. I've put her through a lot. But my mother's tough," he laughed, "I think she's going to outlive me." He blinked his eyes as fast as hummingbird wings and rubbed his index fingers against his thumbs while he talked. I was forced to look away periodically; I couldn't concentrate on what he was saying or hold him in my gaze for long.

"I don't think you're interested in how Emily's doing, are you?" He laughed again. He seemed to laugh at everything he said. But then I saw the dimple in his cheek. He had only one. I remembered Emily and me teasing him about having a sink hole on the right side of his face.

"Honestly, I'm not interested. So please don't tell me anyway, the way your mother did the last time I saw her."

He roared laughing, loud and strong, for a long time. I was so glad when Mr. Lavata told him his order was ready. When he was ready to leave, Johnnie suddenly grabbed me and gave me a big hug.

"We're not that far apart in age," he said, "maybe I'll marry you when you grow up. You're a little thin, but you'll probably fill out in a coupla years. Oh, look...look at what I got a few weeks ago." He pointed to his right foot and lifted his pant leg above his ankle. He was wearing a prosthesis. "I've got two feet again. They're making them better and better all the time. I don't have too much of a limp with this one. Good, huh?"

"It looks great, Johnnie. You had your poor mother really worried about you. You'd better go before your loaves get cold. Don't make her mad at you."

"Maybe *I'll pass over by your house sometimes*, you know, to talk." He grinned, then decided to give his usual laugh. "You still in school?"

"I'm starting Xavier U in a few days. What are you doing with yourself?"

"Construction, what else. Only part time, though. My foot can't take a whole day."

"That's good. I'm glad you're not still crying in your beer."

"Don't drink. So my mother told you about me, huh?"

"She did. But it wasn't just anyone she told, it was me. I've known you almost all my life. I want you to be okay." I noticed his rapid-fire eye movement had slowed and he had stopped rubbing his thumbs.

"Claire, would it be okay for me to come by your house sometimes...to talk?"

"Ah...su...sure, Johnnie...anytime." Oh God, I thought, what have I done!

"Okay, I'm gonna hold you to it." As he left, he pulled my hair and his laugh was a slow teasing rumble in his chest. "Remember when I used to do that to you and you'd run and tell my mother?" He didn't wait to hear my answer. "Bye."

With all he'd been through, Johnnie was still as handsome as he'd always been. Only the deep, dark circles under his eyes told the story of his pain. And of all the places on his body that could have been changed by suffering, why did it have to be his beautiful eyes? Those big, round, dark-brown balls of chocolate didn't melt; they melted you. I remember having a huge crush on him when he used to pull my hair. I was about eleven. Neither he nor Emily ever knew that was always the highlight of my day. When he went to college, he became too busy to pay attention to "snotnoses" as he called us. He never knew he broke my heart.

While Mr. Lavata was frying the oysters for my loaf, I picked up his newspaper. The headlines screamed:

NEW ORLEANS POLICEMAN MISSING AND FEARED DEAD.

Michael McArdle, an eighteen year veteran of the police department with a wife and seven children has been missing for almost two months. The department has kept it under wraps because it believes Officer McArdle was on the take. Someone at his precinct leaked the story...

My oyster loaf was ready.

Even though I was weighted down with my load of packages, I walked the ten blocks from Lavata's to the house as fast as I could. I didn't stop to look behind me or around me. The moment I entered the house I yelled, "Miss Menard? Lena?" I mumbled, "Please, not Lena!"

"I'm in the kitchen," Miss Menard shouted back. When I appeared, she looked at me quizzically. "Lena's gone already. What's wrong? Why are you yelling?"

There she was sitting at the table calmly sipping a cup of tea and I had become completely unraveled. "Did you read the paper this morning?" I asked panting.

"Yes...yes I did. Why?" Not one sign that she knew what I was talking about.

"Didn't you see who's missing?"

"Officer Michael McArdle?"

"Why are you trying to be cute with me, Miss Menard? Yes, Officer Michael McArdle. Why didn't you tell me before I went to Canal Street?"

"It wasn't worth mentioning. That lousy bastard got what he deserved."

"But he's only missing, not dead. What if he shows up here?" I got shaky and had shortness of breath again.

"Believe me, he won't show up here. He's a dirty cop, Claire, on the take. I'm sure you know what that means. I'll bet he crossed the mob and that was his undoing. He's probably in a swamp or a bayou somewhere. And with all those alligators out there, there's nothing left but his bones. The mob is thorough and it doesn't give second chances." Her tone was unaffected, matter of fact. It was as if she was telling me how to make bread pudding with a whiskey sauce.

"Miss Menard, please tell me you and Leonard Stern had nothing to do with that cop's disappearance."

"Good Lord, cher. Who do you think we are? Do you think we're Al Capone and his moll? What in the hell would make you believe we're powerful enough to make something like that happen? Is it hard for you to accept that we know powerful people?"

"No, it's the way you acted the night the incident happened and right now. You don't seem a bit surprised he's missing and you're sure he's not going to come back here. Why?"

"I called Leonard Stern that night. He told me he'd get the police commissioner to issue a reprimand. When Leonard learned McArdle was the cop arrested in the next block, he pressed the commissioner to do something about an out of control policeman. He was told the police department would handle it. In light of today's paper, I have to assume the department must have had an idea he was dirty and was waiting to nail him, but the mob got to him first." Miss Menard resumed sipping her tea. I got the impression the subject was closed; she'd said all she was going to say.

150

Her denial did nothing to quell my fear that she might indeed be that powerful. And if she was, she'd done it on my behalf. Didn't that make me have to carry part of that guilt? I looked down at the table afraid to let her see my face for fear she'd suspect what I was thinking. In fact, I wanted...I needed to stop thinking about it altogether. Not even going to Confession would unburden me. I couldn't tell a priest what had happened.

"Claire. Claire!" Miss Menard banged her empty cup on the table. "Haven't you heard a word I've said?"

"No, I'm a little shell-shocked right now."

"Let's move on and not dwell in the past. Let all that old stuff become history, cher. I was asking you if you'd heard from Donovan."

"I found out he moved to California about two weeks ago. Father O'Mara told me. Well, so much for being driven to school every day. Guess it's not my year to be chauffeured." I was trying desperately to lighten my mood.

The phone rang and Miss Menard answered it. "Yes, she's here. Who is this? Gina Marie Auberge? Oh yes, Donovan's sister. Just a moment, please." She handed me the receiver. "How's that for timing?" she grinned and shook her head.

"Gina Marie, this is Claire. This has been one helluva crazy day, so I hope you're not calling me with bad news." My stomach tightened while I waited for her to answer.

"Not exactly. It's just that my brother hasn't been acting like himself since we got here. We think he misses New Awleans and you. My mama asked me to call you. She thought you might be able to talk some sense into him. Do you think you can call and talk to him?"

"Listen, Gina Marie, your brother and I are just friends. I don't know what I could say to him to cheer him up if he doesn't want to be in California. He might think I'm meddling in his business." I had no intention of becoming a junior shrink. I liked Donovan and felt sorry we didn't have a chance to know each other better, but I didn't want to be his "play mama." All of a sudden, I wondered if he'd put his 15 year-old sister up to calling me because he was too timid to do it himself. God, he's eighteen! It was time to be a man, or at least try to be one. I was from a school of hard knocks; there was no time for timidity. "Gina

Marie, I think your mother has to keep on trying to talk to him. I'm not doing it."

"Please, Claire. He won't listen to my mama. Here's our number..."

"No, I don't want it. I'm not going to call your brother. If he wants to talk to me, he'll have to call me. He has my number. Sorry, Gina. Nice to talk to you. Bye."

Miss Menard had continued to sit in the kitchen during Gina Marie's call. "Sorry to meddle in your business, but aren't you being a little hard on Donovan. You don't really think that boy has gotten over losing his father, do you, Claire? Don't be so hard on people."

"I can't help it. I think he needs someone to think for him. I remember the time he told me why his mother wanted to leave New Orleans. 'Too many bad niggers,' he said. "He didn't try to clean up his mother's words nor was he embarrassed. He was being the typical light-skinned Negro. I hate that! It reminds me of my grandmother and Bobby and their Creole crap."

"Don can't change who he is, nor could your grandmother and Bobby...neither can you! What matters is he's a friend, a bit wounded right now, but still a friend who seems to care."

"He couldn't have cared too much; he didn't even call to say goodbye. He wasn't sure how I was going to act toward him, so he asked his sister to call me. I think he thought he'd play on my sympathy. Well, he can't. To tell you the truth, Miss Menard, I'm a few days away from starting college. I don't have time for games - Don's or anybody else's." I'd said it and I couldn't take it back. I hadn't started the sentence with her in mind, but it had landed full of thorns and nettles right in her lap. It seemed I was injuring the person who held the key to my future.

- 20 -

LIVING IN THE BIG HOUSE

Quietly, I slipped into the house without Lena knowing. I needed to try to unwind for a few minutes before I faced the mean old cat in the kitchen. Lately it seemed, she always had her claws ready to strike at me. I sat in the living room like a tired little mouse not wanting to be eaten just yet.

As I looked around, I thought: Here I am...me...in this big house. How did I get here and when will it all be taken away? Surely my being here with someone taking care of me was some kind of fluke, a mistake, an accident. Maybe I was dreaming and hadn't yet awakened.

The transition from high school to college had been seamless. My first year at Xavier University gave me an enormous infusion of confidence. The day after school started two of the school's administrators, Sister Marie Claire and Sister Magdalena, paid us a visit to meet Miss Menard. They were curious to meet the woman with whom they'd spoken on the telephone; the woman who would be responsible for any expenses that weren't included in the scholarship and the person with whom I lived. When they learned the whole story about what had happened to me, the nuns decided to include all my books into the four-year scholarship. Sister Marie Claire and Sister Magdalena took me under their wings and counseled me through the year – everything from help with my assignments to what classes to take next. I could ask them for any kind of help, day or night.

Everything else I needed, Miss Menard provided and many times before I asked. She had an uncanny way of knowing just what I needed or wanted, no matter what it was. Of course what I really wanted was to know all about her life. She'd tell me little tidbits, then she'd steer the conversation around to my life and what I should do not to end up the way she had – alone. It seemed she didn't trust me any more than I trusted her. More and more I thought about what she might be hiding and wondered if that something would affect me in some way. And as for Miss Menard being alone, that was no longer the case. I had certainly filled a big, empty space in her life. Lena now worked full time for her. And what about Leonard Stern? Who was this man and what other role had he or did he now play in her life? I only knew him to be the one who handled her finances. What baffled me most was that the whole time I lived there and even before, I never saw the man nor did I ever hear his voice. But I know he had to come and go in order to get cash to Miss Menard and take care of her other banking needs. He must have paid everyone who performed a service for her because I never saw her do it.

It was also very easy to convince myself that I was the reason Miss Menard's arthritis had gone into remission. Her energy level and ability to walk a little and enjoy lemonade and cookies on the porch again caused me to heap silent praises upon myself. I had given her life an extension! She needed me; I needed her. It was an excellent example of a new word I had learned: symbiosis. I hurried to the house everyday anxious to get to my new home and family.

This was my second year at the university. I was much less dependent on my benefactors, the nuns, and I excelled in my studies. There was no doubt in my mind that the feeling of contentment with Miss Menard as my family was at the core of my achievements. But I couldn't shake the feeling that something hovered over me and was waiting to pounce. So living on Esplanade Avenue in that big house often made me close my eyes and shake my head in disbelief. Then when I'd open them again and realize that it wasn't a daydream like the ones I'd had when I first knew Miss Menard, I'd hug myself with hesitant happiness. And even while feeling somewhat joyful, I silently waited for the next crushing wave to roll over me.

Although Miss Menard's arthritis was on hold, another problem had developed. She was diagnosed with congestive heart failure and needed to take several naps a day to replenish her energy. I always tried to be quiet whenever I entered or left the house so as not to disturb or alarm her. I didn't like the fact that she locked herself in her room, but no amount of persuasion worked in getting her to keep her door unlocked. Her classic retort was: "If I take too long to answer when you knock, either call the fire department or take the door off the hinges."

The telephone rang only once. The noise startled me out of my reverie.

I got up and started down the hall when I heard Lena's loud voice float out of the kitchen and up the hallway. The only reason Miss Menard couldn't hear her was because she closed the door which separated that part of the house from the kitchen whenever Lena was working there. Miss Menard and I occupied those rooms and hers was on the far side.

The original owners had been a large family with several servants. The servants' quarters had consisted of four rooms: two sleeping rooms, an extra pantry, and a laundry room. Now it had a small sitting room and two bedrooms with their own bathrooms. I felt very comfortable with the way it was set up.

The second floor of the house was off limits. Lena told me when she was hired she found everything upstairs covered with white sheets. She'd tried several times to sneak up there to find out what was under the sheets, but Miss Menard seemed to know each time she tried and she'd call her to the kitchen. Miss Menard eventually had a gate put up at the top of the stairs and padlocked it. Lena was obsessed with finding out what was up there. So every chance she got, she tried to coerce me into finding out where Miss Menard hid the key that opened the gate. "Ain't you wonderin bout what's up those stairs?" she'd ask. "If you want, Ah'll go and snoop around with you." I wasn't as curious as she was and I never looked for the key.

Lena's grating voice brought my mind back to the present situation as I stood in the hall hugging the wall. I don't know what possessed me to listen to her conversation instead of walking straight into the kitchen.

"Girl, this ol woman love her little, café au lait nursemaid. You'd swear they was kin or somethin. Huh? What? No girl, she ain't here na. She at school and Miss Menard sleep. Oh shit, Earline, hold on. Ah gotta turn off some a these pots Ah got cookin fo they burn."

While I was deciding whether I'd heard enough and if I should enter the kitchen or not, Lena returned to the phone.

"Earline? Hey girl, Ah'm back. Ah got to member not to laugh so loud, Ah might wake up Sleeping Beauty," Lena giggled softly. "Girrrl, lemme finish telling you bout this yella heifa. When her house burn down with everythin that chil had, Miss Menard gave her a chunk a change, honey, to get clothes and stuff she needed right away. Then when she started college las year, she got mo money to buy school clothes. Huh? Xavier University, girl. Claire's smart, yeah, but she weird, girl. She ain't got no man and she nineteen years ol! Either she a dyke, or she saving herself fa somebody." Lena cackled but it was suddenly muffled. "Huh? Yeah, you right. She sho could have somebody and jes don't bring him round here. Ah think she sneaky, if you ax me. "What?" she was silent for a while as if listening. "Oh honey, listen. Ah been scratching my head bout that fa mo than two years na. You know what Ah think? Ah think the powers that be didn't give a damn she was a mina. Girrrl...you know them people don't care bout Colored folk! Ah thought somebody in her neighborhood who knowed bout what happened to her would report her to the welfare people or somebody like that. Ah don't think nobody did. Nooo...body, you hear me. Nobody ever came here and probly didn't go to her school neither. Miss Menard got her free and clear. Ain't nothin nobody can do bout her na; she nineteen. Huh? Yeah, Ah know Miss Menard giving her a lot of stuff, but she still a slave. Claire's gonna be with this ol woman till this ol woman close her eyes. All Claire's youth gonna be gone by that time. Na...tell me, Earline, ain't that a slave?"

The anger rose up through my chest and constricted my throat. I could hardly breathe. This was the same Lena who had stayed with me and had gotten me through Big Mama's death and burial. I wondered how she could say those things about me after helping me the way she had. I tiptoed to the front door, opened it, then closed it with a light slam. By the time I reached the kitchen, Lena was off the phone and changing her shoes.

"Hey, Claire! What's goin on, girl? How you doin?" Lena didn't look up as she used her index finger like a shoehorn to slip on her loafers.

"Okay, I guess." I had decided not to confront her or let her know I'd heard her phone conversation. Confrontation could wait. "School's got me pretty busy. There's a lot of work, but we're getting close to finals. I'm glad for the weekend; I can really use the rest."

"Rest! You don't work at the drugstore no mo – how hard can it be?" Lena looked up at me over the top of her eyeglasses as she lobbed her sarcasm.

I ignored her. "Has Miss Menard been asleep long?"

"Yeah. She oughta be up soon. Tell her Ah made a buncha stuff fa y'all's dinner fa the next three days. Y'all got filé gumbo and a big pot of vegetable soup. Ah cooked y'all a pound of red beans with salt meat and Ah stewed a chicken. All you got to do is cook some rice. That's not too much fa you to do, is it?" She chuckled with her hand over her mouth clearly aware that I knew she was baiting me again. I continued to ignore her.

The door opened and Miss Menard rolled into the kitchen. "Lena, it's 3:00. You're still here?"

"Yes ma'am. Ah been cooking y'all some stuff fa the three days Ah'll be gone. Member, Ah ain't gonna be here tomorra, Sundy or Mondy? My family's all goin to a wedding in the country. Ah tol you a coupla weeks ago." Lena stood up and grabbed her purse and the bag with her apron and shoes.

"That's right, you did tell me. I'd forgotten."

"Okay, enjoy y'all's weeken. See y'all on Tewsdy," Lena said as she was backing out of the kitchen door.

"Claire, does Lena seem like herself to you lately?"

"No, she's different. She seems to have a lot of animosity toward me. I haven't done anything to her. I've always been grateful for the help she gave me when Big Mama died. So what's her problem?"

"I think she's going through an early change of life. She's getting to be that age, you know."

"She's being extremely nasty to me and I don't care whether or not the change is causing it. One of these days I'm going to tell her ass off. But I've been holding my tongue because I don't want her to quit on you. She's getting bolder because she believes I'm timid, but she'll find out what I'm really like if she doesn't cut the crap." I didn't tell Miss Menard about the telephone call I'd overheard. I wanted to fight my own battles.

"Hmm…I'll have to pay closer attention to the way she treats you. She certainly has no reason to dislike you. Do you think she's jealous of you because you live here and you're able to get a college education? She didn't have the opportunities you have, you know. Do you have any idea why she's treating you badly, cher?"

"Now, Miss Menard, you know I don't give a damn what her reasons are. She needs to know she can't intimidate me. And when I let her know how many of her phone calls I can quote, she'll think I know someone at the FBI."

"Claire, has she been stealing from me? A lot of housekeepers steal from the people they work for. What do you know about Lena? Tell me, I think I ought to know."

"Sorry, what I know has nothing to do with you, Miss Menard. She's like a lot of other people in this town. She does a lot of things she has no business doing because there's nothing better to do. Maybe she's bored, I don't know."

I had decided not to tell her Lena's secrets, especially the one about calling Miss Menard names hoping I would laugh. Sometimes she'd refer to her as "Old Moneybags." Other times when she was trying to get me to look for the key to open the padlock to the upstairs, she'd call her "Killer Madam of Mystery." I'd hear her on the phone tell her friends that she had pet names for the old woman. She'd rattle off: "Lady Gimp," "Greta Garbo in a Wheelchair," and "Lucy Liniment."

It was imperative that I keep that secret and all the others I knew about Lena because her absence could bring about other negative changes in my life. She'd called me Miss Menard's slave, and I was convinced that if I got her fired, I might indeed have to quit school and take up her household duties. Here was that lack of trust for Miss Menard again. Of course, if Lena stepped too far over the line, I'd have to dangle what I knew in her face. After all, I had seen her going into a seedy motel on Dumaine just off Claiborne. My bus had broken down and I was walking home. The man who had his arms wrapped around her was not her husband. I'd heard many whispered phone calls to someone who might have been that man. And what I heard was 1954 phone sex. So, I hoped I wouldn't have to resort to blackmail.

"Claire!" Miss Menard banged the tea kettle on the stove. "Where were you, in a trance? Would you like a cup of tea?"

"No, no trance. Still thinking about Lena. Tea sounds great. Thanks."

"I'll bet you're glad the weekend's here and you have some time off."

I grinned. "You have no idea. Plus...the icing on the cake is that I have no papers due. I'm free the whole weekend. I'll start studying for finals in a week or so. Boy, this year has whizzed by. I'll be a junior in September, can you believe it?"

While talking, I was simultaneously thinking that there was no way I was going to let Lena upset my world. Too many things were going the way I needed them to go, and her jealousy, change of life, or whatever the hell was responsible for her behavior toward me would have to stay hidden away. Nothing she could say about me was going to take me off the course I had set for myself.

- 21 -

FINDING EMILY

At breakfast the next morning, Miss Menard was eager to talk. She couldn't wait for me to sit at the table.

"Have I told you lately, Claire, that I'm very proud...?" Miss Menard was interrupted by a loud, urgent knock on the front door.

I ran to open it with Miss Menard on my heels in her wheelchair. I cracked the door a bit to see who it was and saw Emily's mother standing with her eyes closed and her hands clasped in prayer. It was raining hard and she was dripping wet and trembling violently. As soon as I opened the door wider, she fell into the foyer on top of me.

"Mrs. Valcour, what's wrong?" I held her up as she tried to catch her breath.

"It's Emily. Have, have, you...seen her, Cl...Cl... aire?" She was shaking so hard I grabbed Miss Menard's afghan that was folded on the sofa and wrapped it around her.

"You know I haven't seen Emily in a long time, Mrs. Valcour. Nothing's changed."

"I still thought she might have come to you after she talked to Bobby last night. She was visiting me when he called and told her he wanted her to stay with me for a while because he needed a break. When he told her it might be forever, she screamed, threw the phone on the floor, and then ran out the front door. While I was trying to talk to Bobbie, I heard the tires squeal as she pulled away from the curb."

"Didn't you or Johnnie try to stop her? Can she even drive?"

"Emily failed the driving test three times; she doesn't have a license. I didn't know she'd be crazy enough to take my car. She must have grabbed my keys off the dresser when she ran out. She hasn't called and she's nowhere to be found. She's pregnant again,

Claire! I don't think she's been right since she lost the first baby. I have to find my daughter!"

"I'm sorry; I don't have any idea where Emily might be. Bobby knows she's missing, right?"

"He's been helping me and Johnnie look for her. Bobby was still on the phone when I picked it up off the floor last night. That's how I found out what he'd told her. You're the one person I thought she'd come to because she's never stopped talking about you even though you two *fell out*. She's wanted to tell you how sorry she is, but she can't seem to get up the courage to do it."

"I'm sure it must be difficult for her to admit what she did. And I certainly have had no desire to get in touch with her after what happened?"

"But why, Claire? She needed you with all that's happened to her and to our family. She's never been able to talk to me the way she used to talk to you." Emily's mother began to cry again. "She's known all along Bobby doesn't love her and that he's carrying a torch for you. She's had some kinda crazy notion that he's going to ask you to take him back and that you will."

"Look, Mrs. Valcour, I never had him to begin with, so there is no taking him back. Emily was my best friend, but she sacrificed our friendship for Bobby. I wasn't interested in marrying him, so they could have gotten together without all the lies. She could have had a much different relationship with him instead of him going to her on the rebound. You should have discouraged her when you found out what she was up to. But you didn't. So when I found out she was pregnant, I thought she got what she wanted – a man to sit her on her ass and give her five kids. I was actually happy for her and damn glad I wasn't the one marrying that bastard." I knew I should have had more sympathy for the woman, but my tongue seemed to have a mind of its own and I could see my words stung her bitterly.

She recovered quickly. "Well...okay...Claire, if you should hear from her, let me know. She hasn't been a good driver, so I worry that something might have happened to her. She's also been spot-bleeding and that's not good when you're five months along." When I didn't comment, she went on. "Thank you, honey. I wish you were still her friend." She patted my face, dropped the afghan on the floor, and left without ever acknowledging Miss Menard's presence.

As I started to complain about Mrs. Valcour's rudeness, Miss Menard stopped me. "Cher, don't. She didn't have time to exchange pleasantries with me. Her child is missing."

I should have felt more compassion for Emily and her mother, but I knew that through all the trouble I'd had with Bobby, my grandmother's death, and my house burning down, I hadn't received one word of any kind from either of them. Why shouldn't I respond in kind? To me, Emily was getting exactly what she deserved and so was her mother for supporting what she'd done. The spoiled little girl would return home as soon as she thought she'd worried everyone sufficiently. I vowed to erase it from my consciousness.

After Miss Menard put the cup of tea in front of me, I started to tell her what I had been thinking. She didn't wait for me to finish when she began telling me her thoughts.

"I knew that would happen, Claire. Her mother may have let her get away with that behavior, but God didn't." This was one of the few times Miss Menard had talked so openly about God. She rarely spoke of Him. I had no idea if she prayed. "I told you seeking revenge is a waste of time. God always takes care of things like that. Don't doubt me, cher," she said.

"I never doubt you," I laughed while being dishonest. "I just wanted to feel vindicated by doing the job myself. Don't you…"

Before I could finish what I was saying, there was another knock on the door. I headed down the hall again with Miss Menard rolling behind me.

It was Bobby. He was bone dry. The rain had stopped.

"Is Emily's mama here, Claire?" He was looking down at the porch and gasping for breath as if he had been running. I could see his car parked in front of the house so I knew that wasn't why he was on the verge of hyperventilation. Suddenly his shoulders shook, and when he looked up at me, the tears were streaming down his face.

"You just missed her. Has Emily been found?"

"Yeah…yeah…yeah…they found her," Bobby sobbed and covered his face with his hands.

Taken off-guard by his breakdown, I couldn't get the words out to ask where they had found her.

"She was in Bayou St. John," he whispered as the saliva and tears mingled and leaked from his lips. "They think she musta run off the road in the dark last night. Somebody spotted the bumper of the car sticking outta the water. They just pulled her out a few minutes ago. Her mama don't know yet." He wiped his nose and his mouth on the sleeve of his shirt.

"Oh my God!" I muttered. I couldn't keep the tears out of my eyes. Another piece of my childhood was gone. Miss Menard's hand flew up to her mouth and she groaned.

Bobby suddenly threw his arms around my neck and collapsed against me. I wanted to push him away but didn't. I stood ramrod stiff waiting for him to right himself and move away of his own volition.

"It's my fault they're dead. God, what am I gonna do?" He lifted his arms that had been heavy on my shoulders, then dropped them at his sides and stepped away from me.

Miss Menard's voice rang out as she rolled her chair between us. "You didn't kill Emily, Bobby, and don't think that you did. She was driving that car, not you. She left the house in hysterics, not you. Emily was spoiled and in the habit of getting what she wanted and she wanted you."

"It don't matter, Miss Sera, she's still dead. And she's dead because I didn't want her." Bobby didn't look up. He continued to cry and stare down at the floor.

"Look at me, Bobby," Miss Menard commanded. "When you rejected her and asked for a break, she threw a fit of temper thinking that would make you change your mind. Her mama's got to take part of the blame because she always let her get away with those tantrums, probably from the time she was a baby."

"Maybe all that's true, Miss Sera, but I drove her to take that car and run off. Now I got to live with that for the rest of my life" Bobby stepped out of the foyer and onto the porch. I moved aside as Miss Menard maneuvered her wheelchair and followed him out.

"Claire, I'm sorry I slobbered all over you. I know I'm the last person you want touching you," he said sounding genuinely contrite.

"It's okay, Bobby, I understand. Don't worry about me. You should be worrying about how you're going to face Emily's mother and her brother." I knew it was a mean thing to say at a time like that. I hadn't stuck the knife in his gut, but I wasn't above twisting it. I glanced sideways at Miss Menard and saw the disapproval on her face.

"I'd better get on over to Emily's house." Bobby walked off the porch without a backward glance. After he got in his car, he sat for a while before he drove away.

"Was it necessary to treat Bobby that way, Claire? Shame on you!" Miss Menard rolled back into the house. I followed her in and slammed the door.

"Shame on me? Was I supposed to pity that bastard? Well...not in this life or the next one. He's lucky that's all I told him because I was thinking a helluva lot more than I said. When I think of Emily and her baby, I can't even see straight."

Miss Menard spun around to face me. "Bobby has some blame in Emily's death, Claire, but he's not solely responsible. Emily and her mother own a large part of it."

"But what a terrible way to die! She was the sister I never had. I was hoping one day when she had her house and all her kids, we'd forget the past and try to be friends again. Well, that's not possible now. And even though Bobby wasn't driving the car, he's still the primary cause of her death and he should feel guilty. I hope he never sleeps another night in his goddamn life!"

"Why? Is his suffering your revenge?"

"Damn right," I said. "If I could get away with blowing his brains out, I would."

"Claire, please don't say that. You have to learn to forgive. Don't hold on to hurt and anger for so long. They will eat up your life. Please, cher."

"Miss Menard, I usually take your advice, but not this time. I hate Bobby. He not only had a hand in Emily's death, but he sure as hell helped kill my grandmother and Marcel. I'll never forgive him."

"Oh, cher. Why are you still living in the past?"

"Because my grandmother is dead," I screamed at her, "and I still haven't gotten over it. Bobby hurt her, and anyone who hurts me or someone I love, I can't and won't forgive them. And if there's an opportunity to exact revenge, I'll do that, too."

"Sometimes you frighten me, Claire. Maybe one day I'll say or do something that will hurt you. How will you deal with me?" Miss Menard didn't wait for an answer. She wheeled herself down the hall and went straight to her bedroom and closed the door.

I couldn't bring myself to go to Emily's rosary or her funeral. Deep in my heart I knew I still loved my childhood friend and I'd always miss her. Miss Menard begged me to go. She told me I'd probably regret not going in the years to come.

"Listen to me, cher; soften your heart a little. It doesn't cost you anything. You've got too much pride. You don't lose anything when you show people you care about them. I think Emily's mother and Bobby would feel better if they saw you there."

"No, sorry. Every person I've ever cared about leaves me. And if you haven't noticed, it's usually through death. Let them bury her without me. I can't stand to see anyone else I've loved lying lifeless in a coffin." I fought back the tears, but let them go later when I was alone in my room.

– 22 –

LET'S KEEP THIS ONE

It had taken Johnnie Valcour four years to "pass over by my house to talk" as he'd put it. It was the middle of spring, just weeks before my graduation from Xavier U when I found him sitting on the porch with Miss Menard. They were laughing and talking as if they'd known each other for years. It was a beautiful, early May evening and every flower in the garden was in bloom. Their fragrances mingled with the scent of the night jasmine made the air intoxicating.

"What's going on here?" I teased. My college years had mellowed me a bit. I had lost most of my paranoia that some kind of impending doom was just around the corner waiting to pounce. I had learned to laugh more. I didn't mind looking at myself in the mirror now that I wasn't as skinny as I had been. I had filled out in the places that counted.

"Hello, Miss Soublet, *long time no see.*" Johnnie smiled his best toothpaste smile exposing his prominent canines. Right away I knew he wasn't the Johnnie I'd seen in Lavata's.

"Hey, Mr. Valcour. How long has it been?"

"Why, were you marking the days on the calendar?"

"Wow! You've gone from a sweet person to a smartass."

Johnnie smiled ignoring me. "I came to talk and you weren't here, so this beautiful lady's been standing in for you." He winked at Miss Menard.

Her pale cheeks suddenly glowed bubble-gum pink. "Claire, we're going to keep this one," she said, "and shoot all the rest."

Everybody laughed. And to my delighted surprise, Johnnie's chuckle was natural and he stopped before Miss Menard and I did. I began to relax a little. Oh, but what about his eye movement?

Even though I was afraid to stare at him to find out, I knew I had to know.

"So, stranger, what have you been doing for the past four years?" I held his gaze. Oh yes, the hummingbird eyes were gone. My God, he was sooo...handsome! I tried hard to remember how much older he was than me but couldn't. Then I tried picturing him when he used to pull my hair, then when he graduated from high school, and then when he played college football. How old was I at those times? I arrived at a five or six year age difference. I was almost twenty-two, so he had to be about twenty-seven or twenty-eight. Not bad...not bad at all.

"Yoo-hoo, earth to Claire." Johnnie was clapping his hands close to my face. "Have a seat. Don't you want an answer to your question?" He pulled up a chair next to his, took my hand and guided me until I sat.

"I finished my degree in education at Southern, thanks to the G.I. Bill. In September, I'll be teaching history, I think, and if they'll take a chance on me with my disability, I'll be the assistant football coach at Clark High. Okay, close your mouth and congratulate me."

"Oooo...I like this fella," Miss Menard teased.

I gave her a dirty look and to Johnnie I said, "Congratulations. Sorry I looked so shocked. But c'mon now, the last time I saw you, you looked as though you had a long way to go. What happened?"

"You happened. You were the catalyst I needed to alter my pathetic state of being." He sounded every inch the learned man. "I'm here to thank you."

"Well damn, professor, you sure as hell did a 180." I bowed to him from my seated position. "What did I do to facilitate this new state?"

"It was the way you looked at me in Lavata's. You pitied me. You managed to wipe the floor with the rest of my dignity. My kid sister's friend was talking to me as if I were an old friend with a mental problem. And actually, I was. You seemed to patronize me rather than be rude to me. I was angry and thankful at the same time. When I got home that evening, I took a long look at myself, and from that day to this, I haven't looked back."

"Good for you, Johnnie. I think the three of us have a lot in common." Miss Menard was beginning to get too involved in my business. Technically, though, there was no business – yet.

"What's for dinner?" I needed to change the subject.

"I've already eaten. But for you, nothing. Johnnie's going to take you out to dinner, aren't you, Johnnie?"

"Stop, you're embarrassing me!" Now I was angry. She'd gone too far.

"Hey, don't yell at Miss Menard. That really is why I'm here. Where would you like to go?"

It was obvious he was covering for her. I let it go. "Why didn't you call to ask me out?"

"Didn't have a number for you and didn't know how to get it, so I came by instead. You're not going to send me away are you?" His chocolate eyes were caressing my face and I felt so happy I wanted to lick his face like a new puppy he'd just found.

"Well...no...but...," I couldn't think and I couldn't talk. My thinking tool and my voice box had malfunctioned.

"Then it's settled. I think I know a place you'd probably like. Do you need to change?"

"Yes. I'll only be a few minutes." I caught a glimpse of Miss Menard's face as I got up. If she had grinned any wider, the corners of her mouth would have wrapped around her ears.

Looking in the mirror at myself in my Sunday duds was a surreal experience. These were my church clothes – the name I called them at ten and at twenty-two they still had the same title. Going to Mass was the only time I ever dressed up. I had shunned all the social events at Xavier U, except the regular after-class functions on campus and an occasional bite to eat with a couple of the guys at school. I did lunch, never dinner. And every single one of them had in mind an extended relationship and all that went with it, and of course, I ran like hell. It was usually one or two dates and that was it.

Every second I was away from the porch was agony. What was Miss Menard telling Johnnie? Not paying attention to the way I grabbed my purse, I lifted it off the dresser upside down and everything spilled out.

Johnnie glanced at his watch when I stepped out onto the porch. "A few minutes, huh. I didn't think you were the primping type like Emily." When he saw he'd wiped the smile off my face, he tried to correct his mistake. "That's not true, I apologize. I remember you did most of the work for your teenage parties and you'd still get back to my house bathed and dressed before your friends arrived. Emily would still be fussing about what she was going to wear." His voice had grown tentative.

"You managed to get the story straightened out, so I accept your apology." That's what was coming out of my mouth, however inside my head was another story.

As I stared at Johnnie I prayed, "Oh Lord, after all this time, You're not going to send me an impatient man, are You?" Sweep out those thoughts, you ninny. Does God have time to hand pick a man for you? Get real, toots! I laughed to myself about how prompt my ever-present superego was. I could always count on my watchful policeman who was always on guard and ready to battle my conscious mind whenever it threatened to go off the deep end.

Johnnie pushed Miss Menard into the foyer. She sat in the doorway waving as we left. When I turned to wave the last time, I saw my grandmother sitting in the wheelchair. I imagined she was saying, "I'm glad you waited, Claire." I tried to make a quick mental note to ask Miss Menard if those had been her thoughts.

Johnnie held the door of his 1955 Crown Victoria open for me. The blue and white car sparkled like a brand, new, silver dollar. My head was spinning and my nerves had gone haywire. I thought it best to be quiet; I didn't want to hear my voice quiver when I talked. Johnnie must have sensed I was having an anxiety attack because he drove without saying a word. We parked on Orleans St. in front of Dooky Chase's restaurant. Hmm, Johnnie had said he knew a place I'd probably like. Well...this certainly was the place to go for dinner, maybe the only place.

Most people didn't dine out much in those days; we ate at home. Segregation prevented us from eating in restaurants that were not Colored owned. We also had suppers you bought from other people's kitchens, usually on a Friday or Saturday night. You often ordered the number of plates you planned to buy during the week. That gave the cooks an idea of how much food to prepare. On Fridays, they served a plate of fried fish, macaroni and cheese, potato salad, sometimes smothered greens or other vegetables – it depended on who was doing the cooking. On Saturdays, you got everything served on Fridays, but they substituted fried chicken for the fish because it wasn't a Catholic meatless day. For $1.50, sometimes $2.00, you received a heaping plate of food that usually fed two people. We frequented "little holes in the wall" that only served boiled seafood and raw oysters, or you'd go to places like Lavata's that sold oyster loaves or Joe Sheep's for special po boy sandwiches. But when you wanted gumbo, red beans and rice, jambalaya or baked mirlitons – you ate at home. These were on your table daily; you couldn't get these dishes any better prepared than what you got at home.

After we parked, Johnnie jumped out of the car and ran around to my side to open the door and help me out. The bells and whistles went off again. Not only was he handsome with a terrific car, but he seemed to be every bit the gentleman. His assets just kept piling up.

As soon as we were seated in the restaurant Johnnie asked, "Is this place okay with you? I guess I should have asked you when we first pulled up, but I was too busy trying to shake the jitters. I think you were having a few yourself, weren't you?"

"A few," I admitted. "I've never been here. I've heard the food is good, though." I watched Johnnie's head jerk and his eyes flash in disbelief.

"Really? You've never been here? Don't you go out?"

"No, I don't," I said. "You're my very first dinner date. I'm a virgin...dinner-dater, that is." We both covered our mouths trying not to laugh out loud.

"That was a good one, Claire. I'll never, never let you live it down."

I closed one eye and pumped my right fist at him, "And I'll have to hurt you," I said.

"You're not so tough. By the way, you look beautiful tonight. The last time I saw you, you weren't so...ah...filled out." He rolled his eyes toward the ceiling, then bit his bottom lip and screwed up his face to look as if he was afraid of me. I liked the biting of the lip thing.

"I remember. You told me I was thin and I'd probably fill out in a couple of years. I follow orders well. I did exactly that."

"Yes...you...did!" Johnnie punctuated every word. "Look at you. You've got stuff in all the right places. You're no longer a *skinny galoot.*"

"You're embarrassing me."

"No, I'm complimenting you. That's what nice guys do when they take a beautiful woman to dinner. Oh, sorry. I forgot you have no experience with this sort of thing. You're a virgin dinner-dater."

"Not after tonight, you smartass. Let's talk about something else before I forget all the good things I've been thinking about you, and for good measure, douse you with this glass of water." I knew I really didn't mean what I was saying. It was the same nasty habit I needed to break – always being on the defensive.

"Would you care to elaborate on those good things you've been thinking about me. My ego could use a boost right now." Johnnie tried to look as pathetic as his face would allow, but his ego was as intact as the image of the Holy Ghost in the stained glass window at Corpus Christi Church.

"You haven't mentioned your foot. Did you get a new prosthesis?" I ignored his request.

"You didn't remember I had a missing foot, did you? C'mon, admit it. I'm so charming I swept you off your feet and you couldn't think of anything else but those good things, right?" He had the upper hand and he was milking it.

"I admit it, but not for the reasons you say. Your limp isn't as pronounced as it was before and I did forget about it until just this minute." Of course that wasn't true, but since I'd been asked to boost his ego, wouldn't the content of my lie qualify?

"Let's talk about my foot after we order. I think we should get something we rarely get at home. What do you think?"

I agreed.

Waiting for our dinner to arrive was the perfect opportunity for me to excuse myself and go to the ladies room. I needed a chance to breathe and to stall having to answer Johnnie's request for a list of things I liked about him. Caterpillar...chrysalis... which stage was I in?

Would I ever become a butterfly? Didn't I think I was ready to fly? I washed my hands six times before I got the nerve to go back to the table. The drinks had already arrived and the waiter was on his way to our table with our seafood platters.

"Are you okay?" Johnnie looked at me suspiciously. "I hope you're not having second thoughts about coming out with me."

"Don't be silly," I managed to get out. I stuck the straw in my mouth to shut myself up.

I hated catfish; Johnnie hated softshell crab. We traded our fried sea creatures like ten-year-olds. I stole one of his hush puppies; he stole four of my French fries. When he gulped down his coke and then poured part of mine into his glass, I was forced to dump ice water into his stolen goods. He had to order another drink.

We laughed all through dinner and found ourselves too stuffed for dessert. We'd both had our minds set on the bread pudding with whiskey sauce. Johnnie said it was even better than his mother's. He said we'd have to come back, just for the bread pudding.

In between eating and laughing, our personal adult histories, our goals, our likes and dislikes were laid bare across the table. There wasn't too much information withheld because there wasn't anything we couldn't talk about. Although I hadn't learned to fish and crab with my grandfather, I was excited to know those were some of Johnnie's favorite pastimes. He promised to take me with him in the fall when the "r" months came round again. I had forgotten the guide rule about the safest seafood for eating was said to be caught in the months spelled with r. The other months were considered risky, especially the hot summer months.

We were avid readers and movie buffs – *Phantom of the Opera* with Claude Rains our favorite movie. Outside of the trip to Korea during the war, Johnnie hadn't done any other traveling and he was desperate to see the world. Like me, he wanted to see the places he'd read about. How was it possible that after dreaming all of my life about the places I wanted to see, someone was sitting across the table from me with that same dream? It was hard to believe we'd lived around the corner from one another most of our lives but only now had we gotten to really know each other.

When we left the restaurant, Johnnie drove as slowly as the car would go. I asked if there was something mechanically wrong with it that we couldn't go any faster.

"No, I'm trying to keep you with me as long as I can. Is that okay with you?" He reached for my hand, but I quickly slipped it under my purse.

"Claire, I know what's going on with you and it's okay. I learned patience when I was being rehabilitated after Korea. You can only do things when you're ready and not before. So when you're ready to be touched, I want you to take my hand. Okay?"

172

Too embarrassed to lift my head, I twisted it toward the window so that he couldn't see the tears glistening in my eyes. I managed to thank him for the nice evening and tell him goodnight when he walked me through the garden. I ran up onto the porch and slipped into the house as quickly as I could to avoid having to say anything else. As soon as I closed the door, I realized I hadn't given him my telephone number. I opened it again as fast as I could and called out to him as he was opening the gate.

"Johnnie, wait. I forgot to give you my phone number."

He closed the gate and walked back toward the porch. "I already have it. Miss Menard gave it to me before you came home this evening."

"Oh."

"Is that all you wanted?"

"No," I said and walked down the steps to where he was standing. I took his hand in both of mine and held it tightly. Gently he raised my chin, kissed me lightly on my lips and then held me close to him for a few seconds.

"Thank you," he said as he let me go. "I'll call you soon. Goodnight, Claire."

Sandwiched between my finals and graduation, Johnnie and I found time to see each other as often as we could. He was usually waiting for me on the porch with Miss Menard at his side. He no longer lived on Laharpe St. near Anne Marie Bogass. The house had become too big for his mother, especially when he was living and going to school in Baton Rouge. She'd sold it and bought a smaller house in the Gentilly area near Dillard University. Johnnie invited me to Sunday dinner several times but I always declined. Finally, he stopped asking.

Miss Menard adored Johnnie and she told us as often as we'd let her. And every time she said it in front of him, he tried to keep his lips in check, but they'd widen across his face, anyway.

My trust in him grew quickly. So much so, that I told him all about my life before I met Miss Menard and after she took me in. Eventually, I even told him about the policeman, Michael McArdle, and his subsequent disappearance. There was no need to tell him I believed Miss Menard was somehow involved; he said he'd gotten that impression while I was telling him the story. He asked if there had been any other news releases about the missing cop. I had never heard or seen any. Johnnie felt I had gotten through the last four years in spite of my feelings of guilt, and as long as Miss Menard was unwilling to talk about it, then he suggested I let it go forever.

Now that I planned to stay home for the summer and Johnnie was coming to the house as often as he was, I encouraged Miss Menard to cut Lena's hours to mornings only and just have her cook. Father O'Mara quickly found a woman to do house cleaning for us twice a week even though he had never found anyone to replace me at the drugstore. Mr. Colari's wife assisted him in the store after I left. When she died suddenly two years later, he sold the drugstore and his home and moved to New York to be near his daughters.

Graduation was everything I had wished for. Johnnie brought Miss Menard to the cap and gown ceremony. He had to carry her to and from the car and to all the other places her wheelchair couldn't go. Sisters Marie Claire and Magdalena remembered Johnnie from his days at the university and seated them in the faculty section. Miss Menard enjoyed every moment and never once said she was tired. When my name was called to receive my diploma and it was announced that I was graduating summa cum laude, Johnnie whistled and stomped his feet as I walked across the stage. When I looked out into the audience, Miss Menard and all the nuns were clapping and stomping their feet along with Johnnie. I was so happy to have a family, even a makeshift one, my feet must have given off sparks as I crossed the platform. By the time I got back to my seat, the front of my gown was soaked with tears.

- 23 -

COMING APART
AT THE SEAMS

It was pleasant around the house in the afternoon without Lena's wisecracks and snide remarks. She had mounted an all-out assault on me when Johnnie began to spend a lot of time at the house. And when Miss Menard asked her to cook a little more because Johnnie usually had dinner with us, she was beside herself. After her hours were cut, we expected her to quit at anytime. She didn't. Johnnie wanted to know how I'd managed to ignore her for such a long time. He didn't buy that I was a patient person and I wouldn't tell him the real reason. I figured if he guessed why, I'd admit it.

Without warning, I had no energy. I was tired all the time and often couldn't put one foot in front of the other. Food didn't interest me; I just wanted to sleep. In order to feel rested, I needed ten to twelve hours every night. After several weeks, Johnnie and Miss Menard insisted I see a doctor. I hadn't been to one in so long, I could only think of the one I'd known all my life. I called Dr. La Croix's office and made an appointment. He was in the same office he'd always been in on Gentilly Boulevard near Elysian Fields. Johnnie drove me to his office the next morning.

Dr. La Croix recognized me immediately and gave me a hug. I told him what had brought me to his office.

"Are you pregnant?" he asked.

"Pregnant? I haven't done anything to get pregnant." I replied.

When he burst out laughing, I knew I'd made a mistake in going to him.

175

"How old are you, Claire?" He was still laughing. "Have I seen you since your grandmother died?"

"I'm twenty-two, and no, you haven't seen me since then. In fact, you didn't see me that day; you talked to me on the phone." I'd never been made to feel so cheap and disrespected. So along with my energy, my self-worth was now flagging.

He stopped laughing. "You're Iris' girl and you're trying to make me believe you haven't been with a man, yet? I remember your mother very well. She had a reputation in this town as a real hot mama."

"I'm not my mother, and frankly I don't give a damn what you believe or what you remember about her. If you weren't such a dried up old son-of-a-bitch, I'd knock you on your ass. The one you should be laughing at is your daughter, the one in California who's married to my father, Lester." Dr. La Croix's eyes opened wide and his brows almost receded into his hairline.

"Oh, you're shocked. Didn't think I knew, huh. Well, let me tell you what else I know. When Lester, his wife, his three kids, and his father moved to California, they moved to an all White area. And then his last two kids were born looking just like your son Junior - too brown to pass for White. They had to move to the New Orleans ghetto, you know, that special section in Los Angeles where all the Creoles of color settle. How am I doing so far, doc? This is the Seventh Ward in New Orleans, remember, there ain't nothing secret here."

"Get out of my office," he yelled at me. "Find another doctor to treat you. I'm damn glad Philomene isn't here to see this. You're just like your mother." His face looked like a big, red boil and his balled up fists were shaking in the air above his head.

I jumped off the examination table. "Don't worry, I'm leaving. But remember, all five of your Menard grandchildren have half the same blood as me, Lester's blood. Maybe what you see in me is Lester, not Iris." I opened the door and slammed it into the wall, marched through the office, then through the waiting room and out to the street. Johnnie didn't say a word; he simply got up and followed me out. When we reached the sidewalk, he grabbed my shoulders to make me stop, then spun me around to face him.

"Is it bad, Claire? How could the doctor know what's wrong with you that fast? Tell me!"

I couldn't tell him because I couldn't talk. I fell sobbing into his arms. The past twelve years had just exploded inside my brain and the eruption had hurled every piece of boiling hurt through my body scorching my heart and all of my nerve endings. I clung to Johnnie as if the end of the world was upon us. He couldn't pry me loose. Somehow he managed to walk to his car with me hanging onto him as I stumbled backwards.

"You don't have to talk right now," he told me. "Just get in and I'll sit and hold you until you're ready."

The tears refused to stop. I drenched Johnnie's neck with tears and slobber. He never moved or winced. Finally he took his arms from around me and started the car. "I'm taking you home with me." When I shook my head he said, "We'll be the only ones there. My mother's working." I didn't protest again.

Johnnie pulled the car into the driveway when we reached the house. "Before we go inside," he said, "I want you to tell me what the doctor told you. If it's something serious, we'll handle it together. I'm not going anywhere."

"No, it's nothing like that. He didn't tell me anything is physically wrong with me." Then I told him what Dr. La Croix had said to me.

"That lousy bastard!" Johnnie pounded the middle of the steering wheel forgetting that was where the horn was. The unexpected loud noise made us both jump. His next door neighbor came out to see who was blowing. Johnnie rolled down the window and told the man that he'd leaned on the horn by mistake.

"Why didn't you call me in there, Claire? I sure as hell would have told his butt off. Did you know that his son Junior, his wife's change of life baby, is just a few years older than me? Junior might be married, but I can take his pappy to the Quarter almost any night of the week and show him his "ac-dc" son in high heels sashaying his narrow ass from one bar to another."

"Oh!" How in the hell did Johnnie know that? That sounded like something he'd heard his mother and her club members discuss. Please God, not another bigot in my life!

"Wait, that's not all. For years the good doctor made so-called house calls right across the street from our house on Laharpe. Remember the nice-looking woman whose husband had a heart attack on the lawn and died...well...ol doc's been going to the widow and giving her his special injections several times a

177

CLAUDETTE CARRIDA JEFFREY

week ever since she buried her old man. Damn, let's get the hell out of this car; I'm beginning to sound like a gossipy, old woman. Stop crying, Claire. That old buzzard isn't worth it. He's got one foot in the grave; you've got your whole life ahead of you. C'mon let's go in, I'll make us some lunch."

I practically grew up in the Laharpe St. house and I never wanted to forget the happy times I'd spent there. This house I didn't know; a house without Emily's ghost. So I decided to relax and shake off what Johnnie had said...but put it on the back-burner.

"Look around if you want. You don't need me to give you the ten-cent tour, do you?"

Johnnie was busy opening Venetian blinds and drapes.

"No, but I don't like snooping around in your mother's house." I remembered how fussy Mrs. Valcour was about the things in the other house. "Your home is beautiful, Johnnie. The rooms are bright and sunny. I like that." I walked into the kitchen and everything looked new. "Wow, who did all this work?"

"I did." He grabbed my hand and took me down the hall to his bedroom. It was the last room off the hall. "Look," he pulled me toward the bathroom, "I'm self-contained. I added this on a few months ago. I used to complain about doing construction work, but it sure came in handy when I saw everything that needed to be done to this house. I did almost everything myself, except for some things I couldn't manage alone." He pointed to his right foot. "Some of my old buddies came to my rescue."

I couldn't let this opportunity pass. "Johnnie, do you realize you've never told me about your foot. You promised the night we went to Dooky Chase's, remember? I've been reluctant to bring it up. I thought you hadn't talked about it because you didn't want to."

"I don't. But I did promise, didn't I? Okay, here goes: Lecture on Artificial Limbs 101. This class deals with a SACH foot," he raised his pant leg to expose it. "It's new and hot off the mold." He looked at the expression on my face and realized I didn't think he was being funny. Raising his pant leg higher so that I could take a better look, he continued without the comedic flair, "I didn't have this one the night we went to dinner. I just got it last week and it's not that comfortable yet."

178

"I would never have known. You put on such a good front. Does it hurt your...umm...the bottom of your leg?" I couldn't look at him. I looked at his foot.

"My stump, Claire, you can say it. You won't offend me. That's what it is." He realized he was hurt and being defensive. "I'm sorry; this is a sore subject with me." I saw his eyes briefly cloud over with tears.

"SACH is an acronym for 'solid ankle, cushion heel.' It's really light. The fact that they're fairly inexpensive means I can buy a couple of them to wear with different shoes. Of course, there's always a drawback. I'm still limited as to what I can do with it."

"How did you find out about it?" I asked.

"Through the Veteran's Hospital. UCLA developed it and the hospital ordered it through the university. They tell me in a few years there'll be lots more on the market even more technologically advanced. So, I'll have to be patient. Okay, that's the last word about my foot. Lie down on my bed and rest if you like. Hell, take a nice warm bath. It'll help you relax. I need to get started on lunch." When I didn't answer fast enough he said, "Follow me into the kitchen, then. You can think about my foot some more." There was no smile when he said it.

"Johnnie, your foot doesn't bother me. I asked because I'd like to know everything about you. What's wrong with that?"

"Nothing, but...you haven't had the privilege of seeing me without it."

"It won't matter when I do. I won't recoil in disgust."

"How do you know you won't?"

"I just do. I'm not a fair-weather friend."

"With all the kissing and touching we've been doing, is that all we are, Claire? Friends?"

"Don't start with me, Johnnie Boy. I've had enough shit for one day."

"What a mouth! I'm going to have to wash it out with soap if you keep that up." And in a flash, he threw me down on his bed and flopped down beside me. We were both on our backs looking up at the ceiling. The urge to get up and run was strong, but not overpowering.

Something held me in place until the feeling subsided.

"I suddenly have a flash of brilliance, Claire. I know what's wrong with you. You're not physically sick; you're suffering from something like battle fatigue. You've had to fight against all sorts of enemies your whole life, and just when you think you've fought your way to what you think is a safer place, you collapse from exhaustion. You're battle weary. Your mind and your body have reached a breaking point. I know; I've been there, too."

"I once told you I follow orders well, so what do you think I should do, doc?" I was handling the whole thing as if it were jest, but I wasn't so sure it was.

"You have to fight against letting the weariness get the best of you until you're strong again. One way may be to get away from the problems for a while."

"Can't do that. Not only do I have to get my master's, I can't leave Miss Menard. She depends on me now. Plus, she's done too much for me for..."

"Claire, Claire! I didn't mean for you to go away. I meant for you to change the way you're living your life. Not to be so closed off from everything. See the world around you. You haven't done that in a long time, maybe you never did. Does that make sense to you?"

I partially sat up, then propped myself up on my elbows. "I hate to say it, but you actually do make sense. Why didn't that occur to me?"

"Because you're not as smart as I am."

"Bullshit! Remember, I'm the one who graduated summa cum laude."

"And I'm the one who graduated volumma cum laude, that's a 4.5 average."

"Oh shit, really?"

"No, I just felt like pulling your leg."

"You liar!" I looked around for something to hit him with. I grabbed one of the pillows on the bed and started to whack him with it. He batted it out of my hands and pulled me on top of his body. As he wrapped his arms around me, I nuzzled his neck with my nose and started to kiss him gently on the side of his face near his ear. I felt him tremble.

"Do you know what you're doing to me, Claire?"

"Oh yeah! I know you're excited; I felt you trembling. I'm not six years old, Johnnie. Maybe I haven't been with a man, but I do know what goes on during sex. What do you think I've been reading all these years, *Alice in Wonderland?*"

"Damn, you're a long-legged brat. Do you realize that if you keep doing what you're doing to me, you may find yourself wrapping those long legs around me? We'll end up making love."

"Okay." I shrugged my shoulders in a so-what attitude.

"Okay doesn't cut it, Claire. Listen to me carefully, I love you." He threw me off him and sat up. "I love you and I think you know I do. Don't take advantage of that. Do you love me? Even better...can you love me? Can you love a man with a missing part?" He sounded pathetic.

"Is that the only goddamn thing you ever think about – your foot? There's more to you than your foot. Its gone, Johnnie, and I don't give a damn...it doesn't matter to me. Everything that I love is still intact." Before I could think about what I'd just admitted, he fell on top of me. He held my face between his hands and kissed me until I couldn't breathe.

"Can we make love, Claire? Are you ready?"

"Yes and yes."

"It's your first time, aren't you afraid?"

"I'm not afraid – apprehensive maybe – not afraid. If I can admit that I love you, then I should be able to make love with you."

"Please don't sound so matter-of-fact about it. Say it with a little passion, please. For your information, Miss Soublet, you didn't tell me you loved me; you said you loved things that I have. Whatever that means."

"Same difference. What should I say to be passionate...let's fuck, big man?"

"You're putting on a comedy show to stall for time. You're not kidding me. You're not as brave as you pretend to be."

"Right, again. I confess. I haven't any idea what I'm supposed to do now. Help!"

"Ssssh. I'll show you," he told me. I sat obediently and waited.

Johnnie turned on the fan and darkened the room by closing the drapes over the Venetian blinds. He pulled me off the bed and stood me beside it and started to undress me. I grabbed his hands and held them. This time I was the one shaking.

He whispered, "It's all right, Claire, I love you. Please let me." I let go of his hands and closed my eyes.

He removed my skirt, my blouse, and my sandals. Then my bra. I quickly covered my breasts with my hands. When he tried to remove my panties, I grabbed his hands again. He let go, then pulled back the spread and lifted the top sheet for me to slip in. I watched him as he took off his shoes, his SACH foot, and then his clothes. He presented himself to me. "Here I am, he said softly, "all 90% of me. Do you still love me? Do you still want to make love with me?"

"Even more than I did before you took your clothes off." I pointed to his extraordinary erection. "I've read that no matter what anyone says, size does matter. So, big man, and I mean that literally, I can see what a very lucky girl I am. Damn, Johnnie!"

He laughed so hard, he lost what I had been so proud to be receiving. He crawled into bed, grabbed me and held me until we both stopped laughing. "Now, brat, we have some work to do to restore me to my former self. So, be quiet!"

For someone who just months before didn't want to be touched, I shocked myself. I allowed Johnnie to explore every nook and cranny of my body. I was a little timid to explore his, so he took my hands and guided me. He winced when I touched his stump. "It's okay," I whispered, "I want to touch it."

I tried to watch him put on a condom, but he turned his back to me. When he was ready, he pulled me under him and gently pushed inside my body. I don't remember if there was any discomfort. I only remember feeling Johnnie and the overwhelming release of loneliness. I seemed to intuitively know what to do to give us both pleasure. We made love and talked for hours forgetting about time, food, and the world around us. I knew I'd started a new phase of my life. There'd be fewer tears. I'd be stronger and tougher going forward.

"All good things must end, my sweet. We have an hour before my mother gets home. Let's take a quick bath. Is it okay if we eat at your house?" Johnnie started to get out of bed.

"It's okay, but wait. How did I do in Lovemaking 101, professor?" I vamped for him.

"You're volumma cum laude, baby. C'mon you spoiled brat, get up." He dragged me out of bed and held me away from him to look at me. He sighed. "Let's clean up fast and get out of this house or we'll be crawling right back in bed for more Lovemaking 101. C'mon, hop to it."

Miss Menard had a sheepish grin on her face when she saw us. I wondered if she could tell we'd just made love. I knew I was emotionally different, but did I look physically different? Did I have a glow? I was feeling some discomfort and a little stiff in a couple of areas of my body and I wondered if I walked funny because of it. She didn't make any comments about how I looked or walked or how long we'd been gone. She didn't even ask what the doctor had said.

After a short conversation, she excused herself and left us alone to eat.

Lena had baked mirlitons. While I heated them, I prepared a lettuce and tomato salad.

We were equally ravenous, so we split the pan down the middle and ate the whole thing. Only after the fact did I wonder if Lena had intended it to last more than one day.

"You must have great metabolism, Claire. You eat like a horse and yet you don't seem to gain any weight." Johnnie had watched me polish off the last of the salad right out of the bowl it was made in.

"I don't usually eat that much. Blame yourself - you and Lovemaking 101. I'm not complaining, mind you, just stating a fact." I fluttered my eyelashes at him. "How often do you suppose our class will meet?"

"Uh oh, the comedienne's back. Are you covering up regretting what we did, or are you really excited to do it again? You puzzle me sometimes, Claire. I don't think you always say what you're thinking."

Hey, this guy is good. He watches closely. For me, though, maybe that's not so good. I had to think for a few seconds how I wanted to tactfully word my answer.

"There's no doubt that in the morning some part of me will regret today. I guess that part doesn't want to be sidetracked ...away from my ultimate goals. You know, all the things we talked about on our first date."

"What about the other part of you?"

"That part...I guess it could let love and all that comes with it take over. Sometimes I think if I let it loose, I'll be wild."

"What in the hell are you talking about? Anyone with a tendency to be wild wouldn't be a virgin at twenty-two. You're talking crazy; you must be tired. I'm going home so you can get to bed early." Johnnie got up looking perturbed and worried at the same time.

"Sit, please." I pushed him down gently. "I'm not delusional or anything else. I've been thinking about what Dr. La Croix…"

"I knew…I knew it! I knew you still had that crap rolling around in your head."

"Let me finish. Maybe I am like my mother and that's why I've fought so hard to be clean, pure and chaste. I didn't want to be like her, but half the blood coursing through my veins belongs to her. I can't get new blood and new genes the way you got a new foot."

Johnnie grabbed me and tried to hold me but I pulled away. "You're not your mother, Claire. You'll never be her. What would make you think that?"

"I had too much fun today. I really, really enjoyed making love. I think I could do it every day." Even though I was dead serious, I had to smile just thinking about how good it had been.

"Isn't a part of that sentence missing? Shouldn't you have said enjoyed making love with me? Wasn't I involved?"

"You're getting a wee bit touchy. I think we're both tired. Why don't you go home." I started clearing the table and stacking things in the sink. "Lena's going to have a shit-fit when she finds these dirty dishes waiting for her tomorrow. Too bad."

Johnnie stood up again. His tall, lean frame fooled the eye. With his clothing peeled away he was a perfect form, one akin to a cheetah – sinewy, muscular, and agile. He was spare but strong. The missing foot did not diminish his prowess. I realized I would be hungry for him every time I looked at him. He literally filled me up with no room to spare. At that moment, I dared not hold him to say goodbye. I'd have to wait until I saw him in a private setting to touch him again. Damn, I thought, that would never satisfy me in the long run.

"I'll see myself out, Claire. Call me tomorrow when you get up." There was no embrace, no kiss. Did he know what I had been thinking? Had we had the same thoughts?

I needed to examine myself before I went to bed. I tried to see what I thought Johnnie saw when he held me away from him and sighed. I had breasts now. They were mid-size, but seemed to have given him a veritable feast. Very long legs that I knew he liked. No butt. Well, you can't have everything. Hair didn't matter; we both had the same type - a bit rough but manageable. I had learned to keep mine long so that I could pile it on top my head in summer, wear a beret in winter, and when I wanted it straighter, I got a reverse permanent.

When I removed my panties, there were several, small spots of blood on them. Boy, I thought, my hymen must have been almost dried up. It had, after all, waited a long time.

Sleep was out of the question. I tossed and turned. I got up and got a warm glass of milk. I counted sheep. I read a few magazines. Nothing worked. I finally sat up in bed in the dark and made an attempt to recreate, in my mind's eye, making love with Johnnie. I felt like an intruder. It was no substitute for the real thing. I needed to be there, in the thick of things…participating. Had I finally outgrown daydreaming?

Then fear set in. Were my ultimate goals taking a backseat to passion? Did I love Johnnie or was he my savior? I remember feeling that well of loneliness empty out when I was in his arms. Was the empty well just temporary and would it fill up again when I realized Johnnie wasn't really who I wanted? Would he let me maintain my independence or would he bring possessiveness - he the possessor; I the possessed? After all, he was that "Creole I didn't want to marry." He was, however, educated. Would that make a difference? Did he just want to travel but live in New Orleans permanently? I wanted to get out forever!

Sleep finally came…I don't know when.

– 24 –

GENES: NO EXCHANGES
OR REFUNDS

The run-down, tired, always-out-of-energy feeling persisted. Johnnie took me to one of his friends from his Xavier University days who had a new practice in the same building as Dr. La Croix. I hoped I'd have better luck with a younger doctor and with someone who didn't know me.

Dr. Beauchamp had a wonderful bedside manner and showed complete interest in what was troubling me. He examined me and ordered a blood test. He asked me to return the next week for the results. The test revealed I was severely anemic. He recommended I take an iron supplement, drink about four ounces of red wine every day and eat calf's liver two or three times a week. He also suggested I wait a year before going on for my master's degree. The doctor asked if I felt depressed or had suffered any traumatic events recently. I gave him a condensed version of my life. Not being a psychiatrist, he said, he wasn't going to speculate about my mental or emotional state. But he thought the stress may have built up over the years and was just now surfacing. He recommended I see someone and that I try Flint Goodridge and Charity Hospitals to find out if any of the psychiatrists on their staffs were available. I didn't say it to him but I knew that wasn't an option.

I asked how long it would be before I'd see a real change in my overall, energy level. The doctor thought if I was diligent about taking my iron supplement and following his diet recommendations, I should begin to see results in six to eight weeks. He thought I should expect to be "back-to-normal" in about three months.

It was already the end of July and school would be starting in about six weeks. I had to make a decision soon. There was no point in discussing my dilemma with Miss Menard or Johnnie. I had a good idea what they'd want me to do. I already knew the back-to-normal process would be slow and that I could do nothing to expedite it. I had to wait it out. Still, my decision took a whole month.

I talked to Miss Menard first. She was just making her afternoon cup of tea.

"I've decided to take a year off as the doctor suggested," I told her.

"I'm so glad. I think you've made the right decision, Claire."

"Well...yes and no. It's right because I don't think I can get my energy level up to where it should be with all the pressures of school. I'm physically not able to handle a heavy load right now. On the other hand, a year off will put me a year behind schedule." I got up and put the kettle back on the stove to make myself a cup of tea.

"Let your schedule go for a while and enjoy life a little bit." Miss Menard got a cup and saucer for me.

"What I think I'll do is take the whole three months the doctor talked about to just rest, that would go through October. In November, I'll get a job and earn some money to help pay for my tuition. This is grad school; I don't have a scholarship. Sister Magdalena told me they'd give me a break on tuition, though."

"Claire, that's terrific news. They've been very good to you."

"I know, but so have you. That's why I want to earn some money so that I can relieve you of some of your responsibility for me. It's time for me to start paying you back. I need to show you how much I appreciate what you've done for me." It was the first time I had given her such a detailed outpouring of appreciation. I surprised myself. Tears threatened to spill down my cheeks. I quickly blinked them back.

"Job...I won't hear of it. Every day you've spent in this house with me has been pay back. Having you here has meant more to me than I can ever tell you. I was not obligated to you any more than you were to me. We traded services. I didn't give you any more than you've given me." Miss Menard sighed heavily as her eyes grew moist.

"That's not true. After the house burned down, I came to you with a bag of clothes and a bag of family heirlooms. Everything else I owned was gone."

"I know what it is to have a hard life. I haven't always been in these circumstances."

"But Miss Menard, you never let me pay for anything, even when I've worked. I've done nothing but go to school. No cleaning, no cooking, no taking care of you. In fact, I can't cook. In my whole life I've never done anything but make coffee and tea. Oh, I forgot, I can scramble eggs, make toast and heat cooked food."

"I've never complained, have I?"

"No, you haven't. There's something else I want you to know. I never squandered the money you gave me. I've saved a lot of it."

"That's what I hoped you'd do. I may have to leave you one of these days and I want you to be able to take care of yourself. The money your grandmother left you and the money you've saved will give you a start."

"What kind of 'leave me' are you talking about?" I thought the term sounded too vague.

"Die or become senile. Dying is forever, but living and being senile is a long hard road. I don't want anyone to have to live with me, much less take care of me if that happens."

"I remember my great-aunt. She was senile. My grandmother had a hard time taking care of her before she died."

"I wouldn't want to be that kind of burden to anyone. I've told Leonard to make sure I'm put in a good nursing home if I should become senile - not like the one across the street from your old house. I really would like to die here, in my own bed. I hope God let's me. Leonard is older than I am and he's been very ill lately. I hope he outlives me so he can make sure things go the way I want them to when my time comes. I know that sounds selfish, doesn't it?"

"Not really, but do you mind if we talk about something else? I'm getting really depressed. The thought of you dying or becoming senile is more than I want to ponder right now." I busily stirred my tea looking down at the table. I was beginning to get choked up.

"One last thing, I want you with me when the time comes. I'd also like to know you have Johnnie in your life and I'm not leaving you alone." She sniffed and suddenly found it necessary to look in the refrigerator. Then she closed it as quickly as she'd opened it.

"My future doesn't depend on Johnnie or any other man. I think he knows that, at least I hope he does."

"I think you need to talk to him about that. I get the impression he wants to marry you." She wrinkled her nose and pursed her mouth clearly signaling she'd divulged a secret. "Listen, don't tell Johnnie I said anything to you."

Oh shit, they'd discussed it! This was happening to me again. First my grandmother with Bobby, now Miss Menard with Johnnie.

"I won't say anything. But don't be surprised if…" Someone was knocking.

"Hello. Were your ears burning?" I teased Johnnie as I let him in. "We were just talking about you."

"Good or bad?" he asked.

"Neither. Miss Menard had just asked when I expected you and before I could answer, you knocked. It's 2:00 in the afternoon, what are you doing here so early?" I got a good look at his face then and realized something was wrong.

"I had to take my mother to the hospital this morning. Her leg's been feverish and swollen for two or three days. But you know my mother. She insisted on treating herself because she didn't want to miss work."

"What's wrong with her leg?"

"She has a blood clot in it. The only reason she went to the hospital was because she couldn't walk at all this morning and I forced her to go. She's in Flint Goodridge."

When we got to the kitchen, Miss Menard had gone to her room. I made a pot of coffee for Johnnie.

"I was supposed to go to Clark High today," Johnnie told me, "to interview with the football coach. The other teacher vying for the assistant coach job was supposed to be there, too. When I called the principal to tell him why I couldn't make it, he told me that in light of my mother's illness, he thought I should concentrate on her and not the coaching job. So, I took the hint and I bowed out."

"He was right, though. Don't you think so?"

"I dunno. I think I'm upset because I was counting on that pay from the extra job. I'd planned to save every penny of it."

"Look around at other schools. Maybe one of them has a position open. It might even be a better offer. School doesn't start for a few weeks. You might get lucky."

"That's an idea. But you know what, I think the principal used my mother as an easy out. He really didn't want a coach with one foot; the others might not either."

"Oh shit, Johnnie! Never mind. Guess what I did today?" It was pointless to argue with him when he was feeling sorry for himself. "I decided to take the year off the doctor suggested. I told Miss Menard a little while ago. She doesn't want me to work, but I think I will anyway. After I get better, I'm going to find a job. Are you hungry?"

"Yes, a little. I'm going back to the hospital when I leave here."

"I'll go with you if you want me to."

"Okay, that sounds good. I could use some moral support right about now."

"What about a plate of red beans and rice?" I started rummaging in the refrigerator to see what else there was. "Oh, here's some pork chops and gravy."

"My stomach is growling. I'll take some of everything."

While I changed, Johnnie washed and dried the dishes. I fully expected to see Miss Menard in the kitchen when I returned, but she hadn't come out of her room. I walked back there and knocked on her door to tell her what had happened and where I was going. She called to me through the door that she was on the phone and she'd see me later.

On the way to the hospital I asked Johnny how long his mother would be hospitalized. Maybe a week, he thought. I invited him to eat with us as long as he needed to. I was sure Miss Menard wouldn't mind. When I asked him if there was anyone he needed to call, he swung the car around and headed toward his house.

"Thanks, Claire. I had forgotten my mother asked me to call my aunt in Chicago."

"I didn't know you had an aunt in Chicago." In all the years I'd known his family, I had never heard Emily or anyone else mention anyone in Chicago.

"My mother's sister. They haven't spoken in over thirty years. My mother stole my aunt's boyfriend and then married him."

"You're kidding!" I tried hard not to grin. Hmm, Mrs. Valcour, that little devil had set the example. No wonder her daughter didn't hesitate to take what she thought was mine.

"I wish I was kidding. And get that 'I know a secret' grin off your face. My aunt took my grandmother and moved to Chicago right after the wedding. Neither of them ever wrote or spoke to my mother after that. All my mother's folks are in Chicago." Johnnie looked at me as if he was sorry he'd told me.

"Who did you live with in Baton Rouge while you were at Southern University?"

"My father's people." Johnnie pulled into his driveway and turned off the ignition, He quickly started the car again. "I don't know who to really ask for when I call. The hell with it."

"Johnnie, c'mon. Your mother asked you to do this. Don't disappoint her."

"The number I have is about five years old. One of my cousins was visiting from Chicago and gave my mother the number. My cousin asked her not to tell anyone where she got it."

The number was disconnected and there wasn't a forwarding one. Johnnie was relieved.

"You know what this call is all about, don't you, Claire? My mother's scared she's going to die. Why in the goddamn hell did she wait this long to get in touch with them? It's a little too late to think about going to hell." He slammed the receiver on its cradle. I had never heard him use the Lord's name in vain. He sure complained when I did.

I followed Johnnie to his room. He said he felt hot and sticky and needed to take a quick bath. I asked if I could bathe with him. No, he said, he needed a couple of minutes alone.

So used to being alone and rejection free, I wasn't too happy he had refused me. I told myself I understood why he'd done it, but it didn't make me feel any better. I plopped down on his bed on my back and stared up at the ceiling. What was wrong with thinking we could make a little love since we were already there? He didn't seem to be in too big of a hurry to get to the hospital. That didn't seem selfish to me. I liked being with Johnnie and we'd made love only once after the first time. It was the day he'd taken me to my appointment with Dr. Beauchamp.

Why was he rationing lovemaking? He knew I liked to do it, so what was the problem? He couldn't believe I was too fragile to do it often. And if he did, why didn't he ask me if I was? We would get into heavy petting after Miss Menard went to bed, but it never went any further than that. He was teaching me to drive, and after we'd finish my lesson, we'd often park near the lake if the mosquitoes weren't too bad. We'd kiss and touch but never get...beyond...that...

"Claire! Claire! Wake up!" I opened one eye and looked at Johnnie. "I'm glad you're taking a year off. I think you need a lot more time to get your strength back. Do you want to stay here and sleep while I go to the hospital?" He started to pull back the spread.

"No, don't." I put the spread back over the pillows. "I just need to wash my face." I stumbled to the bathroom where I put a cold towel on my face, combed my hair, then put on some lipstick.

Neither of us said a word on the way to the hospital. Johnnie seemed agitated and I was still in the process of waking up. I didn't know if he was aggravated with me, his mother, or the loss of the coaching job.

There was no parking on the hospital lot or in the immediate vicinity. We had to park four blocks away. The area around the hospital was notorious for its crime, so you had to walk looking over your shoulder.

I wanted to wait in the downstairs lobby for Johnnie, but he insisted I go up with him.

When we got to the nurses station on his mother's floor, I told him I'd rather wait there while he went in alone. If his mother asked to see me, then I would come in. About fifteen minutes later, he came out to get me. He was beaming.

"Your mother must be better," I said.

"She is. Whew!" Johnnie ran his index finger across his forward as if removing sweat. "That's a load off my mind. The clot is in her calf, which is good. They're giving her blood thinning medication and she seems better already. C'mon, she wants to see you."

Mrs. Valcour was sitting up in bed with her leg elevated. With her eyeglasses on the tip of her nose, she turned her head slowly toward the door like a cobra when it's coming out of a basket. I had never seen her without makeup and was stunned to see how old she looked. Not even a hint of a smile greeted me.

"What possessed you to come here, Claire? You couldn't come to my house for dinner when I invited you, but you can come here. Why? Did you want to see me sick and old looking? Or did you think I was dying? You'd like that, wouldn't you? You're..."

Johnnie cut his mother off. "Mother, what's the matter with you?" he yelled.

"You don't think I know this cheeky little bitch has been in my house screwing you when I wasn't home. Old man Danneau told me; he saw her." She turned to me again. "You're a trifling, slant-eyed wench. You ain't got no Creole pappy. It musta been some Chinaman, cuz your mammy screwed anything with a set of balls." Mrs. Valcour had switched to the vernacular. She sounded just like Emily. "You the fruit from your mammy's tree and you been trying to make everybody believe you so pious and that you such a good, little girl. I ain't forgot how you tried to make my poor dead Emily look like a slut. I don't want you in my house, you hear me? Don't come to my house to fuck my son...no damn mo!" Gasping, she threw her head back on her pillows.

Johnnie rang for the nurse just as she was entering the room.

"What in God's name is going on in here?" She went to check Mrs. Valcour's intravenous feeding pole and then asked us to leave. Johnnie told his mother he'd be back after he took me home. The nurse suggested he come back in the morning.

I hadn't opened my mouth the whole time. My eyes had been downcast; I looked at the foot of Mrs. Valcour's bed. Every arrow pierced me. I flinched as I felt them wound me.

"I'm sorry, Claire," Johnnie told me on the elevator. "I never would have asked you to go into my mother's room if I had known what she intended to say to you. I'm not going to ask you to forgive her because she's sick; nothing can ever excuse what she just did to you." He didn't say anything more except goodnight when he dropped me off.

I remained silent because I had no words. I had been muted.

"Claire," Miss Menard was calling me and knocking on my door, "Johnnie's on the phone.

"I don't want to speak to him," I told her. There wasn't anyone I wanted to talk to, I just wanted to be alone to have time to lick my wounds and regroup.

"Is that what you want me to tell him?" she asked in a chastising voice. "Did something happen between you two yesterday?"

"Ask him." I could hear her wheelchair rolling away from the door. Johnnie would tell her, of that I had no doubt. He had told her everything else. I wasn't sure how to face her after he filled her in. I needed to get out of the house. It was Sunday. There was always Mass.

I dressed for church. I didn't want to go to Corpus Christi for fear Johnnie might wait around the church for me. I decided I'd go to St. Peter Claver instead. It was in the opposite direction.

Miss Menard was waiting for me with my place at the table set with coffee and toast. Why? I never ate before Mass – I usually took Communion. Did she think I wouldn't be taking the sacrament because I'd been screwing lately? Actually I wasn't going to take Communion because I hadn't had the courage to go to confession and tell the priest what I'd done – but how could she know that? I was angry with the world and that included her.

"Good morning." My greeting was flat, almost threatening.

"Good morning, Claire. Sit down, please. I want to talk to you. Can you go to a later Mass or skip it this Sunday. I think this is important and God will understand. Please, cher."

"I need to go to Mass with the way I'm feeling, Miss Menard. This is not a good time for me to talk. I don't want to rehash what happened last night. I'm angry and humiliated and that makes me dangerous."

"Listen to me, cher. You haven't done anything to be ashamed of. Johnnie's mother is a lonely, bitter, old woman. She knows her son loves you and she's jealous. And because it's you, it makes it that much worse. Ignore her."

"I can't, Johnnie lives with her. She depends on him. She'll need him even more now."

"Let her need him and let him do what a son is supposed to do for his mother. That shouldn't have anything to do with his relationship with you."

"Oh, but it will. She'll find a way to get between us. Every chance she'll get, she'll make him feel guilty for neglecting her or for something else. And he'll be too damn blind to see she's manipulating him."

"Johnnie's not a fool, Claire. If he loves you the way he says he does, he won't let her wreck things for the two of you. And if you love him, then make love with him – that's your right. It's no one's business, certainly not his mother's. You don't have to do it in her house. You have a house of your own. And you making love with Johnnie is all right with me. I'm not a prude."

To say I was shocked would truly be understating what I was feeling at that moment. "I think right now all of my desire to make love is gone; it's been zapped away. If I'm not careful, I'll end up being a man hater." I slammed the coffee cup so hard on the saucer, I made Miss Menard jump. "Every goddamn nasty and bitter thing that's happened to me has involved a man. Let's run them down: my father Lester, Uncle Gus, the bishop, Bobby and Michael McArdle. Did I forget anyone?"

"Do you count Donovan?" Miss Menard cautiously asked.

"No, he was too wimpy. Him I should have kept. I could have snapped my fingers and he would have begged like a dog. In fact, I think that actually happened once." I had to smile when I pictured him doing that the day he followed me after church.

"Don't count Johnnie in that bunch…yet. His mother's youth is gone; that's why she envies you and calls you names. She knows you're beautiful and knows her son knows it, too. So don't fall out of love with him so fast, and certainly not because of her. Love him in spite of her."

I knew she was right. But did I love Johnnie enough to go up against his mother? I didn't think I had the stomach for it. Life had been tough enough already. Why should I have to engage that old witch in battle in order to secure her son's love?

As usual Miss Menard seemed to know what I was thinking. "Nothing in life is easy, Claire. I'm going to surprise you one day soon when I tell you my life story. Well, not really tell you; you'll read it. I think it's about time, don't you?"

"Yes, it's about time. You've promised me for years. So frankly, I'm not sure I believe you. And what do you mean I'll read it? Have you written your autobiography?"

"I guess that's what you'd call it. Leonard has been cleaning up my English and typing my story for me. I'm not too good with writing. Remember, I'm not formally educated like you."

"That's crazy! You're smarter than anyone I know. You didn't need a formal education. Look what you've accomplished without one." I'm sure she knew I meant her house and her seemingly infinite bank account.

"Thank you, cher, but remember these are only material things. Anyway...Leonard tells me he needs some more time to finish it. If he wasn't sick so much of the time, it would have been finished months ago. I hope we're not both dead before it's completed."

"Wow, I can't wait. After all this time, it had better be spectacular, my good madam. In fact, it better be juicy, raw and full of sex!" I stomped my feet on the floor a couple of times and pounded on the table. I had forgotten all about Johnnie and our problems. "And you and Leonard had better be alive when I get it because I'm sure I'll have a thousand questions."

Miss Menard laughed hard. "Okay, so you're anxious to read it, huh. I hope you'll feel the same way about me after you do. I promise to give it to you as soon as it's finished. You might say...hot off the press."

– 25 –

BLESS ME FATHER FOR I HAVE SINNED

School had started without me for the first time in sixteen years. I wondered how I could have allowed myself to be talked into taking a year off. Less than a month into my hiatus and boredom was already nipping at my heels.

Miss Menard seemed to grow weaker by the day. Even though she slept through the night and well into the morning, she didn't arrive in the kitchen for our morning coffee until almost 10:00. After lunch, she returned to her room for a long nap and didn't come out again until after 5:00. When I told her how concerned I was about how much she was sleeping, she shrugged it off and told me the doctor had informed her that as congestive heart failure progressed, she'd need more and more rest. She said the illness now controlled her life.

Alma, the woman who cleaned for us, was the only person allowed in Miss Menard's room now. Lena and I had to speak to her through the door if we couldn't wait for her to come out to the kitchen. I often wondered if she was actually sleeping all those hours or if she was up to something she wanted to keep private. With Lena always snooping around, I didn't blame her.

In recent months, Lena seemed to be a changed woman. She was still nosy but she'd finally stopped being so antagonistic toward me. She'd cut her work schedule to two days a week and spent all her time cooking and cleaning the kitchen. There were no more of those strange phone calls. With her hair dyed a reddish brown, she looked ten years younger. Her clothes were all updated and her fingernails and toenails were polished. When Miss Menard commented on how great she looked, Lena smiled and said because all her kids, except one, were "out of the way," she had a few dollars to spend on herself.

Johnnie's mother had finally been released from the hospital. She'd been kept additional weeks after developing a second clot behind the knee in the same leg. Johnnie didn't want to leave Mrs. Valcour home alone when he started his teaching job, but when he suggested she remain in the hospital for two more weeks, she refused. And it didn't take much for her to convince him to pass on the job at Clark High. She told him how expensive an extended hospital stay would be and then reminded him what the principal had done to him with the assistant coaching job. He also knew there was no one else they could call upon to help them, nor would his mother allow a stranger in her house.

Mrs. Valcour claimed to be in constant pain and unable to put any weight on her leg. Most of her time was spent in bed while Johnnie waited on her like the nurses at Flint Goodridge Hospital – to her no request was unreasonable. He rented her a wheelchair, but she wouldn't use it unless he pushed her wherever she wanted to go, even from her bedroom to the living room. He complained but did nothing to change the situation.

Johnnie's only free time was Sunday afternoon when his mother's club members came to visit her after they went to Mass. They'd arrive with hot glazed donuts from McKenzie's Bakery and then make the coffee to drink with them. They spent the afternoon gossiping and laughing with Mrs. Valcour while Johnnie used that time to come and have lunch with Miss Menard and me. And this was the only time Miss Menard mustered enough energy to spend an hour or so sitting with us on the patio. Johnnie had built a wooden ramp for her to get from the kitchen out to the patio. Mr. Dejean's magic hands had turned the gardens around the house into a feast for the eyes. He'd filled them with magnificent trees and blooming flowers. The patio was a wonderful place to sit and enjoy it all, even in the fall when the leaves were falling.

While we were waiting for Miss Menard to join us one Sunday afternoon, Johnnie was unusually quiet and lost inside himself. I asked him if there was anything wrong.

"I know it's a lot to ask, Claire, but please be patient. I know my mother's taking advantage of me, but I don't know what else to do right now. I can't let her fend for herself all day. If something happened to her because of something I did...or didn't do, I couldn't live with myself." He couldn't look at me. He looked down as he played with the crease in his pant leg.

"Patience, huh. I'm trying, Johnnie. But I think you know by now patience isn't one of my virtues. At least you know you're being taken advantage of. What I really feel, though, is your absence. I miss you."

"Boy, am I glad to hear that! Because lately, you've been coming across as cold and disinterested. Sometimes I wake up during the night touching the other side of the bed hoping you'll magically appear beside me. That's crazy, isn't it? Especially when we've never spent the night together."

"Uh huh, that is crazy. What exactly do you miss about me?"

"Your enthusiasm for making love...you spoiled me. I miss that, Claire."

"Oh, so you don't miss the whole me; you miss my vagina. Damn, that makes me feel great."

"That's not what I meant and you know it." Just as Johnnie pulled me up from my chair with plans to hold me close, Miss Menard opened the kitchen door and rolled down the ramp.

"Oh my, poor timing. I'm sorry." She chuckled and spun her wheelchair around to head back into the kitchen.

"No, no," I said as Johnnie and I sat down again, "come back. You're not intruding. We can save it."

Miss Menard looked at Johnnie for confirmation. He winked at her and used a hand signal. "Come on back, we were just killing time until you got here."

As she rolled onto the patio, she asked Johnnie how his mother was getting along, something I never did.

"She's doing okay. It's a slow process, but she's walking a little more these days. She wants to be back in the kitchen by Thanksgiving."

"I'm glad to hear that. I suppose you'll start looking for a job soon, won't you?'

"Yeah, in a couple of weeks. I want to wait to see if my mother's going to sell the house and move to Lafayette. A friend of hers just lost her husband and the house is too big for her now. She wants my mother to move there."

My fingers and toes began to tingle. Hallelujah! The old bag was going to move hundreds of miles away from New Orleans. That was too good to be true.

Miss Menard's voice brought me back to reality. "Cajun country, huh. Are you going to stay in the house in Gentilly?"

"No, she's expecting me to move to Lafayette with her. But...ah...ain't no way."

Needless to say my head shook from shock. The hesitation seemed to suggest he was unsure. I stared hard at Johnnie waiting for him to state with certainty he was not going. Instead he laughed, then quickly changed the subject. "This is 1956, ladies, when are you going to put a television in your house? No one lives in this day and age without a TV."

"We've been too busy to spend time in front of a silly, little box. I'm reading quite a bit, so I don't have a need to be entertained beyond that. My life has been full of entertainment; I haven't missed much. What do you think?" Miss Menard pointed to me.

"Umm...I've seen TV a couple of times, but like you I've been too busy. While I was in school, I didn't have time for anything else. I did turn on your TV once, Johnnie, and I think I must have gotten one of those ongoing stories, a serial of some kind." I was talking about television, but still thinking about Lafayette. After 22 years I had given myself to someone, body and soul, and now he may walk right out of my life. Feeling more contrite than usual, I knew I couldn't put off going to Confession any longer.

"That was probably *The Guiding Light.* My mother watches it religiously every day. All of her friends watch what they call 'their stories.' I run for the hills when that crap is on."

"You don't have to run for the hills; why don't you come here?" Miss Menard chirped. I could sometimes let things pass without comment but not her. I imagined she was one helluva businesswoman.

"Now, Miss Menard, why do you want to put me on the spot?"

"Because we don't see enough of you now. We miss you, don't we, Claire?"

"He knows," I said, "so please stop massaging his ego. He believes in 'absence makes the heart grow fonder.' Sunday-only visits seem fine with him."

Johnnie ignored my jeer. "I think you should get a TV. You'll both have a new toy to occupy your time. I know you'll enjoy having one, especially you, Claire, now that you're home more often."

"What do you watch, Johnnie?" Miss Menard wanted to know.

"News shows mostly. I like to know what's happening in the world. I used to like to listen to westerns and some mysteries on the radio. Now I watch them on TV."

"My God, news shows! How can you listen to all that propaganda? Those news people just try to control the way you think. I get my fill of what's wrong with the world when I read the newspaper every morning and that's enough."

"Careful now. You're sounding like a commie. Don't force me to inform on you. I just might be secretly working for Joe McCarthy." Johnnie tried to keep a straight face.

"Well, Johnnie Valcour, if there's one thing I'm an expert on...that's people. I would have known you to be a spy the moment I laid eyes on you. Claire would have had to bury you under that magnolia tree over there because I would have put a bullet through your heart before I learned your name." Miss Menard's face glowed red hot. Her hands were twitching.

Johnnie didn't seem bothered by what she'd said. "Maybe the two of you would like variety shows. There's *Ed Sullivan, Milton Berle and Jack Benny.* But with the way you think, Claire, you probably wouldn't like Jack Benny's show."

"Why wouldn't she?" Miss Menard snapped, still perturbed at his last statement.

I answered. "Because Rochester has that 'Yassah, Mistah Binny' shit...that 'Uncle Tom' kind of crap. I didn't listen to him on radio, so you know I don't want to see him on TV."

"Oh," was all Miss Menard said.

"See, I knew it. Well, maybe you like Elvis Presley. He's always a guest on one of those shows." Johnnie stood up and made believe he was strumming a guitar.

"Do the rest," I urged him. "Gyrate those hips, baby, or you ain't no Elvis Presley!"

"Sorry, I can't; I'm out of prac..." Johnnie's mouth stayed open but the last syllable never made it out of his mouth. Miss Menard and I howled.

Johnnie waited for us to stop laughing. "Claire, how do you know what Elvis does with his hips?"

"C'mon now, I do read the paper. Some people like his swivel hips; others think he's vulgar and disgraceful. I think he's a good-looking White boy who spent a lot of time around those juke joints in Mississippi listening to Colored musicians. Now he's getting rich singing their kind of music. Don't get me started, okay?"

"Yes, ma'am."

"Johnnie, no man should ever be out of practice. You've got to find the time to do it, right, Claire?" Miss Menard winked at me.

"Yup, that's right." I looked at Johnnie. "Sorry, old chap, I had to call a spade a spade."

He drew up his mouth in something between a smile and a smirk, "Can we get back to discussing television? Listen, there's a lot of different kinds of shows on. It depends on what appeals to you."

"I like comedy and I guess variety. Are we getting a television now?" I expected Miss Menard to say she'd think about it because she seemed to have given up on how much of the outside world she allowed to get inside her home.

"We'll have a TV as soon as one can be delivered," she said. "I'll have Leonard take care of it this week."

"Damn that was too easy. Are you sure you want that squawk box in your house? Why don't you think about it for a few days before you call him?" I didn't think she had considered how much time she spent sleeping. When would she ever watch it? Then it occurred to me she was probably getting it for me.

"No, no mulling it over. I will be up and about more. I promise I won't spend as much time in my room now."

We heard the front gate open and close. The hinges had rusted from the rain and humidity. As I walked to the front of the house, I made a mental note to ask Mr. Dejean to oil them. I met Morris Hebert, Lena's husband, as he rounded the front porch.

"Ah heard talkin, so Ah was comin back dere. I need to talk to Miss Sera, Claire."

"Okay." I walked back to the patio and Morris followed me. Johnnie pulled up a chair for him but he shook his head.

"No, thanks. Ah cain't stay."

"You look troubled, Morris. Has something happened to Lena or one of your children?" Miss Menard asked.

"Yes, ma'am, Ah guess you could say dat. Lena didn't tell y'all she was quittin and leavin town?"

"No," Miss Menard and I blurted out in unison.

"Dis mornin, Lena sen me to Mass wif ma youngist girl...da only chil we got at home na. Lena say she sick. When we got back, she gone. Lef me a letta tellin me she so misable wif me, she had to go. Say not to try to fine her, cuz she ain't comin back."

"She left her five children, Morris; I don't believe she'll stay away. Even if she claims to be tired of you, she wouldn't leave those children." I wondered if Miss Menard believed what she was telling Lena's husband or if she was trying to give him a modicum of hope. I believed the opposite. After all the phone calls I'd listened to, plus seeing Lena with another man at the motel, I felt she had been waiting for the right opportunity to be free of Morris as well as her kids. After all, they were all out of the house and on their own, except the last girl who was about sixteen.

"Ma'am, Lena don want to be married no mo. She been changing fa a lon time. Y'all neva notice dat?"

"I did but I thought it was the change of life. Women do funny things during the change, Morris." Miss Menard looked at me hoping I'd concur. "Claire?"

"I'm the wrong one to answer that question, Morris. Your wife wasn't always kind to me, so I tried to steer clear of her as much as possible. There were times when I wanted to send her home with her face caved in." I said that rather than tell him she had probably run away with the man she was with at the motel or someone else. I suddenly remembered one of Lena's phone conversations when she told one of her girlfriends what a dumbass, country boy she'd married and that he'd never know she was running around behind his back. "He ten years older than me, girl," she'd said. "In a few years, he won't be able to get it up. If the trut be tol, he ain't wurt nothin na."

"Ah'm sorry, Miss Sera," Morris said, "Lena shoulda tol y'all she wasn't comin back so y'all coulda got somebody else to cook and clean everyday."

"Lena wasn't coming every day. She was only here two days a week. I have a woman who comes in to clean. Lena only cooked when she was here." Miss Menard looked at me out of the corners of her eyes and her look told me she now had an idea what I'd refused to tell her years ago about Lena.

Morris nodded several times as if something suddenly made sense. "She never tol me she work ony two days. Evey day she leave da house like she workin and she got even mo money den befo. When Ah ax her bout it, she say she got a raise."

"Oh, Morris, I'm sorry she did that to you."

"Don be sorry, Miss Menard. She gon; she jes gon, dat's all dere is to it." Morris closed his eyes and shrugged his shoulders. "When ma girl gits outta school, we gon go back to da country to live. Ah'm mo happy dere, anyway."

"Good for you, Morris. You're still young enough to find another wife and I hope you do."

"Ah sho am, Miss Menard, Ah'm gon git a country girl dis time. Say, do y'all need somebody to cook fa y'all? Ah could probly fin y'all somebody."

"Thank you, Morris, but I think we'll be all right. I'm sure the cleaning lady wouldn't mind working a few more days."

"Okay, Miss Menard, but if you eva need us for anythin, jes holla. You been good to Lena, Ah know, so dat mean you was good to me and ma churen. Ah won forgit. Good evenin, y'all." Morris quickly walked away from the patio.

"That poor man. Marriage, huh. Damn marriage!" Miss Menard smacked both arms of her chair and left that pronouncement hanging in the air as she flipped herself around and rolled up the ramp. "Excuse me, I need to rest."

Rest...indeed! First Johnnie's teasing comments about Miss Menard being a communist, then Morris arrived to tell her about Lena. It had been too much. I had only seen her that angry once before – the night of my encounter with the policeman.

"Is she going to be okay, Claire?" Johnnie looked worried.

"I don't know; I hope so. With her bad heart, she sure as hell doesn't need to get as angry as she is right now." I thought about asking him why he liked to call people names like commie or the names he'd called Dr. La Croix's son, but I didn't. I realized that he and Emily were apples that hadn't fallen far from the tree.

"How's about getting a couple of oyster loaves for lunch? That might cheer her up."

I thought about all the food Lena had prepared on Friday. No wonder she'd cooked so many different dishes. She must have had a touch of conscience when she thought about leaving us high and dry. Her good deed didn't mean much to me; she was still a lousy witch for leaving her husband and her kids the way she had. It would serve her right if she got dumped by her new man and had to crawl back to New Orleans only to find her husband had moved back to the country and had found himself a new wife. Too bad I didn't believe in voodoo. If I did, I'm sure for a few dollars an old hoodoo woman would be only too eager to burn a black candle and do some chanting to put a curse on Lena.

"Claire!"

"Sorry. I was thinking about all the cooked food we have," I half-lied. "Lena made a lot of different things when she was here Friday; we need to eat some of it."

"You have all week to eat that stuff. C'mon, let's go. I think Miss Menard will enjoy a loaf, don't you?"

"I don't know, Johnnie. I can't speak for her." My answer was acerbic.

Johnnie jumped out of his chair. "Well, tell you what. I'll go home and have lunch and you and Miss Menard can eat what you have in the refrigerator. But I'm not stupid, Claire. Whatever is wrong with you has nothing to do with food. You've got a bug up your butt for some other reason. Care to talk about it?"

"Not really. I'll wait to see what you do. If you choose to move to Lafayette with your mother, I can't stop you. So there's nothing to discuss."

"Didn't I say I wasn't going? What else do you want from me? You want it in writing? Should I have it notarized, too?"

"Don't be so goddamn nasty about it. You sound guilty...like you're really considering it. How do you think I feel after I let you...let you...oh, you know what I'm trying to say? You introduce me to sex and then you don't have time for it anymore. And now you're talking about moving away." My voice went up several octaves. I was screeching.

"Oh shit, Claire, go to confession. Ask God to forgive you for losing your virginity. You're twenty-two goddamn years old; you're not sixteen. I didn't take advantage of you; we both wanted it. I think you probably wanted it more than me and you'd be ready to do it every damn day if I agreed!"

"You lousy bastard! So now I'm oversexed."

"No, damnit, I'm just the bastard telling you the truth. Your problem is you're paranoid. You're so used to everyone leaving you that you think I'm going to leave you, too. I don't intend to leave you, Claire, unless you insist on keeping up this 'you took my virginity' crap."

I was humiliated. "Go home, Johnnie. We've said enough. All this shit isn't getting us anywhere. Do whatever you want; I don't give a damn."

"Okay," he said. And without another word, he stormed off the patio.

I sat for a long time trying not to think, trying to keep the fear and rage out of my head. There was really only one thing that would make me calm. I wondered if Father O'Mara was in the rectory. I left a note for Miss Menard and headed for the priests' house at Corpus Christi.

Mrs. Lenoir, the housekeeper, was off on Sunday, so I had to ring the bell for a long time before I heard footsteps approaching the door. Father Pitou, the new young priest, answered the door.

"I'm sorry to disturb you, Father, but I was wondering if you'd hear my confession right now?"

"Here?" the priest asked stunned.

"No, oh no, Father, in the church. Is that okay?" I was glad he'd come to the door instead of Father O'Mara. It was better to have a priest who didn't know me. Father O'Mara had known me all my life; I didn't want to have to confess to him what I'd done.

"Yes, yes of course. I'll be there in a few minutes." The priest looked a bit frazzled. His curly blond hair was tousled on his head. He slammed the door.

It was dark in the church and my old fear took over. I couldn't go in to wait. I stood with my back against the partially open door and held it that way until I heard the priest's footsteps as he descended the rectory stairs and started across the driveway toward the church. When the sound grew closer, I let go of the door and stood in front of the first confessional. When Father Pitou entered and saw me, he motioned to me to go in behind the curtain.

"Bless me Father for I have sinned. It's been ...a long time since my last confession."

"How long?"

I didn't remember exactly, but I said, "A couple of months, Father." I waited but the priest's silence told me he was waiting for me to continue. "I'm twenty-two, Father, and because I think I love the guy I've been going out with, I had sex with him." When I finished, there wasn't a drop of saliva in my mouth.

"Do you intend to marry this man?"

"I don't know because he just told me today his mother wants him to move with her to another city." I tried to be as ambiguous as possible so that the priest couldn't automatically know who I was talking about. Johnny had told me his mother went to the priests with all of her problems. She might have already confided in Father Pitou.

"And now you're afraid. Something tells me you weren't planning to come to confession until you received the news that this man might leave. Are you pregnant?"

"No, Father."

"If you're truly sorry for what you've done, then don't allow yourself to be in situations where you know you won't say no. That may mean this man should not be a part of your life if he's causing you to sin. You'll have to be the strong one and be prepared to see him leave you and not come back when you say no. Can you do that?"

"I'll try, Father."

"You must save yourself for marriage. Find a man who is willing to wait."

As the priest lectured me about marriage and sex, my thoughts were bouncing all over the place. He was spouting off about the church's doctrine...well, what the hell did I expect? He was telling me to stay pure until I married. Wasn't he listening? I had already given that up. And to make matters worse, how could I stay away from sex when I liked it? I liked it so much that every time I saw Johnnie, I wanted to jump on him like a bitch in heat. I suddenly remembered the conversation I'd had with Emily about how much she wanted to have sex and how meaningless it was to me back then.

"Do you see how important it is to do the things we've talked about in order to be a good Catholic and to go to your future husband clean and untouched?"

"Yes, Father." We hadn't talked; he had talked.

"If you have difficulty abstaining and you need ongoing counseling, I want you to come to me. Don't be afraid. That's what I'm here for."

"I'll remember, Father."

"For your penance, say the rosary. Now go in peace, my child."

"Father, do you mind if I say my penance at home? The church is too dark. I'm afraid to stay in here alone."

There was no answer. And then I heard the door close. Father Pitou had quietly left the confessional and the church.

So I went in peace and said the rosary on my knees in my room. That night I slept better than I had since Johnny had shown up on my front porch.

PART THREE

– 26 –

SPECIAL COUNSELING

"Claire? Is this Claire Soublet?" A man's hesitant voice asked when I answered the telephone.

"Yes, this is Claire. Who's calling?"

"This is Father Pitou, Claire. I thought I'd better check to see how you're doing. It's been more than a month since I've heard from you. Have you been strong? Have you kept the promise you made during your confession?" The priest's voice was soft and a bit paternal, even though he wasn't much older than me.

"I haven't seen or spoken to the person we discussed, Father. But I'm stunned and more than a little curious as to why you're calling me. Are you in the habit of making follow-up calls to people who've confessed to you? I don't think Father O'Mara ever did – why are you?" Father Pitou was supposed to be from France; maybe he had been trained differently. Perhaps he had been taught to be more empathetic. I was still skeptical.

"I do...occasionally," he said. "But sometimes special problems deserve special treatment." Father Pitou must have been in the States a long time; he had almost no accent.

"I didn't tell you my name when I confessed. How did you find out who I was?"

"I described you to Father O'Mara and he immediately knew who you were."

I wondered how he had described me and wanted desperately to know but there was no way I'd ask. Thoughts of the cop I'd had to fight off and the way he had addressed me flooded my brain and raised goose bumps on my skin. Yet, somehow I knew Father Pitou was no Michael McArdle and neither was Father O"Mara.

"Now I'm really embarrassed. It was hard enough discussing my problems in the confessional, Father; I'm definitely not ready to do it by phone." I spoke as softly as I could. The kitchen door was open and I was afraid my voice would travel down the hall.

"There's no need for you to be embarrassed. I'm calling you as a spiritual counselor, Claire. I think you need to talk about what's happening to you. You need help. Is there someone in your life to whom you normally confide such personal things?"

"No. I've always been my own counselor."

"You don't have to be. This is a time you need to take advantage of the services the church has to offer, and I'm offering you my counsel. Please accept it, Claire."

This was a new breed of priest. He intended to help you whether you wanted him to or not. It seemed saying no wasn't an option.

"Claire? Did you hear me?"

"Yes, Father, I heard you. I just don't know what to say to you."

"Say you'll let me help you. Are you busy right now?"

"Not really. I was just reading."

"Can you come to the rectory? I have a few hours this afternoon before I visit the sick. I can use that time to talk with you."

"Talk! Talk about what, Father? There isn't anything more to say about my problems. I confessed and then I did my penance. I said the rosary, remember? Now all I have to do is wipe my thoughts clean." Why wasn't he accepting the fact that I was capable of getting over Johnnie without help? His help. "Father, I'm not interested in counseling."

"I can't accept that. I won't accept that. Because whether you know it or not, you're crying out for help. And if you won't come to me, I'll come to you."

"No! You can't come here." He must know more than my name. Did he know about how I lived and with whom I lived? Was that the reason he was pressuring me into counseling? But why? Was I his experimental dummy? Did he need to practice his newly acquired skills on me? Could Father O'Mara or Johnnie's mother have spoken to him? Had she, in all her evil wisdom, asked the priest to take care of me while she whisked her son away? Of course not, I knew that wasn't the case. There had to be some other reason and I was itching to find out what it was. I was suddenly calm.

"What time should I be there, Father?"

"Is now a good time, Claire?"

"Yes. I'll be there in about twenty minutes."

Father Pitou answered the rectory door without his white collar and black frock. He was wearing dark trousers and a starched, white shirt open at the throat with the sleeves rolled up. This time I noticed his clear blue eyes and full lips. "Come in, Claire. This way, please." The priest walked through the living room, then went down the hall. I followed behind the six-foot man of God and for a moment I took in his whole frame and thought about how attractive he was. But then enormous shame flooded over me. He's a priest, you idiot!

By the time I reached the priest's office, my hands were sweating and I was sorry I'd let him talk me into coming. He invited me to sit on the leather loveseat under the large, draped window across from his desk. Instead of sitting at his desk, he sat beside me. Fear suddenly gripped me and I sprang to my feet.

"Your office...is...is beautiful, Father," I stammered. I walked around the office touching everything I could while trying to suppress the urge to run from the room and the rectory without looking back. I knew this visit would have nothing to do with counseling, but I decided to let things play out. I spent a long time studying the silver pitcher on his desk.

The housekeeper! Where was she? It was a weekday afternoon and she should have answered the door. "Where is Mrs. Lenoir?" My voice was a bit trembly.

"Her father is ill. She's across the river nursing him for a few days. Father O'Mara and I have to fend for ourselves while she's gone." The priest used his benevolent, soothing voice trying to allay my fear. He chuckled softly.

"Where's Father O'Mara?"

"Attending a seminar at Loyola. I've got the whole place to myself today."

I tried to swallow but the saliva got hung up in my throat and I started to choke. Father Pitou jumped up and ran to me. He lifted both my arms above my head the way my grandmother used to do when I was a child. "Keep them up until you stop coughing," he told me.

He poured a glass of water from the decanter on his desk and handed it to me. "Here, drink this. Slowly now, don't gulp it."

The priest walked behind me and gently patted the center of my back. He took the glass from my hand and set it down on the desk. Then as fast as a lightning strike, he pulled me into his arms and kissed me.

"Father! What the he..."

"Jean-Michel, please."

"Jean-Michel, my ass! Are you crazy? Is this what you had in mind when you lured me here to counsel me? You're a priest, goddamnit!"

"You've got a right to say that to me, but please don't use God's name that way, Claire. Yes, I'm a priest, but I'm also a man. And a Frenchman, to boot. I needed to touch you. I wanted to touch you when you were here for confession and I've thought about you constantly ever since that day. I felt compelled to call you." Jean-Michel was searching my face probably hoping to find a hint of forgiveness. When he saw none, he continued. "I don't think you're as shocked at my behavior as you pretend. You were skittish when you arrived. I think you knew the counseling lure was a ruse. Didn't you?"

My legs were numb. I didn't know if they were capable of holding me up much longer. My body was shaking, and once again, my mouth didn't work. Jean-Michel gathered me in his arms and held me close. I didn't pull away. To me, in that moment, all that mattered was there was comfort and safety in his warm and tender embrace...something I'd had so little of in my life. Whatever sins we were going to commit and the punishment that would surely follow did not frighten me.

Jean-Michel led me to the back of the rectory to his bedroom and lay down with me on his bed. When I began to cry, he kissed me until I was calm. Neither of us spoke. We made love as if we were condemned to death and would go to the gallows the next morning.

"Claire, are you feeling better now?" Jean-Michel turned his back while I put on my clothes, then he hurried and pulled on his, too.

"At this very moment, Father Pitou, I hate both of us. You for breaking your vow, and me for not only helping you to break it, but for being vulnerable in the first place. God help us! How could we have done such a thing? Who do I confess to now? And what about you?"

"No one has to know, Claire."

"God knows!"

"Yes, but God is the only one besides you and me who has to know."

"Jesus, you're a collar-wearing hypocrite. You took a vow of celibacy, remember? You're not supposed to covet the flesh. You're a priest first, and then you're a man."

"I know who I am, Claire. I do everything else the priesthood asks of me, except occasionally taste the flesh. I'm a good priest and I know God forgives my weakness and he forgives yours, too."

"Well, I don't forgive either of us. I'll never be the same as long as I live." The punishment had already begun – I would flog myself every chance I got. I could blame Johnnie for what I'd just done, but I didn't dare. I, alone, was guilty.

"Are you telling me we can never make love again?" Jean-Michel came toward me smiling, ready to put his arms around me.

"Don't," I told him as I quickly moved out of his reach. "What do you want, Father, a full blown affair?"

"Yes, I can't think of a reason not to."

"God, you're an arrogant bas…man. Your occasional taste of the flesh did not fall on deaf ears. You're a priest for all of five minutes and you're bragging that I'm not the first woman you've been with. After all, you're a Frenchman," I sneered.

"It's only happened a few times, Claire. I'm not the only priest who covets the flesh, as you put it. It's more prevalent than you might think."

"Oh God, shut up!" He was so smug defending his dirty deeds; there was nothing else I could think of to say. Why did I feel so dirty and he didn't?

"Me thinks the lady doth protest too much. Did you enjoy making love with me, Claire? Please…be honest." The priest ran and blocked the doorway as I started toward it.

"Be honest, huh. Okay. Yes, I enjoyed having sex with you. And it was having sex, not making love, Jean-Michel. I like sex. In fact, I love having sex. That's why I needed to confess. I realized that because John..." I stopped and wondered if I should finish saying the name. There seemed nothing left to hide now, so I started again. "I figured out missing sex with Johnnie would hurt more than missing him. Perhaps you came to the same conclusion about me and that's why you pounced."

"Listen to you, an experienced woman of the world. You were crying less than an hour ago; now you're assertive and bold enough to tell me the real reason you came to confession." The priest looked at me with squinted eyes as he screwed up his mouth into a strange kind of smile. "Something tells me I may have grabbed a live wire with more voltage than I can handle."

"Did I make you sin, Father...Jean-Michel? I don't know what to call you now. The more we talk, the more confused I become."

"Jean-Michel, Claire. And no, you didn't make me sin. When I first saw you, I couldn't believe how beautiful you were. I loved your long hair and your long lean body. Your slightly hoarse voice excited me. When I rushed from the church after your confession, it was to get away from temptation. But I couldn't get you out of my mind. Father O'Mara told me about you and what a difficult time you had growing up. I was even more fascinated then and knew I had to know you, to be close to you. I wanted to be the one to bring some happiness into your life."

"You haven't brought me happiness; what you've brought me is guilt. How in the hell will I ever go to Confession again...receive Communion?" I wanted to cry again, but realized I was well beyond tears. I put the palm of my hand on my forehead and the priest rushed toward me. "No, please don't touch me."

"Let me help you, Claire. You need me more than you realize."

"As my priest or my lover? Or maybe my psychiatrist. Do you think I have mental problems? Is that why I need you more than I realize?"

"One answer should do it. I'll be all of those people for you."

"Why?"

"Because you want me to be, but you're afraid to let me. Don't be afraid. We'll pray and ask God to forgive us and help us. And He will, Claire, you'll see."

I wanted to believe Jean-Michel. I knew he was telling me in a round-about way that I had some emotional problems that he was willing to help me address. And I was tired of trying to carry them alone. I was tired of fighting demons all of my life, all of the time. I walked over to him and threw myself into his arms. After we made love again, we knew there was no turning back.

On my walk home, I realized how hungry I was. I detoured and went to George DeBlanc's grocery on Galvez and Laharpe and bought a half-pound of boiled ham and a loaf of French bread. Boiled ham on French bread with mayonnaise was Miss Menard's and my favorite sandwich. And while I was in a hungry mood, I bought a half-pound of hot sausage to make sandwiches with the other half of the loaf.

I took the long way home. I walked the block where my old house had burned. It had been rebuilt a few years after the fire. It looked just like the old one, except it had only one stoop and the front yards had merged. Bobby had turned it into a one family home. All of his brothers and sisters and their children had moved out to California, so the house had gotten too big for his parents. When his father died, Bobby moved his mother in with him and rented out the house.

Before I left Johnson St., I went back to the old, sycamore tree to look at the names I'd carved on its trunk. Lady Blue and Wobble would never know they had been immortalized.

It had been a long time since I'd walked around the neighborhood. I forgot how hungry I was and decided I'd walk a few blocks in on Columbus, then on Prieur and then on Kerlerec. Very little had changed. The thing that stood out most was how many of the White families had moved away. The civil rights movement was starting to accelerate and the Whites had taken flight. Many of the Creoles of color had moved to California and most of their houses had new families in them. It was December and getting chilly, so there weren't many people on the street. Only a few did I recognize.

I suddenly felt melancholy. Change was all around me, but I had moved only a few blocks away from the old house. It seemed change had skipped over me. I wanted desperately to get my turn.

After the front door closed, I heard, "Claire?"

"Yes, Miss Menard, it's me." She sounded full of anxiety. As I rushed down the hall and into the kitchen, I wondered, once again, if she'd be able to tell by looking at me what I'd been doing. "What's wrong?" I asked.

"You weren't here to get Johnnie's call. Someone bought their house and he came back to get the rest of his and his mother's things." Her voice had a cutting tone.

"Okay, so what was he calling me about? Did he want to say the goodbye he failed to say when he left town? Well, he can keep it and shove it."

"He wanted to talk, Claire." Miss Menard's demeanor changed abruptly. She looked at me with pleading eyes that asked me to give Johnnie a chance to explain why he hadn't come or called to say he was leaving. She desperately wanted to get us back together.

"It's been more than a month since Johnnie stormed off the patio. He had already made up his mind when he told us what his mother wanted him to do. When I confronted him, he lied about it. Then he quietly left New Orleans. Not even a 'goodbye dog' from him. I'm through with Johnnie. There's nothing for us to talk about."

"You're wrong, Claire. He's sorry about the way he left and he wants to tell you that. He hasn't stop loving you or wanting to marry you. Talk to him, cher, please." Miss Menard was pleading Johnnie's case. He must have given her a sob story when he called.

"Too bad! I'm not interested in hearing a damn thing he has to say. He and his mother can go straight to hell and I'll tell him that to his face. Is he still in New Orleans?"

"No. He had to get on the road while it was still light. After his second call, he said he'd call you from Lafayette in a couple of days. In case you want to get in touch with him, he left his address and telephone number." Miss Menard handed me the information.

"No thanks." I took the paper, tore it in half and threw it on the table.

Miss Menard squeezed her hands tightly together in her lap obviously trying to control her meddling and her temper. She knew she'd have no luck in convincing me to keep Johnnie's address and phone number. "Where were you, Claire? I looked for a note but you didn't leave one. That's very unusual for you. What's going on, cher?"

"I went to see Father O'Mara, but he was at Loyola attending a seminar. So I talked to the new priest, Father Pitou."

"You were at the rectory all that time? Do you want to tell me what has you so troubled that you had to spend all those hours talking to a priest?" Miss Menard rolled her wheelchair right up to the tips of my toes and stared up at me. She was searching my face for clues because she knew there was only so much I was going to divulge.

I smiled down at her. "Now you know how secretive I am. But I'll tell you this: I, like you, have trouble with my faith sometimes. I needed a little counseling from Father Pitou to get through a rough patch, that's all."

"Did you get it? And did it help?"

"Yes, I got it and it did help. Why?"

"My counseling never did. That's why I have no trust in the church now. I just got a bunch of pats on the head telling me to pray hard. But never mind that, the reason I asked you if it helped is because you looked a little wild-eyed when you walked into the kitchen. Did the priest upset you with all his religious mumblings?" Miss Menard's voice was full of contempt.

"No, he didn't. In fact, he helped me quite a bit. You should try talking to a priest again; it may help this time. Don't you want the last rites when you die?"

Miss Menard didn't answer the question. She simply glared at me and said, "This isn't about me. We're talking about your need for counseling."

I wished I could have taken back what I'd said, but since I couldn't, I wondered if a partial truth would satisfy her and smooth things over a bit. It might also help her to let go of forcing Johnnie and me together. "I feel content to let Johnnie go now; I don't really need him," I told her. "He's not the only streetcar on the tracks. I'll catch another one soon enough." I sounded as smug as Jean-Michel.

The shocked look on Miss Menard's face said it all. Johnnie was history as far as I was concerned; she had to give up the fight for him. Her eyes were filled with disappointment and tears. I dropped down on my knees and took her hands and held them in mine. "Don't worry about me. I'm okay. Stop thinking about

219

what's going to happen to me when you die. You're worrying just like my grandmother used to do. You can't control or safeguard my future any more than she could. Whatever is to be...I'll handle it. Besides, you know how I feel about you dying. I'm not letting your butt go anywhere." I gave a nervous little laugh; Miss Menard managed a half smile.

Ignoring my sloppy attempt at humor she said, "I am worried. I'd be less concerned if you were a little more vulnerable."

"No, you can't want me more vulnerable. I've been easy prey all my life. It's about time I become the hunter – not the hunted."

"You used to be hard on the outside and soft inside, Claire. I watched Johnnie soften that outer shell...just a little...just enough. But lately, you're cold inside and out. Don't let that happen, cher. If you let the coldness take over, you'll always be unhappy and alone. Look at me. Don't imitate me. If it weren't for you and Leonard Stern, I'd be an old, sickly woman completely alone in this world."

"Right now Johnnie is responsible for my hard heart. Christmas is almost here and we'd talked about driving to Baton Rouge to meet his father and that side of his family. He wanted to invite you to go with us and he said he wouldn't let you refuse. Now Johnnie is history and so is the first Christmas I've been looking forward to since my grandmother died." I couldn't hold the tears back.

I knelt beside her with my head down. For the first time in all the years we'd been together, Miss Menard threw her arms around me, then put her head in my neck and began to cry. I held her close and realized how much more thin and frail she'd become. I could feel the bones in her chest and back.

"Oh, cher," she cried, "why didn't you ever tell me Christmas is important to you, or that you missed celebrating the holidays?"

"You took me in. I wasn't going to make demands on you. Plus, we didn't always have unusual things for Christmas or any of the holidays. I really enjoyed them at Emily's house."

"This is one time you need to hear a little about my life. When I was fifteen, my father sent me to live with his sister in the Garden District. My aunt had converted to Judaism when she married. Not only didn't her husband celebrate Christmas, he didn't believe any holidays should be observed. And when his parents died, he stopped observing the Jewish ones. I lived many years of my life without celebrating holidays, and I continued that tradition…even after you came here to live. I am sorry. Please forgive me. It's not too late for this year, is it, cher?"

"There isn't anything to forgive. And no, it isn't too late for this year, but only if you feel comfortable doing it."

"Let's talk about it later. I'm out of energy and need to rest my tired bones." Miss Menard spun her chair around and left the kitchen. I stood silently and watched my benefactor, my surrogate grandmother, the only person besides my grandparents who truly loved me, roll herself to her room probably feeling she hadn't given me enough.

For a long time I sat in the kitchen and stared out into the yard as a gentle breeze lifted the magnolia leaves from the grass and blew them about in the air. I thought about Jean-Michel Pitou, my new priest, my new lover, my new confidante – a man who excited me not only when I was vulnerable, but even as I sat looking into space. I could still feel his hands touching me, his warm lips as he kissed my neck. I remembered and relived every moment of those passionate hours I spent with him. And I wanted more of him even if it was wrong.

I went to my room, got on my knees and asked God to forgive me for what I had done and for what I was going to continue to do. But most of all, I asked Him not to take Jean-Michel away from me. I spoke to God out loud, "You've taken everyone else, Lord; please let me keep him. Don't make me bitter like Miss Menard. You know when she dies, and I think she's getting close, I'll have no one. I'm not as tough as I make myself out to be. I'm scared to be alone in this world. It's not such a great place; it's cruel. Sometimes I really do think I need some mental help, but then I think of Marcel and what a miserable life he had being mentally disturbed and alone, and it makes whatever is wrong with me seem trite. I tell myself I'm okay. I just don't ever want to feel how I felt the day Big Mama died. Please, don't let that happen to me again. Please…hear my prayer!"

I stayed on my knees for a long time with my upper body lying across my bed. I was too weary to move.

That year we trimmed a medium-size tree. Alma baked us a ham, made candied yams and several vegetables and baked two pies. Miss Menard taught me to make home-made eggnog and pecan pralines. We ate in the dining room for the first time since I'd been living there and used the beautiful, gold-trimmed china and the crystal glasses. Then we exchanged presents. I gave Miss Menard a new robe and a pair of slippers to match. She gave me money because she couldn't shop for me.

I spent a few hours with Jean-Michel on Christmas Eve day and I felt happier than I'd felt in a long time.

– 27 –

JEAN-MICHEL PITOU

"According to you, I am first a priest and then a man, but most of all I'm a hypocrite. Why do you insist on calling me that, Claire?" Jean-Michel was lying on his back with me cradled in the crook of his arm with one of my legs thrown across his mid-section.

I tried to prop myself up on one elbow, but he begged me not to move. "Talk to me where you are. You don't have to always look at me, do you?" he asked.

"But I like looking at you," I pouted, "the same way you like looking at me." I attempted to move again only to have Jean-Michel grab me and hold me forcing me to stay put.

"Okay, okay." I settled back into my original position, "I call you a hypocrite because you're not following your vow of celibacy or the vow you made to serve God for the rest of your life. What you're doing is disloyal and unfaithful to God and the church. Go ahead, defend yourself...again."

"Yes, again. That's why I'm bringing it up because I want this to be the last time we discuss it. Do you realize that you carry around more guilt than I do, Claire? I serve God and the church community and at no time do I neglect them to be with you. Stop judging me and enjoy me. By the way, when are you going to tell me you love me? I've told you how much I love you countless times." Jean-Michel finally let me move. Realizing I wasn't going to answer him, he turned his back to me and I curled around him resting my chin on his shoulder.

"Tell me about your family, Jean-Michel. You have never told me anything about them or how, even where, you grew up."

"Oh, I don't like talking about myself."

"Well hell, you know just about everything about me. Don't you think I'm entitled to know about the man I'm having sex with."

"I really don't like when you say we're having sex and not making love. You make it sound so vulgar. It's either that you really do think of it as dirty or you're afraid to use the word love in my presence."

"It is what it is, my dear. C'mon, tell me about yourself, please."

"I'll give you the short version. I was born in a little town just outside of Paris. When I was about five, my family moved to Marseilles because my father went into the shipping business and wanted to live where he had his office. My mother hated Marseilles, so when I was eight she took my two sisters, my brother and me and moved to the States. We lived with my mother's parents in Connecticut."

"Your mother's American?"

"Yes. She met my father when she spent a year as an exchange student in Paris. She went back and married him when she finished college. After we went to the States, she'd often go to Marseilles to spend time with my father. She always left us with my grandparents so that our education wasn't interrupted. When I was fourteen, she took my brother and sisters and returned permanently to Marseille. I was given a choice; I chose to stay in Connecticut."

"When did you decide to become a priest?"

"My grandparents were very religious, so I think they were my greatest influence. But they encouraged me to go to Marseilles and live with my family for a while before I made my decision. I went back when I was nineteen after I'd finished two years at university. I hated the shipping business. My brother was already working fulltime helping my father and so was one of my sisters. The other one had already gotten married. I got out of there as fast as I could. My father was hurt and angry, but my mother gave me her blessing. Sometimes, though, I wonder if I gave myself enough time between Marseilles and the seminary."

"Oh my God! Do you regret becoming a priest?" I thought I was on to something. Maybe that was why he had broken his vows so easily.

"No, Claire, I don't regret it. I can think of only one other thing I'd like to do more than being a priest. I'd like to grow grapes and make wine...in France."

"Do you think you'll ever leave the priesthood and do that?" Hmmm...I wouldn't mind being a winemaker's wife in France.

"Claire, I've only just become a priest...not quite three years. I was placed in New York for two years for my first assignment. Then I was sent here to New Orleans. So who knows what life holds for me. And as for leaving the priesthood, well...I guess I should never say never."

We were in the upstairs part of a small house in the Lower Garden District. About six months before, Jean-Michel had helped an elderly widow save her house. She was eighty years old but still did the laundry for the rectory. Josephine Gagnier had spent every penny of her savings taking care of her dying husband. Their house had been neglected, she'd told Father Pitou, and it was falling down around her ears. She had no money to fix it and no place to go if she had to move. The priest told her not to worry that he'd find a way for her to get her house repaired.

Father O'Mara refused Jean-Michel the funds from the church coffers saying Corpus Christi couldn't help people who lived in other parishes. It didn't matter that Josephine had worked for the church rectory for over twenty years and used to live in the parish, he'd said, she no longer lived there and wasn't eligible to receive any of the church's money. Jean-Michel's grandparents were dead now so he couldn't ask them for help. He decided to call France and ask his parents. Without any questions, they sent him fifteen thousand dollars. He hired a team of house builders from Corpus Christi's parish to renovate Josephine's house. When I asked their names, I realized many of them were the sons and grandsons of my grandfather's friends.

Jean-Michel and I spent three hours every Wednesday afternoon in Josephine's camelback house. The renovators had done an excellent job. They replaced the roof, all the doors, even the shiny wire fence around the entire property. Her kitchen had been rebuilt with new cabinets and appliances and they'd built her a separate laundry room in her back yard, just steps from her back door. Jean-Michel beamed when he gave me a tour.

There were two bedrooms and a bath upstairs. We always drove into the side yard and entered through the pantry door which was under the stairs that led up to the second floor. It was so private that even when Josephine was at home, we didn't disturb her; she didn't disturb us.

Jean-Michel never fully explained why Josephine, a devout Catholic, had allowed him to bring me to her home so that we could carry on our affair. In her own way, Josephine told me.

When we arrived at her home for the first time, I was embarrassed because I thought she might make a point of showing me how much she disapproved of what we were doing. Never had I been so wrong. She welcomed us like family.

She put her arm through mine, "So, you Fatha Pitou's girl, huh. He tell me bout you all the time. "Ah feel Ah already know you."

Josephine patted my cheek and glanced up at Jean-Michel and winked. "She pretty jes like you say, Fatha. I don blame you one bit fa lovin this chil. And don you worry neitha, sugah," Josephine patted my cheek again, *"God is good* and He fair. He know who to punish and who to fagive. All them folks that treat us bad cuz we are who we are, they the ones gonna answer to the Lawd. You and the Fatha ain't got nothin to worry bout, jes like me. Me, Ah bin a washawoman fa half ma life, but Ah bin good to folks. So Ah know where Ah'm goin when Ah leave this earth. Lissen to me preachin to y'all befo y'all git in the house good."

Josephine was a tiny woman. She probably weighed less than a hundred pounds and wasn't five feet tall. She rocked to one side as if she had a bad hip. Her wiry silver hair was caught up in a bun on top her head; clear brown eyes sparkled like a six-year-olds in her dark face.

"Y'all go on up. Ah set up the room nex to the bathroom and made y'all a lunch with a pitcha a lemonade. Ah'll be back in a couple hours; Ah got to make me some groceries." She slipped out of the front door and quietly closed it behind her.

There were two major problems that had to be solved in order for Jean-Michel and I to be together. It had taken a great deal of ingenuity and lies to pull things off.

We needed to account for our time away. Jean-Michel told Father O'Mara he was helping a group of students at Xavier University prepare for a debate for several hours every Wednesday. He said Father O'Mara never questioned it and would never think of checking on his subordinate as if he didn't trust him. He also thought because he had been volunteering to relieve Father O'Mara of many of his duties when he was too drunk to do them himself, the elder priest had no fault to find when Jean-Michel wanted to spend a little time away doing things that personally satisfied him. In fact, he said, Father O'Mara praised him for his willingness to extend himself outside the parish. And Wednesdays were usually quiet at lunchtime, and on most of those afternoons, Father O'Mara took a long, cognac nap. Jean-Michel solved his problem easily.

My lie was more convoluted. Miss Menard was not as easily fooled and much more curious and suspicious. With Jean-Michel's help, we concocted a plan the week before our first visit to Josephine's.

He called me during breakfast when we knew Miss Menard would be in the kitchen listening to my phone call. He asked if it would be possible for me to take over a catechism class for a group of children who were scheduled to make their First Holy Communion at the end of May. The lay person who'd been teaching the class had been stricken ill suddenly and he needed a replacement for her. The class would be held in the school's auditorium from twelve to three o'clock every Wednesday. I agreed to do it.

Miss Menard was overjoyed. Finally, she said, I was going to do something constructive with my brain and my energy; I wouldn't be hanging around the house all day reading, watching TV or simply vegetating. I was apparently so convincing she never raised an eyebrow, and never mentioned Johnnie to me after that. I don't know whether he ever called me again.

This was the boldest and most creative lie I had ever told Miss Menard. The thought of her not deserving to be lied to and how embarrassing it would be if I were to be found out, weighed heavily upon me. Except for Wednesday afternoons and necessary errands, I stayed close to home. I went to Mass on Sunday mornings but only to the ones officiated by Father O'Mara. I put Confession and Holy Communion on hold. I felt unworthy to receive them, but mostly I was too gutless to confess my sins. Jean-Michel constantly reminded me that until I forgave myself, I would never believe God had already done so. I didn't believe him. I thought he was telling me that to relieve some of his own guilt.

The other problem was getting to Josephine's, particularly for me. Not having a car, I'd have to take two busses and then walk through a bad area of town. But to meet Jean-Michel anywhere in the Seventh Ward was out of the question. We'd surely meet fifty people we both knew who would stare into the car wondering what I was doing in the priest's car in the middle of the day. How long would it take for that to circulate?

We decided I'd take a bus to the French Quarter and Jean-Michel would pick me up behind Jackson Square. He always wore his open-throat, white shirt with the sleeves rolled up and a pair of black trousers. Somewhere along the way to the Vieux Carré, he'd slick back his curly, blond hair behind his ears, don a black beret that covered one ear and then put on a pair of horn-rimmed glasses. He looked every bit like an artist in an area where artists thrived.

When he was out of the Seventh Ward and in an area where he was sure he wouldn't be recognized, Jean-Michel would stop at a drugstore to buy a package of condoms.

My hair had grown longer and hung a few inches below my shoulders. With a reverse permanent I kept it bone straight, and unless you knew me well, you wouldn't know my hair wasn't naturally silky straight. I wore it in a pony tail most of the time. I couldn't wear a beret as part of my disguise because I wore them all the time to go to Mass. Once I'd get on the bus and didn't see anyone I knew, I'd put on eyeglasses with a big blue and white frame and lots of makeup, especially the fake mole on my left cheek. I wore what was in fashion at the time: wide, felt skirts with stiff crinolines under them and white buck oxfords or ballet flats. The last thing I'd do was remove the rubber band or ribbon from my hair, part it on the right side and comb it to hang straight down partially covering my eye.

I carried a sketch pad and pencils in my canvas bag with the catechism manual Jean-Michel thought I should never forget when I left the house to meet him. I'd sit on the steps of St. Louis Cathedral and sketch Jackson Square. I could draw a little, so if anyone looked at my sketch, I believed I could pull off being a beginning artist. When Jean-Michel picked me up, I simply looked like an exotic-looking, young woman with a blond Frenchman. We'd embrace, and in his authentic, French accent and my fake one, we'd greet each other, hug and kiss, then walk off together to wherever he'd parked his car. In the Vieux Carré, we didn't look all that unusual.

Things changed when we almost got caught. The bishop was visiting the Cathedral to assess the work that needed to be done on the exterior of the church. He and one of the priest's from the cathedral were discussing that as they stood behind me at the entrance to the church. I saw Jean-Michel as he started across the cobblestones toward me with his usual long strides and his arms wide open ready to greet me. I leaped up and frantically pointed behind me. He understood my signal and abruptly made an about-face. As quickly as I could, I put away my sketch book and pencils and walked a short distance behind him until we were out of sight.

That incident put an end to our clandestine, French Quarter meetings. From then on, Josephine picked me up at Decatur and Esplanade and returned me to that corner after Jean-Michel left her house. Josephine was at the end of her driving life and I closed my eyes and feared for my safety more than once in her old jalopy. Sometimes when it was hot and sticky I'd take the bus, but usually I liked to walk the rest of the way home.

– 28 –

THE IDES OF MARCH

The last Wednesday in March had been a particularly wonderful day. Its highlight had been Jean-Michel and me having lunch with Josephine. He had called her earlier that morning and asked her not to put a lunch in our room but to set it up in the dining room so that she could eat with us. It was the first anniversary of her husband's death and he didn't want Josephine to be alone on that day.

Easter was less than two weeks away. Jean-Michel suggested we dye eggs when we'd meet the next week. He gave Josephine money to buy the eggs and dye. She wasn't surprised, she said, because we acted like teenagers. I knew that wasn't the only reason he wanted to do it. I thought because she had no children or family, he wanted to do it for her more than for us.

I tried hard to prevent myself from loving Jean-Michel, but I knew how special he was and I simply let myself go. I knew I wasn't yet a winemaker's wife, or if I'd ever be, but I did feel like a priest's wife. We didn't live together nor did we spend a lot of time together, but I loved every stolen moment of it.

Josephine dropped me off shortly after three and I walked home slowly. I wanted to savor that day and relive how happy I felt being with Jean-Michel. About two blocks from the house, I became more aware of where I was and less involved in my reverie. Looking straight ahead, there appeared to be some sort of commotion happening in the block of my house: flashing lights and what looked like a crowd of people gathered on the sidewalk. The closer I got, I could see an ambulance and a group of people...in front of my house. I ran as fast as I could, but when I reached the house and pushed through the crowd, the fireman at my gate refused to let me in. When I told him I lived there, he said he'd have to check. He asked my name then disappeared inside the yard. Mr. Dejean had let the hedges grow higher so it was impossible to see over them. The fireman returned within seconds and held the gate open for me to enter.

Miss Menard was lying on her back in the flower bed to the left of the front steps. Her wheelchair was turned over on its side near her feet. One of the ambulance attendants told me a passerby heard Miss Menard moaning and came into the yard where he found her trying to get up. He told her to lie still and he ran to the corner firehouse for help. She was conscious when the ambulance arrived and told the attendants she did not want to be transported to a hospital. The attendant told me she kept saying my name over and over again, but then she began slipping in and out of consciousness.

I knelt beside her, held her hand, and called her name. She opened her eyes and looked at me, but I don't know if she knew it was me. Her eyes closed again and she didn't reopen them.

I called her doctor and he came right away. Dr. Reilly determined she had no broken bones, but had probably suffered a stroke and her heart was extremely weak. After I got her bed changed and her room set up the way the doctor had asked, the emergency team put her on a gurney, brought her into the house and took her to her room. The doctor released the ambulance crew and asked me to wait in the front room until he called me.

Through the living room window I could see a man trying to straighten the bent wheel on the wheelchair. When he saw me watching him, he brought the chair up on the porch and beckoned to me to come out of the house. I walked out onto the porch.

"Uh, miss, I think I know how that lady come to fall," the man told me. "She musta been rolling close to the edge and couldn't put on her brakes fast enough. See, the brakes ain't on." He pulled the chair forward to show me the brakes were unlocked, and then he locked them in place. "Oh, uh, miss…I found her. My name is Earl Lamont. Me and my family just moved about two and a half blocks away on Kerlerec. I'm real sorry about your gramma, miss." The man looked sincere when he put out his hand to touch my shoulder, but my hand flew out in front of me as I moved out of his reach.

"She isn't my grandmother, Mr. Lamont. She's my employer. It was my day off, that's why I wasn't here. Thank you for what you did for her. I'm very grateful you heard her and saved her life." What right did I have to sound defensive? Guilt! I could hear it in my own voice. I wondered what he'd think of me if he knew the real reason I wasn't here.

"Can I do anything else to help you?"

"No, but thank you. It's nice of you to ask," I said.

"Well, I hope the lady gets better. I need to be on my way. So long, miss." Earl Lamont made his way to the gate as he spoke to me, then he tipped his hat. I didn't respond because I was suddenly aware of how quiet it had become. Not only had the firemen and the ambulance disappeared, but so had the few people who had remained after Miss Menard was removed from the yard.

I walked back into the house and closed the door behind me. I listened in the hall for a long time but couldn't hear a sound coming from Miss Menard's room, so I returned to the front room. Even though it was a warm spring evening, I felt icy cold. I grabbed the afghan and covered myself as I balled up in a knot on the sofa.

Here it was...that major catastrophe that for years I'd been expecting. I put my head on my knees and prayed. But deep inside, I knew God was going to take Miss Menard. Only this time, I wasn't the good girl I was when I'd asked Him to heal my grandfather's heart. This time I knew the reason He might refuse to hear my prayer.

Two hours later, the doctor walked slowly into the room.

"Miss Menard never regained consciousness after she was brought into the house, Claire." The bigoted doctor, who had refused to treat me, had called me by my name. "I called Leonard Stern," he said. "I know them both and their relationship. But because he's confined to bed since his last heart attack, his grandson, Joshua, will be handling Miss Menard's affairs. He'll be here about 8:30 tomorrow morning. Mr. Stern arranged for her body to be picked up in an hour or so. I'm sorry; she was a lovely, kind woman." The doctor sounded as though he really meant it. "I'm sure if anyone knows, you know how kind she was, don't you?" His tone had turned hostile and he glared at me as he opened the door, walked through it and left it open behind him. I was too distraught to even acknowledge his hostility.

For me, the end of the world couldn't have been more cataclysmic. I started to shake. My teeth knocked together so hard,

I thought every tooth would be chipped. I couldn't bear to think that I hadn't gotten to say goodbye to the woman who had loved me unconditionally even though she'd never told me, and who had possibly had someone killed to avenge me. I hoped she'd died in the yard the moment she lost consciousness when I was kneeling next to her and not in her room with the unethical Dr. Reilly who hadn't taken his Hippocratic Oath seriously.

I started toward the back of the house. Every step was painful and filled with dread because I was still afraid of the dark and the dead. It seemed I hadn't matured in twenty-two years. Miss Menard's door was open and I approached the room cautiously as if afraid to wake her. She lay peacefully on top her crisp, white sheets with her hands resting on her abdomen and a slight smile upon her lips. She was beautiful, even in death. That smile? Was she thinking of me when she drew her last breath? I desperately wanted it to be that way…to be relieved of the guilt of not being with her when she'd needed me most.

Before I said goodbye to her, I called the rectory. Jean-Michel answered.

"Father Pitou, this is Claire Soublet. Miss Menard died a little while ago. Can you come to the house, please, to give her the last rites? Please, please hurry! I don't want to fall apart."

I knelt at Miss Menard's bedside and touched her lightly. She was so cold, as cold as my grandmother had been when I'd found her. I couldn't touch her again. I was happy we had hugged that one time in the kitchen a few months before. Though we didn't say it, I knew we loved each other. I'd always be able to feel what her arms felt like around me.

I began whispering and then I realized no one was there to hear me. So I spoke out loud to her.

"I'm sorry I wasn't here when you needed me and that you had to leave before you gave me your final words of wisdom. But don't worry, I remember everything you've ever said to me, and even more, everything you've ever done for me. Thank you for the years you spent with me, for the wonderful home you gave me, and for the education you knew was so important to me.

"I don't know what I'll do now. I have the money Big Mama left me and every penny you insisted I save, so I won't be destitute. I still want to get my master's degree, but not here in

New Orleans. I'd like to see some of the world, but I'm sure I'll come back here to die.

"I lied to you about what I've been doing for the past few months and I'm sorry for that. But I was ashamed to tell you I was involved with a priest. He's wonderful and kind and I tried not to love him, but I couldn't help myself. I've asked God not to take him away, to let me have someone who doesn't leave me. He hasn't answered either of my special prayers, the ones about Big Papa and you. I don't think He'll answer my prayer about Jean-Michel; I think He may punish me because Jean's a priest. Why does my fear of being left alone in the world cause me to make such poor decisions?

"Please stay close to me as long as you can. I don't know if I can get through this alone. I'm going to be so lonely without…"

"Claire?" The voice was coming from the kitchen. I rushed from the room but my sixth sense told me not to call out Jean-Michel's name. When I reached the kitchen, Father O'Mara was seated at the table and Jean-Michel was standing in the doorway waiting for me.

"Thank you for coming," I told them hoping my voice didn't betray my surprise or they hadn't caught the wrinkling of my nose when the smell of alcohol assaulted my nostrils.

Father O'Mara rose from the chair and with a few shaky steps he managed to stand very close to me, put his arms around my shoulders and hold me tenderly for an awkward moment. Nervously, Jean-Michel patted my hand.

Father O'Mara was drunk and had to lean on the table for support. "Was Miss Menard a practicing Catholic, Claire?" he asked.

"Yes," I lied.

"I can perform Extreme Unction, if you'd like?" Father O'Mara looked at Father Pitou who nodded in agreement. The elder priest asked me to take him to Miss Menard's room. He weaved his way inside and I closed the door behind him.

Jean-Michel was pacing and wringing his hands by the time I got back to the kitchen.

"Are you okay?" he whispered and pointed in the direction of Miss Menard's room. "He insisted on coming with me. I couldn't say no."

"I'm numb right now and that gives me the feeling of composure. But I really think I'm okay because you're here. Can you let Father O'Mara go back to the rectory when he finishes? Tell him you'll stay with me while I wait for the undertaker. Please, Jean-Michel."

It took the priest less than ten minutes to perform the last sacrament. I hoped Miss Menard wouldn't be upset because I let him give her the last rights when she seemed to be on the outs with her faith. But it couldn't hurt, I thought. Who knows, maybe I had helped her more in death than in life?

"Father Pitou, would you mind staying with Claire while she waits with the body?" Father O'Mara asked when he returned to the kitchen. "I've had a long day. I need to get back to the rectory to rest."

"Not at all, Father. I'd be happy to stay with her." Jean-Michel took the elder priest by the arm and started to lead him down the hall.

"No, no, I can see myself out. Stay with Claire." He fished a set of keys out of the waistband of his garment and held it out to Jean-Michel. "Here," he said, "I think I'll walk. I need to get some fresh air and exercise."

"No Father," Jean-Michel showed him the keys in his hand. "I drove us here. The keys you have are the keys to the rectory. You'll need those to get in."

"Oh, yes, yes. Hmm, now I know I'm getting old. Claire, if there's anything else we can do for you, don't hesitate to call us. I'm sorry you lost that kind woman. I'll pray for her soul and you must do that as well. Goodnight." Slowly, the priest made his way to the front door.

"Is he going to get back to the rectory okay, Jean-Michel?" I was afraid something might happen to Father O'Mara; maybe it wasn't a good idea to let him go alone.

"He'll be all right. The night air will help sober him up. He often goes out to walk after dark…in that same condition. Don't worry; he'll get there in one piece."

Before we could sit at the table, the undertakers arrived. The two men asked me if I needed to say a last goodbye; I told them I already had. I left Jean-Michel sitting at the table and went out to stand on the patio. I didn't want to see them take Miss Menard out.

How was I going to take the next step and face the future? My life experience was limited. Only in the last two years had I tried to find out what life was about, and the most I had to show for all my worldliness was my taste for the flesh. I had constantly upbraided Jean-Michel about him being covetous of the flesh, and now I was admitting that sex was the only thing I'd learned to do while becoming an adult. What could I do with carnal knowledge? Carnal knowledge, hah! I had to laugh at myself for the use of that term. I really didn't know a damn thing about sex. However, I did know that ever since my grandmother died, except for Miss Menard's affection, having sex was the only time I felt someone really cared about me. For me there was no technique involved; I didn't know enough to be skilled. The warmth and closeness of the bodies locked together did it all for me. I responded to being caressed and told I was loved. That was my enjoyment and I hadn't realized it until that moment.

"Claire, they're gone." Jean-Michel called to me from the kitchen door. He took my hand as I came into the house, then gently held me close. "I knew you wouldn't want to stay here by yourself tonight, so I called Jo. She wants you to spend the night at her house."

"Thank you for doing that. The doctor told me Leonard Stern's been bedridden since his last heart attack, so he's sending his grandson at 8:30 tomorrow morning to settle Miss Menard's affairs. He also told me he was privy to Leonard Stern's and Miss Menard's relationship. Don't know what that's supposed to mean."

"Didn't you ask him?"

"Not that rude, prejudiced bastard! I wouldn't ask him anything. About going to Josephine's...how will I get back here in the morning? Will she be able to get me here on time? God, I hate to impose on her."

Jean-Michel called Josephine again. "She said not to worry," he told me. "She'll get you here around 7:30. Get whatever you need for tonight, Claire. I'll take you up there."

I put a few toiletries, a pair of pajamas and a change of clothes together and Jean-Michel drove me uptown. Except for telling him what had happened to Miss Menard, I was too emotionally spent to talk about anything else. He didn't come in when we got to Josephine's. He said pressing duties awaited him at the rectory and that he was scheduled to say 7:00 Mass the next morning. Before I got out of the car, he kissed me tenderly and then long and hard. He told me not to worry. He looked unreasonably sad, especially if his sadness was tied to my loss. I didn't think it was, but I had to stifle my curiosity. There were too many other difficulties facing me. It would have to wait.

"Where's the fatha?" Josephine asked after she let me in.

"He said he had some urgent problems waiting for him at the rectory."

"Then he tol you what's goin on there. That ol priest got hisself and the fatha in hot wata." Josephine looked at the blank look on my face. Suddenly her hand flew up and covered her mouth. She rolled her eyes and moaned. "Oh, dog caca! Me, Ah'm a real blabbamouth. He didn't tell you, did he?"

"Tell me what?"

"Oh, dawlin, Ah'm sorry. Let me tell you firs how sorry Ah am bout that lady you lived with. Ah'm so mad bout what's goin on at that church, Ah forgot bout what you been goin thew. Fagive this po ol woman, dawlin."

"No, it's all right. I understand, Josephine. But what's going on with Jean-Michel? He didn't mention anything to me about what's happening at the church."

"The archdisee found out the ol priest's bin drinkin and usin some of the collection plate money to buy his licka. They know the fatha bin helpin him hide it. So they gonna replace bot a them. The ol man will probly be put out to pascha and the fatha's gonna be sent to anotha church in anotha state." Josephine sat at the dining room table and grabbed a napkin to catch her falling tears. "He's bin good to me. Ah don want anythin bad to happen to him."

"My God, why didn't Jean-Michel tell me what was happening to him?"

"He probly thought you had enough on your plate, dawlin, and you do. Please don't tell the fatha Ah told you, cuz he might be plenny mad at me. He might think Ah ovastepped."

"I don't think he will. And don't worry; I won't say anything about it until he tells me himself. How did you find out, Josephine?"

"When I delivered some laundry to the rectory yestiddy, Miss Lenoir told me. She know cuz she the one blew the whistle on the ol man. She couldn't take it no mo. He a nasty ol pisstail...pees in the bed cuz he too lazy or too drunk to get up. She bin washin them sheets haself fa a long time so nobody would fin out. She bin knowin bout the licka and the money fa years. Miss Lenoir jes got tired of keepin that secret and cleanin up his piss and puke, so she went to the head office and let them folks know what was goin on."

"You mean Jean-Michel knew this today when we had lunch with you?"

"He sho did."

"No wonder we spent the entire time downstairs with you. God, all those happy smiles and all that jolliness were fake." It was beginning to sink in what it all meant. "There's not a thing either of us can do to help him. What if they send him far away? I can't lose him right now, Josephine." I tried to cry, but couldn't; I was out of tears. Much of my body was in a state of numbness and I was grateful.

"Tonight, you not gonna do nothin. Take yourself a good, hot bath and get you some sleep. Go on up, dawlin. Ah'll bring you up some hot soup afta you git out the tub." Josephine handed me my purse and my bag. "Go on, soak some of that bad stuff outta you."

As I lay soaking in the tub, I remembered Jean-Michel commenting on how quiet Miss Menard's death had been. There had been no family to mourn her passing or any neighbors gathered in the street as her body was removed from the house. When I thought of the people who had gathered at the gate earlier in the day when she lay in the yard, it was clear to me that as long as she was injured it was exciting; once she was dead, they no longer cared. She was aware of how little people cared about each other when she was alive; we'd often talked about it. I wondered if she had any way of knowing how right she was now that she was dead?

My thoughts turned to Jean-Michel and I wondered where they might send him and if it would be a place I'd want to live. I was willing to move anywhere to be with him, but would he want me to do that. Maybe he'd be afraid of being under constant scrutiny, so it wouldn't be wise for me to live near him.

"Claire," Josephine was outside the bathroom door, "Ah put a bowl a soup and a cup a tea on the dressa in your room. Don let them git col. Leave them dishes up there when you finish; Ah'll git them tomorra. Sleep tight."

– 29 –

GENTLY EVICTED

Josephine's powerful coffee was the jolt I needed to fully wake me up. She didn't make café au lait; she made strong coffee with chicory and a little milk and sugar. Having been awake most of the night, I had dressed in a sleepy stupor. I needed that potent potion to kickstart me.

"Take your coffee in the dinin room, dawlin, cuz Ah got a plate of cheese-grits, some bacon and some scramble eggs comin? You want toas?" Josephine was flitting around her kitchen as if she was a short order cook.

"Josephine, please don't go through all that trouble; I can get something when I get to the house," I said.

"Sorry dawlin, Ah already got it cooked. Go sit down, chil." She followed me into the dining room and put an enormous plate of food in front of me. "Eat eva bit a that, you hear. You know you ain't gonna cook yaself a hot breakfas when you git there. Go on, eat."

"Yes, ma'am!" I saluted her. Looking at that full plate, I couldn't imagine how I'd get it all down. It was not the kind of breakfast I was used to. But while Josephine got dressed, I dug into four slices of bacon, two scrambled eggs, a half-plate of cheese-grits and two slices of toast.

Once again, I was being cared for by an elderly person. How could that happen to me time after time? Although in good health, Josephine was still eighty. And to me that meant close to dying. I had to get away as much for her sake as for mine. My grandfather, my grandmother and Miss Menard - I had been in all their lives - look at where they were now. It didn't matter how old they were; all that mattered was that I had been at the desk when they signed out. I was truly spooked.

240

"No, stop thinking like that!" I was drumming my fork on the side of my empty plate and had chastised myself out loud. Why couldn't I think about how lucky I was to have had them in my life? God, what would it have been like had they not been there to take care of me? Would I have been put in an orphanage? Probably not, I was seventeen when Big Mama died. And, anyway, who says Josephine wants to be another grandmother to me?

"Claire," Josephine called to me from her bedroom, "who you talkin to in there?"

"No one, just talking to myself."

"Go ahead then; Ah do it all day long maself."

Josephine dropped me off shortly after seven-thirty. She gave me her phone number and told me to call her if I needed her. How right she had been about me not cooking myself breakfast. I never made it to the kitchen.

I walked around the garden, then went out back to take a look at the patio and the backyard. Everything was beginning to bloom and it was a spectacular sight. I ran back to the front porch and sat on the glider for a few minutes to regain my composure. Finally I went into the house and sat in the living room and allowed the silence and Miss Menard's spirit to wrap around me.

Joshua Stern arrived fifteen minutes later. I heard his footsteps on the porch and I opened the door. He had a key in his hand ready to put into the lock. My eyes took a few seconds to leave his hand...it was the size of a bear's paw. For what seemed an endless distance, my eyes traveled upward looking for his face. He was the tallest man I'd ever seen in person. I guessed he was about 6'10" or taller.

"I guess, judging from the key in your hand, you didn't expect me to be here. I didn't spend the night, but I do still live here." I held out my hand, "I'm Claire Soublet."

His giant hand swallowed mine, "Joshua Stern, Claire. You're just like my grandfather described: tall, willowy and lovely." His small blue eyes with their thick, black lashes looked at me with curiosity. "Grandpa Lenny knows a lot about you. Sera talked to him about you all the time. He knew you wouldn't stay here alone last night." Joshua's smile looked genuinely warm and I began to feel a little less anxious.

He handed me a large brown envelope. "This is for you from Sera. She asked Grandpa to make sure you got this upon her death. There's also her life story he's been working on, but it's not finished and I'm not sure if my grandfather will ever finish it. He hasn't worked on if for quite some time. I'm sure you're aware of how sick he is."

"Thank you." I placed the envelope on the couch. "Yes, I know he's been very ill. I never met him, you know."

"He hasn't been to this house in almost fifteen years. They used the telephone and messengers to communicate."

"That certainly explains why I never saw him."

Joshua chuckled. His deep, resonant, baritone voice matched his height. I wondered if he was an opera singer. "Boy, those two were really something."

"What do you mean by that?"

"Let's be grown up here, Claire. They were lovers for a lot of years. You did know that, didn't you?"

"Miss Menard never said so directly, but I thought they might have been."

"We'd better get back to business. I've yet to tell you some really important things."

"Okay."

"Sera Menard lived a reasonably long life and for almost a third of it, she had no income. When she had no money left, she had to start using up every one of her assets. During that period, my grandfather was forced to sell her jewelry, then everything of real value, and finally the house. He bought the house so that she wouldn't have to move. All of the monies were used to pay her bills and to give her cash from time to time. In the last couple of years of her life, he used his own money to take care of her and he denied her nothing. When my grandmother died in the early 1940s, my grandfather thought they'd finally get married and leave New Orleans. He wanted to move to New York to be near his family, but Sera said she was too old and sickly to go anywhere." Joshua spoke of Miss Menard with fondness. I wondered if he had known her.

"So, you don't live in New Orleans. Why are you here now?" My head was reeling from all the new information.

"I just took the bar exam in New York a couple of weeks ago. While I'm waiting for my results, I thought I'd come down here to spend some time with my grandfather before he dies. Funny, huh, he'll probably die right after Sera. Do you think they planned it or willed it to be that way?" Joshua smiled at me as he waited for an answer.

I didn't answer. Instead I asked, "Did you and your family know Sera?"

"No, we only know what my grandfather told us about her. We did know one thing, though, he really loved her."

"Then why didn't he marry her instead of someone else?"

"That was their secret; no one else knows. I would like to find a love like that one of these days." He paused a few seconds and sighed. "Claire, Sera was cremated last night and this afternoon her ashes are being spread from a boat on Lake Pontchartrain."

"Oh!" I gasped. The finality of it all took the breath right out of me.

"Didn't Sera tell you what she wanted done with her remains?"

"No. She was very private and I didn't pry into her affairs. I wasn't related to her, so I had no right to that information."

"Okay, let's finish up here, shall we? The house will be put up for sale as soon as we decide what kind of touching-up it needs. I'm hoping you can be out by the weekend. How much do you have to move?" He was so matter-of-fact; I felt like I'd just been fired from my job.

"Not much, just my clothes and the contents of my room...minus the furniture. I'm sure I can be out in a day or two. Is that satisfactory?"

"That's fine. I won't be back until Monday, so take your time."

"Okay, I'd better get started packing." I got off the sofa and started to leave the room.

"Claire, please wait. Sit down. There's something I think you should know about why Sera was so important to my family." Joshua put his massive hands on his head and ran them over his kinky-curly, jet-black hair. He looked a bit flustered, yet eager to get something off his chest.

"I like you, Claire, so I feel compelled to tell you the truth, well...as much as I know, anyway. It may not mean much to you now, but at least I'll have cleared my conscience. Maybe that envelope will tell you more about Sera. Grandpa Lenny guarded it with his life, so I know it's important."

"Okay, let's have it," I said through clenched teeth. I couldn't possibly have any more shock than I'd had the day before.

"Sera had a baby for my grandfather about sixty years ago...my father. Grandpa Lenny wanted the child but she didn't. He made her believe he gave the baby to a good family, but he really gave my father to his sister who was unmarried and wanted to raise a child. So the woman I call my grandmother is really my great-aunt. When my father was finally told who his real father was and the circumstances of his birth, he never spoke to my grandfather again."

"Your father doesn't mind your relationship with him?"

"I think he resents it, but it didn't stop me from getting close to my grandfather. After I turned thirteen, I spent many summers here in New Orleans. But you know, the details of my father's birth are a family secret; my mother doesn't even know. She's from a wealthy family of New York Jews, so Grandpa Lenny and the rest of the family decided it best to let that skeleton stay in the closet. And of course Grandma Rose, Grandpa's wife, never knew. The sad thing about that is they never had any children together. There aren't many of us left."

"Your grandfather doesn't have any other relatives in New Orleans?"

"Not one. He had a cousin Daniel, but when he and his wife Pauline died that was the end of the Stern relatives here. We still have a few cousins in New York. When I told Grandpa Sera was dead, he told me it was time for him to go, too. He says he's ready."

So this was Sera Menard. I realized how little I knew about her. I'd had enough surprises in the last two days; I didn't want any more. But then I wondered if there were more in the envelope I'd been given. I sat very still.

"Claire, no reaction; no comment? Surely you have something to say."

"No, no I don't. I thought I knew a little about my guardian, but I was wrong. I didn't know her at all. I think I'll start that packing now."

"While you're doing that, I'm going to look around to see what condition the house is in. Are you staying with friends?"

"No, I'm going to make a call about renting a room from an elderly woman I know."

"Do you have a car?"

"No, why?"

"Because I can take you and a few of your things to wherever you're going this morning, I have the time. Go ahead, make your call, then let me know."

Josephine was delighted to have me stay with her. She didn't know if she'd be at home when I arrived, but if not I'd find a key on the porch under the flower pot near the swing. No, she'd said, she hadn't heard from Jean-Michel, but she'd be delivering his laundry the next day and she'd know something then.

Actually, I had fewer possessions than I'd thought. Joshua was driving a Cadillac and we managed to get everything I owned into it. I didn't have to return to the house ever again. I was in such a hurry to leave; Joshua had to go back inside to get the envelope he'd given me.

After we carried everything into Josephine's house, Joshua asked me for her telephone number. He also jotted down the address. "I'll call you tomorrow. I'm sure you will have opened the envelope by then. I'm curious to know what's inside. I'll also be able to tell you if Sera's manuscript is salvageable."

"I want it even if it isn't. Bring me whatever is there; I'll figure it out."

When Josephine came home, we moved my belongings upstairs. She let me decide which room I wanted. I chose the same room I'd used the night before – the room Jean-Michel and I had always spent our time.

"You can stay here as lon as you like, dawlin. Ah don need no rent money. Just give me somethin on the food and the light and gas bills. That be fin with me. And Ah can wait on that if you ain't got it right na." Josephine's rough hands rubbed my arms and then they went directly to her hips for a fast message. "Gittin up them steps is startin to kill me," she laughed through her pain.

"Josephine, I can afford to pay rent, too. You can use the money to fix your car. I'd also like to help you around the house.

That way I'll be able to keep busy while I take my time figuring out where I go from here. Is that okay with you?"

She didn't have to answer. I could see the happiness in the big smile on her face. "It fin with me. Ah ain't neva had no churen, so you, miss lady, you be the firs. And Ah'm gonna love you to pieces." She handed me a set of keys. "One fa the front do, one fa the side do, and one fa the laundry room do. Member, this your house, too, na. So don be axin me if you can use this or that...just go on and use it. And anythin you see in that frigerator, you eat it. Can you cook?"

"A few things."

"What! A woman gotta know how to cook. You got to feed a man, dawlin. Well, Ah'm gonna show you, how's that?"

"That would be wonderful. Thanks, Josephine." I gave her a big hug and kissed her on her cheek.

Never again would I allow myself to be aloof or keep my feelings hidden from the people who showed me how much they cared about me. Even though Josephine was eighty, and there was a possibility she, too, would die and leave me at any time, I wasn't going to let her go without telling her and showing her how much I appreciated her. I had allowed Miss Menard to die with only one verbal admission of appreciation and one hug, but not Josephine.

While Josephine made lunch for us, she asked what Joshua was like. Instead of telling her the things we'd talked about, I described his physical appearance. I thought I had troubled her enough about Jean-Michel.

"Do you trus him?" she asked.

"I'm not sure; I'd like to. But when I asked him when he thought I might get Miss Menard's life story she'd promised me, he didn't seem too enthusiastic about me getting it. He told me it wasn't finished and he wasn't sure if it would ever be because of his grandfather's illness. That made me suspicious."

"That don soun right to me. Maybe he wan that lady's life story fa hisself. Don trus him, honey." She shook her head, "Uh, uh, uh."

"Jo, whether I trust him or not, there's no way to get it if he doesn't give it to me. I'm sure his grandfather willed the house and everything in it to him. I'll just have to keep positive thoughts that he'll do the right thing."

After lunch I went upstairs to begin putting my things away. There were two things in the center of the bed; the envelope Joshua had given me that morning and the box that held my family's collectibles and the brown paper bag with Lady Blue's shoes. I put the contents of the box in the large hat compartment of the chifferobe along with my berets, two summer hats and three purses. There were no closets in the house, so I hung my clothes on the other side of the chifferobe made for that purpose. There was room under the clothes for all my shoes. I never bought too many pieces of anything. Each season I'd buy several outfits and the next year give them to the church for needy families unless they were timeless and could be worn for several years. Some pieces I kept for a long time.

After I filled the drawers in the chifferobe with the rest of my things, I was ready to tackle the books. By far, they would take up the most space and there was nothing in my room I could use to house them. I had a mantel over the boarded-up fireplace, but there was only room for about twenty books. Then I remembered the small, elevated study nestled next to the other bedroom. It had an antique secretary and over it, built into the wall, a bookcase that almost reached the ceiling. There were also three-shelf bookcases that lined the walls of the study. It was immaculate and there wasn't a book on any shelf. I thought it was a wonderful place to read or study. This was my house now, Josephine had said, so I moved my books to the study and filled most of the lower shelves. All I needed was a desk lamp.

Finally, it was time to open the envelope. I wondered if what was inside would equal the life story I imagined Sera Menard had lived. Even after death my guardian was as mysterious as she was in life. I propped myself up on pillows in the bed before I tore it open and shook out the contents in my lap. Out came a brownish-white, lace-edged pillowcase with something lumpy inside and a smaller envelope addressed to me.

First, I squeezed the pillowcase before I unfolded it. It felt strange, as if it was filled with the braided head of a mop. I was afraid to put my hands in it and pull out whatever was inside. It might be some sort of sick joke of Joshua's or his grandfather's? Maybe they were no better than Miss Menard's doctor. I decided to dump out the contents on the bed. A black plait, about eighteen inches long, tied at the top and bottom with shoelaces, fell out and with it some sort of faded kerchief. The ink-black hair was a heavy, course type and the longest and most beautiful braid I'd ever seen. It looked like a horse's mane. There was not a note or anything else to tell me to whom they belonged or what they meant to me. I returned them to the pillowcase. Maybe the explanation would be in the envelope. I tore it open. There was a short note and a wad of cotton inside. Buried in the cotton was a gold necklace with a large diamond hanging from it.

The note said:

Claire,

The pillowcase contains your great-great grandmother Sanité's braid. The necklace is from a woman who could not pay her clothing bill in cash. My life story will tell you more about these things as well as everything I should have told you. I'm sorry I didn't give you everything while I was alive. That was my plan. Please forgive me.

Seraphine Menard

"Nooo!" My scream pierced the room's quiet and bounced off the walls.

"Oh God...Oh God...Oh God...she was my grandmother's sister...she lied...she lied...she lied to me...she lied to me! She lied to me! Why? Why..." My throat was burning. I could not swallow; I could not breathe.

"Claire! Claire!"

I felt a strong pair of arms tighten around me. I stopped screaming. Josephine held me against her bosom and stroked my hair. She didn't ask me what was wrong; she just held me.

"Shhhh, shhhh, hush, na. Everthin's gon be all right." She pulled the covers back on the bed and forced me to get under them. "You need to sleep, dawlin. Thins won look so bad when you wake up. Go on, na, sleep. Stop that cryin." Josephine patted my back through the covers. "It's bad, na, but it's gonna git betta, you'll see."

– 30 –

SURVIVING A MINI BREAKDOWN

I awakened fifteen hours after my meltdown running a low-grade fever and barely able to stand. Josephine had to help me get to and from the bathroom. She undressed me, gave me a sponge bath, and then helped me put on a pair of pajamas.

When I refused to have her doctor take a look at me, she threatened to call an ambulance and have me taken to Charity Hospital. I realized she wasn't going to relent, so I asked if she'd call Dr. Beauchamp and find out if he was willing to make a house call.

As Josephine was leaving to make the call, I asked if she'd heard anything about Jean-Michel. "Where is he, Josephine? He hasn't even tried to get in touch with me. He has to know what's happening to me. I need him right now."

"No, dawlin, I ain't heard nothin. But I ain't bin to the rectory yet this mawnin. Ah can't leave you til after the docta comes. Member na, the fatha got hisself a whole lot a trouble, too. He probly can't call you." She had put it nicely, but I knew she was telling me to stop behaving as if I was the only one in crisis, not to just think about myself.

"You're right, Josephine. He probably can't call me right now." I felt ashamed.

"Ah'll go as soon as the docta say it's okay to leave you alone."

"That's fine, thanks." I didn't have the energy or the desire to talk anymore. I was glad she had to go downstairs to make the call.

"Ah'll be right back, honey," Josephine patted my hand. "Ah'll git you some breakfas while Ah'm down there."

"No, no, please. I'm not hungry." I was a little hungry, but I was afraid to put anything greasy in my stomach after not eating for such a long time. Grits, bacon and eggs were too heavy; I didn't think I could keep them down.

"You gotta eat somethin. How bout a coupla slices a toas and orange juice?"

"Okay." She must have read my mind.

Dr. Beauchamp arrived two hours later. My temperature had already returned to normal, but I was still a little weak and shaky on my feet.

After he finished examining me, he asked, "Did you ever look into finding a psychiatrist to get some help, Claire."

"No."

"Why not?"

"Because I'm not interested in having someone walking around inside my head, that's why."

"You needed the help then and you still need it. I think you've got to talk to someone now more than ever. Why are you being so stubborn about this? Are you ashamed of needing psychiatric help?" The doctor was looking at me over his eyeglasses as if I were a seven-year-old child who'd brought home a bad report card.

"It has nothing to do with shame; at least I don't think it does. I just think it's time for me to help myself and stop depending on someone else to change my life...my luck. Doctor, I guess you're telling me there's nothing wrong with me physically, correct?"

"That's exactly what I'm saying. Call me Frank, please."

"Your old friend Johnnie Valcour once told me I had something akin to battle fatigue."

"He was right. Lose the stubbornness, Claire. It hurts you more than it helps. Have you heard anything from Johnnie lately?"

"No. I haven't spoken to him since before he moved to Lafayette." I had my mouth pursed to ask him if he'd heard from Johnnie when I decided to let the past stay in the past. I didn't need to rattle the bones of any of my skeletons. "Thank you for making a house call, Frank. How much do I owe you?"

"Nothing, Claire. I hope when you're feeling stronger, you'll consider letting someone help you. Trust me, you cannot do it alone. I'd like to see you in my office in about a month for a follow up. Okay?" The doctor was exasperated and he didn't try to hide it. It was written from his brow to his chin.

"I'm sorry, Frank; I don't mean to be difficult. But so much has happened to me recently that I can't yet absorb it all, much less talk about it to anyone. I need to sort it all out first. In fact, there's more to come in written form. It has to do with my relatives, my ancestors. I hope it will be more informational, than shocking. I don't know how much more stress I can endure, so I'm a little anxious while I'm waiting for it to be completed." I had gotten that out without too much trouble. But then, Francis Beauchamp was a good listener and that made him easy to talk to. He wasn't bad to look at, but he seemed a little shy.

"Whew, Claire, what a life! Someone needs to make a movie about you." The doctor chuckled as he started walking toward the door.

I laughed, too. "You never know. But really, c'mon, I'm not that interesting. Listen, I promise I'll be in to see you in three or four weeks. Thanks, doctor."

I tried to sleep while Josephine was at the rectory, but only succeeded in thrashing about in bed for more than an hour.

I had put off telling her about what happened with Joshua and what I had learned from the contents of the envelope. I didn't want to talk about or even think about Sera...Seraphine Menard. I had temporarily pushed her to the back of my mind. Now that I had the quietude and not much was rolling around in my head, thoughts of her threatened to come roaring back. And then I heard the front door close.

"Josephine?" I called. She didn't answer until she was near the top of the stairs.

"It's me, dawlin." She was huffing and puffing when she entered my room and plopped down at the foot of my bed. "Oh, gimme a minit, honey."

I waited impatiently for her to stop panting. I made a mental note to make sure she didn't climb those stairs too often as long as I lived with her. It took her several minutes to be able to talk.

"Ma news ain't good, Claire."

251

"I figured as much. I could tell by the way you looked at me when you came through the door."

"Ah'm sorry, dawlin. Miss Lenoir tol me she try her bes to fin out where they sen the fatha, but she don fin out. The ol priest, she say, he retire and he gone back to his home town. The only thin she heard is they sen the fatha on a lon retreat befo they give him a new church. Miss Lenoir have to give all they mail to the archdisee. They won give her the place where to sen them letters. The archdisee sen them letters theyselves to the fathas."

I had listened in disbelief. The archdiocese had made it impossible to contact them. "I guess there's nothing I can do to find Jean-Michel, is there? I'll have to erase him from my life as if I've never known him." The tears were running down my face, but there were no sobs, no breaks in my voice and no hanging of my head. These were quiet, angry tears. And I needed my anger to get through it all. For all the changing I'd done, I felt I was being thrust right back to square one – where the old, untrusting, cynical Claire had resided.

"How bout some lunch, honey? You mus be hongry." Josephine got up slowly. I could tell she was in pain.

"You need to rest. I think I'll get a little more sleep. When I get up, I'll come down and make myself something to eat. Go down and rest, Josephine. I'll be okay."

She hobbled out of the room and down the stairs.

I stayed in bed but didn't sleep. My thoughts turned to Joshua Stern. If Seraphine Menard was his grandmother and she was my great-aunt, then he and I were related. We were cousins, I supposed, but I was too frazzled to figure out how close. I wondered if he knew. How could he know if he didn't know what was in the envelope? Then it occurred to me he may have read or was in the process of reading Seraphine's autobiography. Maybe that's why he told me his grandfather hadn't completed it. He might have needed more time to finish reading it. Hmmm, I wondered how he felt when he found out his grandmother was a woman of color...that he is now a person of color? It must have shocked him to his core.

There was no rush to give Joshua information that he might already have. I needed to concentrate on my own mental health and try to figure out what to do next. It was close to the end of the school year and it was too late to apply to universities to get into their master's programs for the fall. I wasn't sure if I'd even be ready to tackle such a grinding project or if I'd be in a better place emotionally and able to handle the pressure.

Then what, Claire? What else can you do with yourself? You need to stay put, and then slowly and deliberately decide what you'll do next. What about a job? A teaching job. Rather than go the public school route, go to Corpus Christi and talk to the nuns. They know you. Call and make an appointment to see the Reverend Mother. I had no one to talk to or ask for advice. I was, once again, my own advisor and psychoanalyst.

School didn't start again until September which meant I had five months to twiddle my thumbs. However, it did give me time to do some physical and mental healing to get stronger all the way around. I could also take a few trips. There was nothing or no one standing in my way.

"Claire, you up?" Jo was calling me from the bottom of the stairs. "How bout a sandwich and some cole slaw?"

"Sounds great. I'll get dressed and come down in a couple of minutes, Jo." Instead of Josephine, I had decided to start calling her Jo the way Jean-Michel used to.

When I got to the kitchen, Jo was making shrimp po boys. I hadn't had one in a long time. I stood still for a second and sniffed the spicy air. It seemed Jo was in the process of spoiling me the way Seraphine had. Whether it was good or bad was a matter of opinion.

"You wan yours dressed, dawlin?"

I nodded and Jo piled lettuce, tomatoes, pickles and mayonnaise on top the fried shrimp. I couldn't wait to bite into the sandwich.

Jo's kitchen was rectangular - long but not wide. Half of it was pantry with the stairs leading to the second floor smack in the middle. There was no place for a dinette set or any way to make it into an eat-in kitchen. I missed that, because unlike the house on Esplanade, everything had to be brought into the dining room and then taken back to the kitchen. But unlike Seraphine's house, the dining room table always had fresh flowers on it and the table was always set with Jo's "good" china.

Every room in Jo's house was filled with antiques. She had done days work for wealthy Whites for many years until her hip problem, and whenever they replaced furniture, china or other household items, they often offered her the old pieces. Most were expensive antiques in excellent condition.

Jo took care of her house the way she took care of the houses in which she'd worked. I never saw her have to fight the man-eater cockroaches I'd helped my grandmother go to war against. They both kept immaculate houses, so the only reason I could find to explain why Jo didn't have those unwanted visitors was because she had a single family house and not a double. Mr. Trevigne, our renter, had lived alone for more than ten years after his wife died. Maybe he hadn't kept his house as clean as he should have forcing us to share his roaches.

"You awful quiet, Claire. Wha cha thinkin bout?" Jo interrupted my musing.

"How lovely your house is and how comfortable it is to live here."

"You can say ma house is lovely afta livin in that big house on Espanade?"

"Sure. Your house has a warm, inviting feeling. Look at your table. There isn't a day that vase isn't filled with flowers from your garden. To me, sitting here eating these sandwiches makes them taste better than a meal at Antoine's in the French Quarter. The first time I came here with Jean-Michel and walked through your front door, I felt instantly at home."

"Crazy talk! You mus still have a feva." Jo tried hard not to smile but she couldn't stop herself. It was obvious she felt embarrassed to receive such a compliment.

"I mean it, Jo. You have a great house. I feel lucky to be here."

"Ah feel lucky, too. Ah bin real lonesome since Ah los ma husban. You bein here makes me real happy".

"Are you busy Sunday, Jo?" I was praying she'd say no.

"Ah go to Mass in the mawning and then Ah go to see some of ma sick friens in the aftanoon. You got somethin you wan me to do?"

"I'd like to go to Mass with you at Corpus Christi. Maybe they'll announce something about the priests. Then I'd like to treat you to lunch after we visit your sick friends. Do you think we can do that Sunday?"

"We sho can, honey. Ah look fawood to it." Jo's eyes got moist. She jumped up and started clearing the table in an effort to hide her tears, but then she suddenly put the dishes back on the table and walked quickly to her bathroom and closed the door.

I followed her and stood outside the door and called softly to her, "Are you okay, Jo?"

"Ah'm fin, dawlin. You jes hit a sof spot, is all."

There was no information about Father O'Mara or Father Pitou from the new priest in the pulpit. After Mass, when he stood outside the door greeting people as they exited the church, he was accosted by several parishioners inquiring about the priests. All he would say was that they had been reassigned.

The following Sunday, Jo and I decided to attend Mass at a church closer to the house. Even though Saint Boniface was only half a mile from her home and considered her parish church in the Lower Garden District, Jo had never been to it. She and her husband never stopped going to Corpus Christi even though they'd moved miles away and they continued contributing to the church. And after her husband died, she still attended Mass at Corpus Christi and she'd put what she could afford in the basket on Sundays. How could Father O'Mara have refused to help her when Jean-Michel asked him for the funds to repair her house?

During those first two weeks at Jo's, I filled my time by helping her around the house and learning to cook a few of the dishes I liked to eat: jambalaya, shrimp étouffée and okra with ham and tomatoes. Learning to make gumbo had to wait; it was too long a process and there were too many different kinds. I was happiest, though, when I was engaged in something I already knew how to do. I planted flower seeds in the front and back yards, weeded the gardens, cut sprigs from the bay leaf tree to give to Jo's friends and neighbors, and took over the job of cutting fresh flowers for the dining room table.

One of Jo's sick friends had a son who was an auto mechanic and he offered to take a look at her car. Jo was furious when he kept it two days. But when he returned it, he had completely overhauled it and it ran like a brand new automobile. And for all the help Jo gave his mother, he only asked for money to cover the parts he'd bought. I insisted she allow me to pay the bill since I too benefited from its use. When she didn't argue, I realized she probably didn't have the money to pay him.

We thought it time for me to get my driver license and from then on we shared the driving, especially when Jo was in pain. I loved driving and knew as soon as my future was clearer, I'd buy a car.

Evenings were quiet and filled with introspection. I watched very little television, only a couple of hours with Jo if I felt she wanted company. Most of the time I read and listened to music in my room. I'd bought a small, table-top phonograph and when I wasn't listening to the radio, I played my own records over and over again. When I played *My Prayer* and *Only You* by The Platters, I'd cry the whole time. *In the Still of the Night* by the Five Satins was another tear-jerker for me. I bought everything Vic Damone and Tony Bennett recorded.

Somehow I coerced Jo into going to the movies. She had only been twice in her life and wasn't too interested in "sittin in a dark room watchin fake people." We usually went every Sunday after lunch and visiting the sick, unless we had chores to do for some of her friends. We sometimes cooked a pot of soup for them or some other dish that would last a few days. We washed clothes or a few dishes, changed the bed linens, mostly for the people who lived alone.

I loved Mario Lanza and saw every movie he made. I dragged Josephine to see *The Hills of Rome* again and again. She rebelled after the third time and told me if I didn't go to see something else that was playing, I'd lose my movie buddy.

I placated her by taking her to see *Rebel without a Cause.* She asked me what was wrong with that crazy boy (James Dean). Next we saw *Magnificent Matador*. Jo gagged and groaned every time the bulls were stuck with the picks and swords. At that point I thought we needed a break from the movies.

After attending Mass at Saint Boniface for the second time, we decided we didn't like the services and wouldn't go back. We returned to Corpus Christi even though it was a long drive. I laughed when Josephine told me she understood why she was set in her ways at eighty, but at twenty-two I was too young to be that way.

– 31 –

A GIANT IN DENIAL

The next Sunday Jo had the sniffles, so we went straight home after Mass. As we pulled into the yard, I could see an envelope stuck in the screen door. It was a letter from Joshua.

Claire,

My grandfather died several weeks ago and was buried next to his wife Rose. I'm sorry to tell you I had to abandon Sera's memoir. I could not muster the mental energy to sort out that disparate stack of papers and make it into a story you could understand. I know how disappointed you must be not to get what Sera promised you.

The selling of both houses is being handled by my grandfather's protégé, Edgar Souté. If there is anything else of Sera's that should come to you, Edgar will contact you.

Since everything seems to be dealt with, there is no need for me to remain in New Orleans. I'm returning to New York this afternoon. It was a pleasure meeting you. I wish you good luck in your future life and whatever you undertake.

Joshua Stern

I sat in the dining room staring at the letter. Jo had quietly undressed and crawled into bed.

"Claire," she called, "come on in here and tell me what's wrong. Ah'm not sleep."

I went in and sat at the foot of her bed. In all the weeks that had passed, Jo had never asked me to tell her about my life before

257

or after meeting Sera Menard. She confined herself to being privy only to my relationship with Jean-Michel.

"This is a bad one, honey. Ah can tell. Don hol that stuff in and get sick again." Jo sat up and patted my knee.

"Oh, Jo, I hate to dump all my problems in your lap before I even get settled in."

"Jes go ahead and dump, honey. Anyway, you ain't got nobody else to tell that stuff to and you need to tell it. So go on, na, tell it."

I told her as briefly as I could about how I grew up and all the people I'd lost, and then about meeting Sera Menard and my life with her until she died.

"Joshua Stern, Jo, is my cousin," I said.

"Lord today, chil! How'd that happen?"

"Sera Menard was my great-aunt, my grandmother's sister. That's what I had just learned the day I screamed upstairs after reading a note from her. For many years she was a passablanc. She had a child for Leonard Stern, Joshua's grandfather, and when she refused to keep the baby, he gave the boy to his sister to raise without Sera's knowledge. That child was Joshua's father." I had to stop and take a deep breath. The story was difficult to tell, so I know how hard it was must have been for Jo to hear that Sera gave away a child when she had been unable to conceive one.

"Go on, honey, finish it." Jo had tears in her eyes.

"Sera promised me her memoir. Years ago, she told me she hoped I'd feel the same way about her after I'd read it. I had no idea what she meant then...now I do. Joshua must have read it and learned she was not only his grandmother but my great-aunt which made her a Colored woman. He didn't want me to know what was in those pages – that he is part Negro. That's why he told me in his letter that he couldn't put the pages together. That way, I'd never find out who Sera really was. But I don't think he knows that she told me in her note and through the contents of the envelope his grandfather sent me."

"Oh, honey, that young man jes got hisself a bunch a demons! Fagive him, chil, them demons ain't gon let him go any time soon. Put him on the hands of the Lord, cuz that's who he gon answer to." Jo made the sign of the cross.

"I can't talk anymore, Jo. Excuse me." I jumped up from her bed and ran upstairs.

There would be no memoir. I had to accept that. I would try to put Joshua in God's hands, but I'd also despise him as I handed him over. He'd robbed me of learning more about my ancestors and that was despicable.

Suddenly a revelation slammed into my head. What hadn't Leonard Stern done for Sera! She'd run out of money, yet because of his money, she had been able to take care of me all those years. Yes, she had nurtured me, but Leonard had put a roof over my head, fed me, and given me all of my material needs. He had generously given to me through her. Now that he was dead, there was no way to thank him. My heart was full and heavy. The tears refused to be deterred.

My thoughts turned to the kind of love there must have been between Sera and Leonard. I wondered if they had only been able to be together long enough to create a child and then never again. I hoped they hadn't died without having reconsummated their great love.

In my life, I had eagerly fulfilled my duties as a lover, but neither of my suitors had bothered to stick around. Johnnie had left town and I hadn't heard a word from Jean-Michel.

"Claire," Jo called up to me and saved me from myself. "are you hongry, dawlin?"

– 32 –

WHERE DO YOU GO FROM HERE?

Dr. Beauchamp was happy I'd come in for my follow-up appointment. He found me in good physical and mental health. He said whatever I had done to get myself in that condition, I needed to continue doing because I was thriving.

"So now what, Miss Soublet?" he asked.

I told him briefly what had happened with my aunt's memoir and how I felt lighter mentally and emotionally even though I hadn't received it. Even knowing my only living relatives were estranged from me, I didn't feel quite as alone in the world anymore. I had Jo and she filled a huge void in my life.

"You have me. Make me a part of your family." He wasn't smiling. He was dead serious.

"Okay, but may I ask why." I was flattered but stunned and curious.

Frank looked away for a moment. When he looked back at me, he was obviously feeling a bit embarrassed. "You haven't heard about a new service I'm offering my patients? And at no extra charge."

"Well…I can't turn down anything free. Welcome to the family, *coozan*." I think Frank was trying to flirt with me, but I hadn't responded in the right way.

"Thank you, I'm honored," he said. Eager to move away from that part of the conversation, Frank asked again, "What now?"

"I think I'm going to take a trip or two. Maybe, New York; possibly, Paris. I've already applied for my passport. I want to spend some time in New York to find out if it's a place I'd like to live. I need to decide soon because I'd like to leave in a couple of weeks or as soon as I can tie up any loose ends." I watched Frank's eyes do a happy dance.

"I'm glad to hear that. Now I can let you in on my secret. I've decided to close my practice. When Dr. Gomes died last year, I took over his practice. He had so many patients I realized I couldn't handle this large a practice alone, but I haven't had any luck finding anyone to join me. The minute they see the age of the equipment and the office furniture, they're not interested. I can't afford to replace all this." Frank touched the blood pressure monitor and it fell off the wall. We laughed. "That was timely," he said.

"How long was Dr. Gomes in this location? He was very old for as long as I can remember."

"About thirty-five years and he never updated anything. I think he was eighty-six when he died. I've always known this was going to be a temporary job but I had to start somewhere."

"What will happen to this office?"

"Dr. Gomes's sons will take it over and sell off everything. I'm free to leave New Orleans as soon as I handle my personal affairs. I've already informed my patients."

"Then what?"

"Two friends in New York have a practice in Manhattan and I'm going to join them. Now isn't that a coincidence! You're going to New York, too. I already have my first patient and you won't have to hunt for a doctor. Gee, Claire, that's the best news I've had in ages!"

Before I could respond, Frank pulled me off the exam table and gave me a bear hug. "I think this news deserves to be celebrated." He looked at his watch. "It's almost lunch time. What about having a bite to eat with me? There's a new restaurant on Elysian Fields that serves delicious po boys."

"Oooooh," I groaned. "I don't think so, Frank." God, not another Creole! My head was exploding. Run, run for your life, you fool!

"Come on, Claire, I don't bite. I'll even pay for your sandwich and soft drink."

"How do you know that's all I'm going to order?"

"I'll buy whatever you order, how's that? C'mon, lady, you're killing my pride here."

261

"Okay, okay, I'll meet you in the waiting room."

I had never laughed so hard in an hour as I did then. I was sorry when our lunch ended. Before we left the restaurant, Frank told me his friends owned a brownstone and rented out apartments. If I planned to stay in New York for a few months, perhaps I'd be interested in renting one. He said he'd call and inquire about vacancies while I finalized my plans and got an arrival date.

"Frank, I don't know how to thank you. Not only was the food great, but you're a terrific lunch buddy. I must admit, I thought you would be shy and boring." I hadn't planned to be so candid, but I had a feeling he could handle it.

"What...shy and boring! Whatever gave you that idea?"

"I...I guess because you're always so serious in your office." I gave him only part of the truth. I didn't think he'd like hearing I had an old bias against Creole men?

"Bedside manner vs. outside the office manner...two different animals, Claire."

"I apologize, Dr. Beauchamp."

"I graciously accept, Miss Soublet." He pulled up alongside my car.

"As soon as I make my decision, Frank, I'll call you."

Instead of going straight home, I drove uptown to the Garden District to see the Prytania house. It was boarded up with a *For Sale* sign nailed on one of the shutters. Then I drove back downtown to the Esplanade house. It was also boarded up with its sign posted on the fence. Without knowing why I'd ever need it, I jotted down the telephone number on the sign.

There was one other thing I needed to do. I went back to Jo's and found a piece of lumber about fourteen inches long in the back yard. With a bottle of black shoe polish, I painted "Thank You" on it. I picked a bouquet of flowers from the yard and tied it securely to the piece of wood. I asked Jo to take a ride with me to Lake Pontchartrain.

Joshua hadn't told me where he'd buried his grandfather, but my feeling was that Leonard would probably have wanted to be with Sera. I wondered if Joshua's anger and revenge had kept them apart. Since Sera was the only one cremated and her ashes put into the lake, I could only thank her and hope she'd get my message to Leonard. I went to the shallow, sandy end of the lake, put my flower boat into the water and watched it float away. I was not only able to say thank you, but I could say a final goodbye to both my guardians.

On the drive home, Jo was so touched by my flower-boat and the respect I had for Sera and Leonard, that for the first time, she talked about her life.

"Ah know misry, dawlin, Ah seen enough of it when Ah was a young girl, so Ah know how grateful you are to them good people. Ah was bawn in south Lousiana, in Houma, that's in Cajun country." It was obvious Jo wasn't used to talking about her life. She spoke very slowly and deliberately. "You eva been to Cajun country?" she asked.

"No, never. But now that I know where you're from, I know why you sound a bit different from the old Creoles here. You have a slight Cajun accent."

"Ah been gon so long from there, Ah ain't suppose to have no accent. My mama sol me when Ah was thirteen to a real, real, ol man. He was Colored, but that don matta cuz he treated me like a slave. He used me fa everthin and Ah mean everthin! But Ah waited fa ma chance to run away and one day it came, the very nex year. The ol man's neighbor was gon travel to Nu Awlins to sell some fur pelts and gator skins. Ah heard him tell the ol man the time when he was leavin. Ah hurried up and got ma few rags together with some food and wata and Ah hid in the wagon. Ah crawled under the covarin and sat between them pelts and skins. Them thins didn't botha me, cuz me, Ah was sleep almos the whole way. Ah only woke up to eat and drink."

"But, Jo, how could you stand the smell all those hours under that covering and eat, too? I probably would have thrown up the whole time. What did you bring to eat?"

"Les see...Ah had a few raw corns, some berled crab, already picked, and two berled potatas. Ah washed it all down with wata. Ah stayed close to the back-end of the wagon. Ah'd lif up a corna of the covarin now and again to git me some good air. When we got to Nu Awlins, Ah jumped out as soon as the wagon slowed down. That ol man neva heard me and neva saw me," Jo chuckled. "But Ah was some scared the whole time. Ah thought when he'd stop to check his wagon whilst on the trip, he'd fin me."

"What did you do after you left the wagon? You didn't know anyone or anything about the city. Where did you go?" I couldn't imagine that kind of courage at fourteen.

"It had jes got dark and Ah started to walk around and that's all Ah member."

"What! Did something happen to you?"

"Ah member fallin on the ground and the next thin Ah know, Ah woke up in Charity Hospital. They say them pelts and skins gave me something, Ah don't member na what it was Ah had. Ah had big, lumpy welps all ova me and a high feva for days and days. They tol me Ah was out of ma head almos the whole time — talkin crazy and cryin and screamin."

"How long did you have to stay in the hospital and where did you go when they discharged you," I asked her.

"Ah think Ah stayed bout eight or nine days. Isaiah worked at the hospital back then and he heard the doctas and nurses talkin bout me not havin a home and no kin. He tol me he had a house and offered me a place to stay."

"Who's Isaiah, Jo?"

"Ma dead husban; he was fifteen years olda than me. Ah was scared when Ah went home with him, but Ah neva regretted it. He married me and Ah was with him until he died las year. He was 95 years ol."

"Oh, Jo, what a great story! You're a very brave woman," I told her.

"Ah don know bout all that; Ah jes know Ah had a get away or Ah'da killed that ol man. Isaiah taught me how to read and write. He was a very smart man. When he got tired a being a janita at the hospital, he opened up a little sweet shop on Claiborne. We made everthin we sol: ice cream, snowballs, peanut candy, caramels, all kinds a cookies, coconut and pecan plarines, fudge — you name a sweet, we made it."

"I remember that shop. It was called Sweet Jo's. Big Mama and I used to stop there when we'd walk home from Canal Street and buy all kinds of stuff. That was your store?" I couldn't believe what a small world it was.

"We had it til Isaiah got sick. It was too much fa jes me, so we had a let the shop go. He had neva let me work, so Ah had a earn some kinda money to take care a us. All Ah could do was clean White peoples' houses and take in washin and ironin. But

Ah neva complained cuz most a them folks Ah worked fa was good to me and ma husban. They helped me bury Isaiah cuz all our money went to doctas and medicine."

Jo was suddenly quiet as if she'd run out of breathe. I didn't ask any more questions, I let her stay quiet. I thought she was probably overwhelmed talking about a part of her life she hadn't thought about for a long time. We drove the rest of the way home in silence.

Insomnia plagued me night after night as I went through the pros and cons of both trips. But what gave me the most anxiety was having to tell Jo about my plans and Frank Beauchamp's sudden interest in me. I chastised myself for assuming his behavior suggested that he was interested in a relationship with me in New York. He might just have been in an exceptionally good mood that day or really glad he'd have a friend from home in a new city. But wasn't that also good for me - a doctor familiar with my medical history and a friend. What was there to complain about? There were many more things that needed my attention.

After I bought my train ticket, I called Frank and told him when I planned to arrive in New York. He had already checked with his friends and they had an efficiency apartment available to me. I thanked him and told him I'd see him when he arrived in New York.

I had dragged my feet for many weeks before making my plans. Now I had to tell Jo I was leaving.

As I reached the foot of the stairs, Jo was on her way up with a letter for me that had just been delivered. There was no return address but the postmark was stamped: Dakar, Senegal. Who on earth was writing to me from Africa?

My hands began to shake as I tore open the envelope. I pulled out one sheet of lined paper with writing on both sides.

July 29, 1957

My Darling Claire,

I have not one doubt that this letter will find you well and beginning to sort through the many opportunities open to you now. Take your time deciding what you want to do.

Enjoy your gift of freedom – the exit from your former life. You've earned it.

My life is now here in Senegal. And because the country is French speaking and I've retained much of my first language, my mission is proving to be easier than I had anticipated. I'm helping to build a church and a school and the rewards are endless. I am grateful to be here.

I chose God, Claire, because I know I could never be happy just growing grapes. I love being a priest and cannot imagine a life doing anything else. You will probably consider me a narcissist when I tell you I enjoy being loved and needed by so many people. The power to be able to help them change their lives and find God is a powerful aphrodisiac.

Don't ever think because I chose Him I don't love you. I think of you when the sun rises and when it sets. You'll never leave my thoughts. And every prayer I whisper to God, I include you. I ask him to guide you and protect you.

Happiness will find you, Claire; you don't have to look for it.

Give my love to Jo. Both of you keep me in your prayers.

Jean-Michel

I put the letter back in the envelope and went into the dining room. I joined Jo at the table and pushed the letter toward her. "It's from Jean-Michel, Jo. Read it." It took every ounce of my strength to keep my voice from cracking and my eyes from welling up.

"No, dawlin. That's persnal. Ah know he ain't coming back. You shows it all ova your face." Jo couldn't look at me. She wrung her hands and stared at the flowers on the table.

"Uh...he said he chose God because he loves being a priest. He's building a church and a school in Africa. I can't blame him for not choosing me, Jo. I always told him he was a priest first and then a man. So I guess I shouldn't be surprised. He sent you his love."

266

"Oh!" Jo had to wait a bit before she continued. "Ah'm glad the fatha didn't jes leave faeva without a word. He wrote and tol us goodbye. He's a good man, Claire."

"I suppose. I do know that his being in Africa completes the job of putting my past behind me. Jean-Michel told me I'm free now and I am." I took a quick breath. "Jo, I've decided to take a couple of trips...first to New York and then maybe to Paris. I want to find out if I like New York well enough to live there." I looked at Jo to see how my news had affected her. She didn't seem upset, in fact, she was calm. It was obvious she had been expecting my departure.

"You go, honey. It's bout time you make a good life fa yourself."

"I'll pay you rent for the room while I'm gone, Jo. That's only fair since my things will still be in it until I have them shipped...that's if I decide to stay in New York."

"No, dawlin, Ah don wan one dime. You use that money to start yourself off wherever you go to live. Ah'm fine today and Ah'm gonna be fine tomorra. Ah got me some new folks Ah do laundry fa. So Ah'll do mo than make ens meet. Don you worry bout me, ya hear."

I took Jo's hands and held them. "I'll miss you, and even though I've wanted to get out of New Orleans for as long as I can remember, I'm going to miss it, too."

"If you miss it too much, then you come on back here as fas as you can pack. Cuz this is your home...this city and this house."

I let go of Jo's hands as I burst into tears. All I could do was put my head down on my arms and sob. Jo stroked my head without talking. I knew she was probably crying, too.

– 33 –

"ALL ABOARD"

Jo and I said our goodbyes the night before I left. I wouldn't let her come to see me off because I hated saying goodbye. That last week before my departure had been hard for both of us. I didn't think we could handle any more heartache. When the taxi arrived the next morning, Jo had already left the house to make her laundry deliveries.

It was early and the streets were empty. The cab got me to the train station in less than ten minutes. I had more than an hour to wait before I could board the train. A handful of people waited with me. I was happy to see that the information I had been given about Tuesday being the lightest travel day was correct. It seemed I would have no problem having two seats together so that I could stretch out my legs at night to sleep.

Carrying one suitcase was all I could manage when I walked the length of the train platform to get to the car set aside for Negroes. Laden with my purse, food for the trip and the suitcase, I was out of breath by the time I boarded and found a set of seats. I put my suitcase on the overhead rack and my purse and bag of food on the empty seat next to me hoping to prevent anyone from sitting in it. I stood up and looked around. The four people seated in the coach with me seemed to be doing the same thing.

Jo had packed more than enough food for my two-day trip. Because Coloreds were not allowed to eat in the dining car, you had to have an ample food supply to last the whole trip. I was curious, so I opened the brown paper bag to see what she'd packed for me. There were several cheese sandwiches, three chunks of French bread and half a dozen pieces of the customary fried chicken. She'd put in a few pieces of fruit, some cookies, gum and some candy bars. There was no mayonnaise to spoil – only

268

mustard. In the bottom of the bag, Jo had put one of her best linen napkins. Inside the napkin were a note and a ten dollar bill. Jo had written: *stay with god and sen me a suvanir.*

"All aboard." The conductor called out. "All aboard." The train suddenly lurched forward and then slowly began to pull out of the station.

"Excuse me, miss. Is this seat taken?" The voice sounded familiar.

"Frank?" I snapped my head around and wrenched my neck. I groaned in pain.

"Oh, I'm sorry. I wanted to surprise you, not cause you to hurt yourself. Turn toward the window, Claire. Sit up straight." Frank quickly massaged my neck and my shoulders. "Relax," he told me as he jabbed his knuckles into the small of my back. He continued to knead the base of my neck until I told him the pain was gone.

"What are you doing here?" I asked him.

"I thought since this is such a long, boring trip and we're going to the same destination, why not keep each other company." He threw his suitcase and a small bag up on the rack and took the seat across the aisle from me. "If I sit here, and not next to you, you'll be able to stretch out to sleep and I can do the same over here. Okay?"

"That was my plan, Frank." I could feel a knot forming in my stomach and my heart began to thump. My palms grew damp. I stared out of the window and watched the outskirts of New Orleans roll by as I wondered, once again, what his intentions were. Please, God, not another caretaker! Make his caring platonic, Lord; that's all I need right now.

"Claire?" Frank leaned over and touched my shoulder. "What's going on in your head?"

"I'm saying a silent goodbye to my hometown – in my head, not in my heart. And I'm wondering if we ever really put our pasts behind us. Something tells me it isn't possible." I knew he had no idea his presence was causing me consternation.

"The trick is to never say goodbye; say so long. Leave the door slightly open in case you want to come back. That's what I'm doing." Frank slid off his seat and knelt in the aisle next to my seat. "You're afraid of the future: that's only natural." He took my hands in his, "But I don't want you to worry. I'm experienced in starting a new life; I'll show you how it's done."

"Will you now, cousin," I chuckled. "I'm going to stay in New York for about a week and then I'm going on to Paris for a week or so. I can handle it, Frank. Don't you trust me to be able to take care of myself?"

"Of course, I do. But I've been thinking, since I plan to take a couple of weeks before I get my practice started so that I can show you New York, why not spend a week of that time in Paris with you? It has nothing to do with you taking care of yourself. I happen to know the city well. I went to medical school right next door in Switzerland, so I spent lots of weekends and holidays walking Paris's streets. You'll love it, especially having a private tour guide. As for me...I'm salivating now when I think of sitting on the banks of the Seine with a loaf of bread, a jug of wine...and thou." He let his eyes roll back in his head as he snickered mischievously.

When I stopped laughing I said, "You seem to be one step ahead of me at every turn, Frank." It was clear he wasn't the Creole type I was running away from. Nevertheless, I was running away.

"Is that a bad thing, Claire?"

"No, not at all." Hmm...I thought. How else could I have answered that question without stepping on his ego? He is quite charming, but I will not be sidetracked from my reality. I'm free now. I intend to enjoy my freedom.

LANGUAGE
and
FOOD GLOSSARY

Armoire – Large closet-like piece of furniture with double doors used for storage.

Back-a-Town - A direction in the city.

Banquette - The sidewalk.

Bay – A term of endearment, like cher.

Bazah – A good time.

Boocoo – A great deal; a lot.

Beignets – Fried donuts smothered in powdered sugar.

Boozan – A good time person; to drink too much liquor.

Bummin – To go out often, especially to a bar.

Café au lait – Half coffee and half scalding milk.

Camelback – a house with one-story front section and a two-story rear; resembles a camel's hump.

Can't Beat That With A Stick – Nothing's better than that.

Cher – Dear; love.

Chifferobe – A closet-like piece of furniture. In that period, houses had no closets.

Chinchy – Stingy.

Chunk-a-change – A good bit of money.

Comass – A disturbance.

Conte – Gossip.

Coozan – Cousin.

Crotay – Dirty.

Dance Hall – Places you rent to have a party.

Do Poppin – Minding other people's business.

Dressed – A po boy that contains lettuce, tomato, pickles and mayonnaise or mustard.

Étouffée - A thick stew made with crawfish or shrimp, fat, garlic and green seasoning.

Fell Out – Stopped being friends.

For True – Is that so? Really?

Gahbe – A light-skinned person; someone who looks Creole like you.

Good Hair – Hair that is not processed in any way; is naturally straight, curly, etc.

Grandmère – Grandmother.

Grandpère – Grandfather.

God Is Good! – A response to something that has happened

Gris-Gris – A powdered substance often used in voodoo charms or amulets; a hex or a spell.

Gros Comme Ça – As big as that. (Use your hands to designate size.)

Gumbo – A stew-like soup made with seafood, meat, chicken, sausage and flavored with myriad other seasonings, usually served with white rice. There are many different varieties of this dish.

Hey La Bas! – Hey you over there!

Hickey – A bump/lump on the head.

Honte! – Shame!

Hoodoo – A person or thing that brings bad luck.

Jambalaya – A rice dish cooked with a mix of diced meat and seafood with tomato and other seasonings.

Looks Like Mortal Sin Dipped In Hell – Horrible looking.

Jesus, Mary and Joseph! – A plea to God for help.

La Shon – Money.

Long Time No See – Haven't seen you in a long time.

Lord Today! – A response to something said.

Lost Bread – French toast.

Magwa – Big mouth.

Make Groceries – Buy groceries.

Mais Non! – But no!

Marie Laveau – Celebrated Queen of the Voodoos.

Mashuquette – gossip

Mirliton – A green, pear-shaped, prickly vegetable (coyote squash).

Mon Dieu! – My God!

Na – Now

Nennaine – Godmother.

Neutral Ground – The grassy middle of a wide street.

Okra – A green pod, a cousin of the cotton plant, was brought to the New World by slaves who hid the seeds in their hair and ears.

Out Of The Way – No longer living at home.

Oyster Loaf – The soft part in the middle of the loaf is removed and the cavity is filled with fried oysters and then "dressed."

Passablanc – Passing for White.

Pass Over By Your House Sometime – Will come to visit you.

Petite Cochon! – Little pig!

Po Boy – A hefty, French bread sandwich filled with meats or seafood.

Praline – A sweet patty-shaped confection made of pecans, brown sugar, butter and vanilla. Often pronounced as "plarine" in New Orleans.

Pull Your Toes Tonight – A dead person, unhappy with your behavior, may pull your toes at night.

Putain, La – Whore.

Put Bad Mouth On – Negative talk that may bring bad luck.

Put Him In The Hands Of The Lord – Pray for a person, then hand him over to God.

Shotgun, Double – A duplex with no hallways and interior doors on each side of the house; rooms are in a straight line. Local folklore: If you fired a shotgun from the front door, the pellet would go through the house and exit the back door without hitting any walls.

Skinny Galoot – A thin, awkward person.

Sweating Bricks – Sweating profusely.

To Do – A party.

Tompee! – The heck with you!

Vieux Carré – The original name of the French Quarter (Means "Old Square").

Voodoo – A blend of West African religion and Haitian Roman Catholicism

You Can't See For Looking – Its right in front of your face and you can't see it.

Yella Heifa – A light-skinned female.

CPSIA information can be obtained at www.ICGtesting.com
Printed in the USA
BVOW021141070113

309990BV00009B/156/P